The Cinnamon Friends' FAVORITE THINGS!

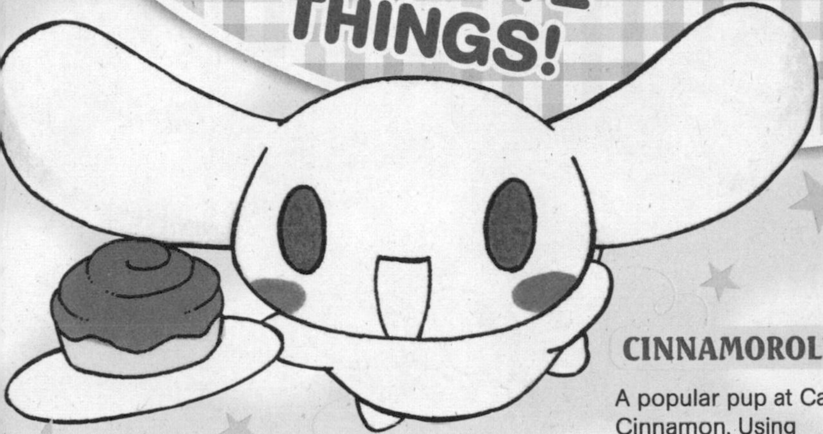

CINNAMOROLL

A popular pup at Café Cinnamon. Using his big ears, he flies through the sky to deliver cinnamon rolls!

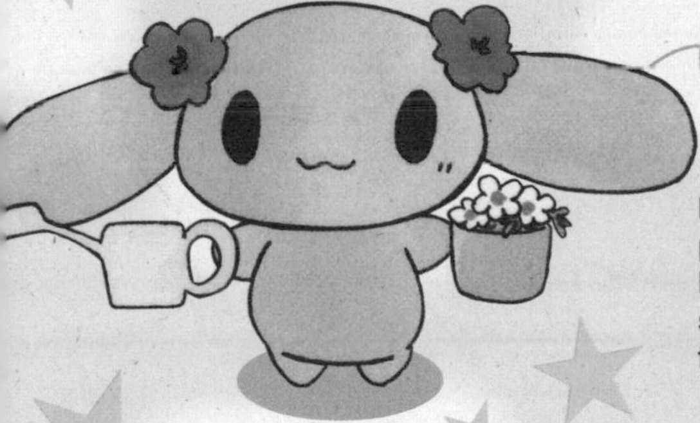

MOCHA

Loves being surrounded by pretty flowers. She works hard to take care of the secret garden of special flowers behind her house.

MILK

Even though he's a baby, Milk always wants to play with the other pups! He drinks lots of milk so he can grow big and strong.

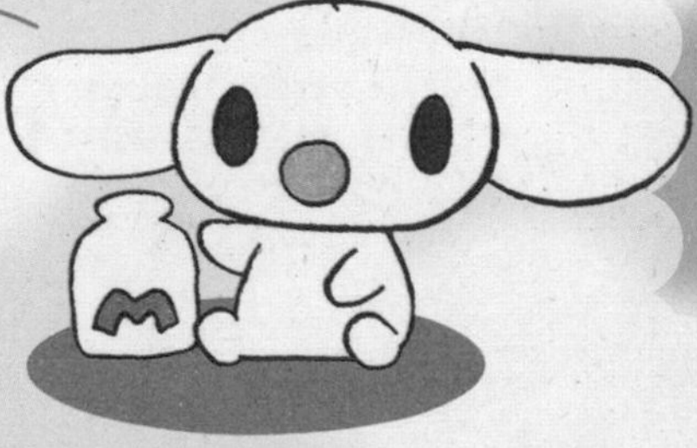

Fluffy, Fluffy Cinnamoroll

4

Story & Art by **YUMI TSUKIRINO**
Original Concept by **CHISATO SEKI**

CHIFFON

Better at sports than any boy. She wants to play outside all day long! She doesn't like rainy days and isn't good at cooking.

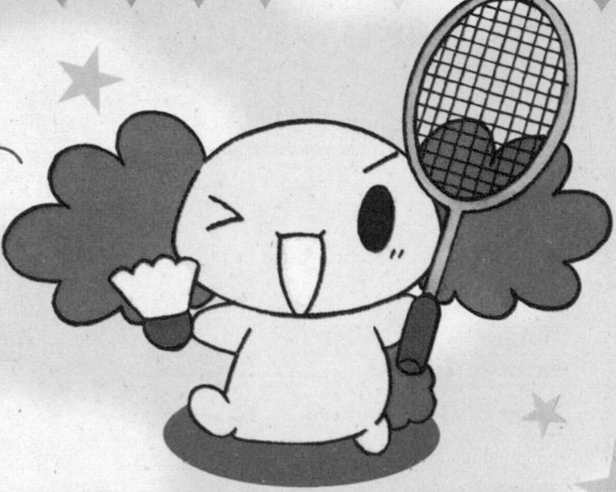

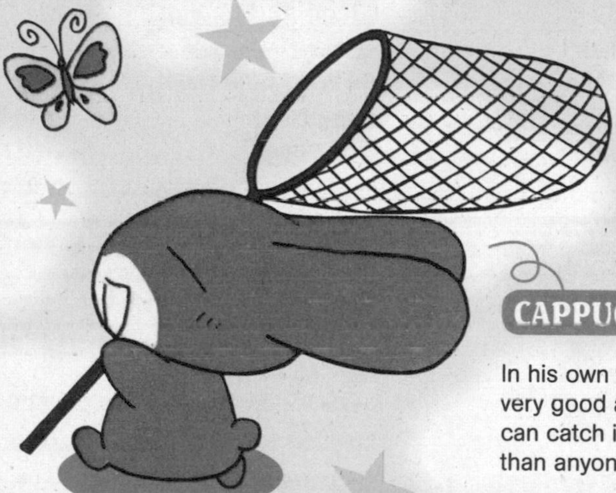

CAPPUCCINO

In his own world. He's not very good at sports, but can catch insects faster than anyone around!

ESPRESSO

An artist inspired by the world around him. He's not just good at drawing, but also music and driving.

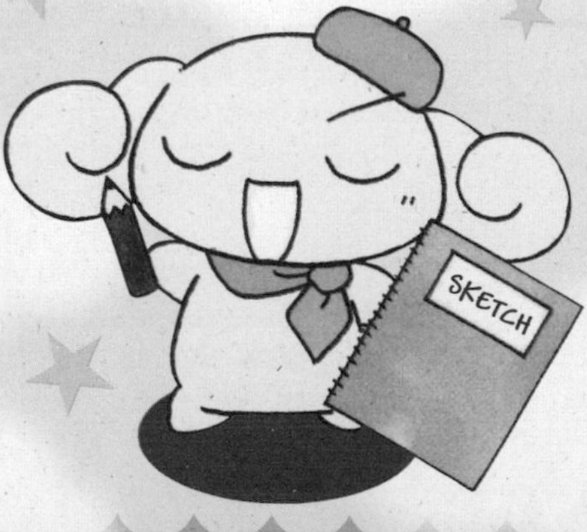
SKETCH

Fluffy, Fluffy Cinnamoroll

4

Contents

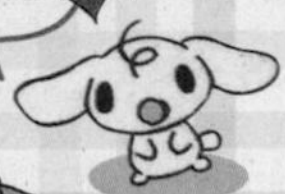

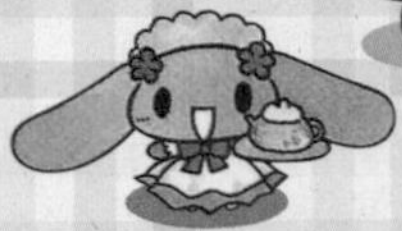

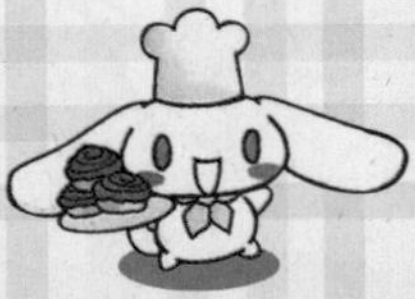

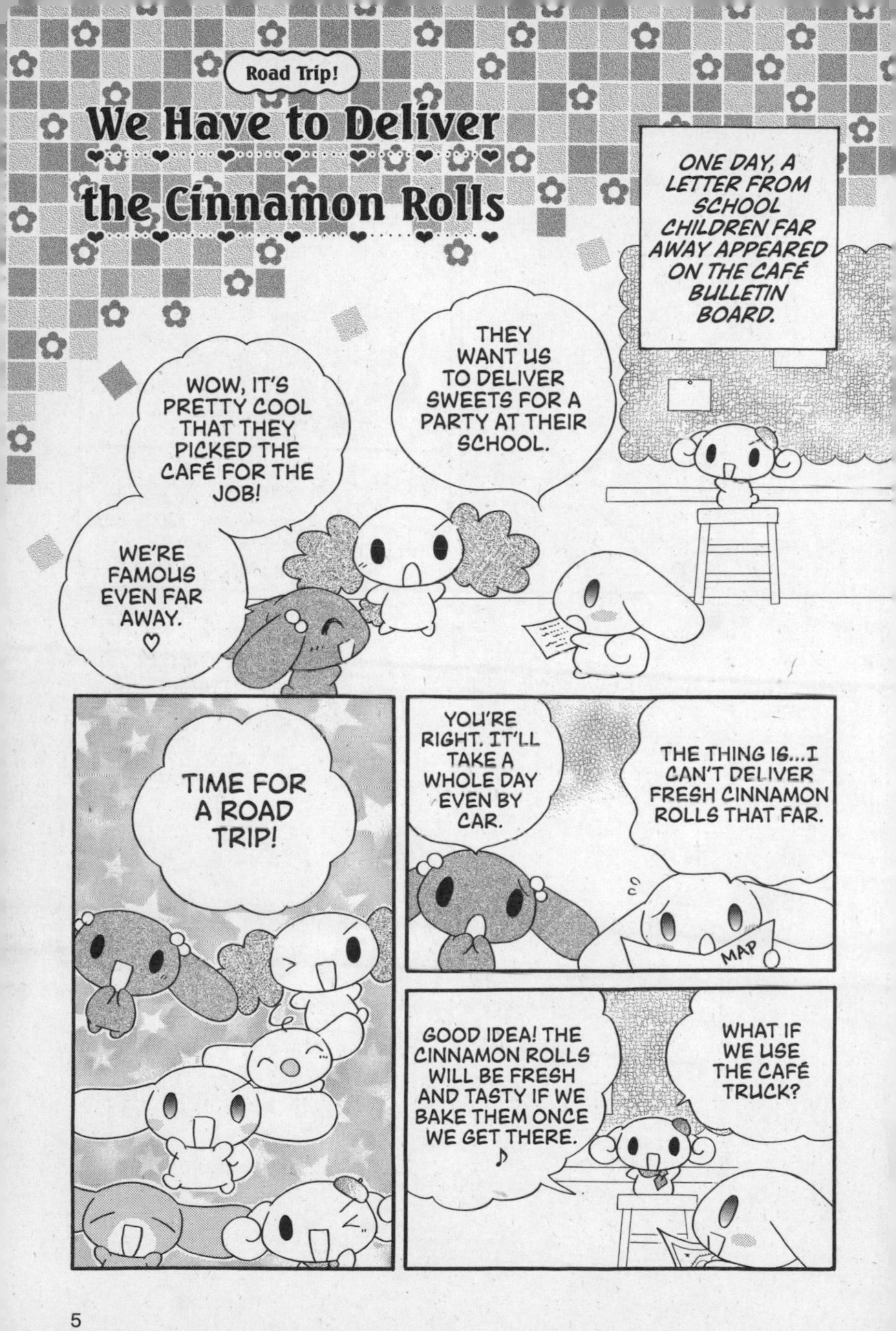
Road Trip!
We Have to Deliver the Cinnamon Rolls
ONE DAY, A LETTER FROM SCHOOL CHILDREN FAR AWAY APPEARED ON THE CAFÉ BULLETIN BOARD.
THEY WANT US TO DELIVER SWEETS FOR A PARTY AT THEIR SCHOOL.
WOW, IT'S PRETTY COOL THAT THEY PICKED THE CAFÉ FOR THE JOB!
WE'RE FAMOUS EVEN FAR AWAY. ♡
THE THING IS...I CAN'T DELIVER FRESH CINNAMON ROLLS THAT FAR.
YOU'RE RIGHT. IT'LL TAKE A WHOLE DAY EVEN BY CAR.
MAP
WHAT IF WE USE THE CAFÉ TRUCK?
GOOD IDEA! THE CINNAMON ROLLS WILL BE FRESH AND TASTY IF WE BAKE THEM ONCE WE GET THERE. ♪
TIME FOR A ROAD TRIP!

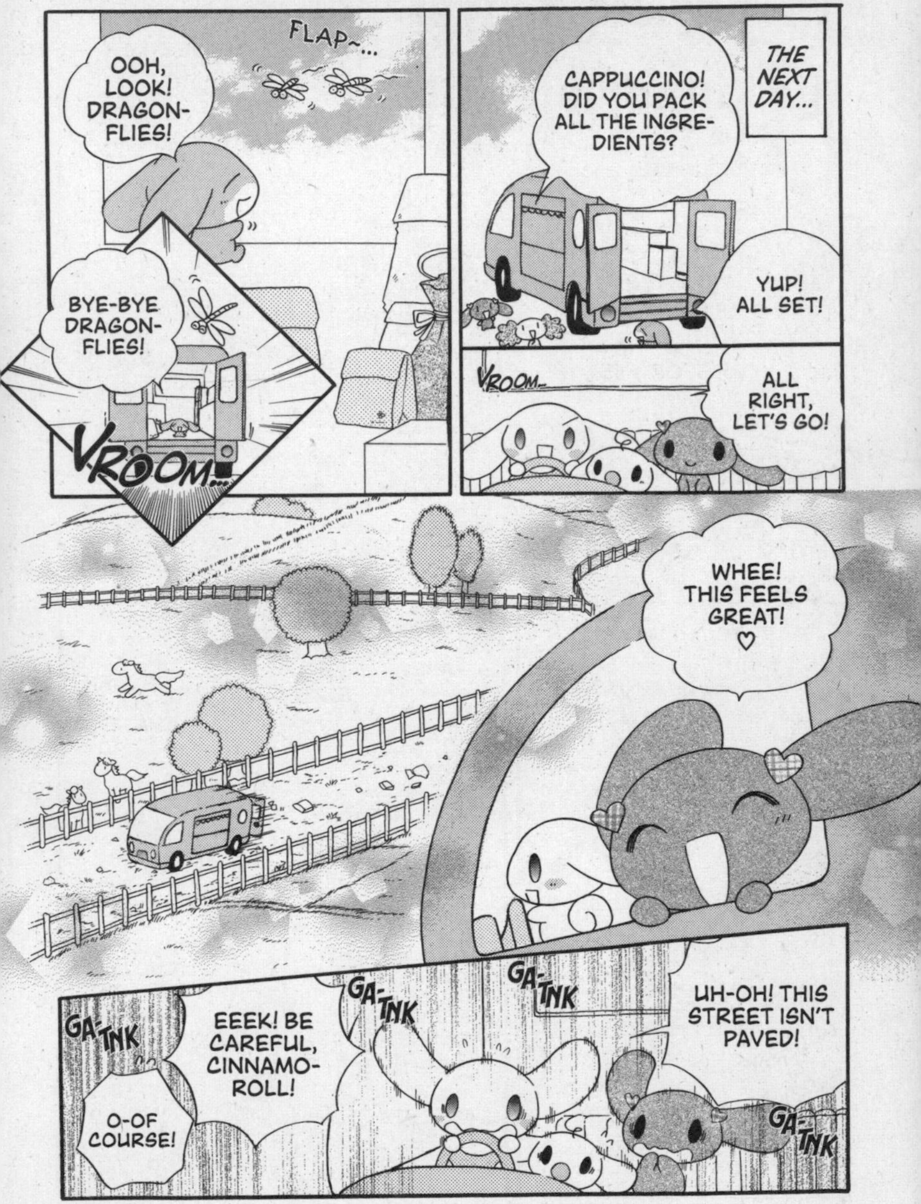
THE NEXT DAY...
CAPPUCCINO! DID YOU PACK ALL THE INGREDIENTS?
YUP! ALL SET!
FLAP~...
OOH, LOOK! DRAGONFLIES!
BYE-BYE DRAGONFLIES!
VROOM...
VROOM
ALL RIGHT, LET'S GO!
WHEE! THIS FEELS GREAT! ♡
GA-TNK
UH-OH! THIS STREET ISN'T PAVED!
GA-TNK
EEEK! BE CAREFUL, CINNAMOROLL!
GA-TNK
O-OF COURSE!
GA-TNK

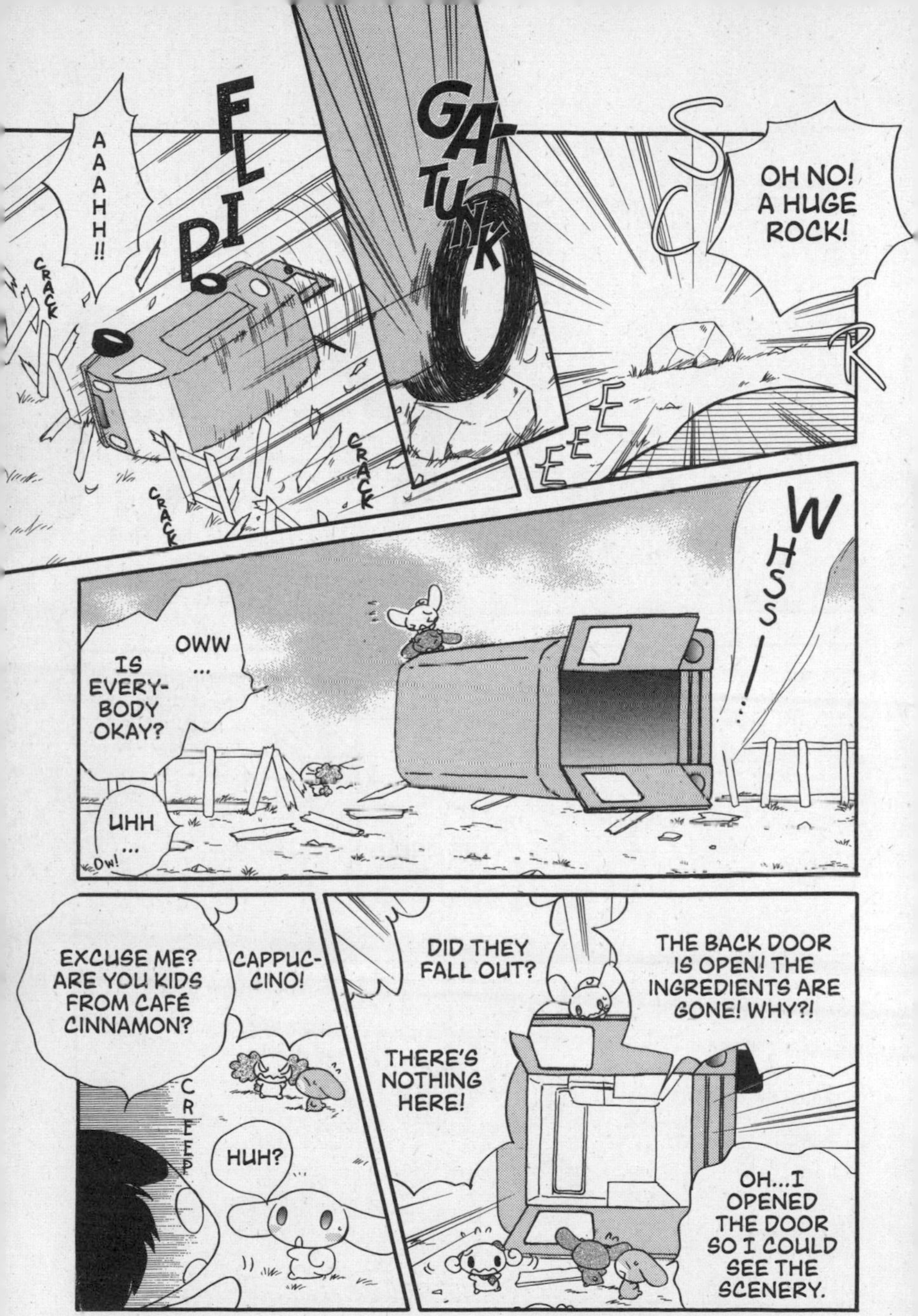
OH NO! A HUGE ROCK!
SCREEE
GA-TUNK
FLIP
AAAAHH!!
CRACK
CRACK
CRACK
WHSS
OWW ...
IS EVERY-BODY OKAY?
UHH ...
OW!
THE BACK DOOR IS OPEN! THE INGREDIENTS ARE GONE! WHY?!
DID THEY FALL OUT?
THERE'S NOTHING HERE!
OH...I OPENED THE DOOR SO I COULD SEE THE SCENERY.
CAPPUC-CINO!
EXCUSE ME? ARE YOU KIDS FROM CAFÉ CINNAMON?
CREEP
HUH?

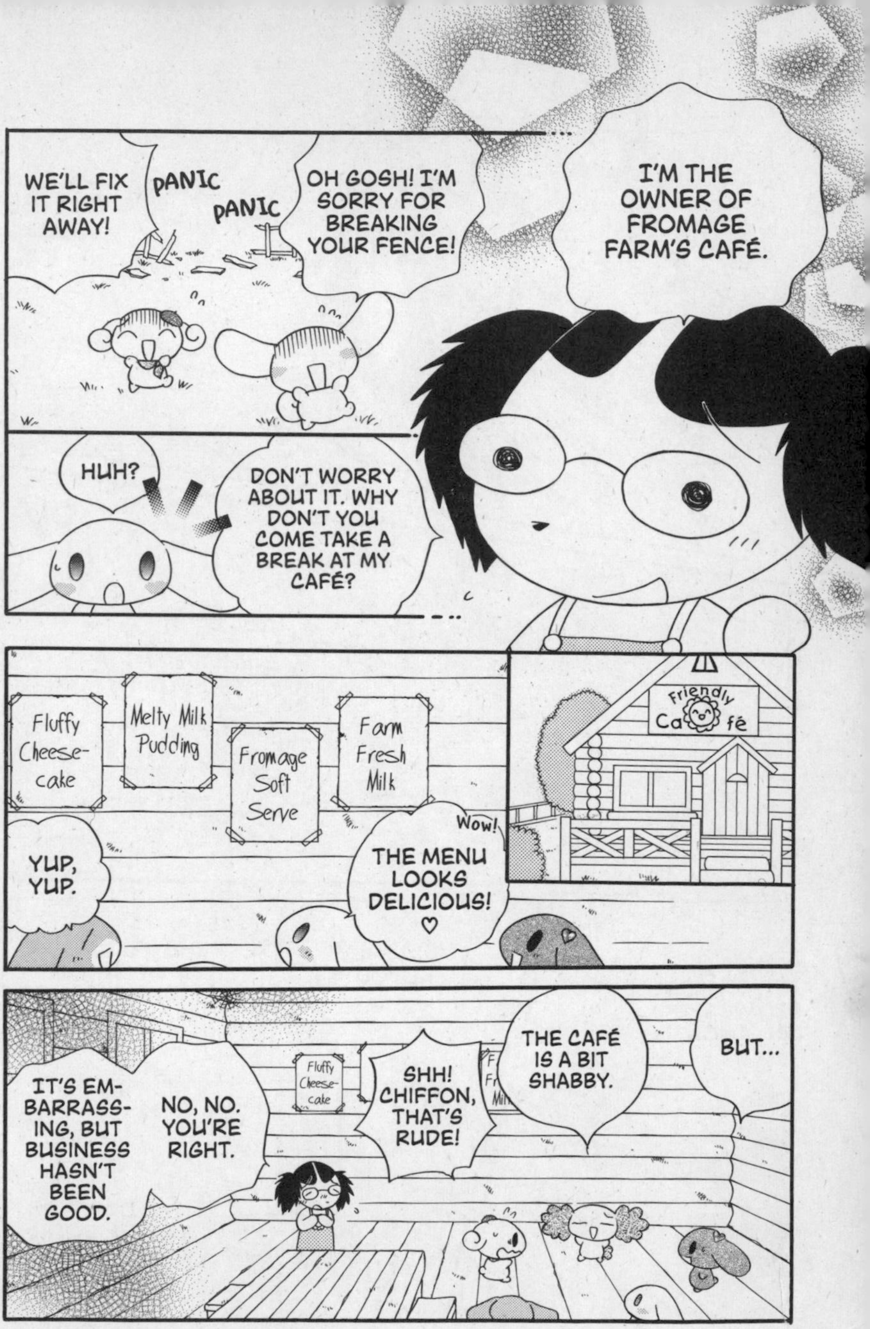
I'M THE OWNER OF FROMAGE FARM'S CAFÉ.
OH GOSH! I'M SORRY FOR BREAKING YOUR FENCE!
PANIC
PANIC
WE'LL FIX IT RIGHT AWAY!
DON'T WORRY ABOUT IT. WHY DON'T YOU COME TAKE A BREAK AT MY CAFÉ?
HUH?
Friendly Café
Farm Fresh Milk
Fromage Soft Serve
Melty Milk Pudding
Fluffy Cheese-cake
Wow!
THE MENU LOOKS DELICIOUS! ♡
YUP, YUP.
BUT...
THE CAFÉ IS A BIT SHABBY.
SHH! CHIFFON, THAT'S RUDE!
Fluffy Cheese-cake
NO, NO. YOU'RE RIGHT.
IT'S EM-BARRASS-ING, BUT BUSINESS HASN'T BEEN GOOD.

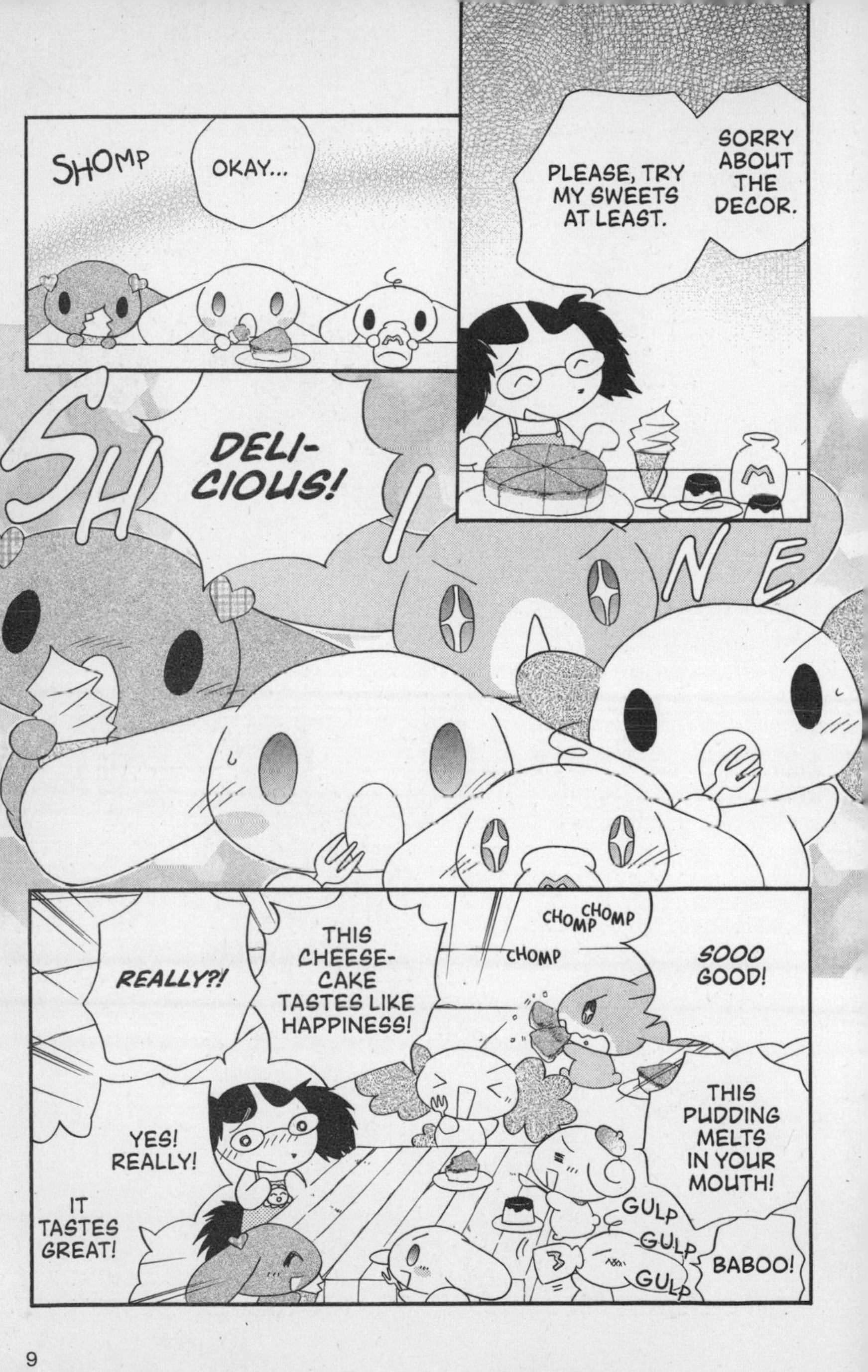
SORRY ABOUT THE DECOR.
PLEASE, TRY MY SWEETS AT LEAST.
OKAY...
SHOMP
SHINE
DELI-CIOUS!
SOOO GOOD!
CHOMP CHOMP
CHOMP
THIS CHEESE-CAKE TASTES LIKE HAPPINESS!
REALLY?!
THIS PUDDING MELTS IN YOUR MOUTH!
BABOO!
GULP
GULP
GULP
YES! REALLY!
IT TASTES GREAT!

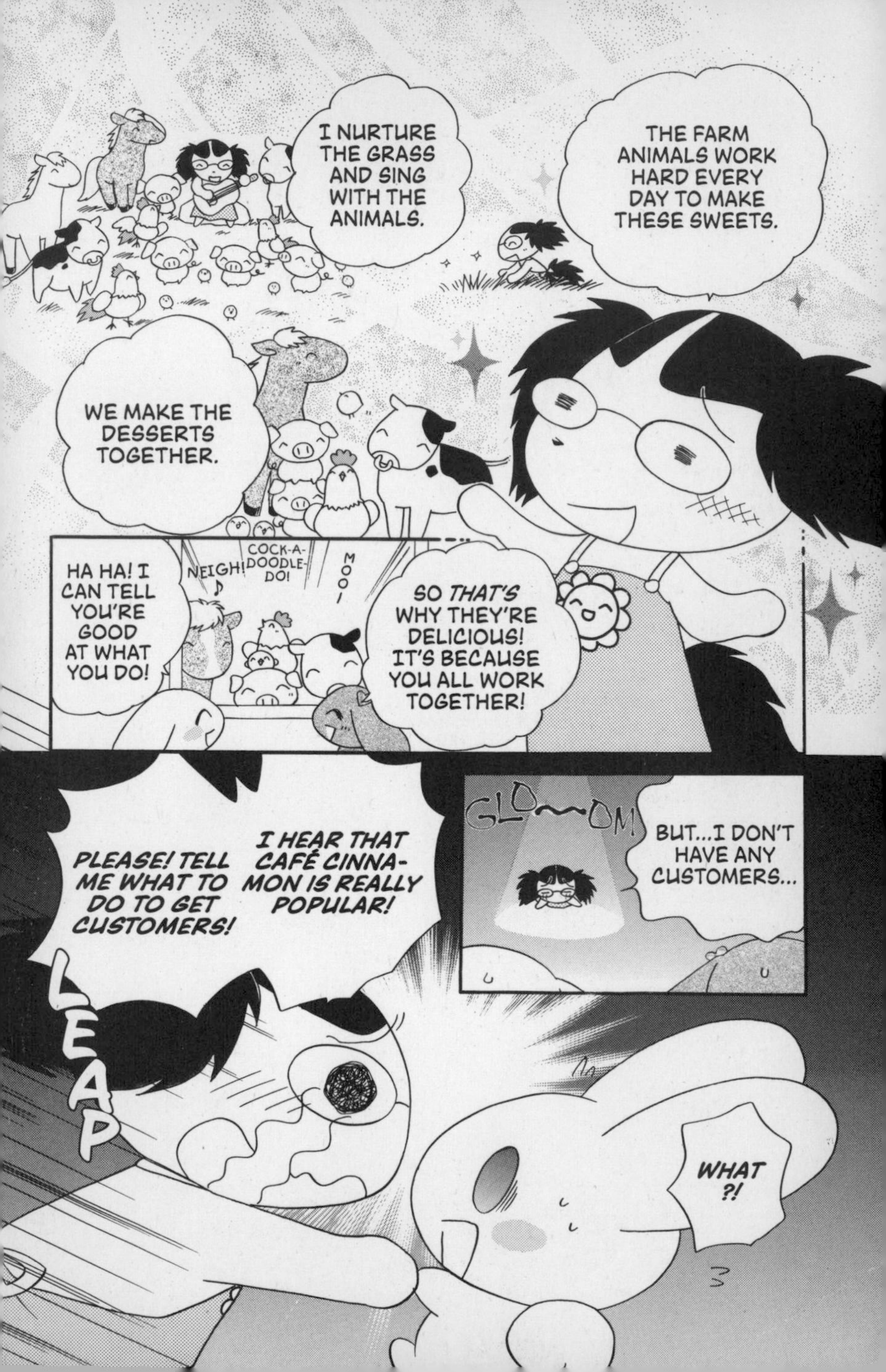
THE FARM ANIMALS WORK HARD EVERY DAY TO MAKE THESE SWEETS.
I NURTURE THE GRASS AND SING WITH THE ANIMALS.
WE MAKE THE DESSERTS TOGETHER.
SO THAT'S WHY THEY'RE DELICIOUS! IT'S BECAUSE YOU ALL WORK TOGETHER!
MOO!
COCK-A-DOODLE-DO!
NEIGH!♪
HA HA! I CAN TELL YOU'RE GOOD AT WHAT YOU DO!
GLOOM!
BUT...I DON'T HAVE ANY CUSTOMERS...
I HEAR THAT CAFÉ CINNAMON IS REALLY POPULAR!
PLEASE! TELL ME WHAT TO DO TO GET CUSTOMERS!
LEAP
WHAT?!

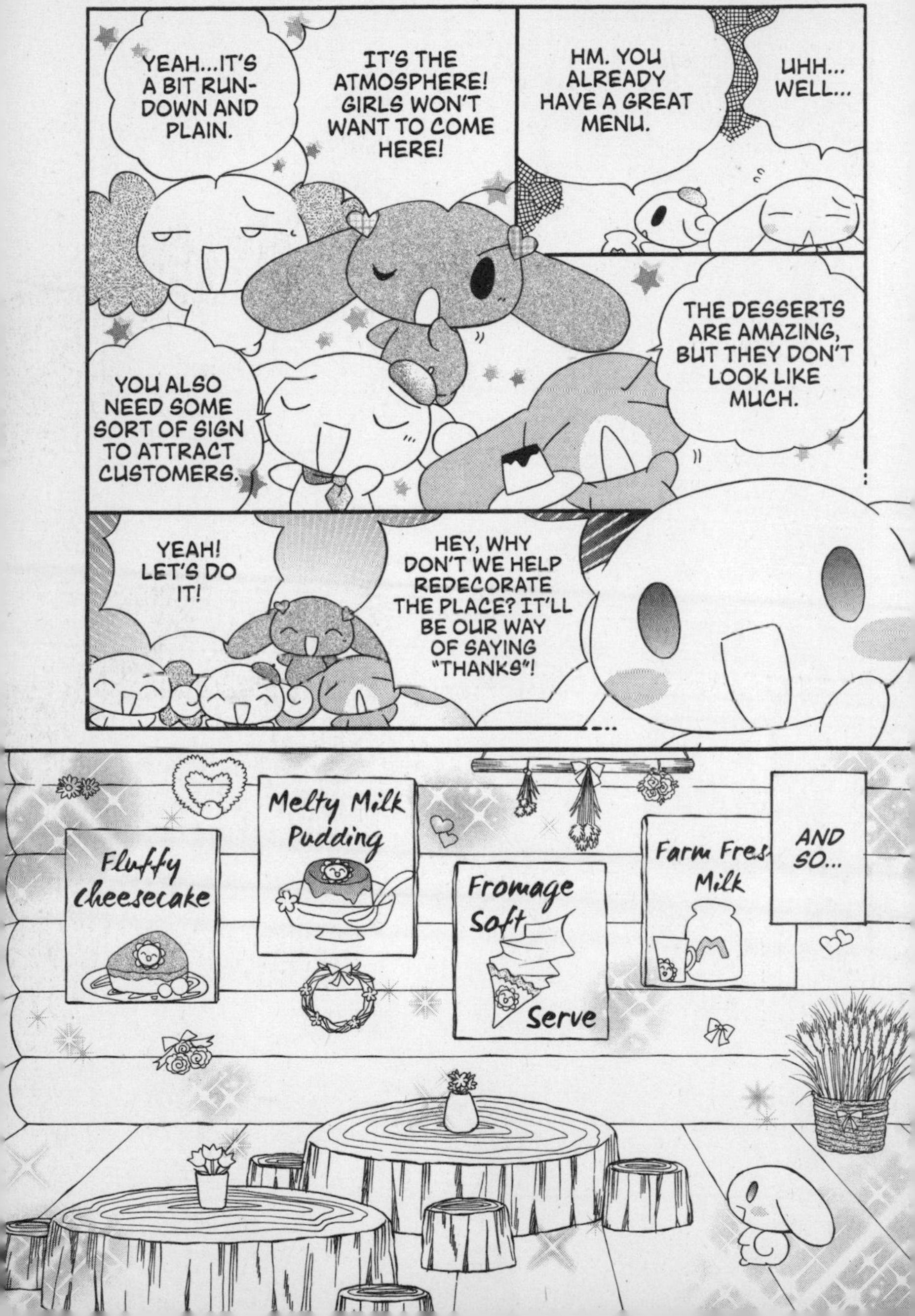
UHH... WELL...
HM. YOU ALREADY HAVE A GREAT MENU.
THE DESSERTS ARE AMAZING, BUT THEY DON'T LOOK LIKE MUCH.
IT'S THE ATMOSPHERE! GIRLS WON'T WANT TO COME HERE!
YEAH...IT'S A BIT RUN-DOWN AND PLAIN.
YOU ALSO NEED SOME SORT OF SIGN TO ATTRACT CUSTOMERS.
HEY, WHY DON'T WE HELP REDECORATE THE PLACE? IT'LL BE OUR WAY OF SAYING "THANKS"!
YEAH! LET'S DO IT!
AND SO...
Farm Fres Milk
Fromage Soft Serve
Melty Milk Pudding
Fluffy Cheesecake

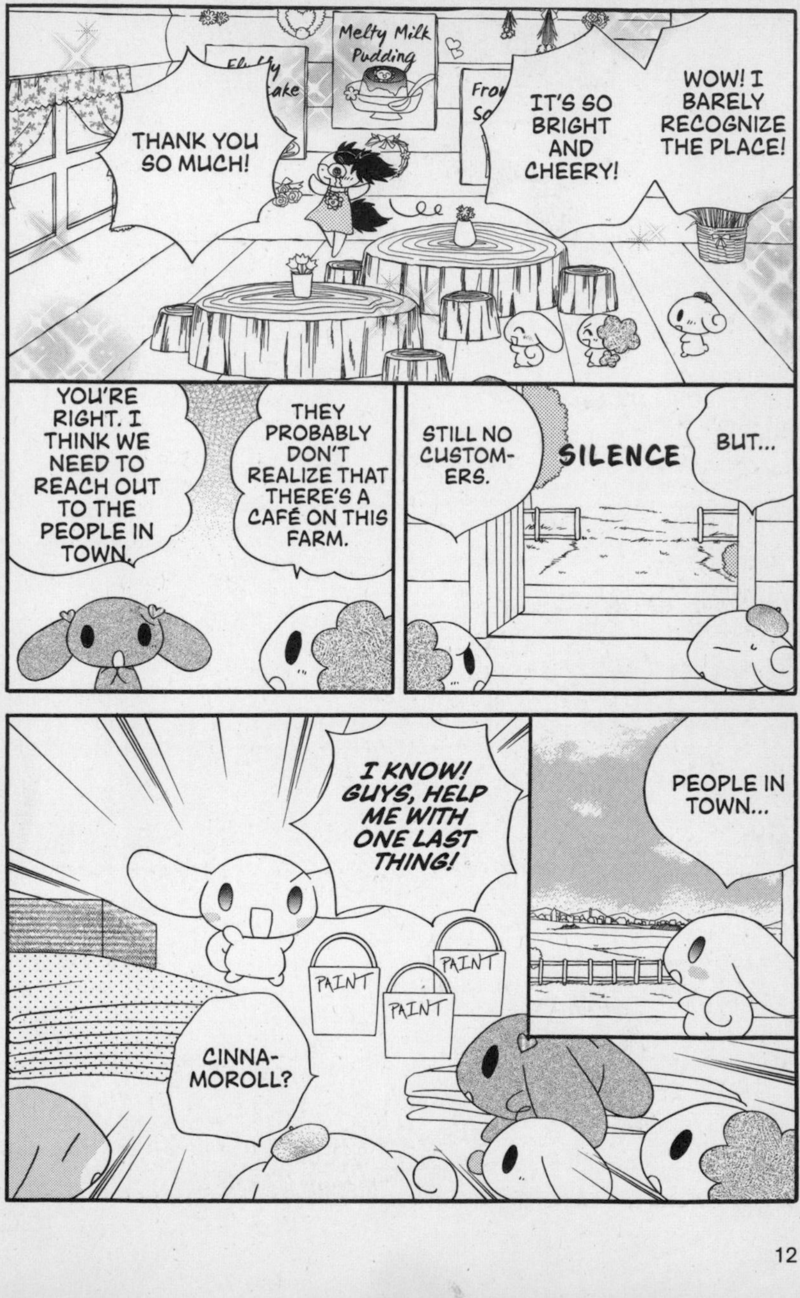

WOW! I BARELY RECOGNIZE THE PLACE!
IT'S SO BRIGHT AND CHEERY!
Melty Milk Pudding
THANK YOU SO MUCH!
BUT...
SILENCE
STILL NO CUSTOMERS.
THEY PROBABLY DON'T REALIZE THAT THERE'S A CAFÉ ON THIS FARM.
YOU'RE RIGHT. I THINK WE NEED TO REACH OUT TO THE PEOPLE IN TOWN.
PEOPLE IN TOWN...
I KNOW! GUYS, HELP ME WITH ONE LAST THING!
PAINT
PAINT
PAINT
CINNAMOROLL?

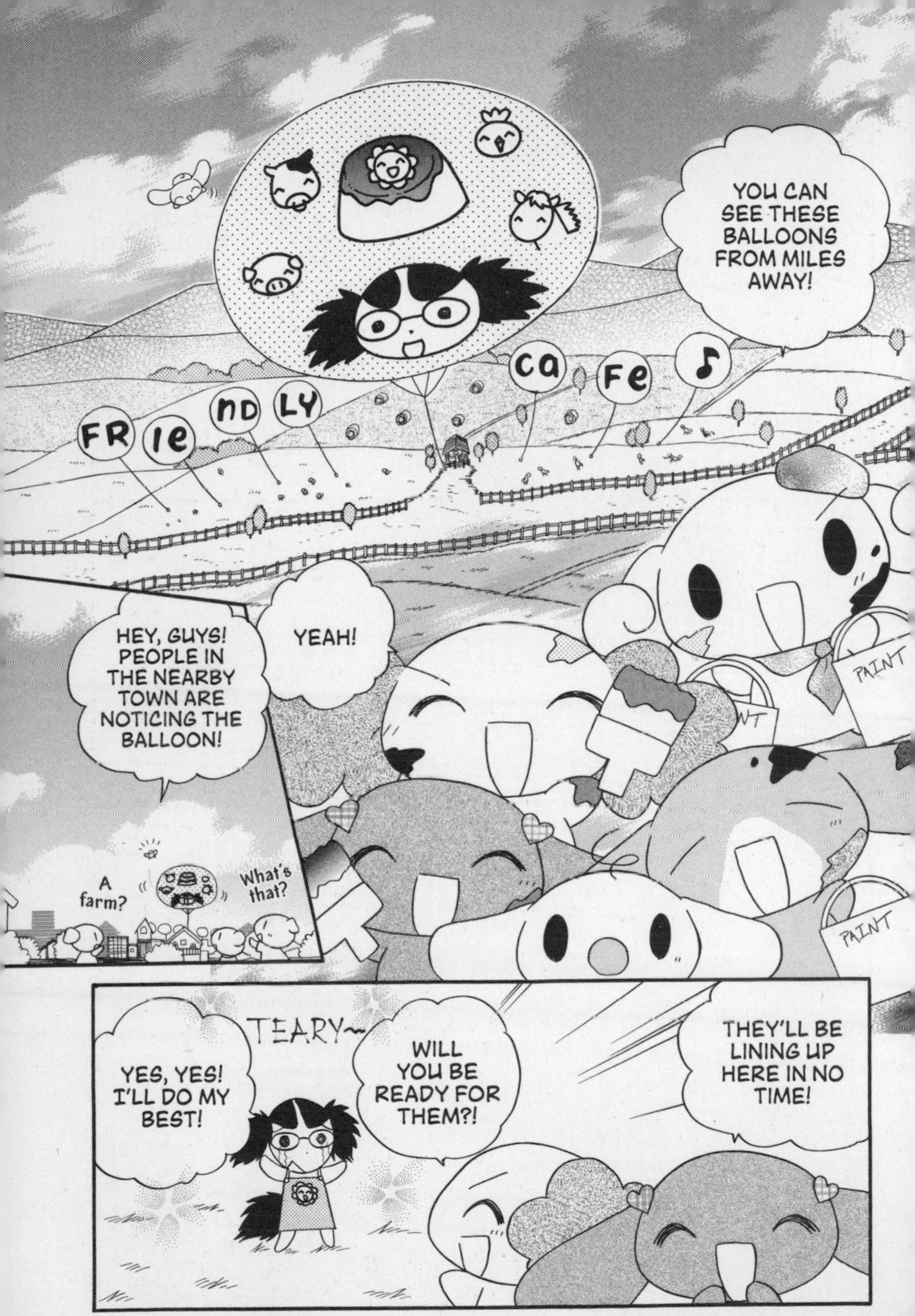
YOU CAN SEE THESE BALLOONS FROM MILES AWAY!
FRieNDLY CaFe ♪
HEY, GUYS! PEOPLE IN THE NEARBY TOWN ARE NOTICING THE BALLOON!
YEAH!
What's that?
A farm?
PAINT
PAINT
THEY'LL BE LINING UP HERE IN NO TIME!
WILL YOU BE READY FOR THEM?!
TEARY~
YES, YES! I'LL DO MY BEST!

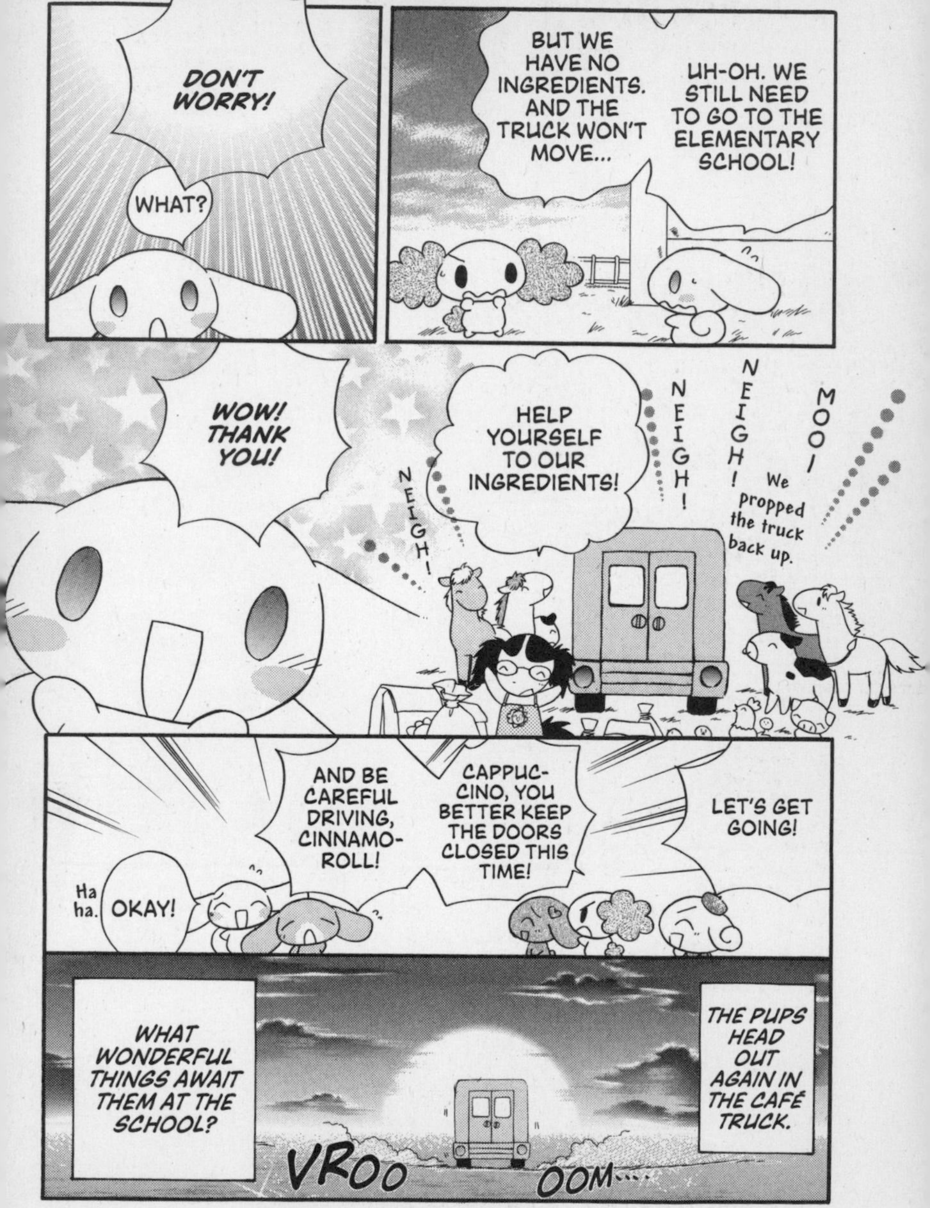
UH-OH. WE STILL NEED TO GO TO THE ELEMENTARY SCHOOL!
BUT WE HAVE NO INGREDIENTS. AND THE TRUCK WON'T MOVE...
DON'T WORRY!
WHAT?
MOO!
NEIGH!
NEIGH!
We propped the truck back up.
HELP YOURSELF TO OUR INGREDIENTS!
NEIGH!
WOW! THANK YOU!
LET'S GET GOING!
CAPPUCCINO, YOU BETTER KEEP THE DOORS CLOSED THIS TIME!
AND BE CAREFUL DRIVING, CINNAMOROLL!
OKAY!
Ha ha.
THE PUPS HEAD OUT AGAIN IN THE CAFÉ TRUCK.
WHAT WONDERFUL THINGS AWAIT THEM AT THE SCHOOL?
VROOOOM...

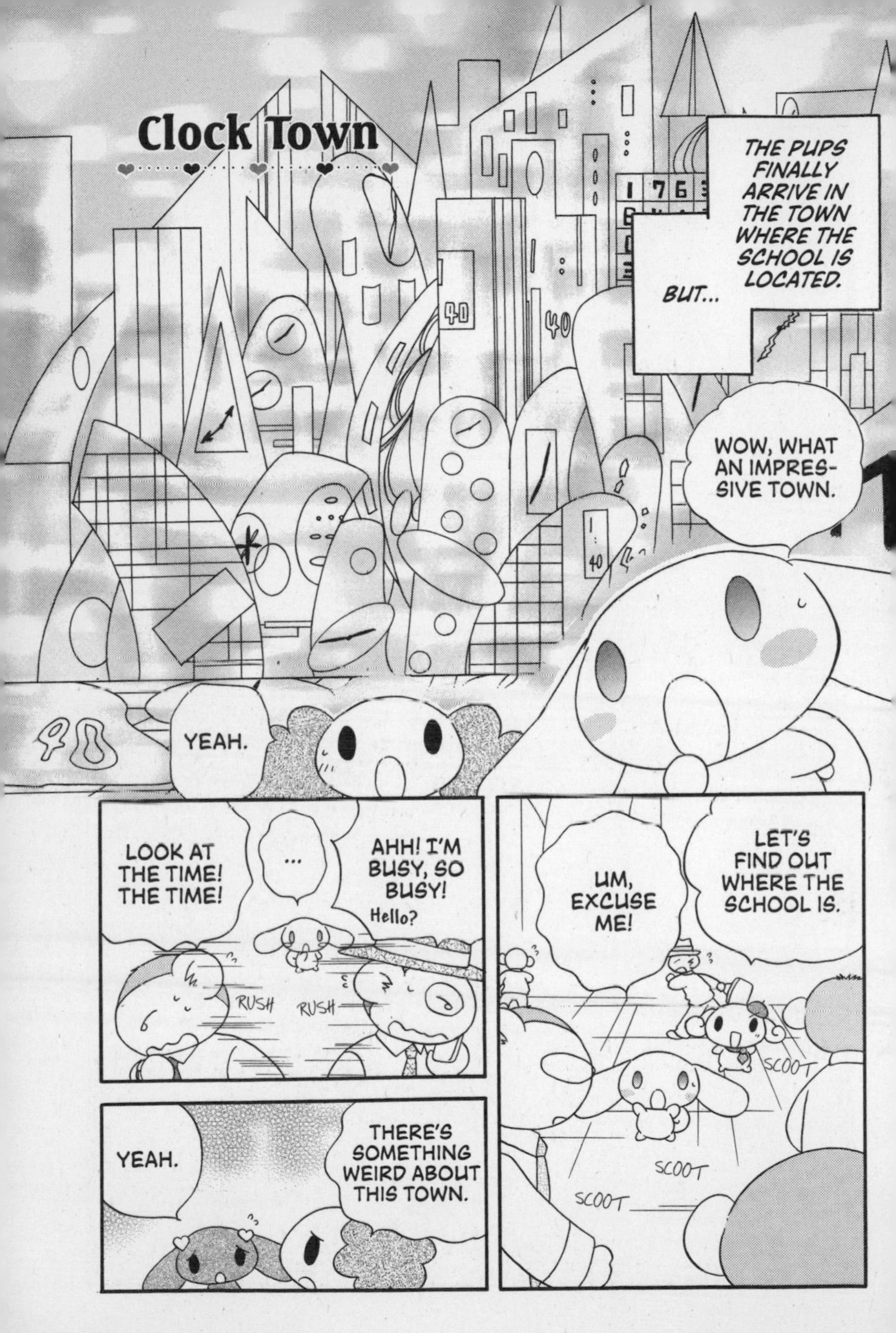
Clock Town
THE PUPS FINALLY ARRIVE IN THE TOWN WHERE THE SCHOOL IS LOCATED.
BUT...
WOW, WHAT AN IMPRESSIVE TOWN.
YEAH.
LET'S FIND OUT WHERE THE SCHOOL IS.
UM, EXCUSE ME!
SCOOT
SCOOT
SCOOT
AHH! I'M BUSY, SO BUSY!
Hello?
...
LOOK AT THE TIME! THE TIME!
RUSH
RUSH
THERE'S SOMETHING WEIRD ABOUT THIS TOWN.
YEAH.

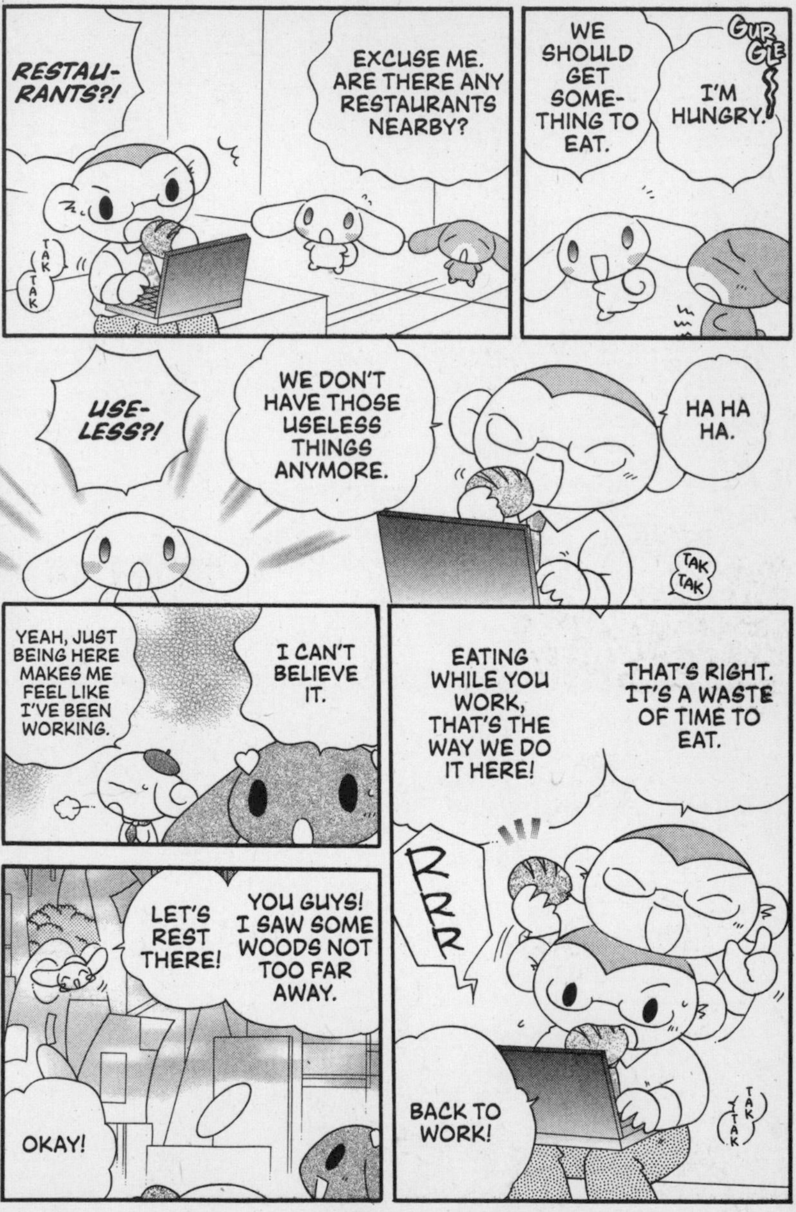
GURGLE
I'M HUNGRY.
WE SHOULD GET SOMETHING TO EAT.
EXCUSE ME. ARE THERE ANY RESTAURANTS NEARBY?
RESTAURANTS?!
TAK TAK
HA HA HA.
WE DON'T HAVE THOSE USELESS THINGS ANYMORE.
USELESS?!
TAK TAK
THAT'S RIGHT. IT'S A WASTE OF TIME TO EAT.
EATING WHILE YOU WORK, THAT'S THE WAY WE DO IT HERE!
RRR
BACK TO WORK!
TAK TAK
I CAN'T BELIEVE IT.
YEAH, JUST BEING HERE MAKES ME FEEL LIKE I'VE BEEN WORKING.
YOU GUYS! I SAW SOME WOODS NOT TOO FAR AWAY.
LET'S REST THERE!
OKAY!

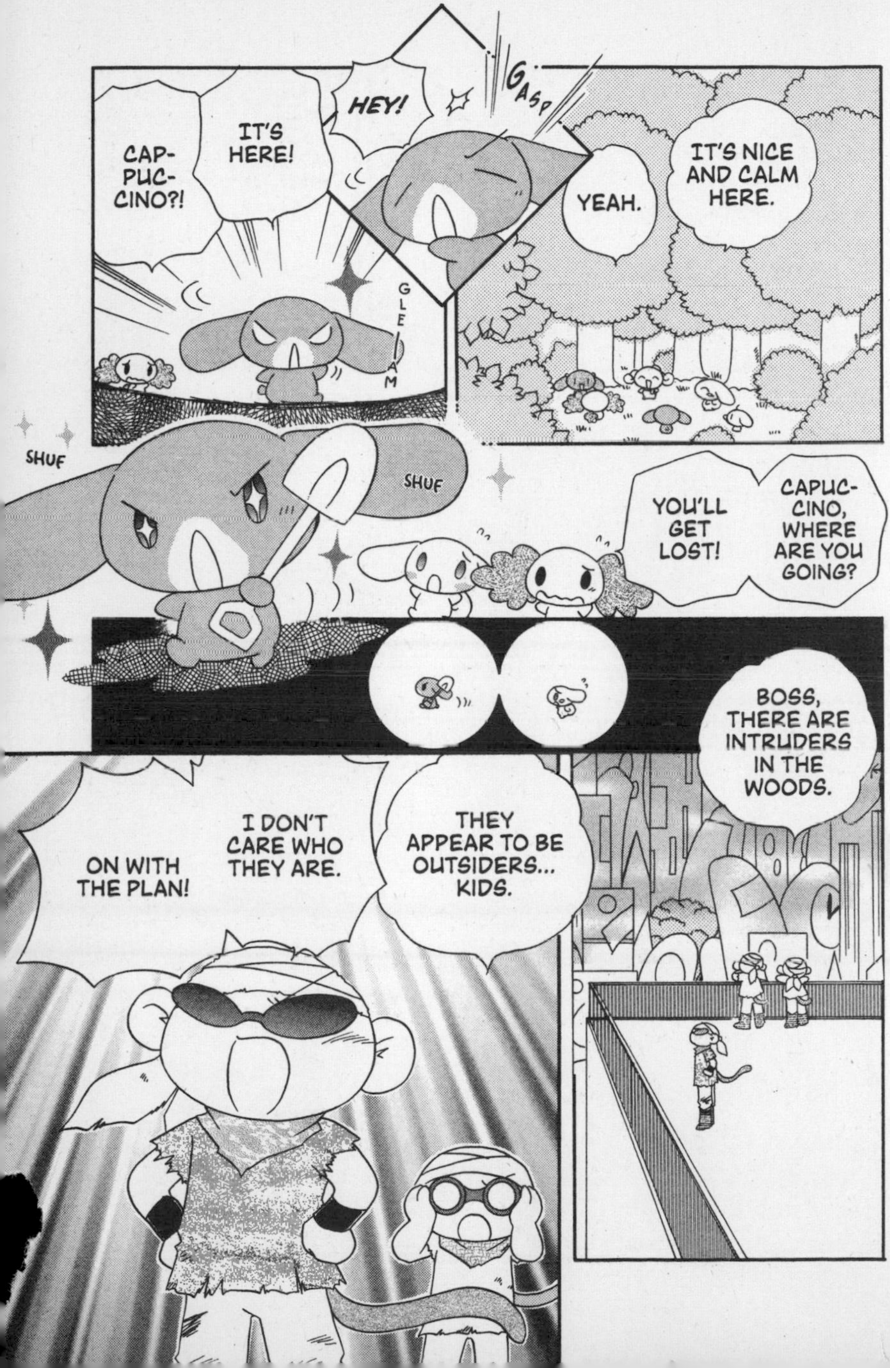
IT'S NICE AND CALM HERE.
YEAH.
GASP
HEY!
IT'S HERE!
CAP-PUC-CINO?!
GLEAM
CAPUC-CINO, WHERE ARE YOU GOING?
YOU'LL GET LOST!
SHUF
SHUF
BOSS, THERE ARE INTRUDERS IN THE WOODS.
THEY APPEAR TO BE OUTSIDERS... KIDS.
I DON'T CARE WHO THEY ARE.
ON WITH THE PLAN!

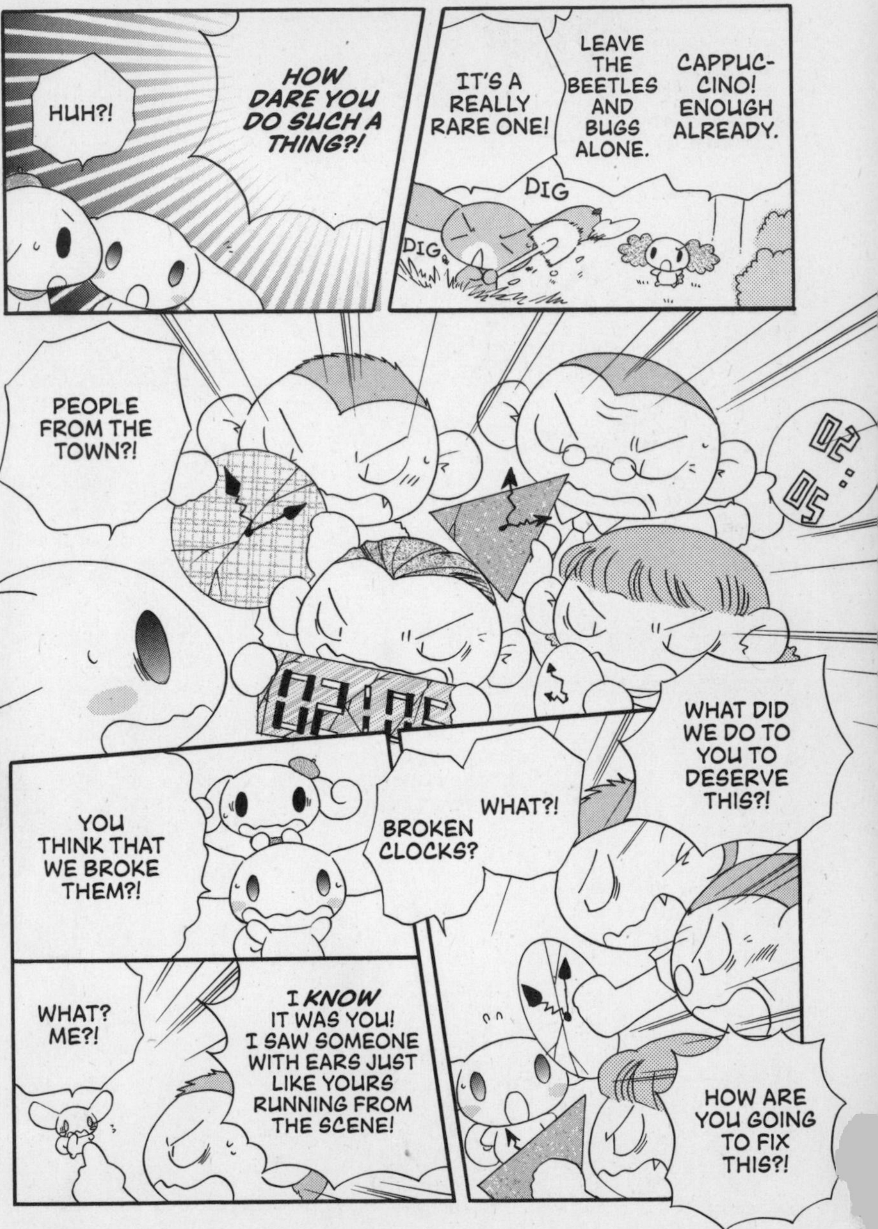
CAPPUCCINO! ENOUGH ALREADY.
LEAVE THE BEETLES AND BUGS ALONE.
IT'S A REALLY RARE ONE!
DIG
DIG
HOW DARE YOU DO SUCH A THING?!
HUH?!
02:05
PEOPLE FROM THE TOWN?!
WHAT DID WE DO TO YOU TO DESERVE THIS?!
WHAT?!
BROKEN CLOCKS?
YOU THINK THAT WE BROKE THEM?!
HOW ARE YOU GOING TO FIX THIS?!
I *KNOW* IT WAS YOU! I SAW SOMEONE WITH EARS JUST LIKE YOURS RUNNING FROM THE SCENE!
WHAT? ME?!

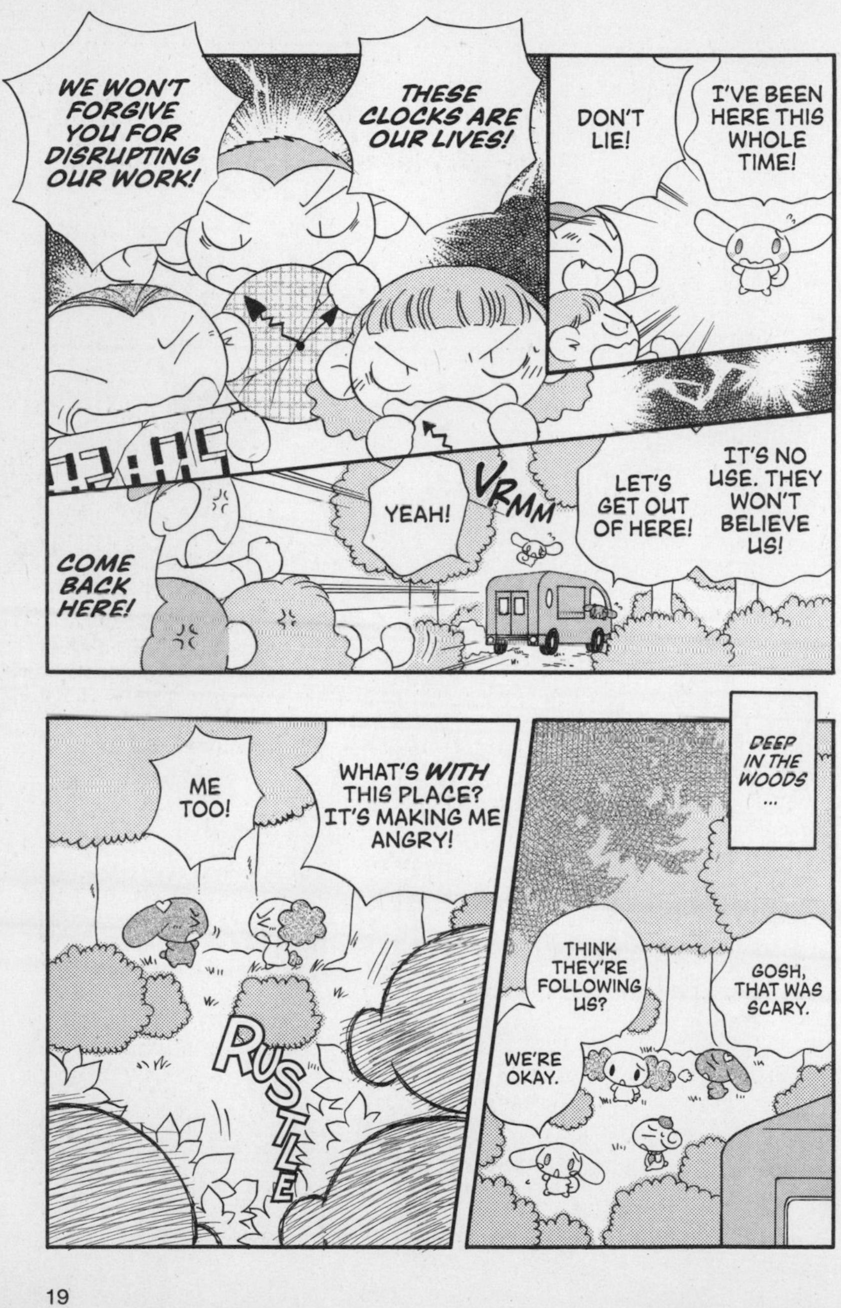
I'VE BEEN HERE THIS WHOLE TIME!
DON'T LIE!
THESE CLOCKS ARE OUR LIVES!
WE WON'T FORGIVE YOU FOR DISRUPTING OUR WORK!
IT'S NO USE. THEY WON'T BELIEVE US!
LET'S GET OUT OF HERE!
VRMM
YEAH!
COME BACK HERE!
DEEP IN THE WOODS ...
GOSH, THAT WAS SCARY.
THINK THEY'RE FOLLOWING US?
WE'RE OKAY.
WHAT'S *WITH* THIS PLACE? IT'S MAKING ME ANGRY!
ME TOO!
RUSTLE

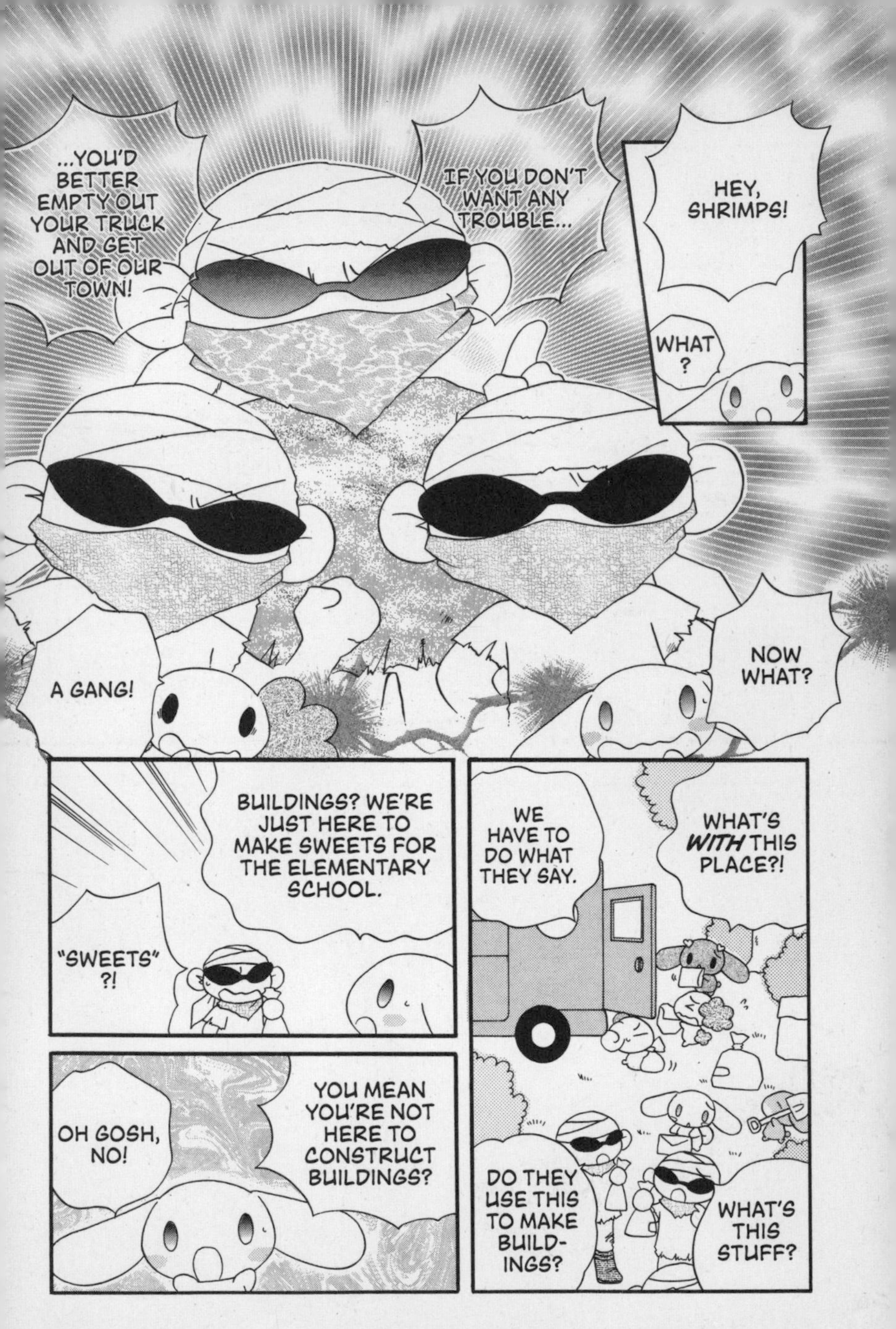
HEY, SHRIMPS!
WHAT?
IF YOU DON'T WANT ANY TROUBLE...
...YOU'D BETTER EMPTY OUT YOUR TRUCK AND GET OUT OF OUR TOWN!
NOW WHAT?
A GANG!
WHAT'S *WITH* THIS PLACE?!
WE HAVE TO DO WHAT THEY SAY.
WHAT'S THIS STUFF?
DO THEY USE THIS TO MAKE BUILD-INGS?
BUILDINGS? WE'RE JUST HERE TO MAKE SWEETS FOR THE ELEMENTARY SCHOOL.
"SWEETS"?!
YOU MEAN YOU'RE NOT HERE TO CONSTRUCT BUILDINGS?
OH GOSH, NO!

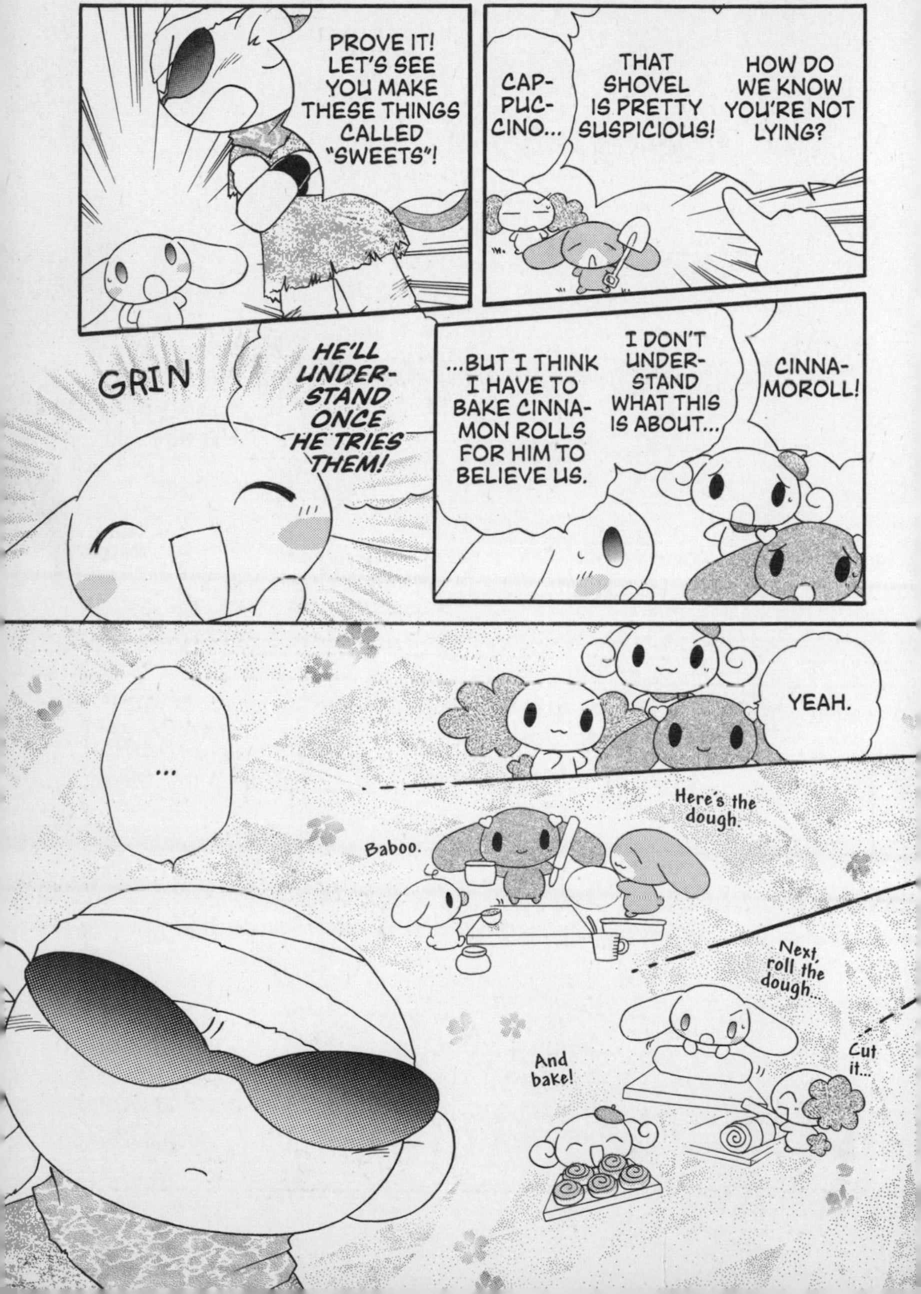
HOW DO WE KNOW YOU'RE NOT LYING?
THAT SHOVEL IS PRETTY SUSPICIOUS!
CAP-PUC-CINO...
PROVE IT! LET'S SEE YOU MAKE THESE THINGS CALLED "SWEETS"!
CINNA-MOROLL!
I DON'T UNDER-STAND WHAT THIS IS ABOUT...
...BUT I THINK I HAVE TO BAKE CINNA-MON ROLLS FOR HIM TO BELIEVE US.
HE'LL UNDER-STAND ONCE HE TRIES THEM!
GRIN
YEAH.
...
Here's the dough.
Baboo.
Next, roll the dough...
Cut it...
And bake!

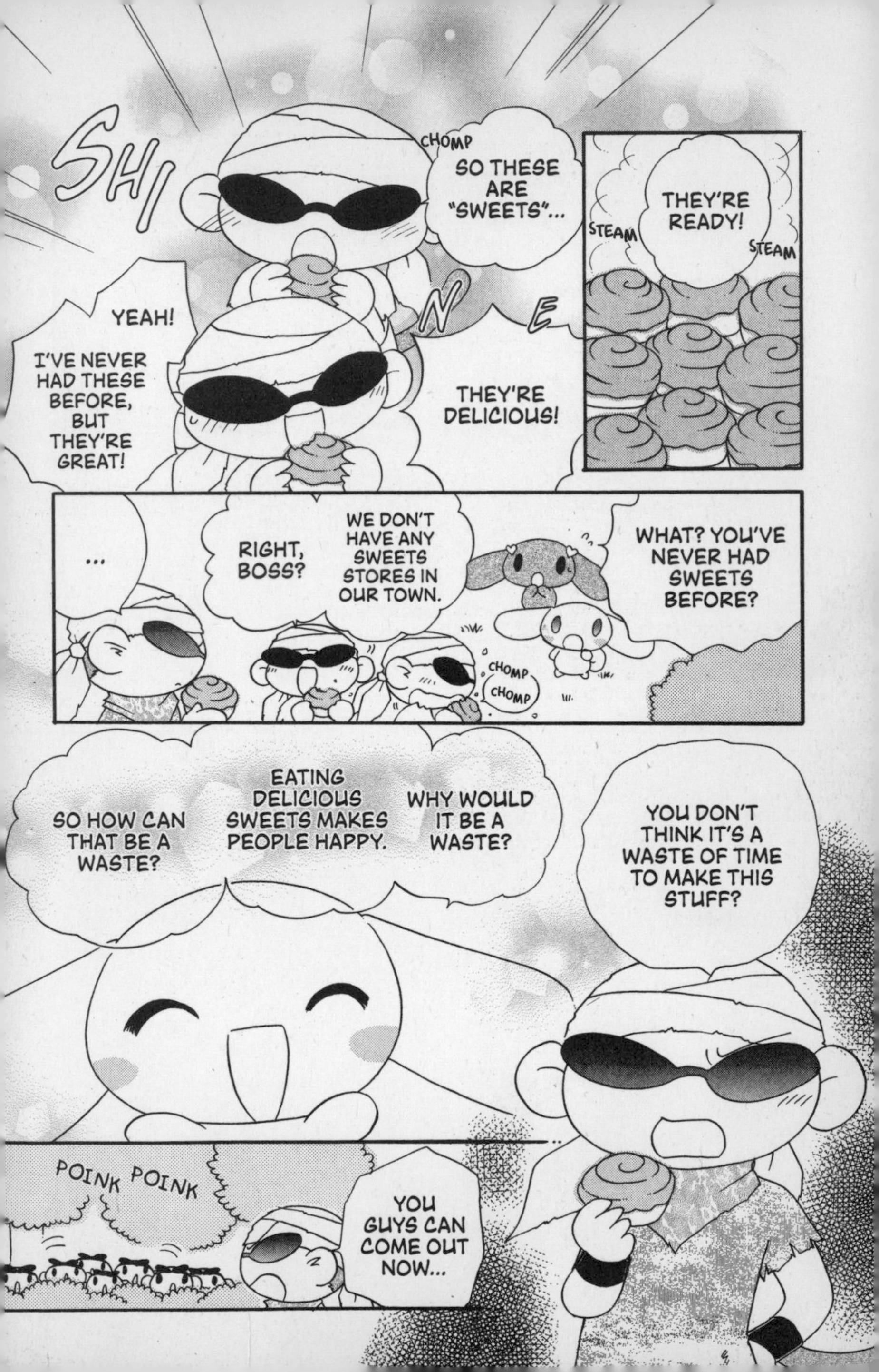
STEAM
THEY'RE READY!
STEAM
SHINE
CHOMP
SO THESE ARE "SWEETS"...
THEY'RE DELICIOUS!
YEAH!
I'VE NEVER HAD THESE BEFORE, BUT THEY'RE GREAT!
WHAT? YOU'VE NEVER HAD SWEETS BEFORE?
WE DON'T HAVE ANY SWEETS STORES IN OUR TOWN.
RIGHT, BOSS?
...
CHOMP
CHOMP
YOU DON'T THINK IT'S A WASTE OF TIME TO MAKE THIS STUFF?
WHY WOULD IT BE A WASTE?
EATING DELICIOUS SWEETS MAKES PEOPLE HAPPY.
SO HOW CAN THAT BE A WASTE?
...
YOU GUYS CAN COME OUT NOW...
POINK POINK

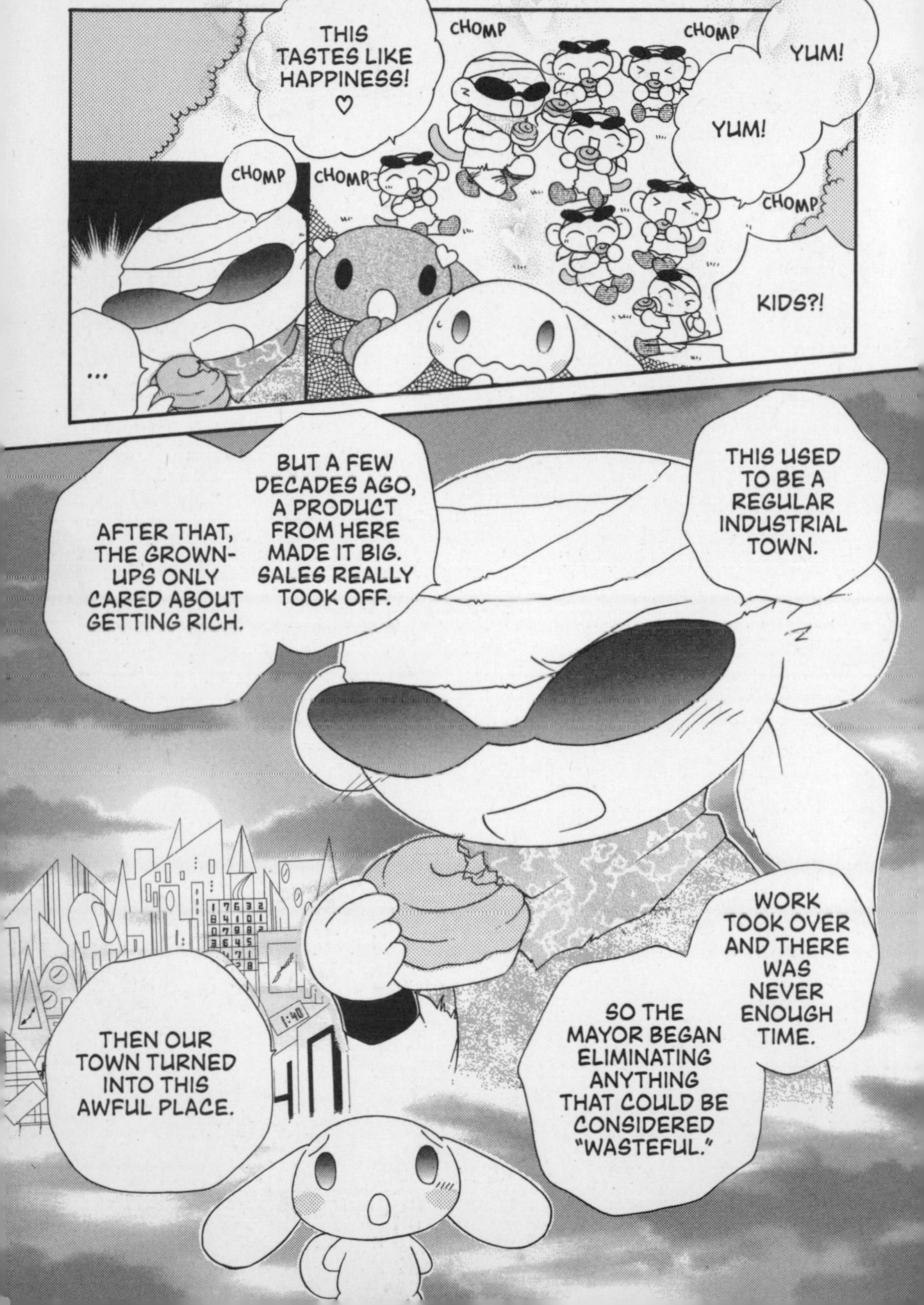
YUM!
YUM!
CHOMP
CHOMP
THIS TASTES LIKE HAPPINESS! ♡
CHOMP
KIDS?!
CHOMP
CHOMP
...
THIS USED TO BE A REGULAR INDUSTRIAL TOWN.
BUT A FEW DECADES AGO, A PRODUCT FROM HERE MADE IT BIG. SALES REALLY TOOK OFF.
AFTER THAT, THE GROWN-UPS ONLY CARED ABOUT GETTING RICH.
WORK TOOK OVER AND THERE WAS NEVER ENOUGH TIME.
SO THE MAYOR BEGAN ELIMINATING ANYTHING THAT COULD BE CONSIDERED "WASTEFUL."
THEN OUR TOWN TURNED INTO THIS AWFUL PLACE.

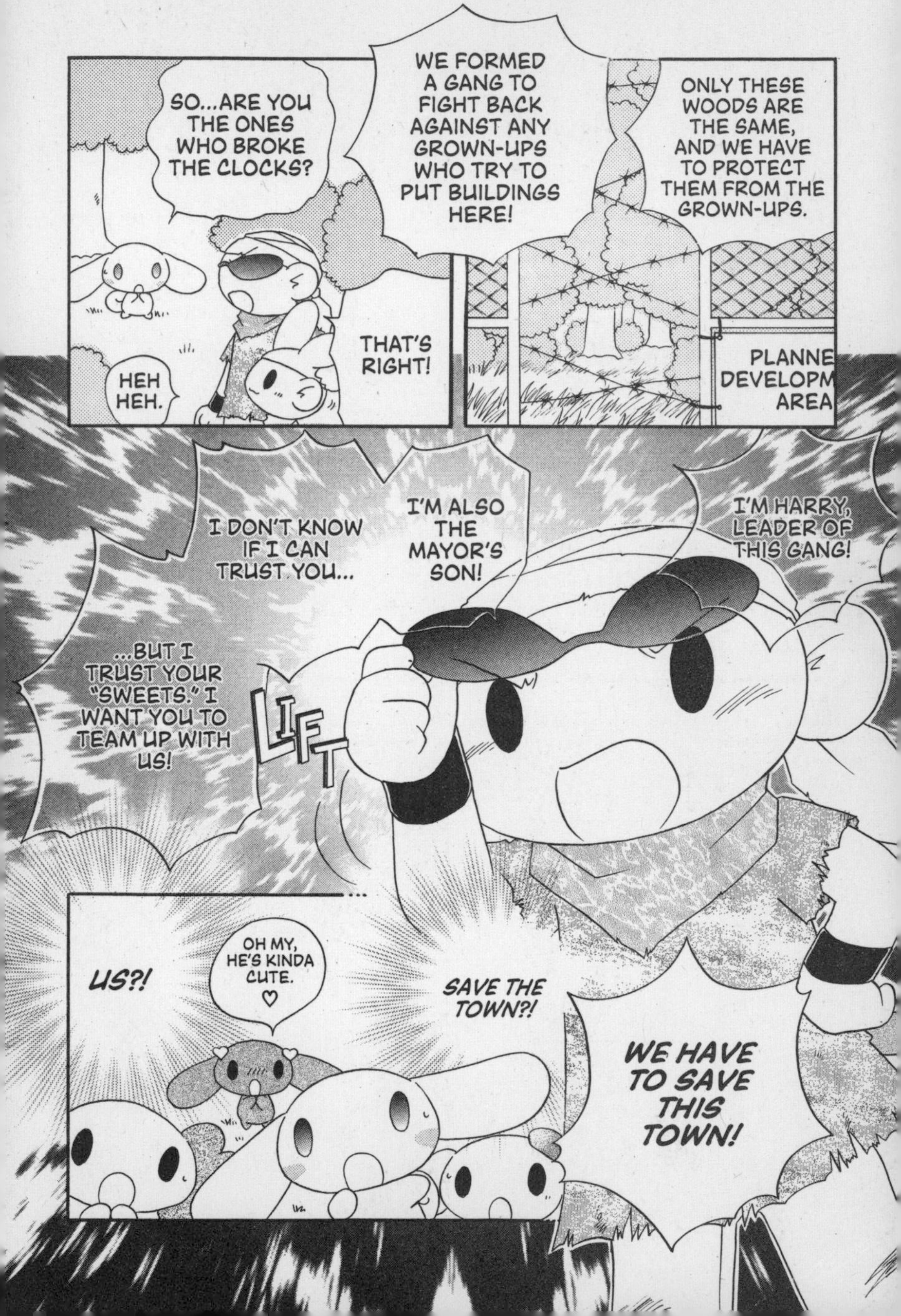
ONLY THESE WOODS ARE THE SAME, AND WE HAVE TO PROTECT THEM FROM THE GROWN-UPS.
PLANNE DEVELOPM AREA
WE FORMED A GANG TO FIGHT BACK AGAINST ANY GROWN-UPS WHO TRY TO PUT BUILDINGS HERE!
SO...ARE YOU THE ONES WHO BROKE THE CLOCKS?
THAT'S RIGHT!
HEH HEH.
I'M HARRY, LEADER OF THIS GANG!
I'M ALSO THE MAYOR'S SON!
I DON'T KNOW IF I CAN TRUST YOU...
...BUT I TRUST YOUR "SWEETS." I WANT YOU TO TEAM UP WITH US!
LIFT
WE HAVE TO SAVE THIS TOWN!
SAVE THE TOWN?!
OH MY, HE'S KINDA CUTE. ♡
US?!

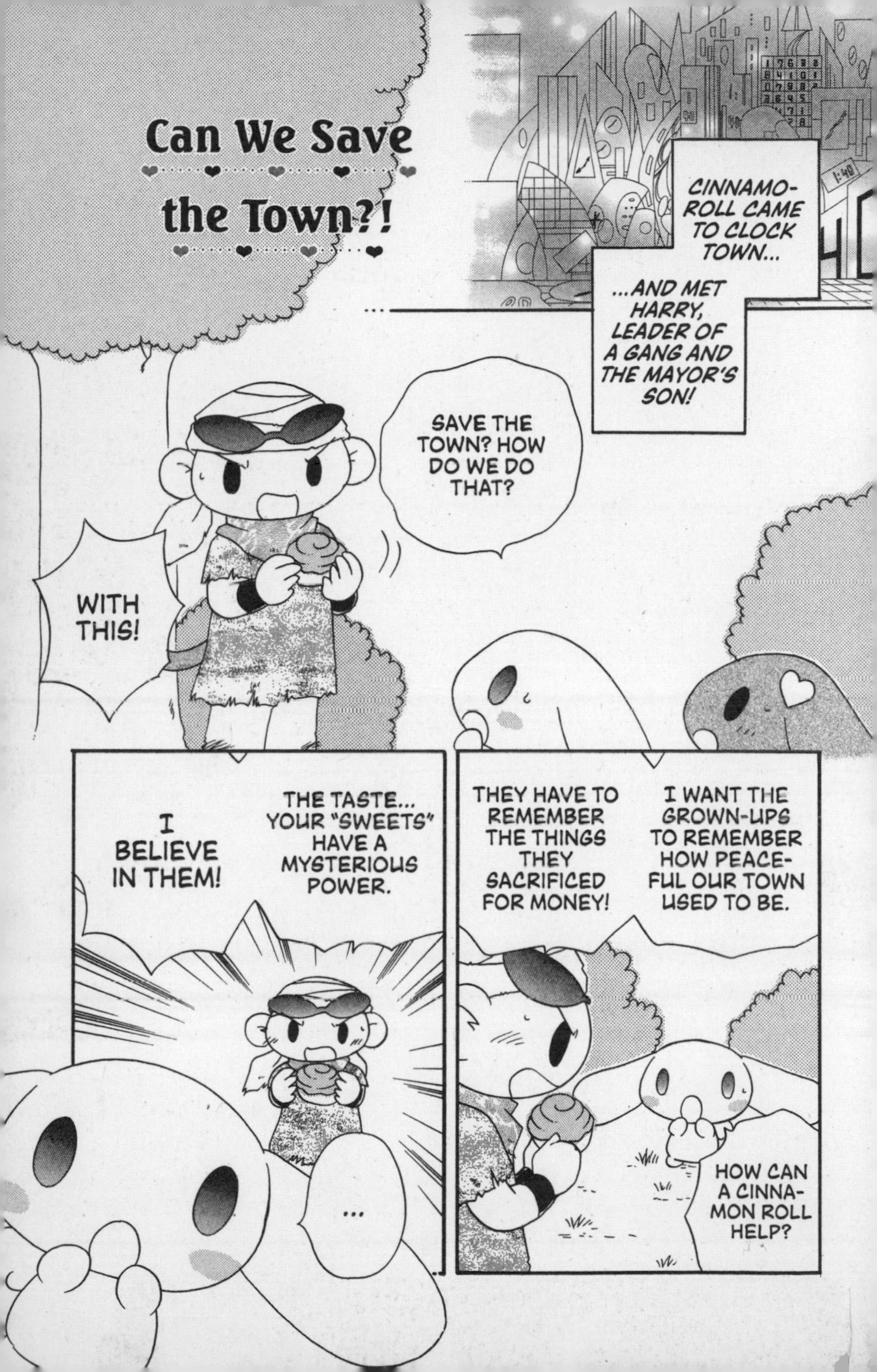
CINNAMO-ROLL CAME TO CLOCK TOWN...
...AND MET HARRY, LEADER OF A GANG AND THE MAYOR'S SON!
Can We Save the Town?!
SAVE THE TOWN? HOW DO WE DO THAT?
WITH THIS!
I WANT THE GROWN-UPS TO REMEMBER HOW PEACE-FUL OUR TOWN USED TO BE.
THEY HAVE TO REMEMBER THE THINGS THEY SACRIFICED FOR MONEY!
HOW CAN A CINNA-MON ROLL HELP?
THE TASTE... YOUR "SWEETS" HAVE A MYSTERIOUS POWER.
I BELIEVE IN THEM!
...

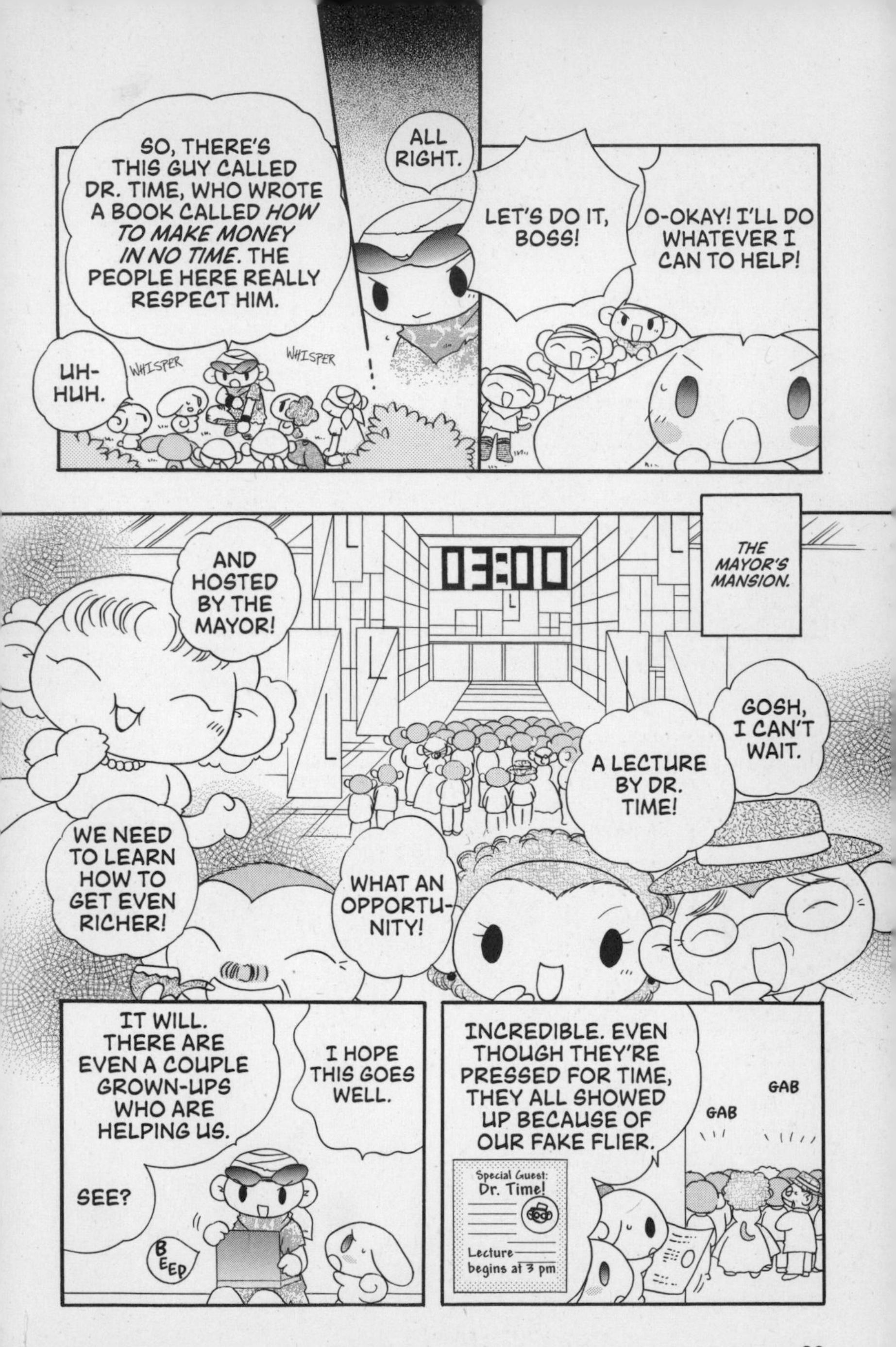
O-OKAY! I'LL DO WHATEVER I CAN TO HELP!
LET'S DO IT, BOSS!
ALL RIGHT.
SO, THERE'S THIS GUY CALLED DR. TIME, WHO WROTE A BOOK CALLED *HOW TO MAKE MONEY IN NO TIME*. THE PEOPLE HERE REALLY RESPECT HIM.
WHISPER
WHISPER
UH-HUH.
THE MAYOR'S MANSION.
03:00
GOSH, I CAN'T WAIT.
A LECTURE BY DR. TIME!
AND HOSTED BY THE MAYOR!
WHAT AN OPPORTUNITY!
WE NEED TO LEARN HOW TO GET EVEN RICHER!
INCREDIBLE. EVEN THOUGH THEY'RE PRESSED FOR TIME, THEY ALL SHOWED UP BECAUSE OF OUR FAKE FLIER.
GAB
GAB
Special Guest: Dr. Time!
Lecture begins at 3 pm
I HOPE THIS GOES WELL.
IT WILL. THERE ARE EVEN A COUPLE GROWN-UPS WHO ARE HELPING US.
SEE?
BEEP

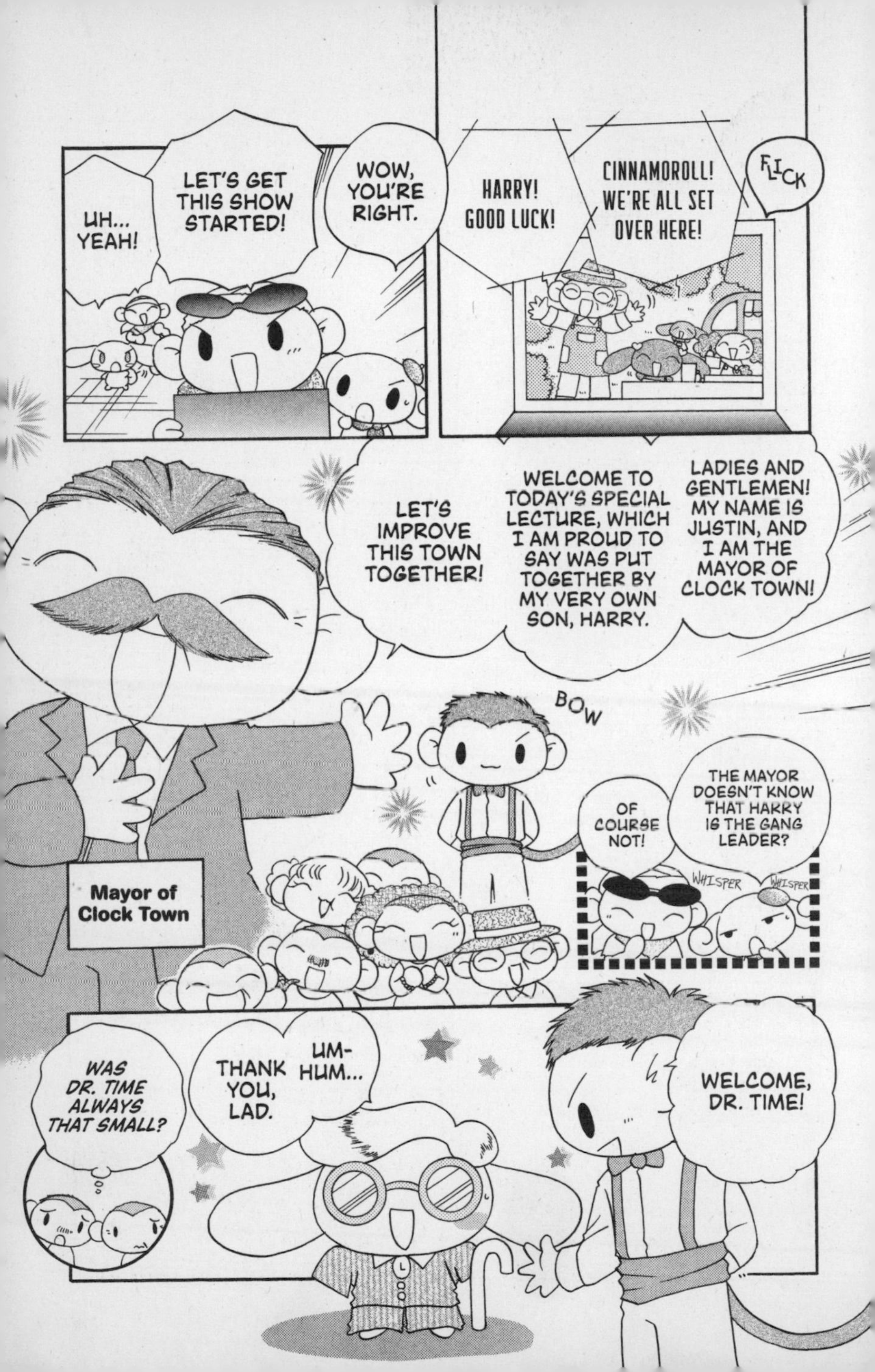
FLICK
CINNAMOROLL! WE'RE ALL SET OVER HERE!
HARRY! GOOD LUCK!
WOW, YOU'RE RIGHT.
LET'S GET THIS SHOW STARTED!
UH... YEAH!
LADIES AND GENTLEMEN! MY NAME IS JUSTIN, AND I AM THE MAYOR OF CLOCK TOWN!
WELCOME TO TODAY'S SPECIAL LECTURE, WHICH I AM PROUD TO SAY WAS PUT TOGETHER BY MY VERY OWN SON, HARRY.
LET'S IMPROVE THIS TOWN TOGETHER!
BOW
Mayor of Clock Town
THE MAYOR DOESN'T KNOW THAT HARRY IS THE GANG LEADER?
OF COURSE NOT!
WHISPER
WHISPER
WELCOME, DR. TIME!
UM-HUM...
THANK YOU, LAD.
WAS DR. TIME ALWAYS THAT SMALL?

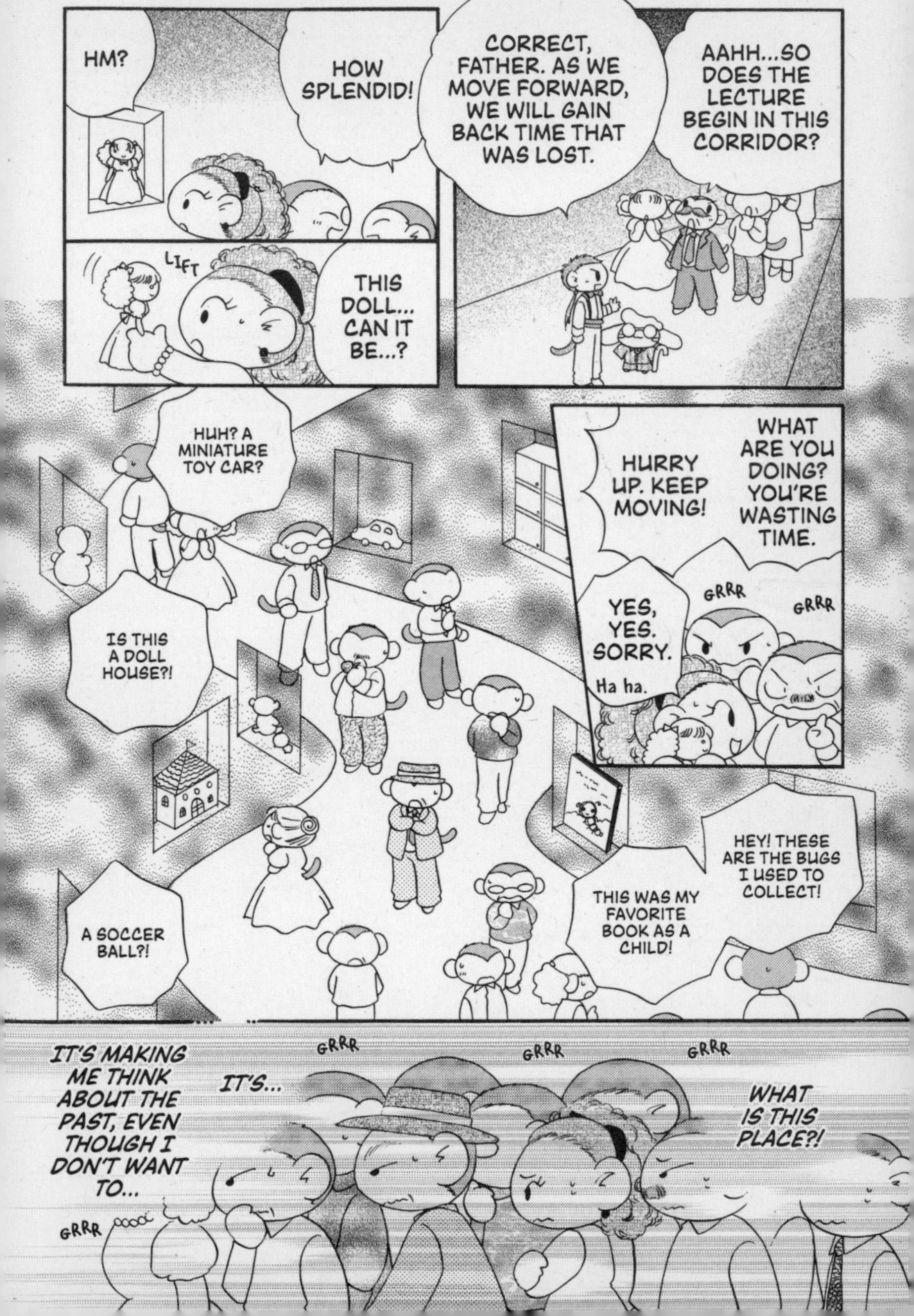
AAHH...SO DOES THE LECTURE BEGIN IN THIS CORRIDOR?
CORRECT, FATHER. AS WE MOVE FORWARD, WE WILL GAIN BACK TIME THAT WAS LOST.
HOW SPLENDID!
HM?
THIS DOLL... CAN IT BE...?
LIFT
WHAT ARE YOU DOING? YOU'RE WASTING TIME.
HURRY UP. KEEP MOVING!
GRRR
GRRR
YES, YES. SORRY.
Ha ha.
HUH? A MINIATURE TOY CAR?
IS THIS A DOLL HOUSE?!
HEY! THESE ARE THE BUGS I USED TO COLLECT!
THIS WAS MY FAVORITE BOOK AS A CHILD!
A SOCCER BALL?!
WHAT IS THIS PLACE?!
GRRR
GRRR
IT'S...
GRRR
IT'S MAKING ME THINK ABOUT THE PAST, EVEN THOUGH I DON'T WANT TO...
GRRR

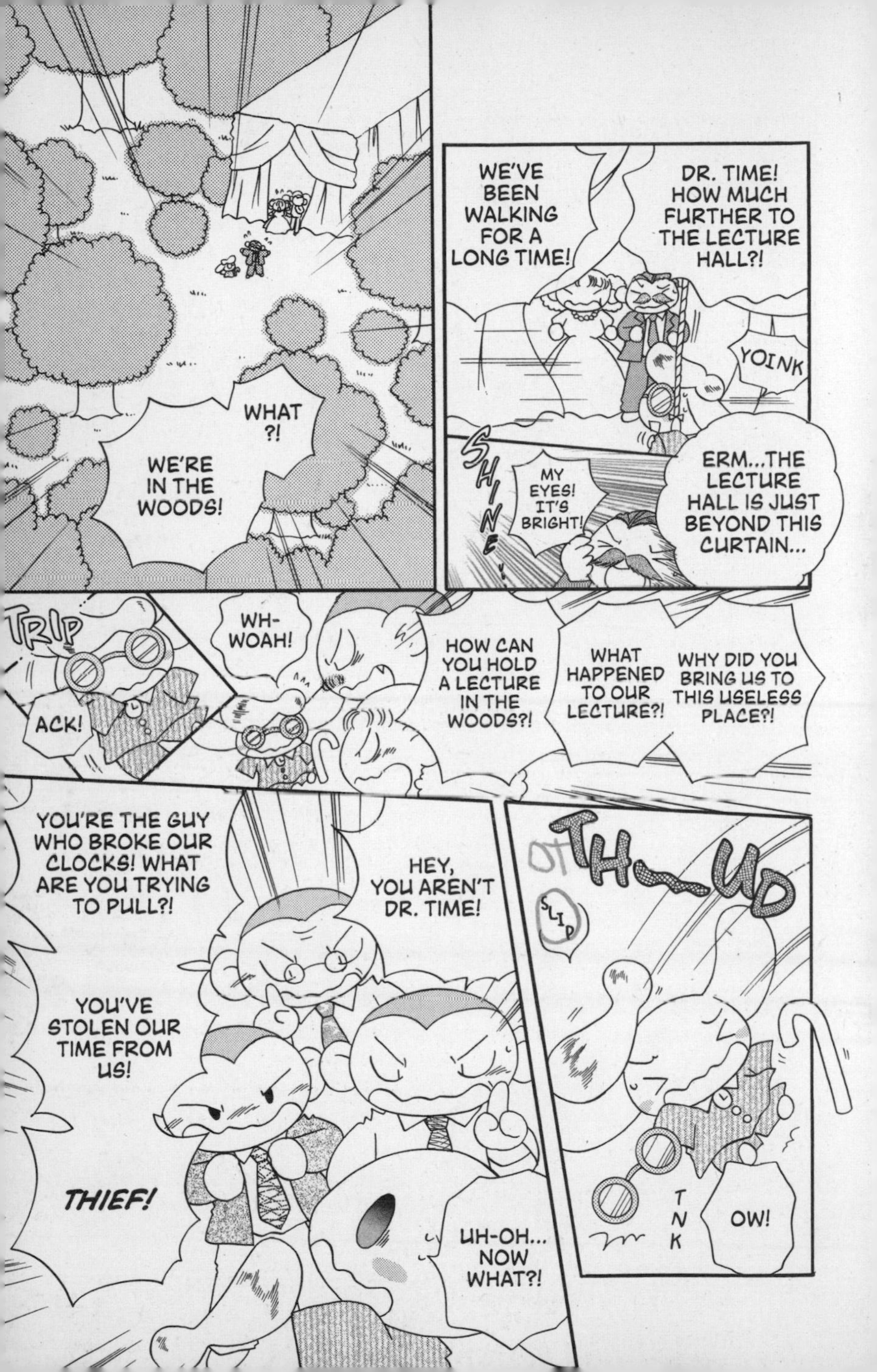
DR. TIME! HOW MUCH FURTHER TO THE LECTURE HALL?!
WE'VE BEEN WALKING FOR A LONG TIME!
YOINK
ERM...THE LECTURE HALL IS JUST BEYOND THIS CURTAIN...
SHINE
MY EYES! IT'S BRIGHT!
WHAT ?!
WE'RE IN THE WOODS!
WHY DID YOU BRING US TO THIS USELESS PLACE?!
WHAT HAPPENED TO OUR LECTURE?!
HOW CAN YOU HOLD A LECTURE IN THE WOODS?!
WH-WOAH!
TRIP
ACK!
THUD
SLIP
OW!
TNK
HEY, YOU AREN'T DR. TIME!
YOU'RE THE GUY WHO BROKE OUR CLOCKS! WHAT ARE YOU TRYING TO PULL?!
YOU'VE STOLEN OUR TIME FROM US!
UH-OH... NOW WHAT?!
THIEF!

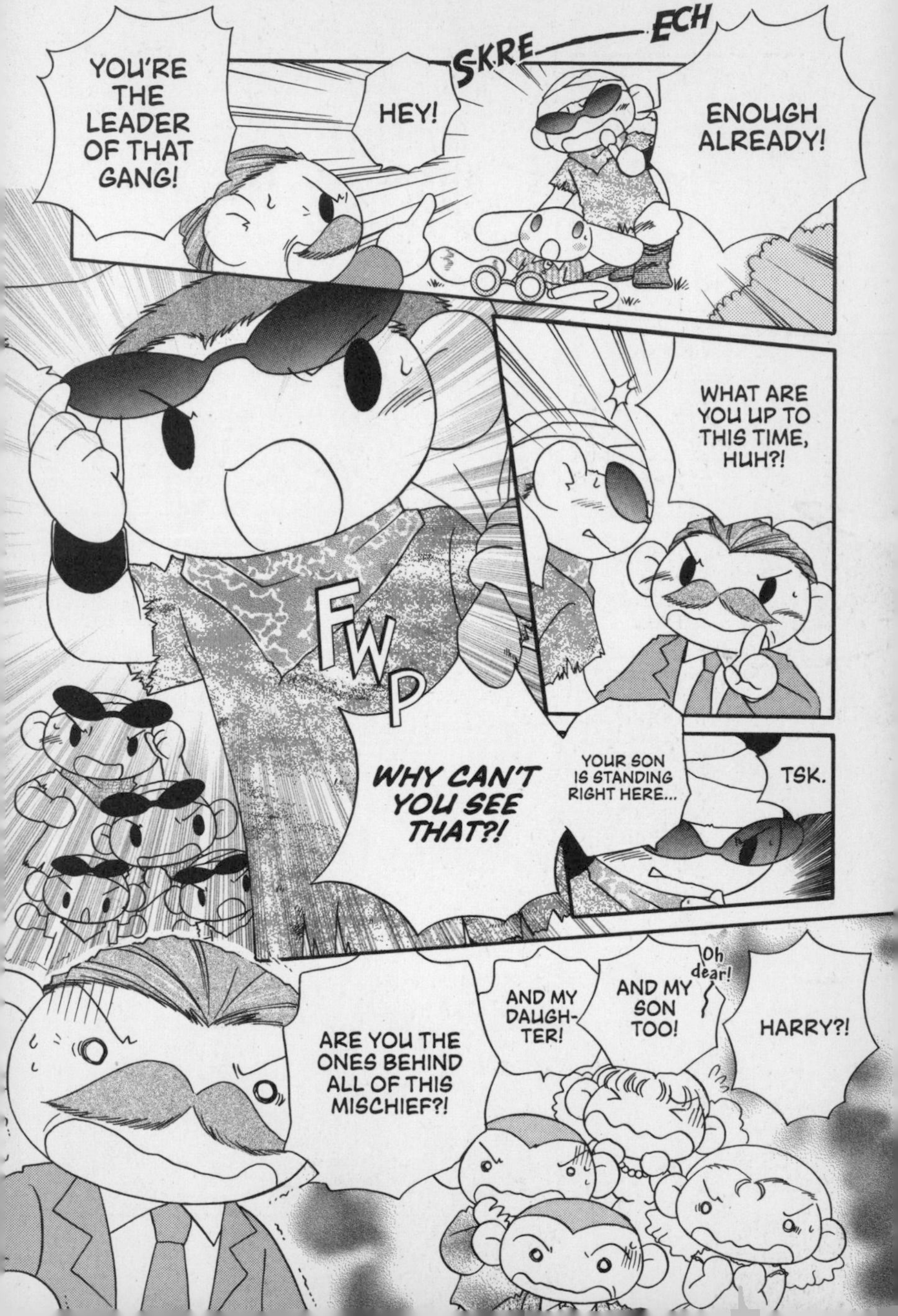
ENOUGH ALREADY!
SKRE—ECH
HEY!
YOU'RE THE LEADER OF THAT GANG!
WHAT ARE YOU UP TO THIS TIME, HUH?!
TSK.
YOUR SON IS STANDING RIGHT HERE...
FWP
WHY CAN'T YOU SEE THAT?!
HARRY?!
Oh dear!
AND MY SON TOO!
AND MY DAUGH-TER!
ARE YOU THE ONES BEHIND ALL OF THIS MISCHIEF?!

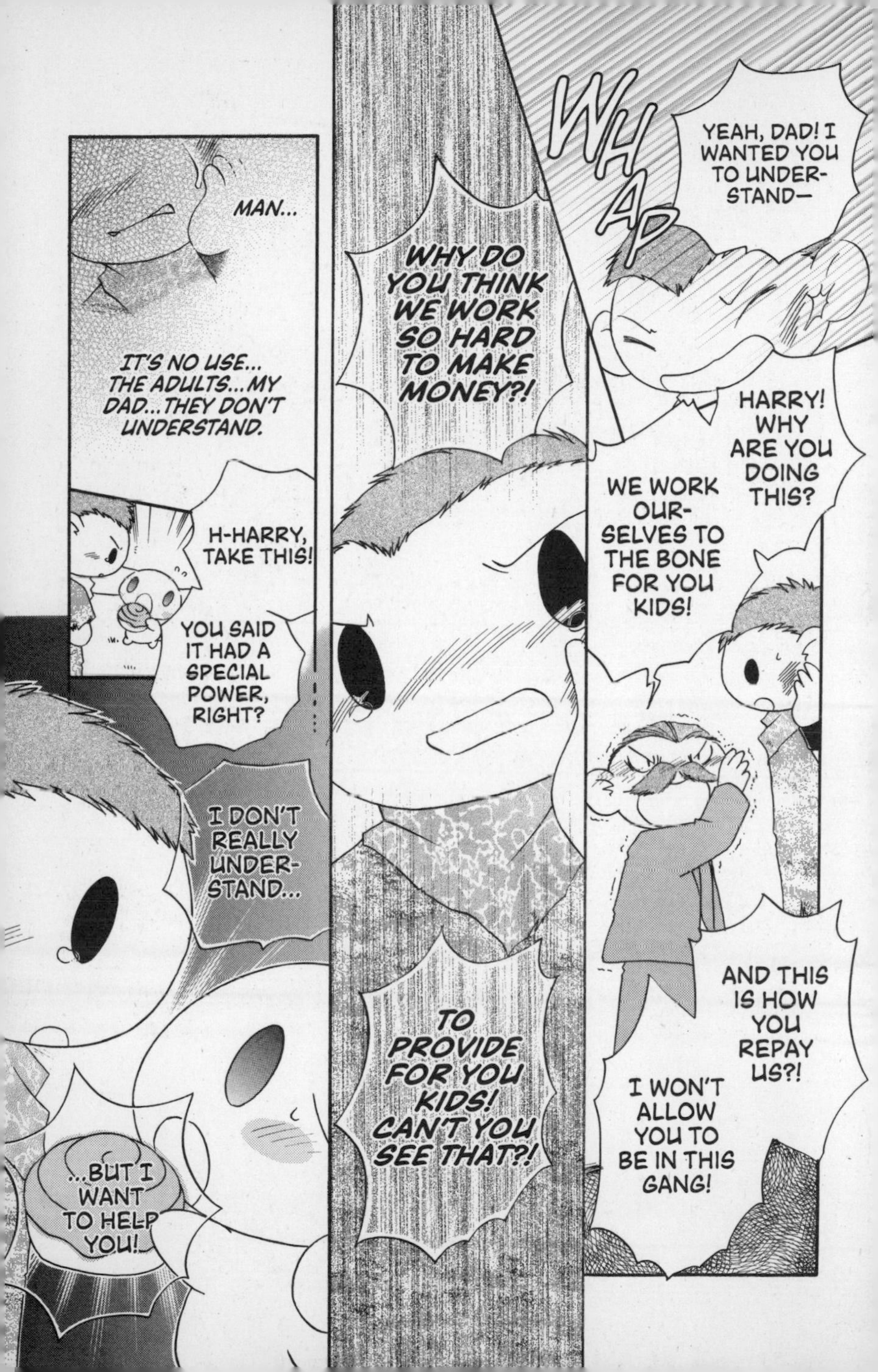
YEAH, DAD! I WANTED YOU TO UNDER-STAND—
WHAP
HARRY! WHY ARE YOU DOING THIS?
WE WORK OUR-SELVES TO THE BONE FOR YOU KIDS!
AND THIS IS HOW YOU REPAY US?!
I WON'T ALLOW YOU TO BE IN THIS GANG!
WHY DO YOU THINK WE WORK SO HARD TO MAKE MONEY?!
TO PROVIDE FOR YOU KIDS! CAN'T YOU SEE THAT?!
MAN...
IT'S NO USE... THE ADULTS...MY DAD...THEY DON'T UNDERSTAND.
H-HARRY, TAKE THIS!
YOU SAID IT HAD A SPECIAL POWER, RIGHT?
I DON'T REALLY UNDER-STAND...
...BUT I WANT TO HELP YOU!

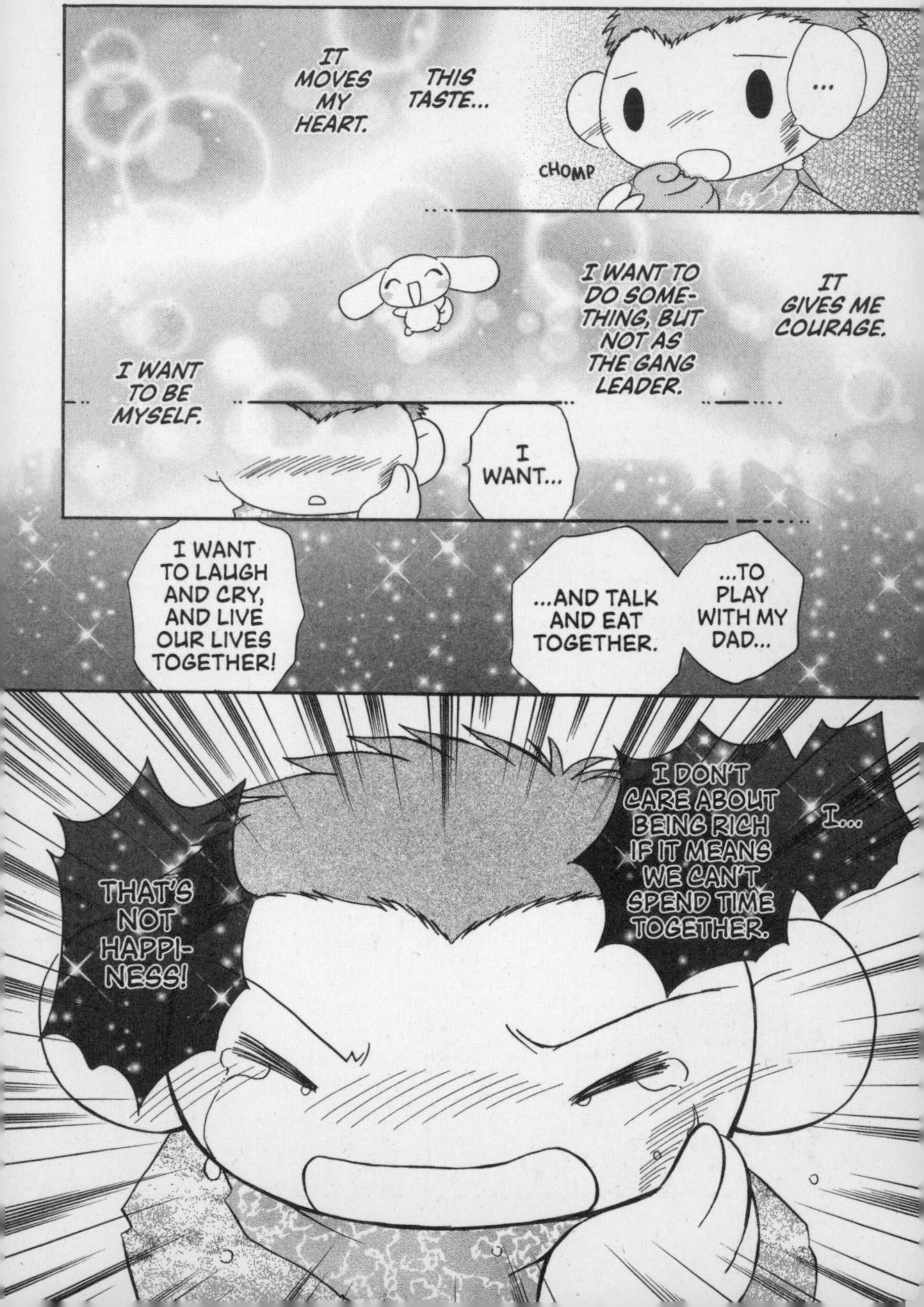
...
THIS TASTE...
IT MOVES MY HEART.
CHOMP
IT GIVES ME COURAGE.
I WANT TO DO SOME-THING, BUT NOT AS THE GANG LEADER.
I WANT TO BE MYSELF.
I WANT...
...TO PLAY WITH MY DAD...
...AND TALK AND EAT TOGETHER.
I WANT TO LAUGH AND CRY, AND LIVE OUR LIVES TOGETHER!
I...
I DON'T CARE ABOUT BEING RICH IF IT MEANS WE CAN'T SPEND TIME TOGETHER.
THAT'S NOT HAPPI-NESS!

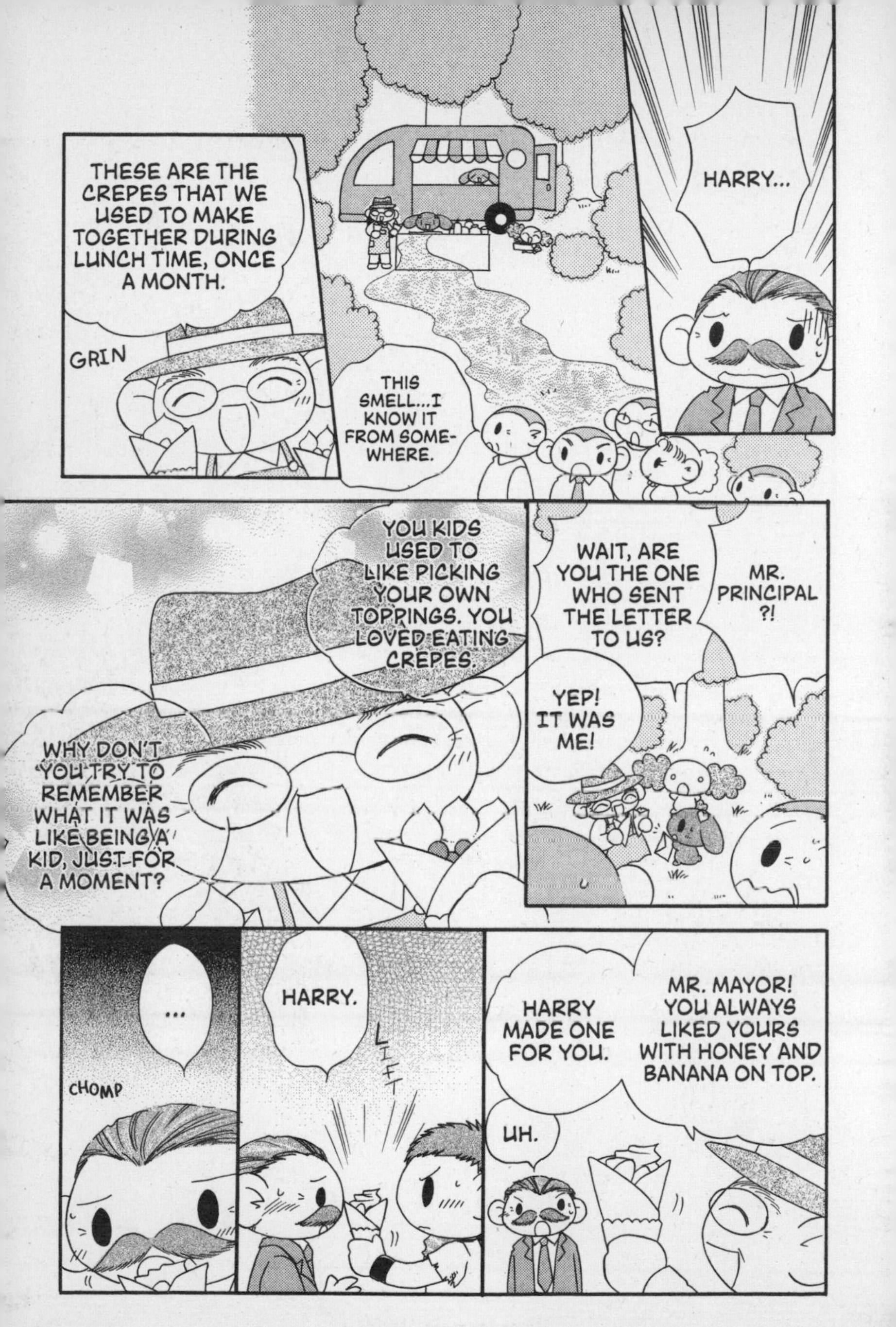
HARRY...
THIS SMELL...I KNOW IT FROM SOME-WHERE.
THESE ARE THE CREPES THAT WE USED TO MAKE TOGETHER DURING LUNCH TIME, ONCE A MONTH.
GRIN
MR. PRINCIPAL?!
WAIT, ARE YOU THE ONE WHO SENT THE LETTER TO US?
YEP! IT WAS ME!
YOU KIDS USED TO LIKE PICKING YOUR OWN TOPPINGS. YOU LOVED EATING CREPES.
WHY DON'T YOU TRY TO REMEMBER WHAT IT WAS LIKE BEING A KID, JUST FOR A MOMENT?
MR. MAYOR! YOU ALWAYS LIKED YOURS WITH HONEY AND BANANA ON TOP.
HARRY MADE ONE FOR YOU.
UH.
HARRY.
LIFT
...
CHOMP

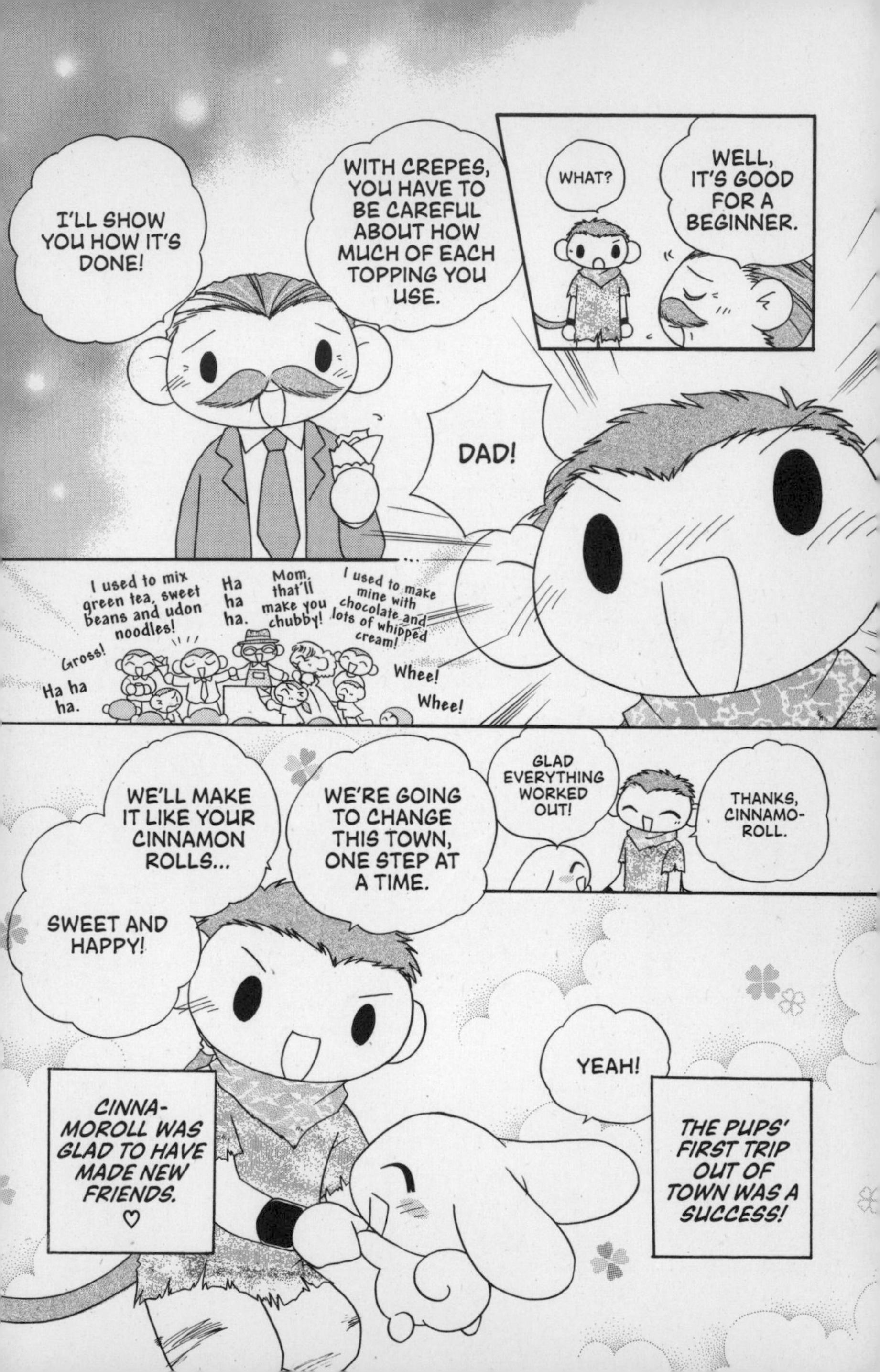
WELL, IT'S GOOD FOR A BEGINNER.
WHAT?
WITH CREPES, YOU HAVE TO BE CAREFUL ABOUT HOW MUCH OF EACH TOPPING YOU USE.
I'LL SHOW YOU HOW IT'S DONE!
DAD!
...
I used to make mine with chocolate and lots of whipped cream!
Mom, that'll make you chubby!
Ha ha ha.
I used to mix green tea, sweet beans and udon noodles!
Gross!
Ha ha ha.
Whee!
Whee!
THANKS, CINNAMO-ROLL.
GLAD EVERYTHING WORKED OUT!
WE'RE GOING TO CHANGE THIS TOWN, ONE STEP AT A TIME.
WE'LL MAKE IT LIKE YOUR CINNAMON ROLLS...
SWEET AND HAPPY!
YEAH!
THE PUPS' FIRST TRIP OUT OF TOWN WAS A SUCCESS!
CINNA-MOROLL WAS GLAD TO HAVE MADE NEW FRIENDS. ♡

★ Fluffy, Fluffy ♥ Cinnamoroll ★

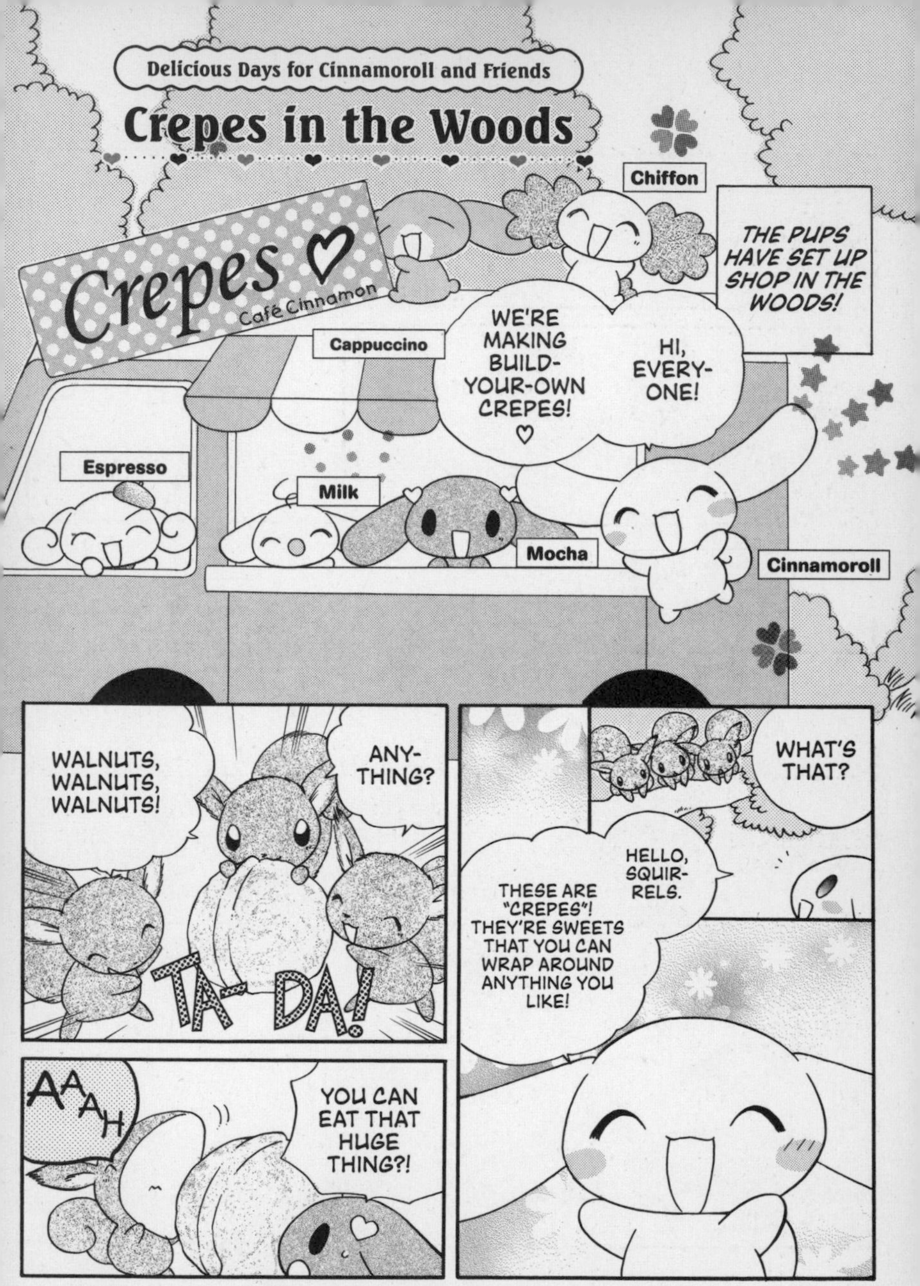
Delicious Days for Cinnamoroll and Friends
Crepes in the Woods
THE PUPS HAVE SET UP SHOP IN THE WOODS!
Chiffon
Crepes ♡
Café Cinnamon
Cappuccino
HI, EVERY-ONE!
WE'RE MAKING BUILD-YOUR-OWN CREPES! ♡
Espresso
Milk
Mocha
Cinnamoroll
WHAT'S THAT?
HELLO, SQUIR-RELS.
THESE ARE "CREPES"! THEY'RE SWEETS THAT YOU CAN WRAP AROUND ANYTHING YOU LIKE!
ANY-THING?
WALNUTS, WALNUTS, WALNUTS!
TA-DA!
YOU CAN EAT THAT HUGE THING?!
AAAH

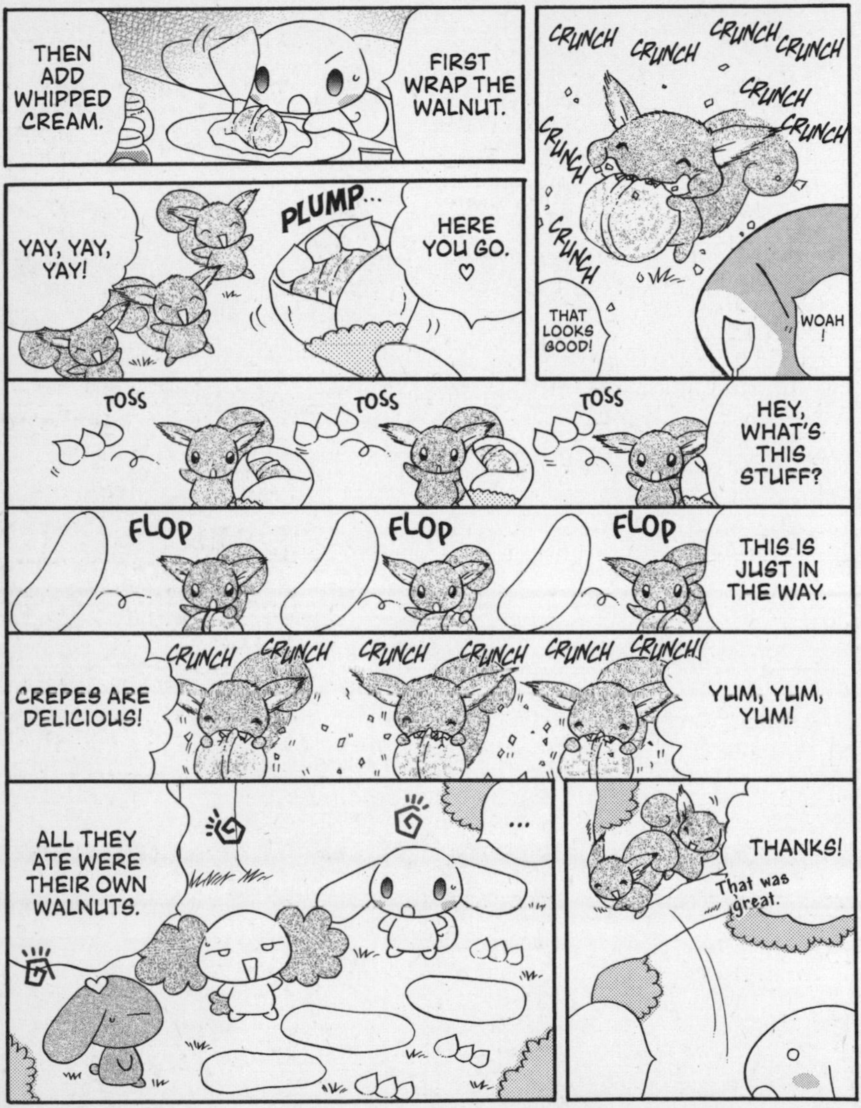
CRUNCH CRUNCH CRUNCH CRUNCH CRUNCH CRUNCH CRUNCH CRUNCH
WOAH!
THAT LOOKS GOOD!
FIRST WRAP THE WALNUT.
THEN ADD WHIPPED CREAM.
HERE YOU GO. ♡
PLUMP...
YAY, YAY, YAY!
HEY, WHAT'S THIS STUFF?
TOSS
TOSS
TOSS
THIS IS JUST IN THE WAY.
FLOP
FLOP
FLOP
YUM, YUM, YUM!
CRUNCH CRUNCH CRUNCH CRUNCH CRUNCH CRUNCH!
CREPES ARE DELICIOUS!
THANKS!
That was great.
...
ALL THEY ATE WERE THEIR OWN WALNUTS.

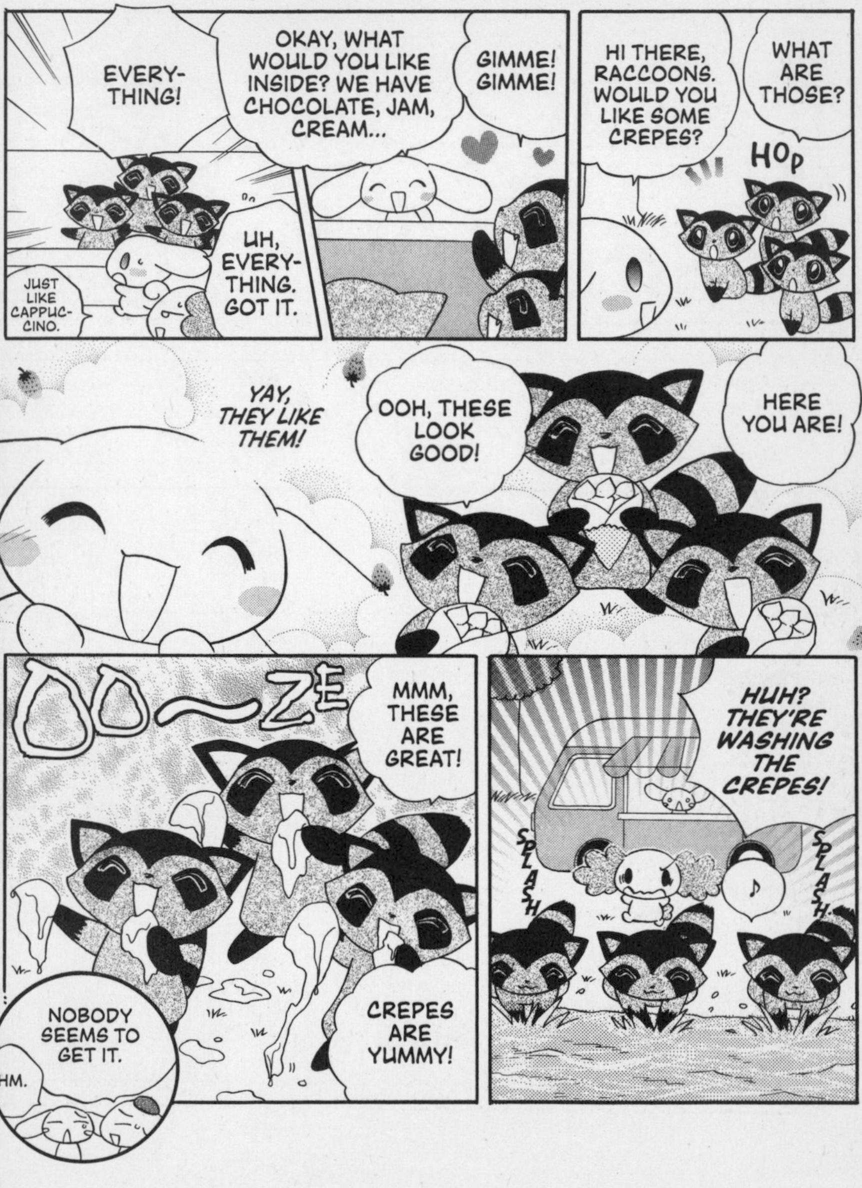
WHAT ARE THOSE?
HI THERE, RACCOONS. WOULD YOU LIKE SOME CREPES?
HOP
GIMME! GIMME!
OKAY, WHAT WOULD YOU LIKE INSIDE? WE HAVE CHOCOLATE, JAM, CREAM...
EVERY-THING!
UH, EVERY-THING. GOT IT.
JUST LIKE CAPPUC-CINO.
HERE YOU ARE!
OOH, THESE LOOK GOOD!
YAY, THEY LIKE THEM!
HUH? THEY'RE WASHING THE CREPES!
SPLASH
SPLASH
MMM, THESE ARE GREAT!
DO~ZE
CREPES ARE YUMMY!
NOBODY SEEMS TO GET IT.
HM.

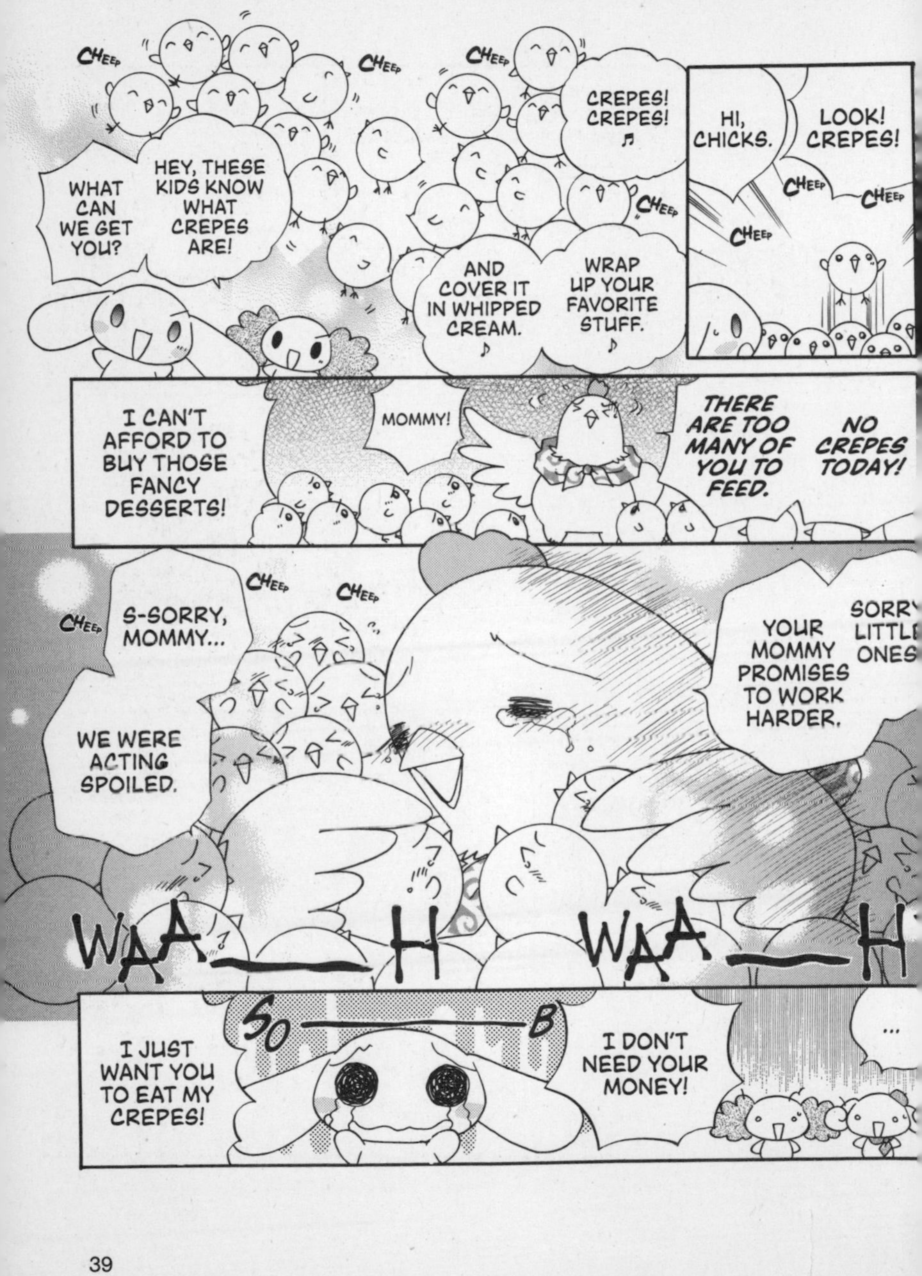
LOOK! CREPES!
HI, CHICKS.
CHEEP
CHEEP
CHEEP
CREPES! CREPES! ♫
CHEEP
CHEEP
WRAP UP YOUR FAVORITE STUFF. ♪
AND COVER IT IN WHIPPED CREAM. ♪
CHEEP
HEY, THESE KIDS KNOW WHAT CREPES ARE!
WHAT CAN WE GET YOU?
NO CREPES TODAY!
THERE ARE TOO MANY OF YOU TO FEED.
MOMMY!
I CAN'T AFFORD TO BUY THOSE FANCY DESSERTS!
SORRY LITTLE ONES
YOUR MOMMY PROMISES TO WORK HARDER.
CHEEP
CHEEP
S-SORRY, MOMMY...
CHEEP
WE WERE ACTING SPOILED.
WAA—H WAA—H
...
I DON'T NEED YOUR MONEY!
SO—B
I JUST WANT YOU TO EAT MY CREPES!

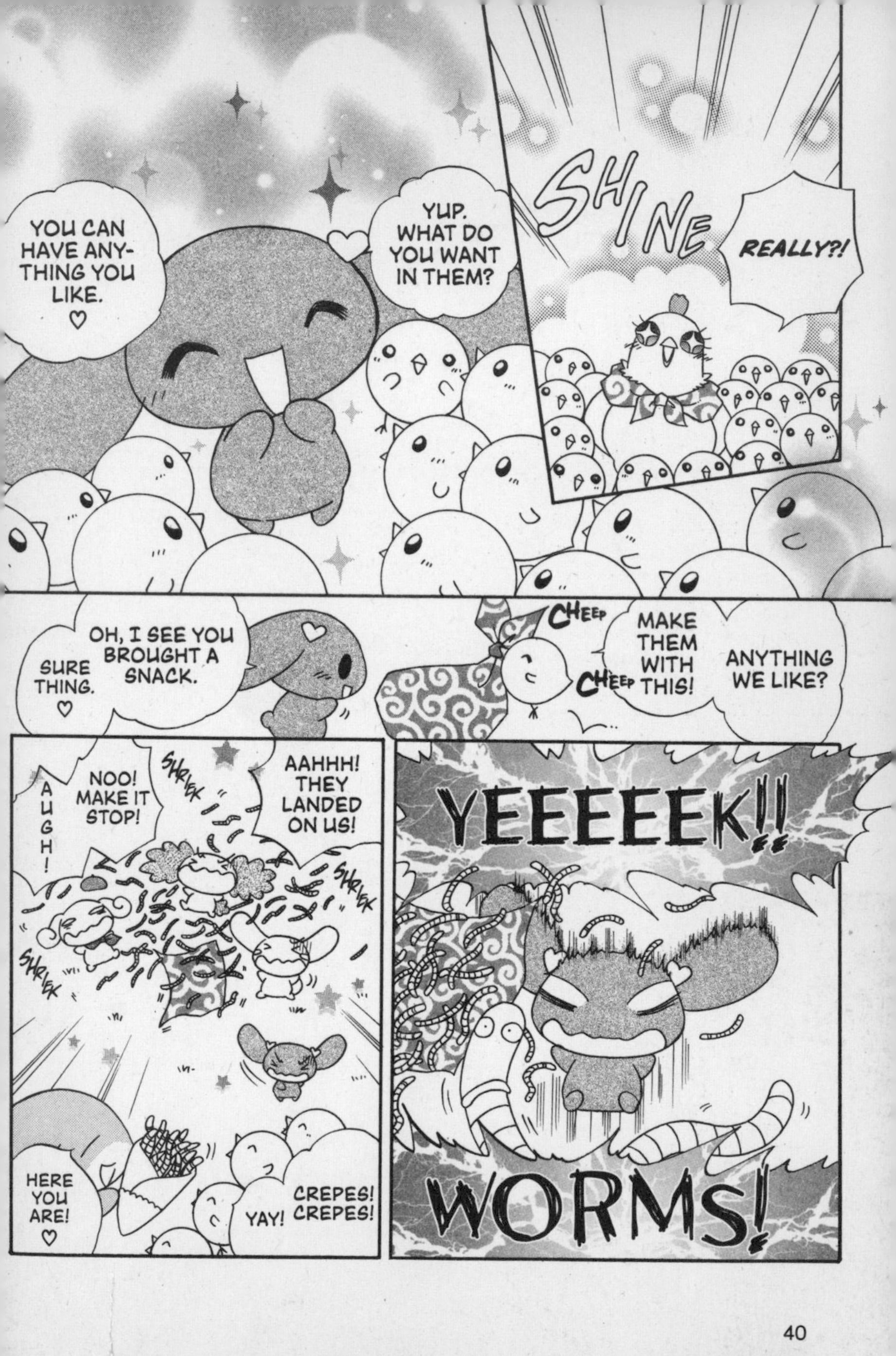
SHINE
REALLY?!
YUP. WHAT DO YOU WANT IN THEM?
YOU CAN HAVE ANYTHING YOU LIKE. ♡
ANYTHING WE LIKE?
MAKE THEM WITH THIS!
CHEEP
CHEEP
OH, I SEE YOU BROUGHT A SNACK.
SURE THING. ♡
YEEEEEK!!
WORMS!
AAHHH! THEY LANDED ON US!
SHRIEK
NOO! MAKE IT STOP!
AUGH!
SHRIEK
SHRIEK
CREPES! CREPES!
YAY!
HERE YOU ARE! ♡

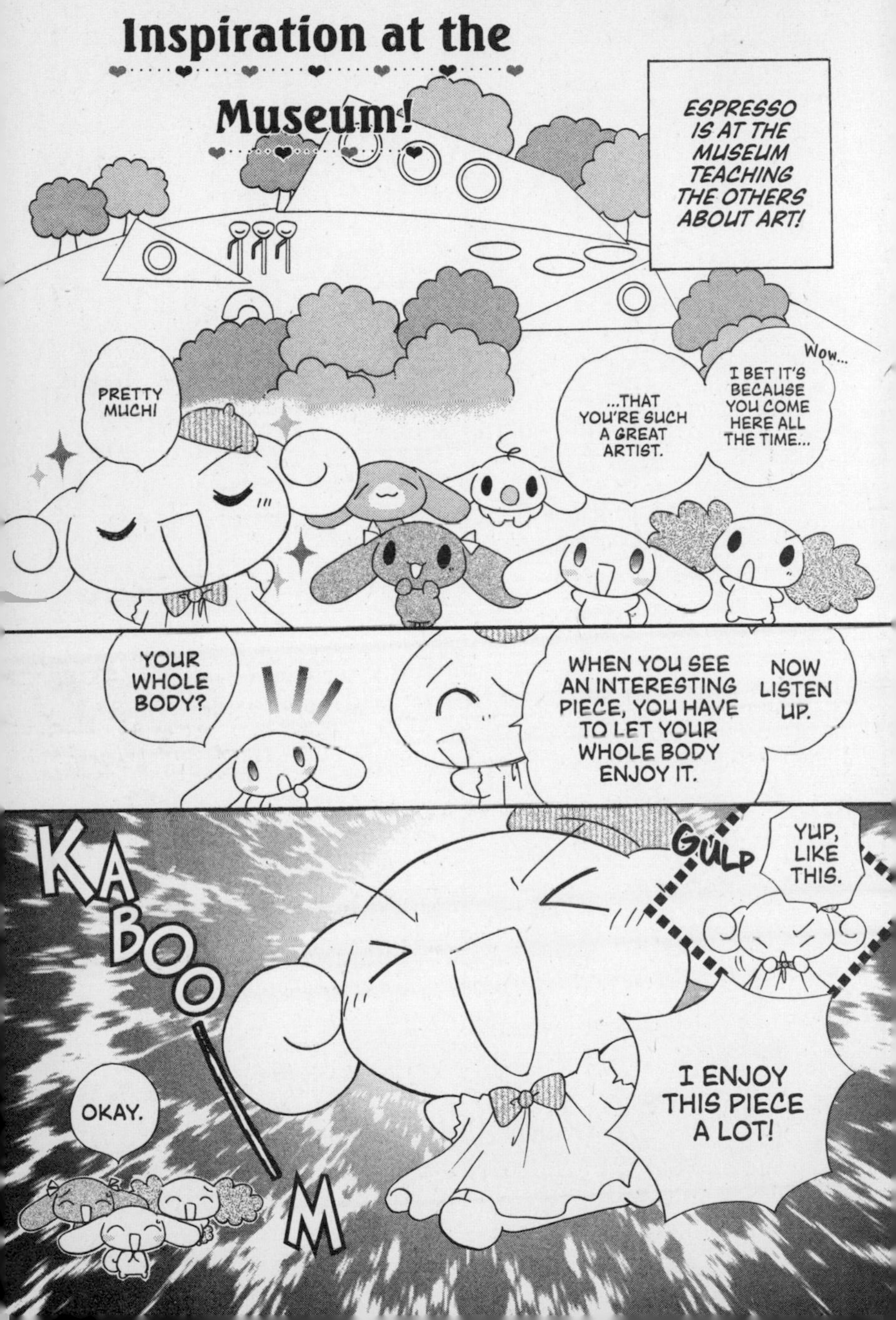
Inspiration at the Museum!
ESPRESSO IS AT THE MUSEUM TEACHING THE OTHERS ABOUT ART!
Wow...
I BET IT'S BECAUSE YOU COME HERE ALL THE TIME...
...THAT YOU'RE SUCH A GREAT ARTIST.
PRETTY MUCH!
NOW LISTEN UP.
WHEN YOU SEE AN INTERESTING PIECE, YOU HAVE TO LET YOUR WHOLE BODY ENJOY IT.
YOUR WHOLE BODY?
YUP, LIKE THIS.
GULP
I ENJOY THIS PIECE A LOT!
KABOOOM
OKAY.

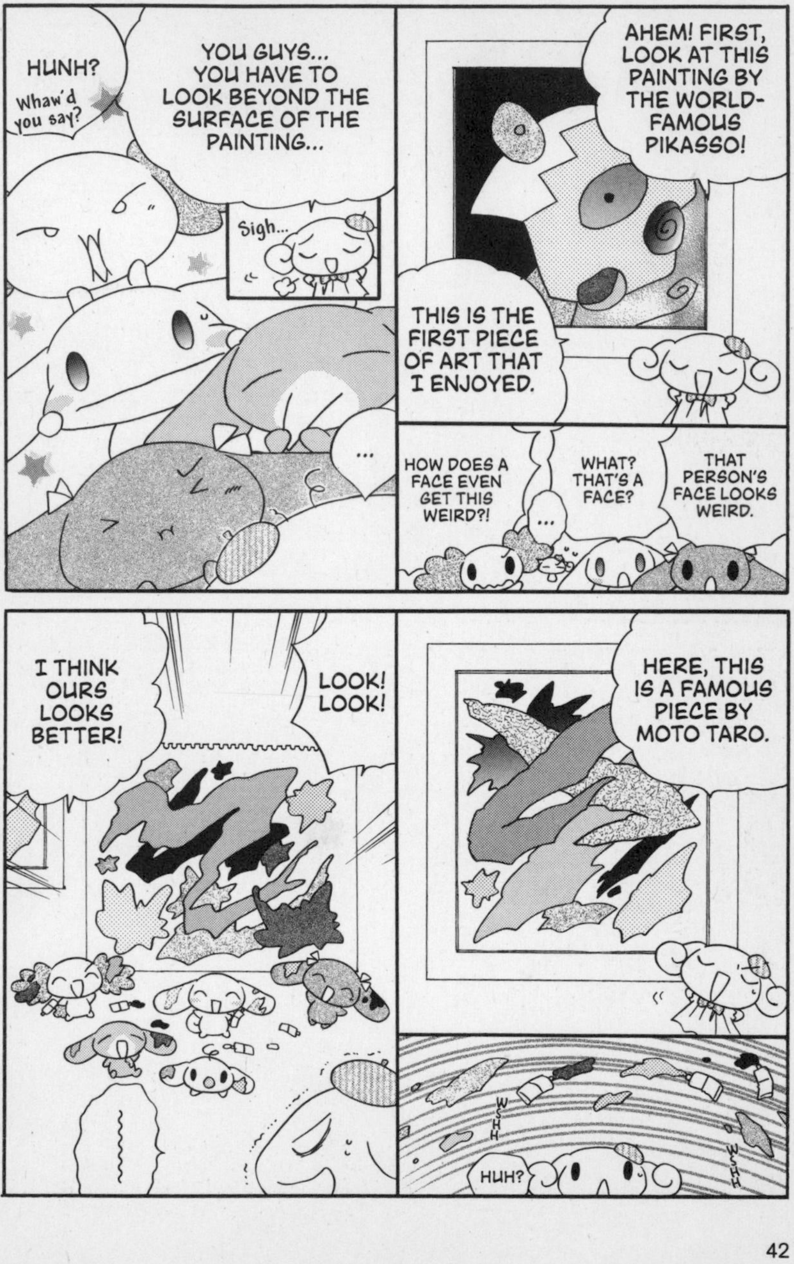
AHEM! FIRST, LOOK AT THIS PAINTING BY THE WORLD-FAMOUS PIKASSO!
THIS IS THE FIRST PIECE OF ART THAT I ENJOYED.
THAT PERSON'S FACE LOOKS WEIRD.
WHAT? THAT'S A FACE?
HOW DOES A FACE EVEN GET THIS WEIRD?!
...
YOU GUYS... YOU HAVE TO LOOK BEYOND THE SURFACE OF THE PAINTING...
HUNH?
Whaw'd you say?
Sigh...
...
HERE, THIS IS A FAMOUS PIECE BY MOTO TARO.
WSHH
HUH?
WSHH
LOOK! LOOK!
I THINK OURS LOOKS BETTER!

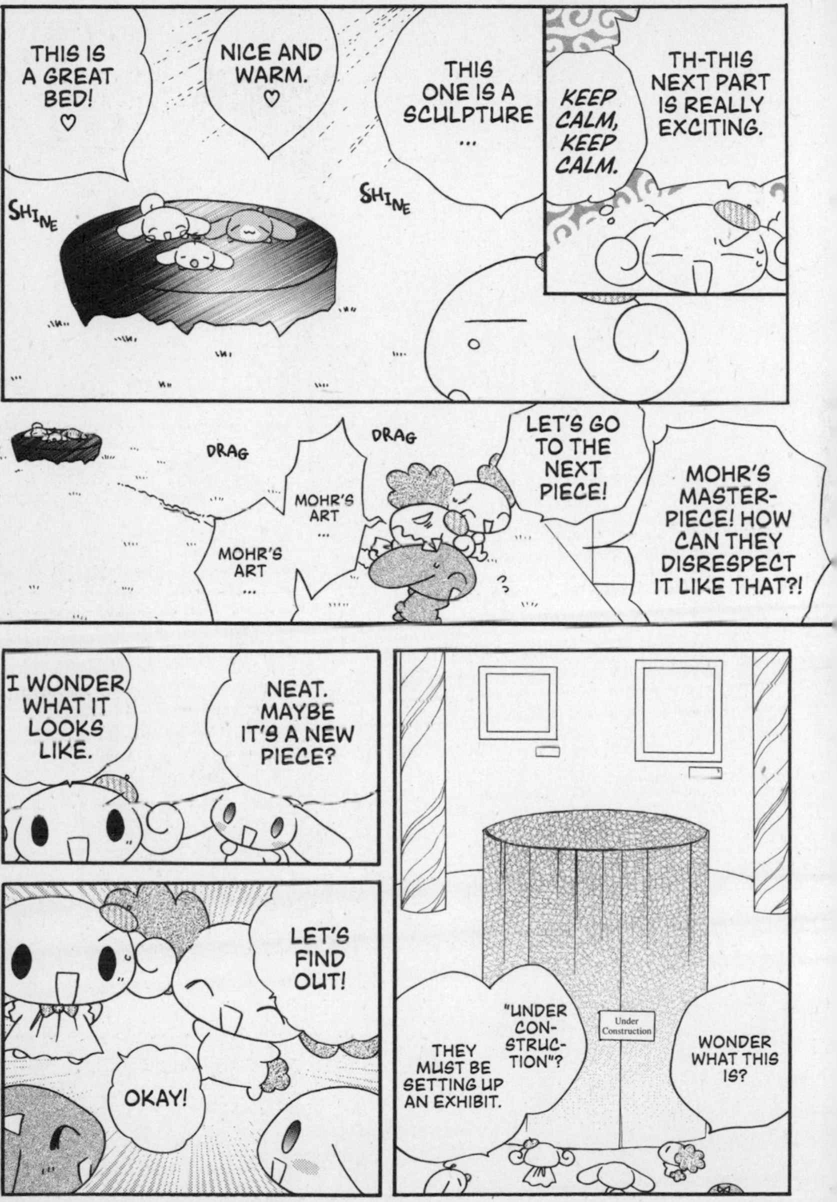
TH-THIS NEXT PART IS REALLY EXCITING.
KEEP CALM, KEEP CALM.
THIS ONE IS A SCULPTURE ...
SHINE
NICE AND WARM. ♡
THIS IS A GREAT BED! ♡
SHINE
MOHR'S MASTER-PIECE! HOW CAN THEY DISRESPECT IT LIKE THAT?!
LET'S GO TO THE NEXT PIECE!
DRAG
MOHR'S ART ...
MOHR'S ART ...
DRAG
WONDER WHAT THIS IS?
Under Construction
"UNDER CON-STRUC-TION"?
THEY MUST BE SETTING UP AN EXHIBIT.
NEAT. MAYBE IT'S A NEW PIECE?
I WONDER WHAT IT LOOKS LIKE.
LET'S FIND OUT!
OKAY!

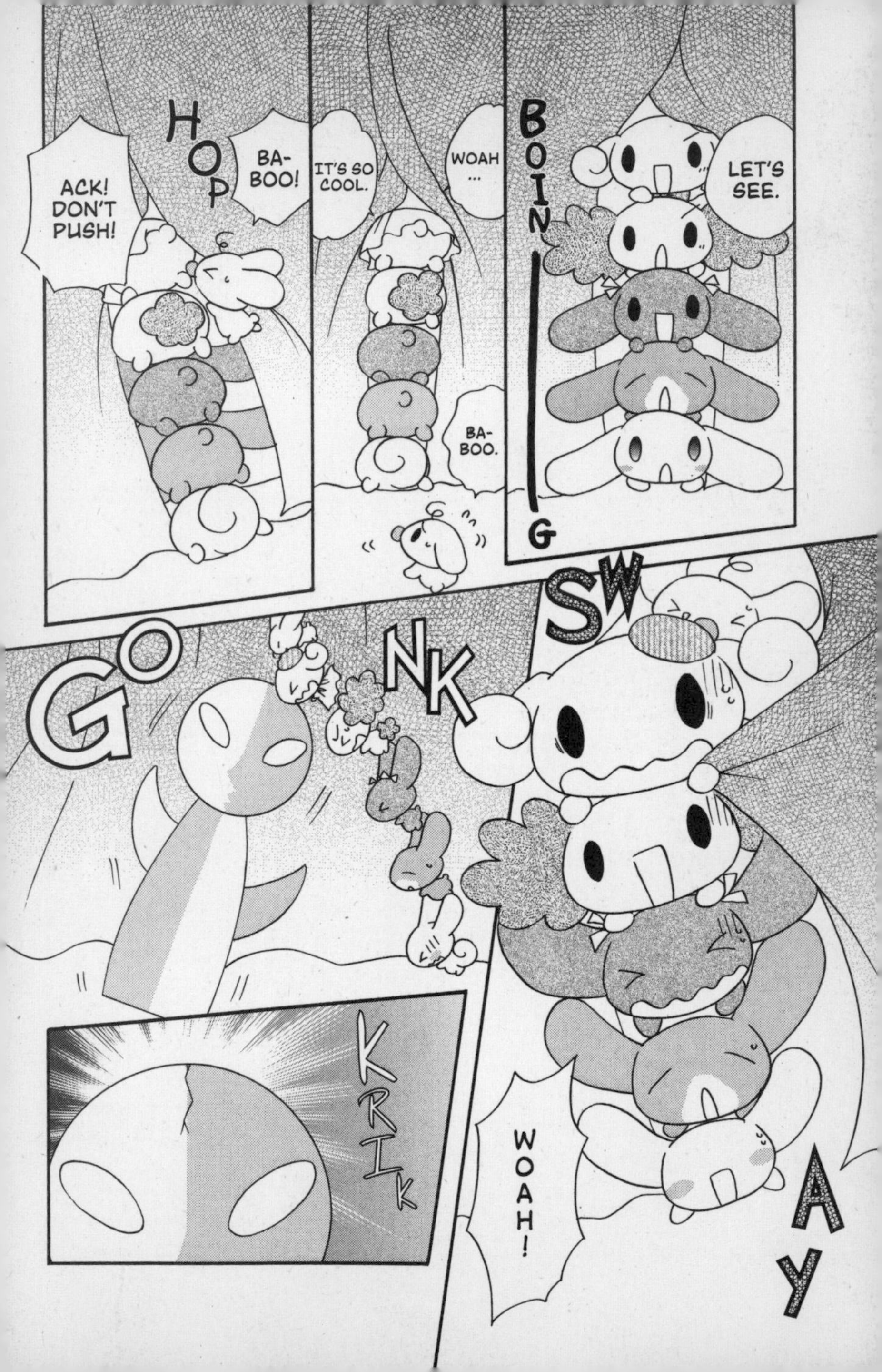
BOING
LET'S SEE.
WOAH ...
IT'S SO COOL.
BA-BOO.
BA-BOO!
HOP
ACK! DON'T PUSH!
SW
WOAH!
AY
GO
NK
KRIK

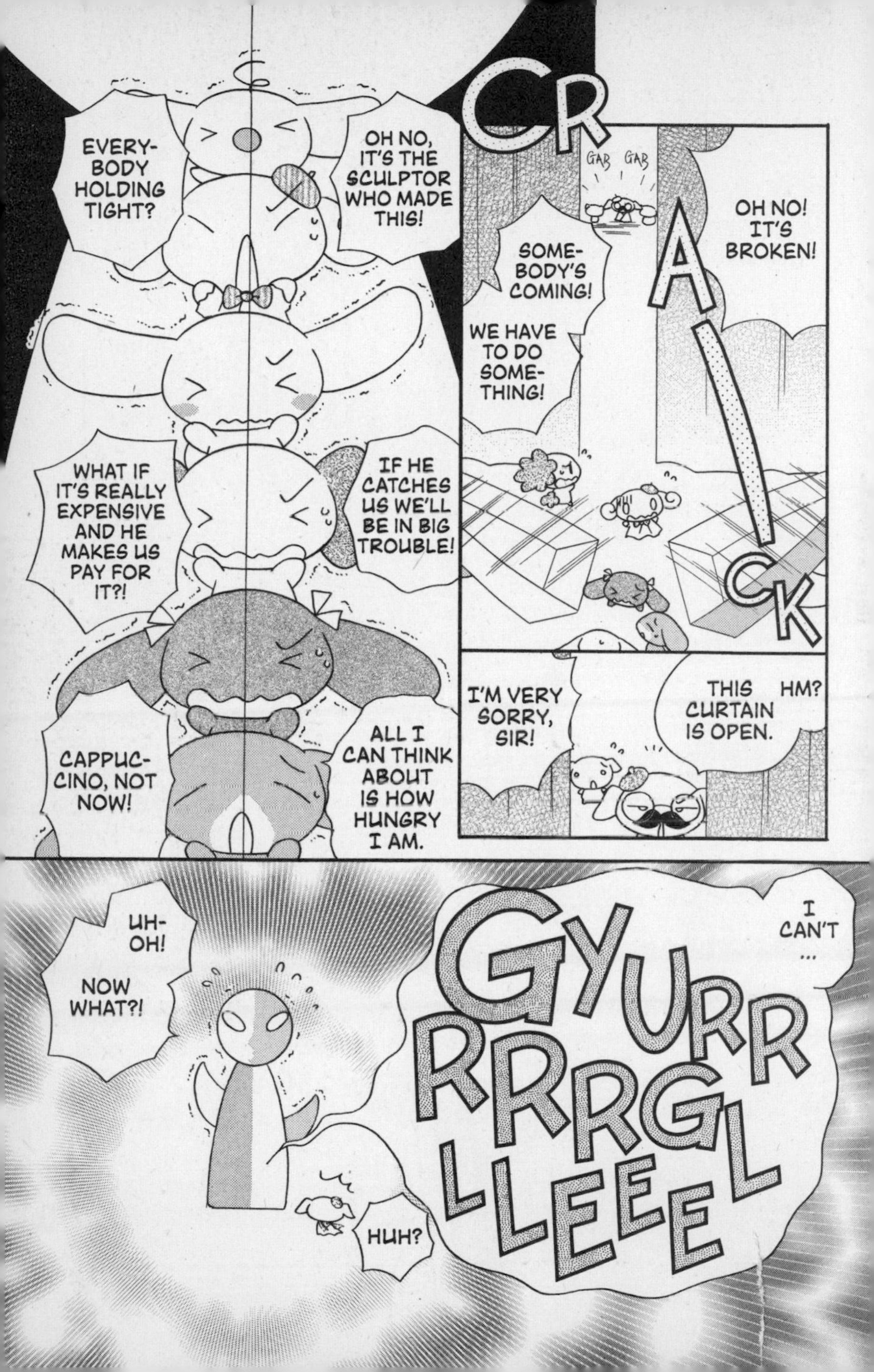
CRAICK
GAB GAB
OH NO! IT'S BROKEN!
SOME-BODY'S COMING!
WE HAVE TO DO SOME-THING!
HM?
THIS CURTAIN IS OPEN.
I'M VERY SORRY, SIR!
OH NO, IT'S THE SCULPTOR WHO MADE THIS!
EVERY-BODY HOLDING TIGHT?
IF HE CATCHES US WE'LL BE IN BIG TROUBLE!
WHAT IF IT'S REALLY EXPENSIVE AND HE MAKES US PAY FOR IT?!
ALL I CAN THINK ABOUT IS HOW HUNGRY I AM.
CAPPUC-CINO, NOT NOW!
I CAN'T ...
GYURRRRRGLLEEEL
UH-OH!
NOW WHAT?!
HUH?

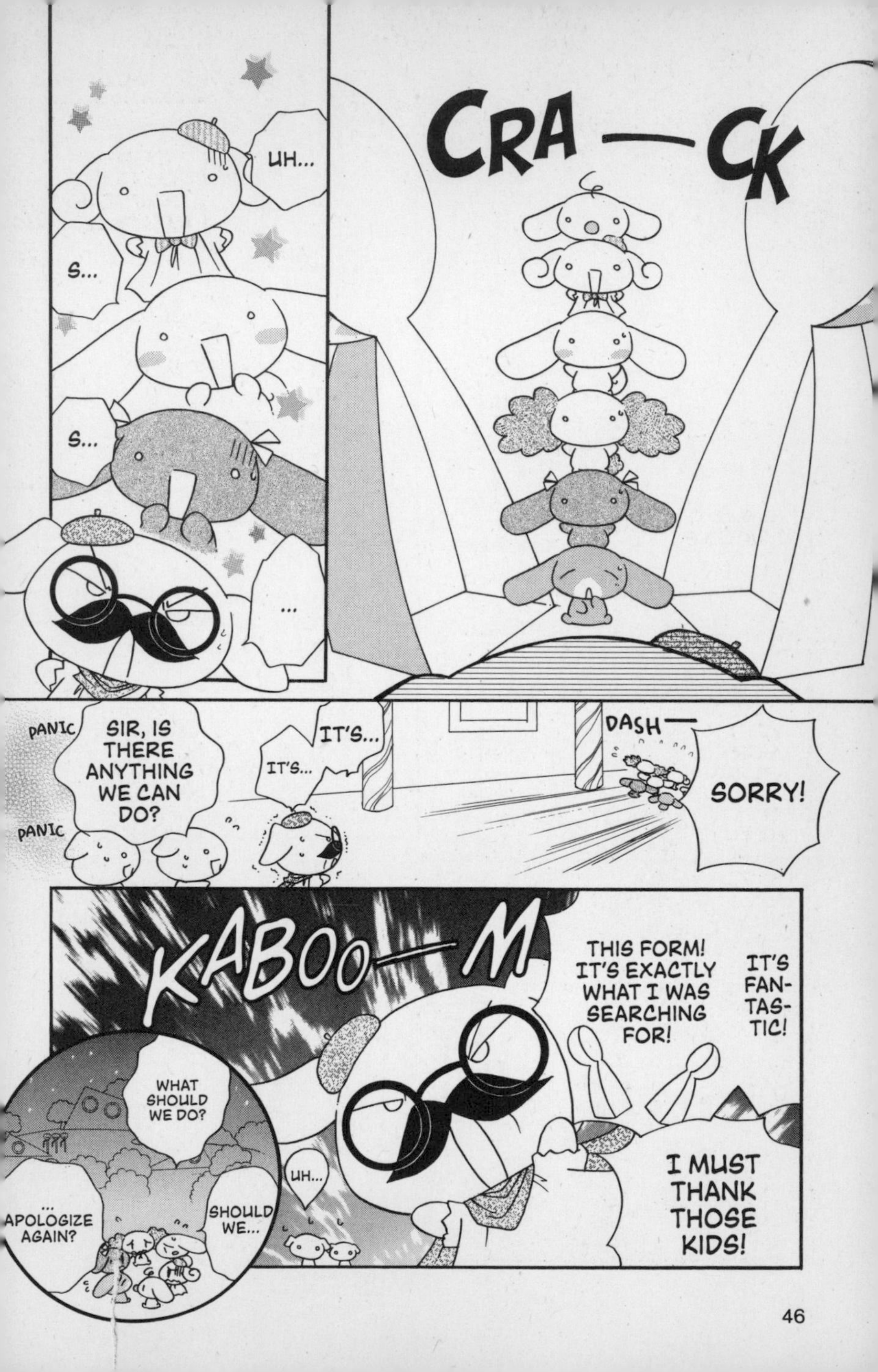
CRA—CK
UH...
S...
S...
...
SORRY!
DASH—
IT'S...
IT'S...
SIR, IS THERE ANYTHING WE CAN DO?
PANIC
PANIC
IT'S FAN-TAS-TIC!
THIS FORM! IT'S EXACTLY WHAT I WAS SEARCHING FOR!
KABOO—M
I MUST THANK THOSE KIDS!
UH...
WHAT SHOULD WE DO?
SHOULD WE...
... APOLOGIZE AGAIN?

A Fun Halloween?!

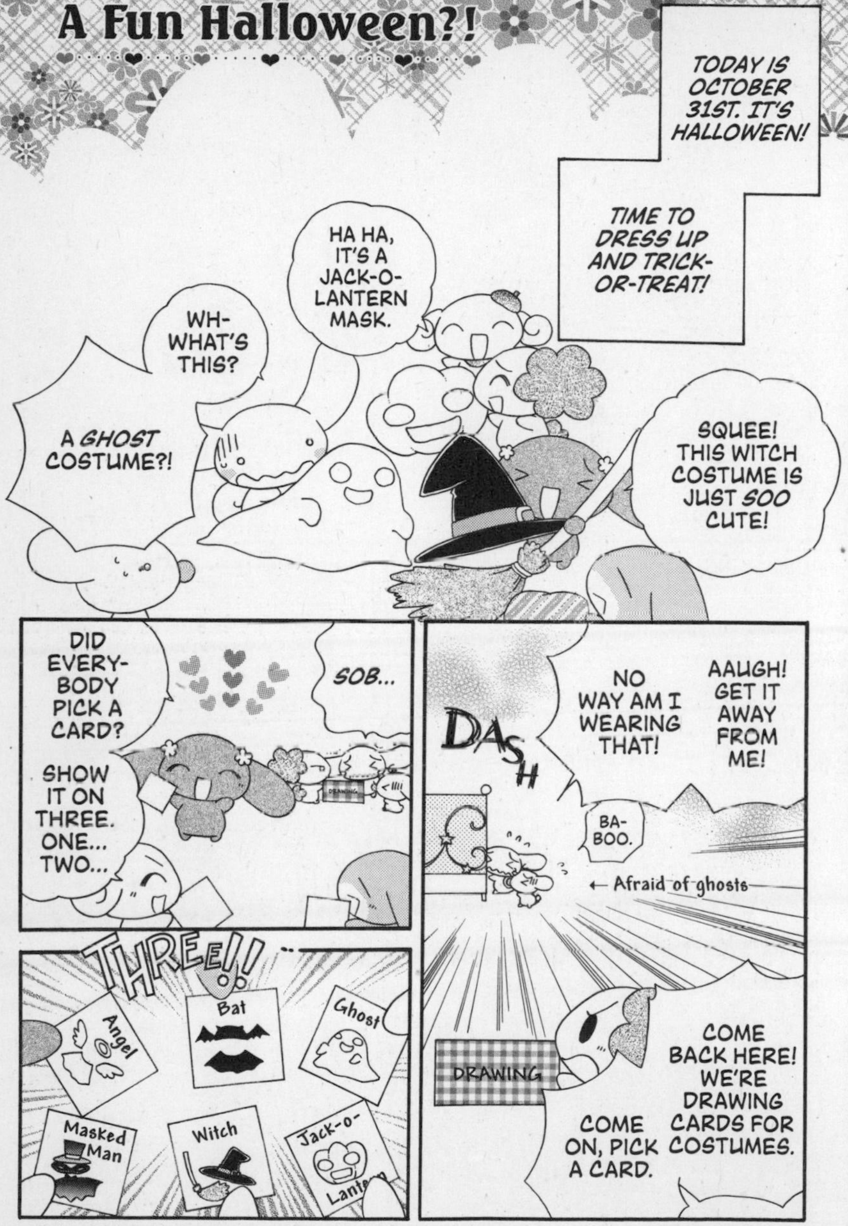
TODAY IS OCTOBER 31ST. IT'S HALLOWEEN!
TIME TO DRESS UP AND TRICK-OR-TREAT!
SQUEE! THIS WITCH COSTUME IS JUST *SOO* CUTE!
HA HA, IT'S A JACK-O-LANTERN MASK.
WH-WHAT'S THIS?
A *GHOST* COSTUME?!
AAUGH! GET IT AWAY FROM ME!
NO WAY AM I WEARING THAT!
DASH
BA-BOO.
← Afraid of ghosts
COME BACK HERE! WE'RE DRAWING CARDS FOR COSTUMES.
COME ON, PICK A CARD.
DRAWING
SOB...
DID EVERYBODY PICK A CARD?
SHOW IT ON THREE. ONE... TWO...
DRAWING
THREE!!
Ghost
Bat
Angel
Jack-o-
Lante
Witch
Masked Man

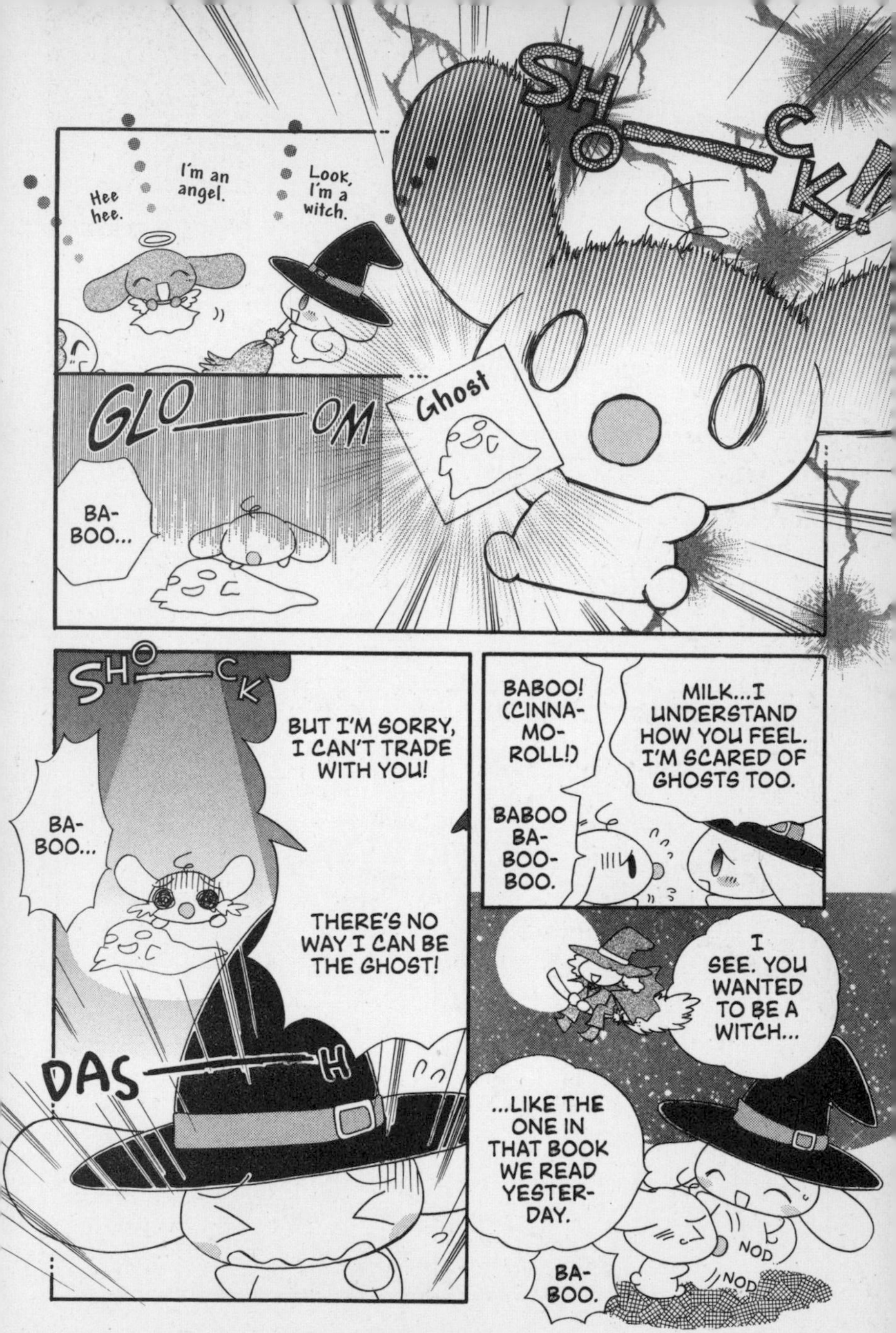
SHO—CK!!
Ghost
Look, I'm a witch.
I'm an angel.
Hee hee.
GLO—OM
BA-BOO...
MILK...I UNDERSTAND HOW YOU FEEL. I'M SCARED OF GHOSTS TOO.
BABOO! (CINNA-MO-ROLL!)
BABOO BA-BOO-BOO.
I SEE. YOU WANTED TO BE A WITCH...
...LIKE THE ONE IN THAT BOOK WE READ YESTER-DAY.
NOD NOD
BA-BOO.
SHO—CK
BUT I'M SORRY, I CAN'T TRADE WITH YOU!
BA-BOO...
THERE'S NO WAY I CAN BE THE GHOST!
DAS—H

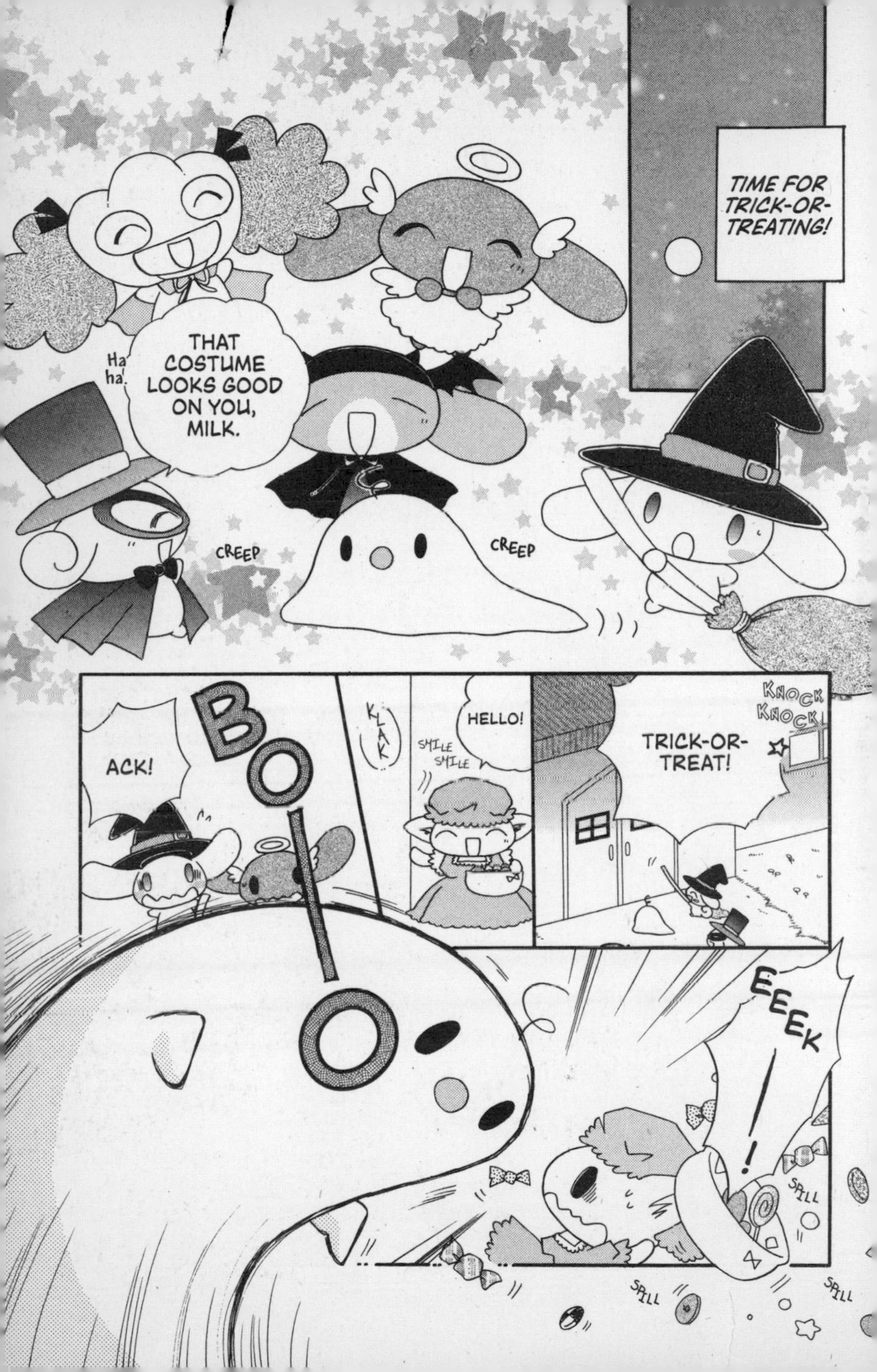
TIME FOR TRICK-OR-TREATING!
THAT COSTUME LOOKS GOOD ON YOU, MILK.
Ha ha.
CREEP
CREEP
KNOCK KNOCK
TRICK-OR-TREAT!
HELLO!
SMILE SMILE
KLAK
BOO
ACK!
EEEK!!
SPILL
SPILL
SPILL

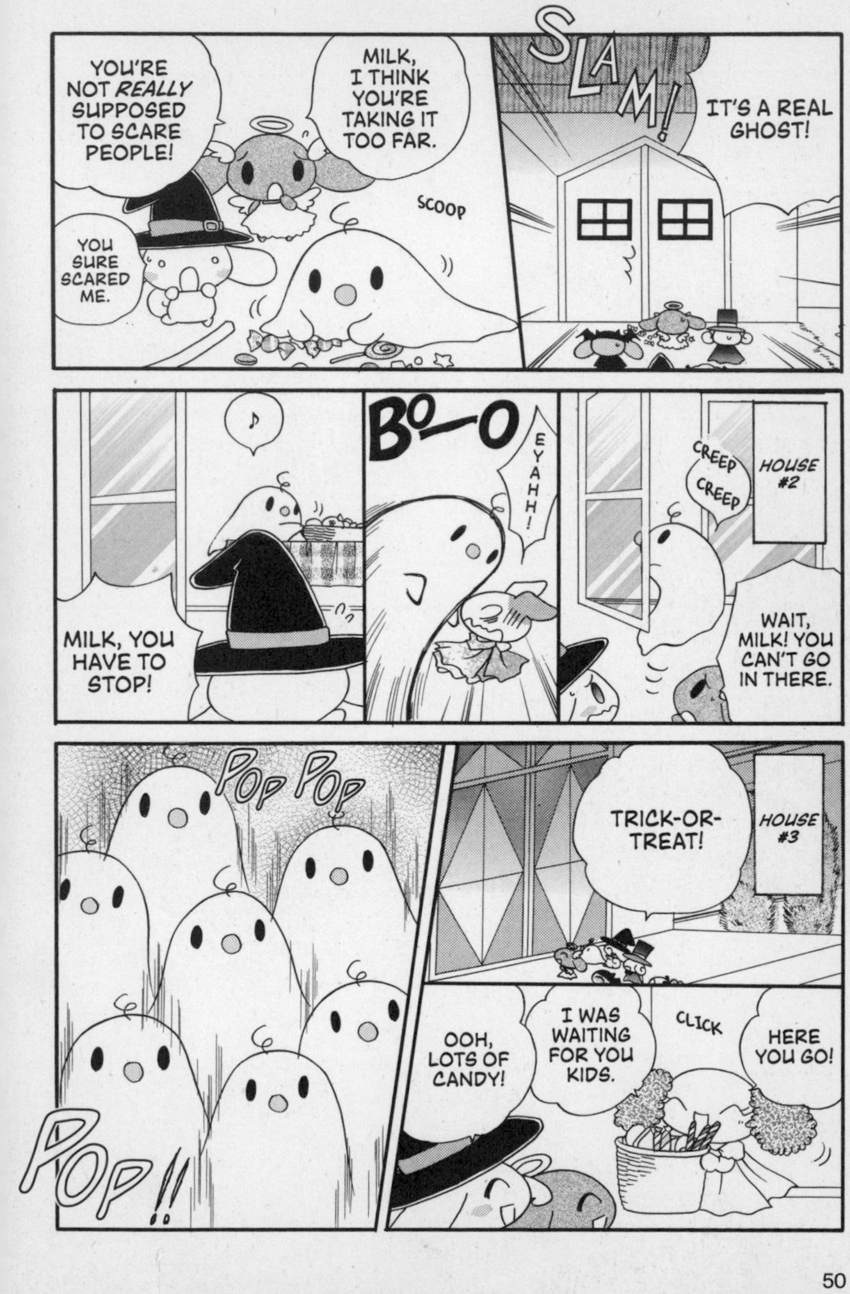
SLAM!
IT'S A REAL GHOST!
MILK, I THINK YOU'RE TAKING IT TOO FAR.
YOU'RE NOT *REALLY* SUPPOSED TO SCARE PEOPLE!
SCOOP
YOU SURE SCARED ME.
HOUSE #2
CREEP
CREEP
WAIT, MILK! YOU CAN'T GO IN THERE.
BO-O
EYAHH!
♪
MILK, YOU HAVE TO STOP!
HOUSE #3
TRICK-OR-TREAT!
HERE YOU GO!
CLICK
I WAS WAITING FOR YOU KIDS.
OOH, LOTS OF CANDY!
POP POP
POP!!

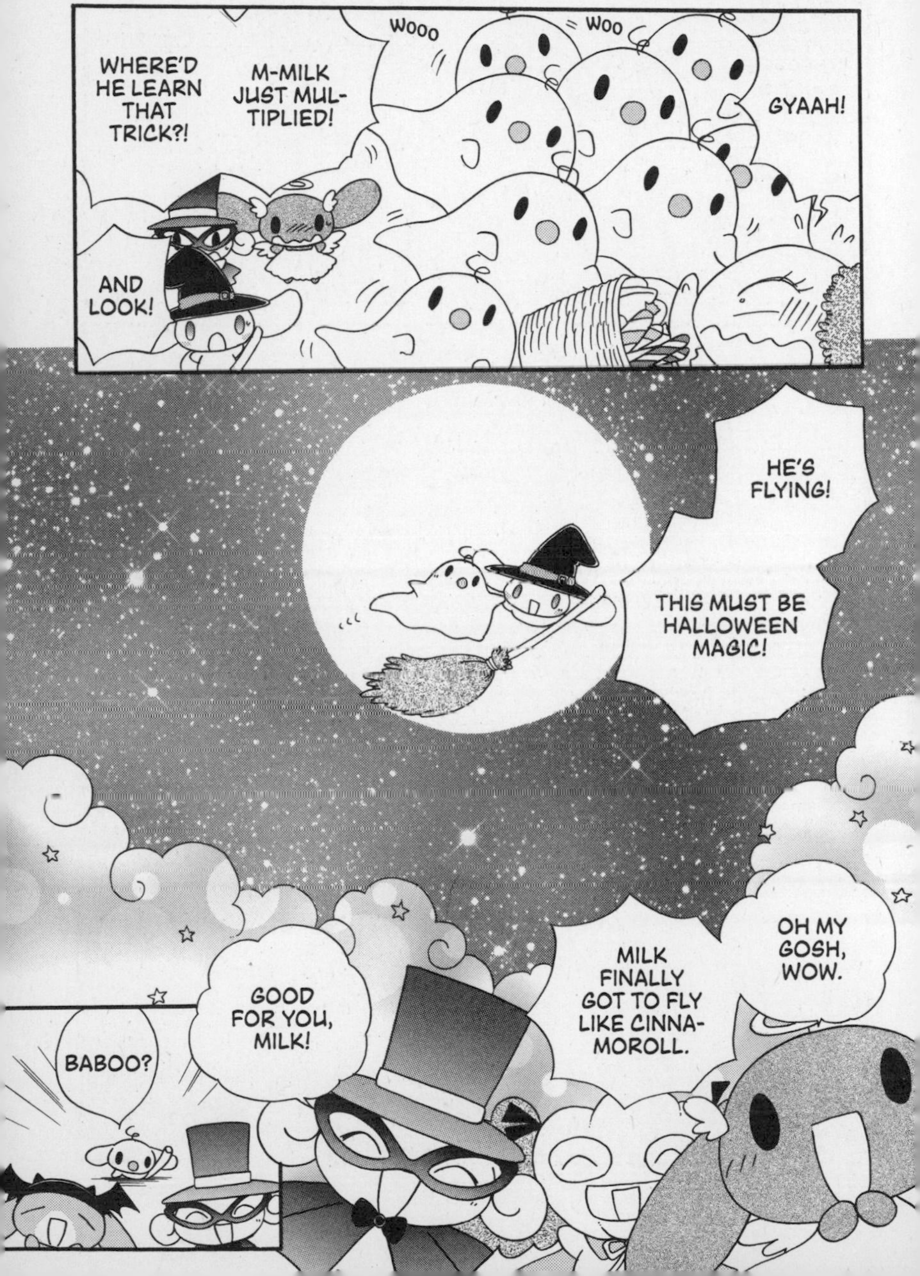
GYAAH!
WOO
WOOO
M-MILK JUST MUL-TIPLIED!
WHERE'D HE LEARN THAT TRICK?!
AND LOOK!
HE'S FLYING!
THIS MUST BE HALLOWEEN MAGIC!
OH MY GOSH, WOW.
MILK FINALLY GOT TO FLY LIKE CINNA-MOROLL.
GOOD FOR YOU, MILK!
BABOO?

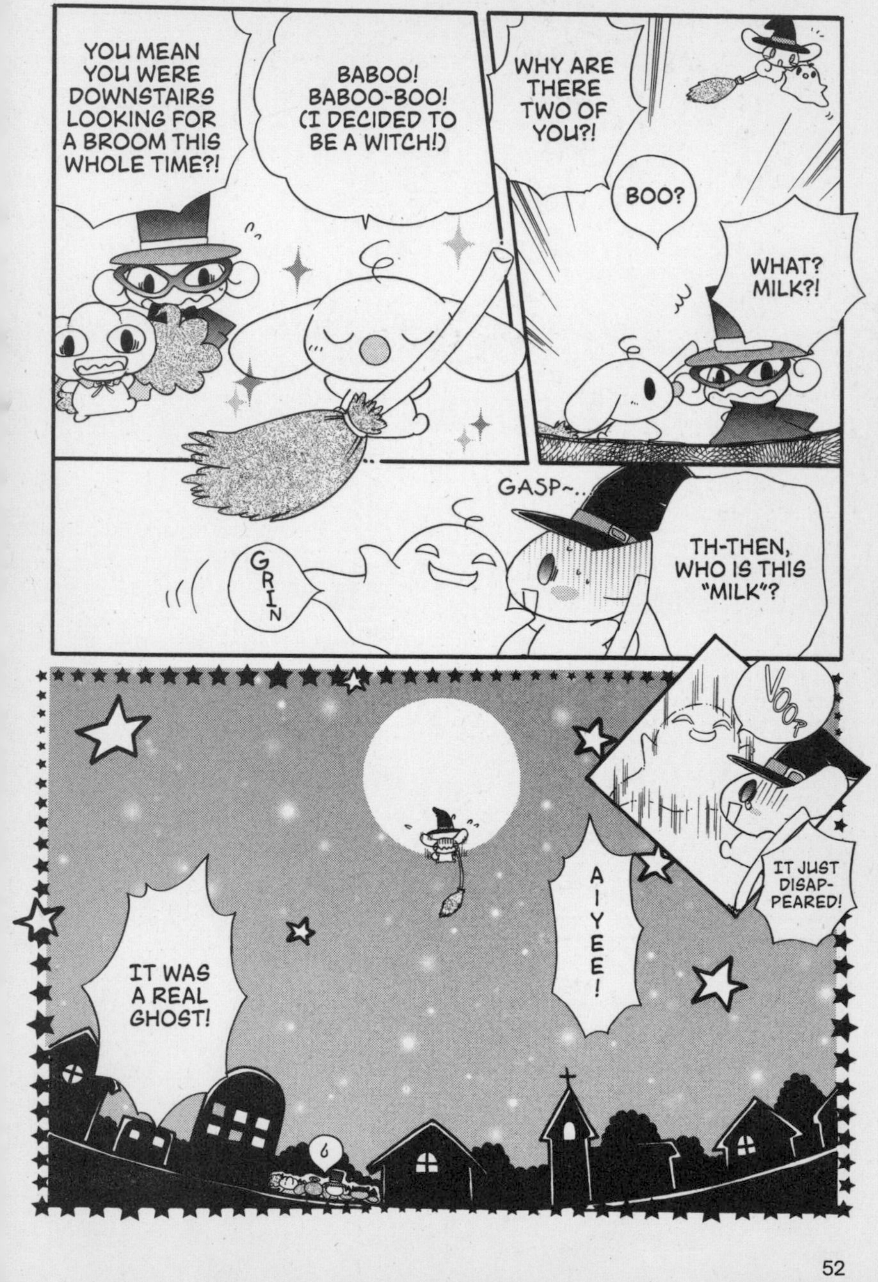
WHY ARE THERE TWO OF YOU?!
BOO?
WHAT? MILK?!
BABOO! BABOO-BOO! (I DECIDED TO BE A WITCH!)
YOU MEAN YOU WERE DOWNSTAIRS LOOKING FOR A BROOM THIS WHOLE TIME?!
GASP~...
TH-THEN, WHO IS THIS "MILK"?
GRIN
VOOP
IT JUST DISAP-PEARED!
AIYEE!
IT WAS A REAL GHOST!

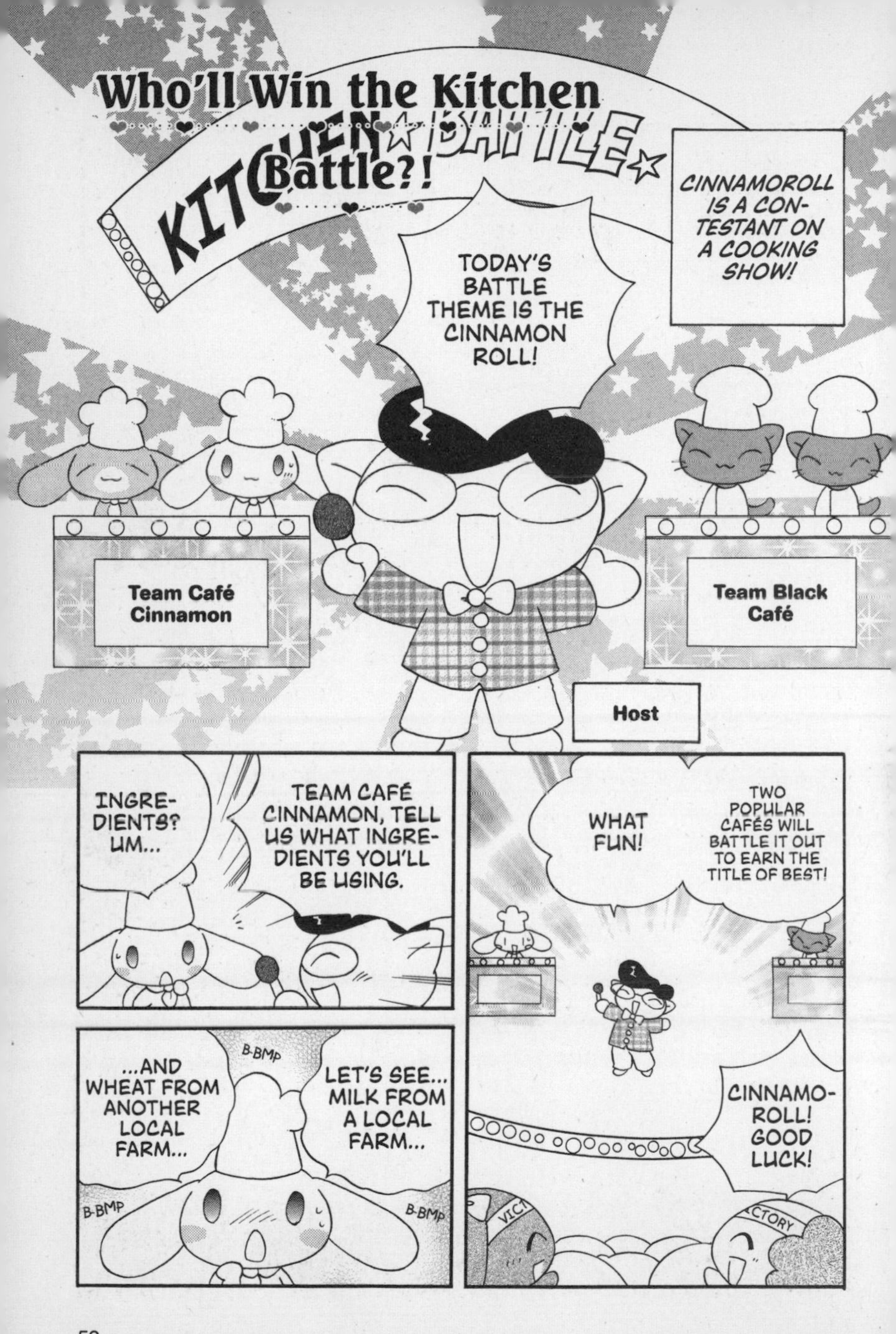
Who'll Win the Kitchen Battle?!
KITCHEN☆BATTLE☆
CINNAMOROLL IS A CONTESTANT ON A COOKING SHOW!
TODAY'S BATTLE THEME IS THE CINNAMON ROLL!
Team Black Café
Team Café Cinnamon
Host
TWO POPULAR CAFÉS WILL BATTLE IT OUT TO EARN THE TITLE OF BEST!
WHAT FUN!
CINNAMOROLL! GOOD LUCK!
TEAM CAFÉ CINNAMON, TELL US WHAT INGREDIENTS YOU'LL BE USING.
INGREDIENTS? UM...
B-BMP
LET'S SEE... MILK FROM A LOCAL FARM...
...AND WHEAT FROM ANOTHER LOCAL FARM...
B-BMP
B-BMP

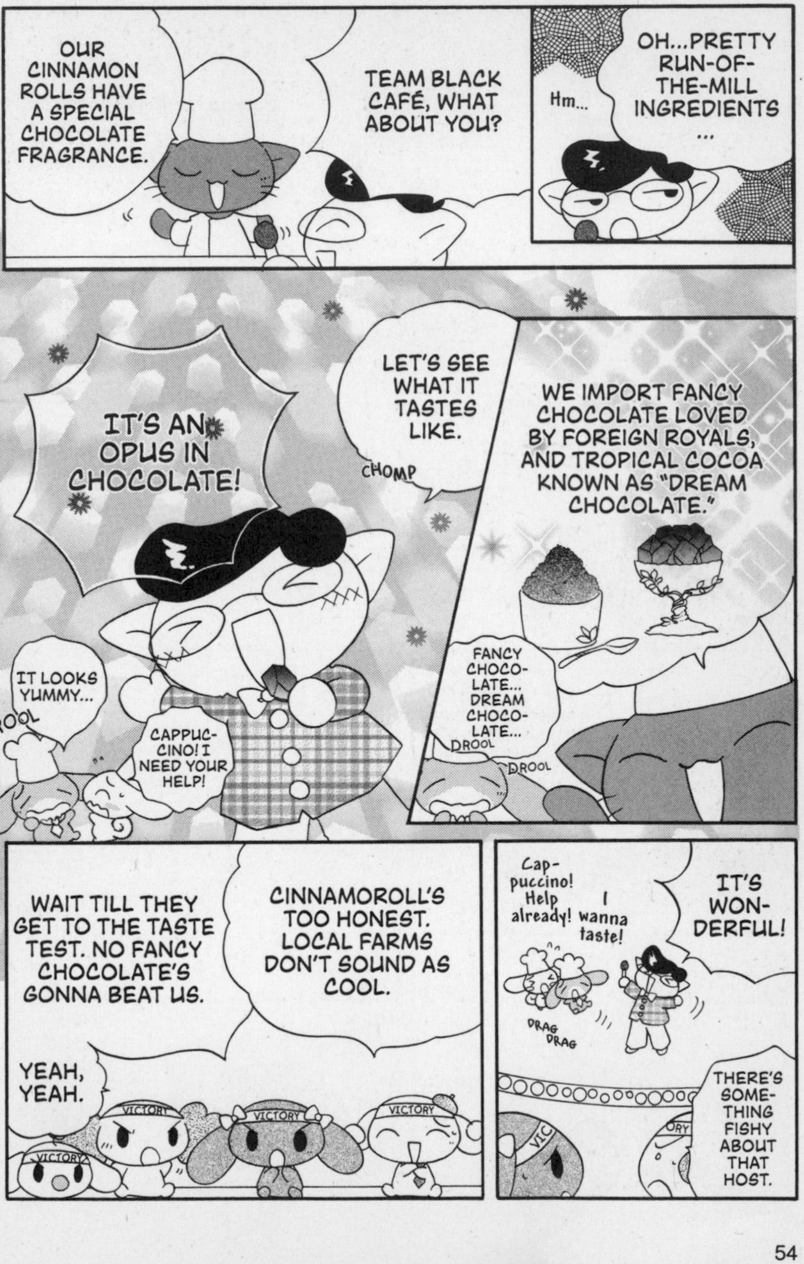
OH...PRETTY RUN-OF-THE-MILL INGREDIENTS...
Hm...
OUR CINNAMON ROLLS HAVE A SPECIAL CHOCOLATE FRAGRANCE.
TEAM BLACK CAFÉ, WHAT ABOUT YOU?
WE IMPORT FANCY CHOCOLATE LOVED BY FOREIGN ROYALS, AND TROPICAL COCOA KNOWN AS "DREAM CHOCOLATE."
FANCY CHOCO-LATE... DREAM CHOCO-LATE...
DROOL
DROOL
LET'S SEE WHAT IT TASTES LIKE.
CHOMP
IT'S AN OPUS IN CHOCOLATE!
IT LOOKS YUMMY...
DROOL
CAPPUC-CINO! I NEED YOUR HELP!
IT'S WON-DERFUL!
I wanna taste!
Cap-puccino! Help already!
DRAG DRAG
THERE'S SOME-THING FISHY ABOUT THAT HOST.
CINNAMOROLL'S TOO HONEST. LOCAL FARMS DON'T SOUND AS COOL.
WAIT TILL THEY GET TO THE TASTE TEST. NO FANCY CHOCOLATE'S GONNA BEAT US.
YEAH, YEAH.
VICTORY
VICTORY
VICTORY
VICTORY

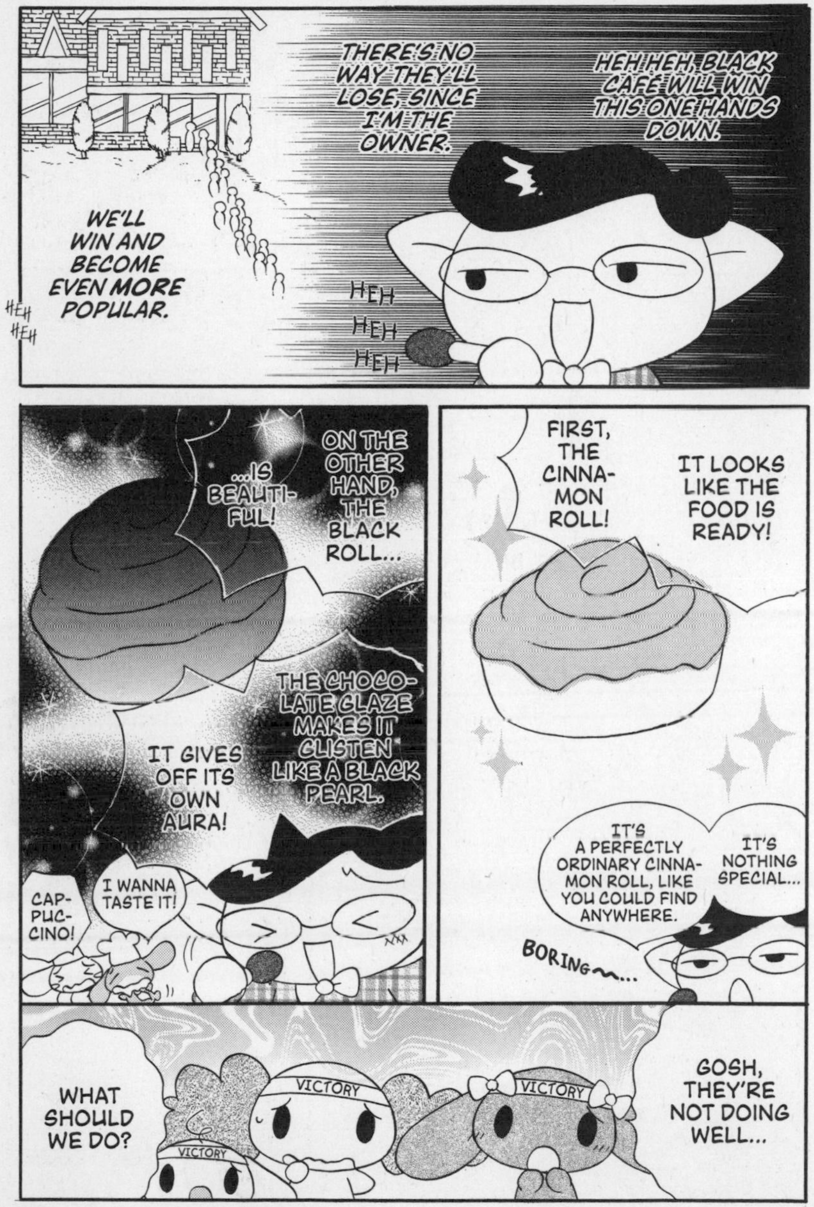
HEH HEH, BLACK CAFÉ WILL WIN THIS ONE HANDS DOWN.
THERE'S NO WAY THEY'LL LOSE, SINCE I'M THE OWNER.
HEH HEH HEH
WE'LL WIN AND BECOME EVEN MORE POPULAR.
HEH HEH
IT LOOKS LIKE THE FOOD IS READY!
FIRST, THE CINNA-MON ROLL!
IT'S NOTHING SPECIAL...
IT'S A PERFECTLY ORDINARY CINNA-MON ROLL, LIKE YOU COULD FIND ANYWHERE.
BORING~...
ON THE OTHER HAND, THE BLACK ROLL...
...IS BEAUTI-FUL!
THE CHOCO-LATE GLAZE MAKES IT GLISTEN LIKE A BLACK PEARL.
IT GIVES OFF ITS OWN AURA!
I WANNA TASTE IT!
CAP-PUC-CINO!
GOSH, THEY'RE NOT DOING WELL...
VICTORY
VICTORY
VICTORY
WHAT SHOULD WE DO?

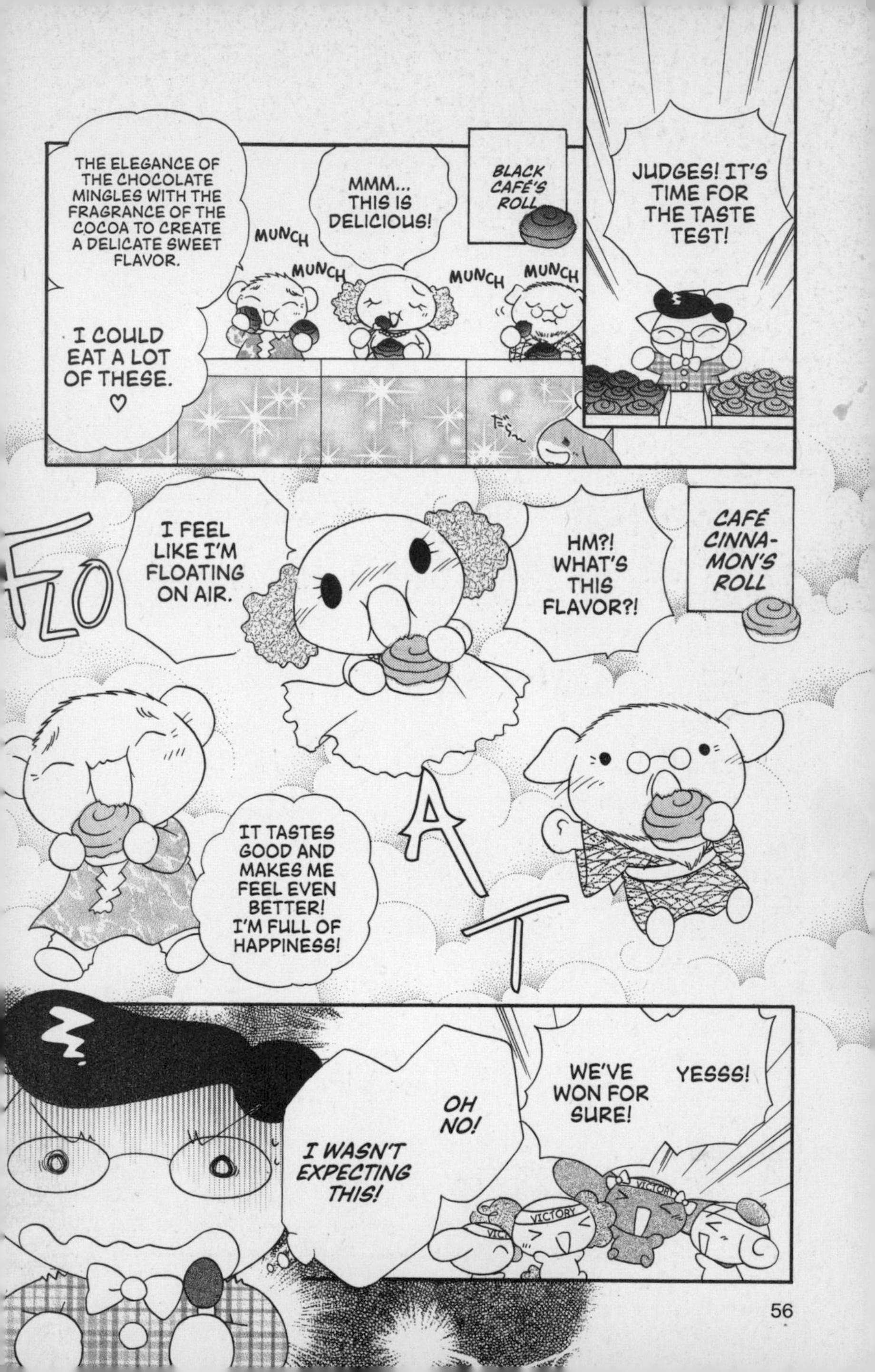
JUDGES! IT'S TIME FOR THE TASTE TEST!
BLACK CAFÉ'S ROLL
MMM... THIS IS DELICIOUS!
MUNCH
MUNCH
MUNCH
MUNCH
THE ELEGANCE OF THE CHOCOLATE MINGLES WITH THE FRAGRANCE OF THE COCOA TO CREATE A DELICATE SWEET FLAVOR.
I COULD EAT A LOT OF THESE. ♡
CAFÉ CINNAMON'S ROLL
HM?! WHAT'S THIS FLAVOR?!
I FEEL LIKE I'M FLOATING ON AIR.
FLOAT
IT TASTES GOOD AND MAKES ME FEEL EVEN BETTER! I'M FULL OF HAPPINESS!
YESSS!
WE'VE WON FOR SURE!
VICTORY
VICTORY
OH NO!
I WASN'T EXPECTING THIS!

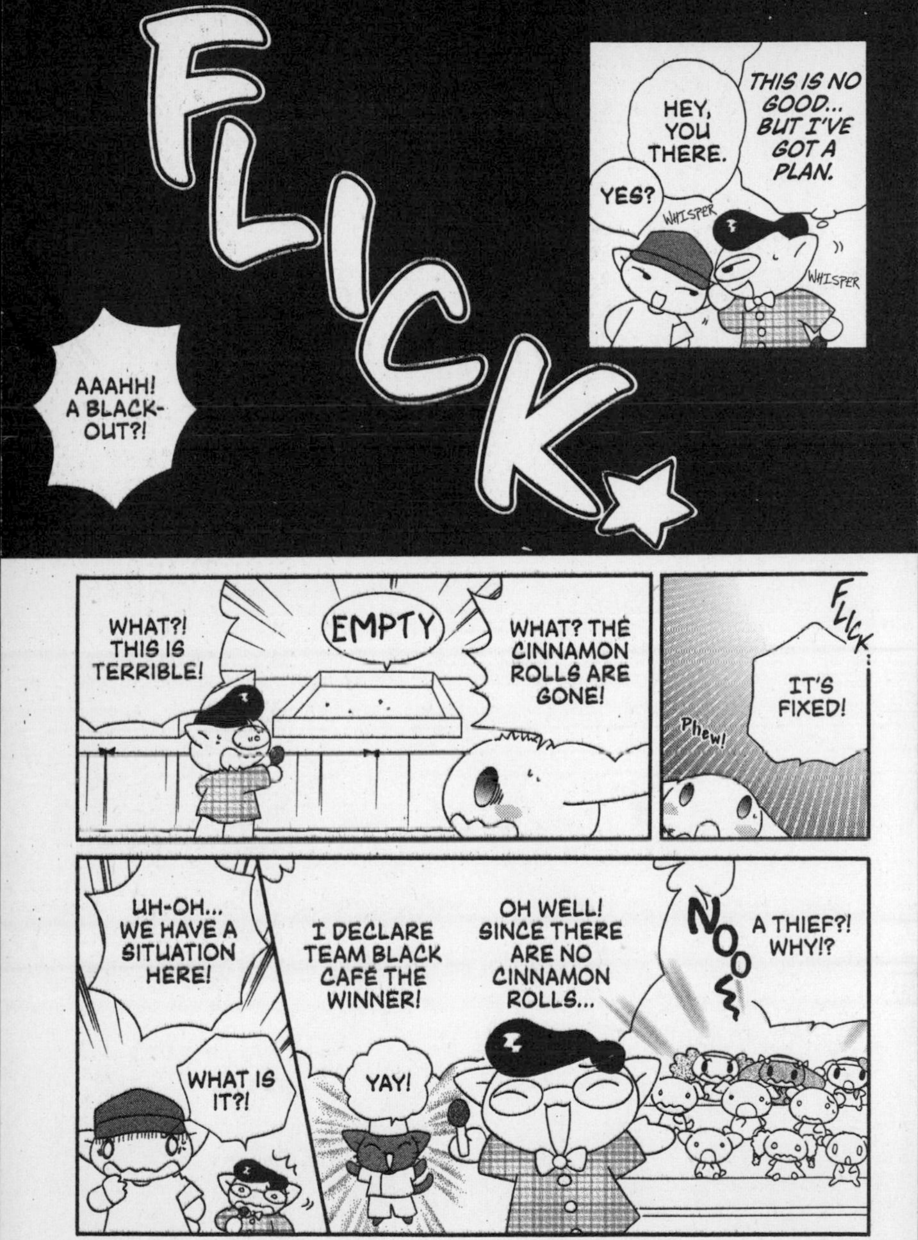
THIS IS NO GOOD... BUT I'VE GOT A PLAN.
HEY, YOU THERE.
WHISPER
WHISPER
YES?
FLICK
AAAHH! A BLACK-OUT?!
FLICK
IT'S FIXED!
Phew!
WHAT? THE CINNAMON ROLLS ARE GONE!
EMPTY
WHAT?! THIS IS TERRIBLE!
A THIEF?! WHY!?
NOOO
OH WELL! SINCE THERE ARE NO CINNAMON ROLLS...
I DECLARE TEAM BLACK CAFÉ THE WINNER!
YAY!
UH-OH... WE HAVE A SITUATION HERE!
WHAT IS IT?!

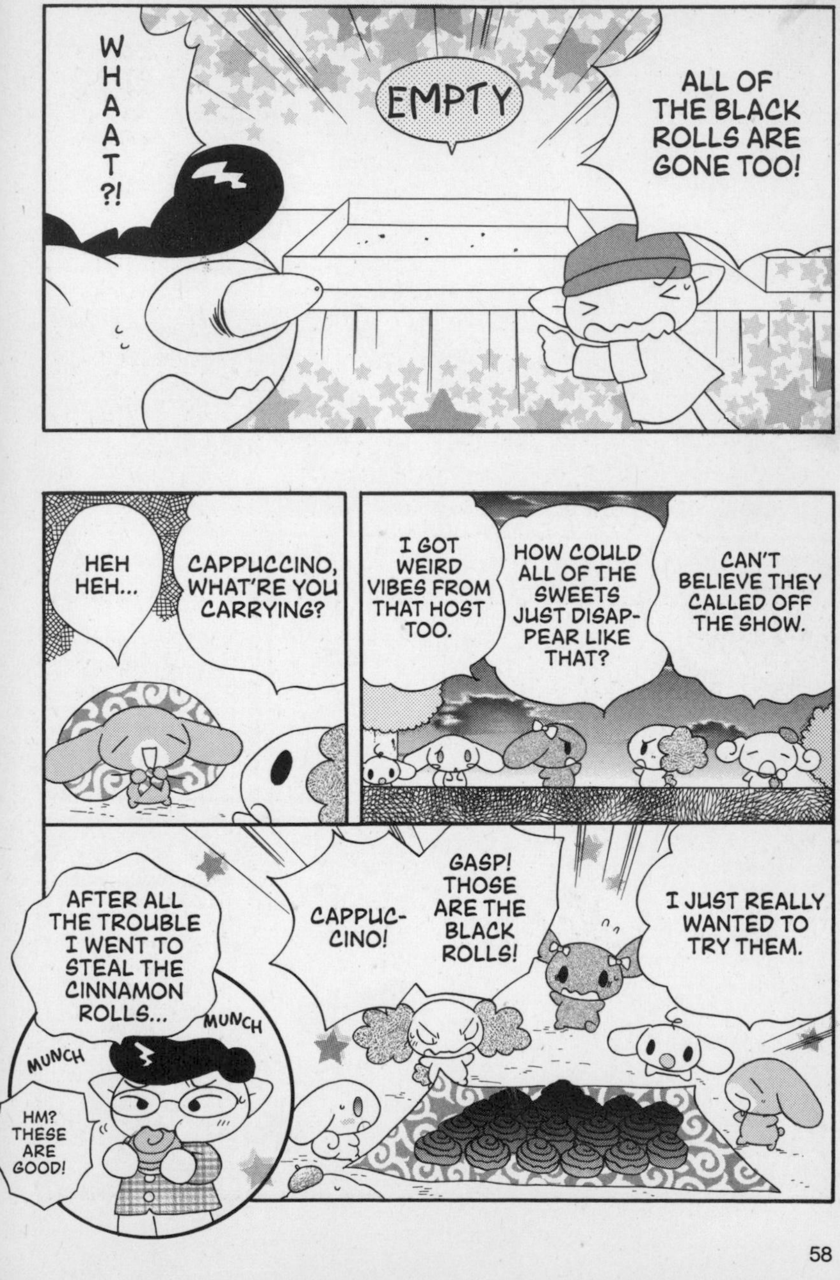
ALL OF THE BLACK ROLLS ARE GONE TOO!
EMPTY
WHAAT?!
CAN'T BELIEVE THEY CALLED OFF THE SHOW.
HOW COULD ALL OF THE SWEETS JUST DISAPPEAR LIKE THAT?
I GOT WEIRD VIBES FROM THAT HOST TOO.
CAPPUCCINO, WHAT'RE YOU CARRYING?
HEH HEH...
I JUST REALLY WANTED TO TRY THEM.
GASP! THOSE ARE THE BLACK ROLLS!
CAPPUCCINO!
AFTER ALL THE TROUBLE I WENT TO STEAL THE CINNAMON ROLLS...
MUNCH
MUNCH
HM? THESE ARE GOOD!

Ice Contest

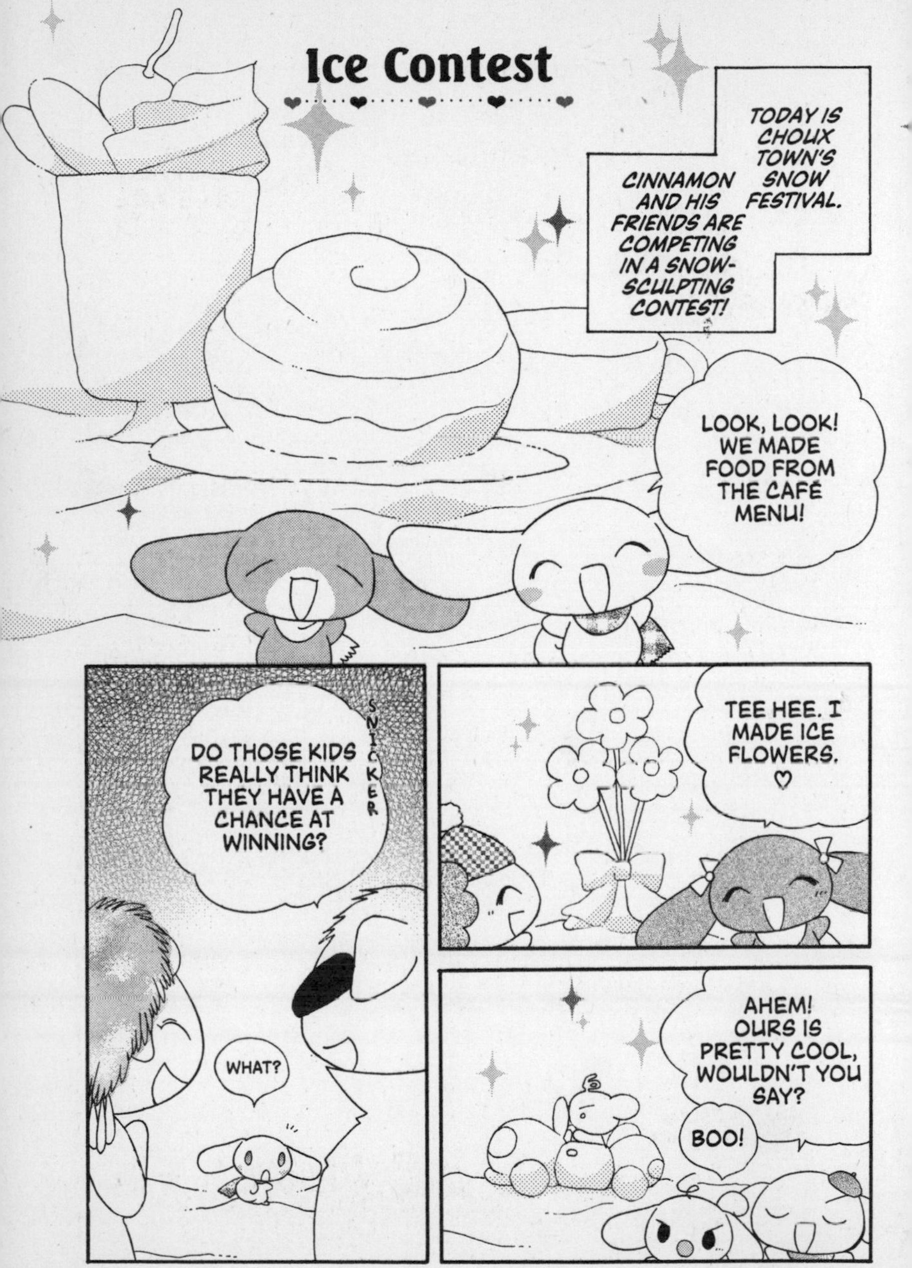
TODAY IS CHOUX TOWN'S SNOW FESTIVAL.
CINNAMON AND HIS FRIENDS ARE COMPETING IN A SNOW-SCULPTING CONTEST!
LOOK, LOOK! WE MADE FOOD FROM THE CAFÉ MENU!
TEE HEE. I MADE ICE FLOWERS. ♡
AHEM! OURS IS PRETTY COOL, WOULDN'T YOU SAY?
BOO!
SNICKER
DO THOSE KIDS REALLY THINK THEY HAVE A CHANCE AT WINNING?
WHAT?

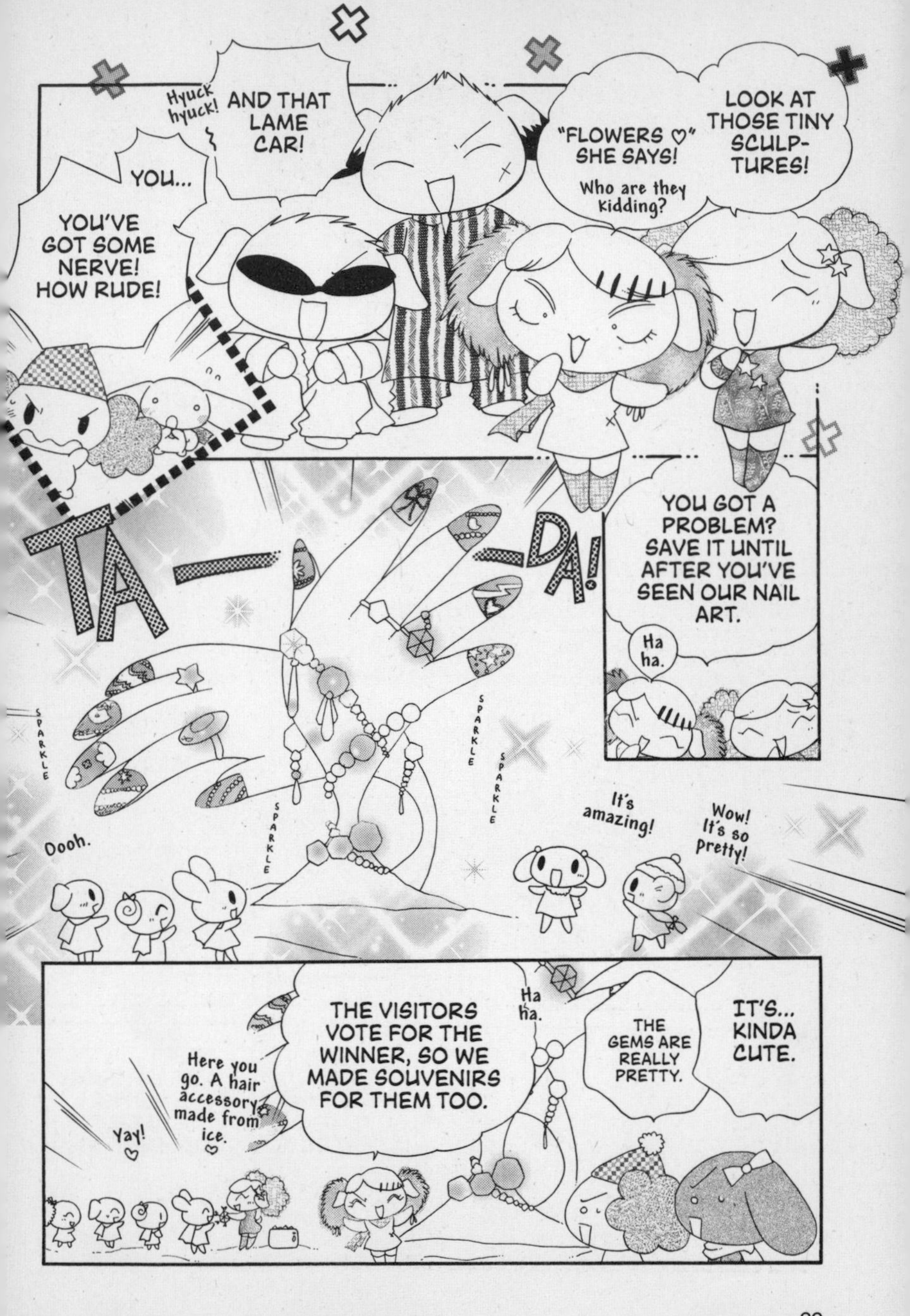
LOOK AT THOSE TINY SCULPTURES!
"FLOWERS ♡" SHE SAYS!
Who are they kidding?
AND THAT LAME CAR!
Hyuck hyuck!
YOU...
YOU'VE GOT SOME NERVE! HOW RUDE!
YOU GOT A PROBLEM? SAVE IT UNTIL AFTER YOU'VE SEEN OUR NAIL ART.
Ha ha.
TA——DA!
SPARKLE
SPARKLE
SPARKLE
SPARKLE
Wow! It's so pretty!
It's amazing!
Oooh.
IT'S... KINDA CUTE.
THE GEMS ARE REALLY PRETTY.
Ha ha.
THE VISITORS VOTE FOR THE WINNER, SO WE MADE SOUVENIRS FOR THEM TOO.
Here you go. A hair accessory made from ice.
Yay! ♡

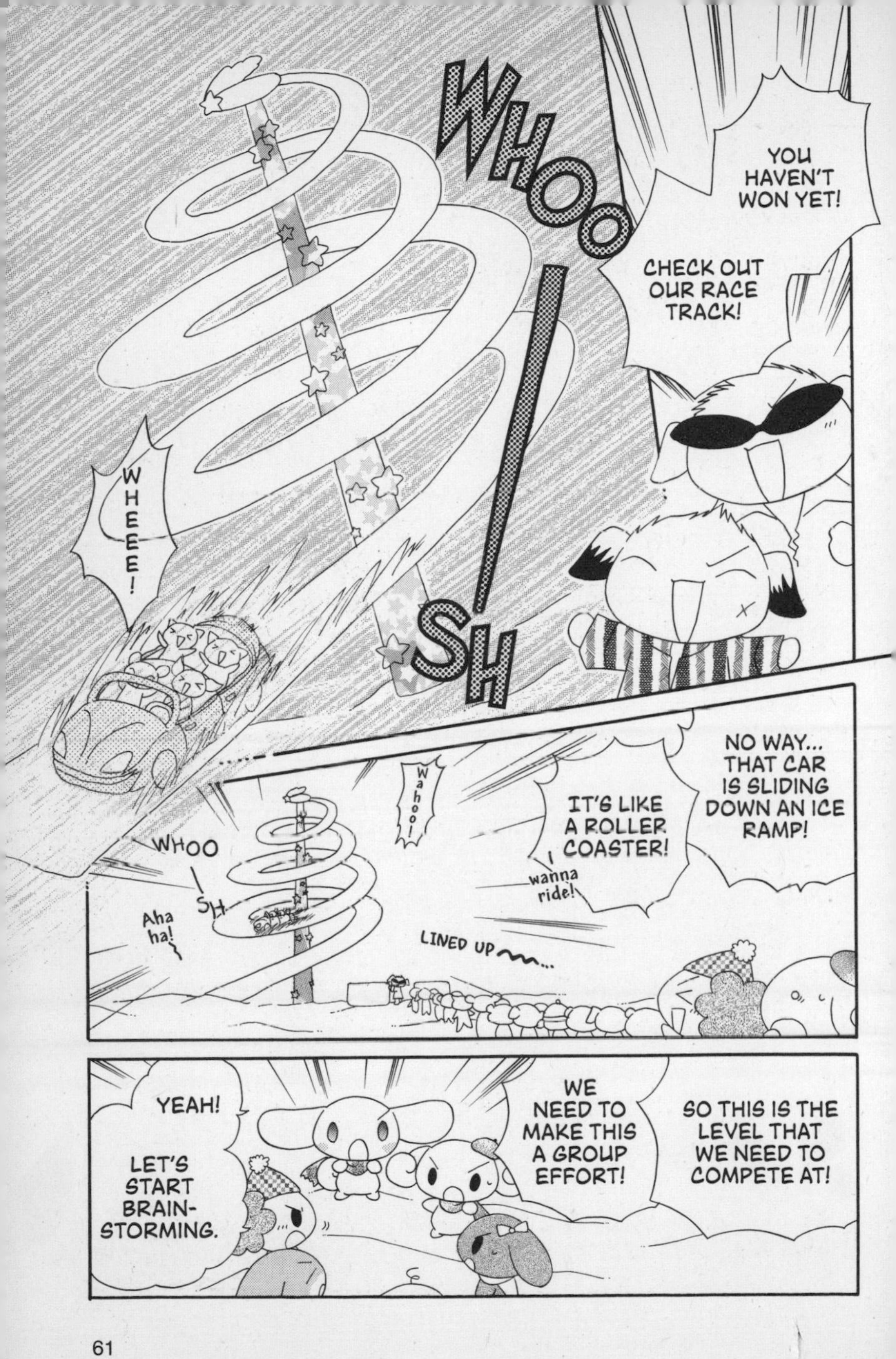
YOU HAVEN'T WON YET!
CHECK OUT OUR RACE TRACK!
WHOOO-SH
WHEEEE!
NO WAY... THAT CAR IS SLIDING DOWN AN ICE RAMP!
IT'S LIKE A ROLLER COASTER!
I wanna ride!
Wahoo!
WHOO-SH
Aha ha!
LINED UP...
SO THIS IS THE LEVEL THAT WE NEED TO COMPETE AT!
WE NEED TO MAKE THIS A GROUP EFFORT!
YEAH!
LET'S START BRAIN-STORMING.

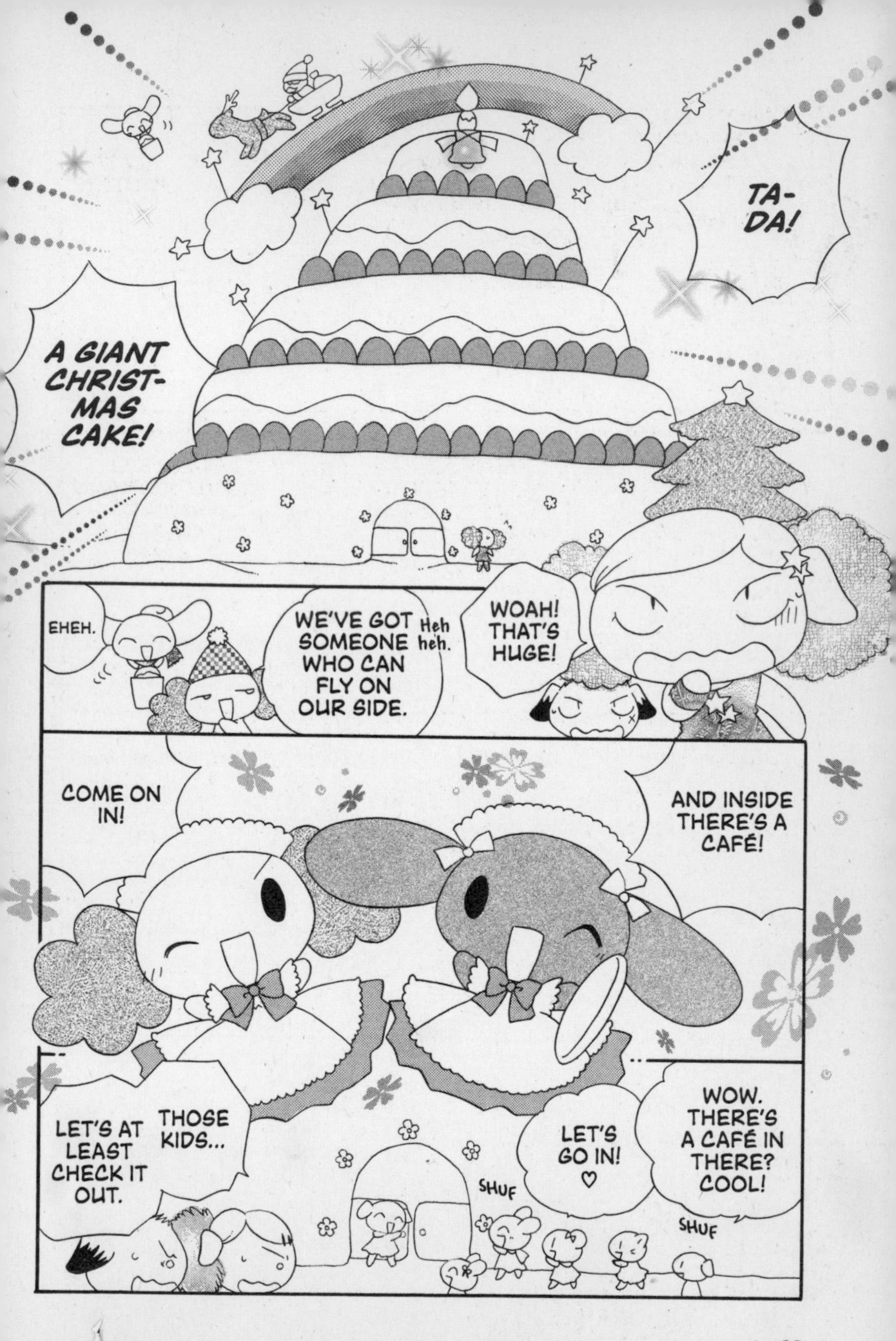
TA-DA!
A GIANT CHRISTMAS CAKE!
WOAH! THAT'S HUGE!
WE'VE GOT SOMEONE WHO CAN FLY ON OUR SIDE.
Heh heh.
EHEH.
AND INSIDE THERE'S A CAFÉ!
COME ON IN!
WOW. THERE'S A CAFÉ IN THERE? COOL!
SHUF
LET'S GO IN! ♡
SHUF
THOSE KIDS...
LET'S AT LEAST CHECK IT OUT.

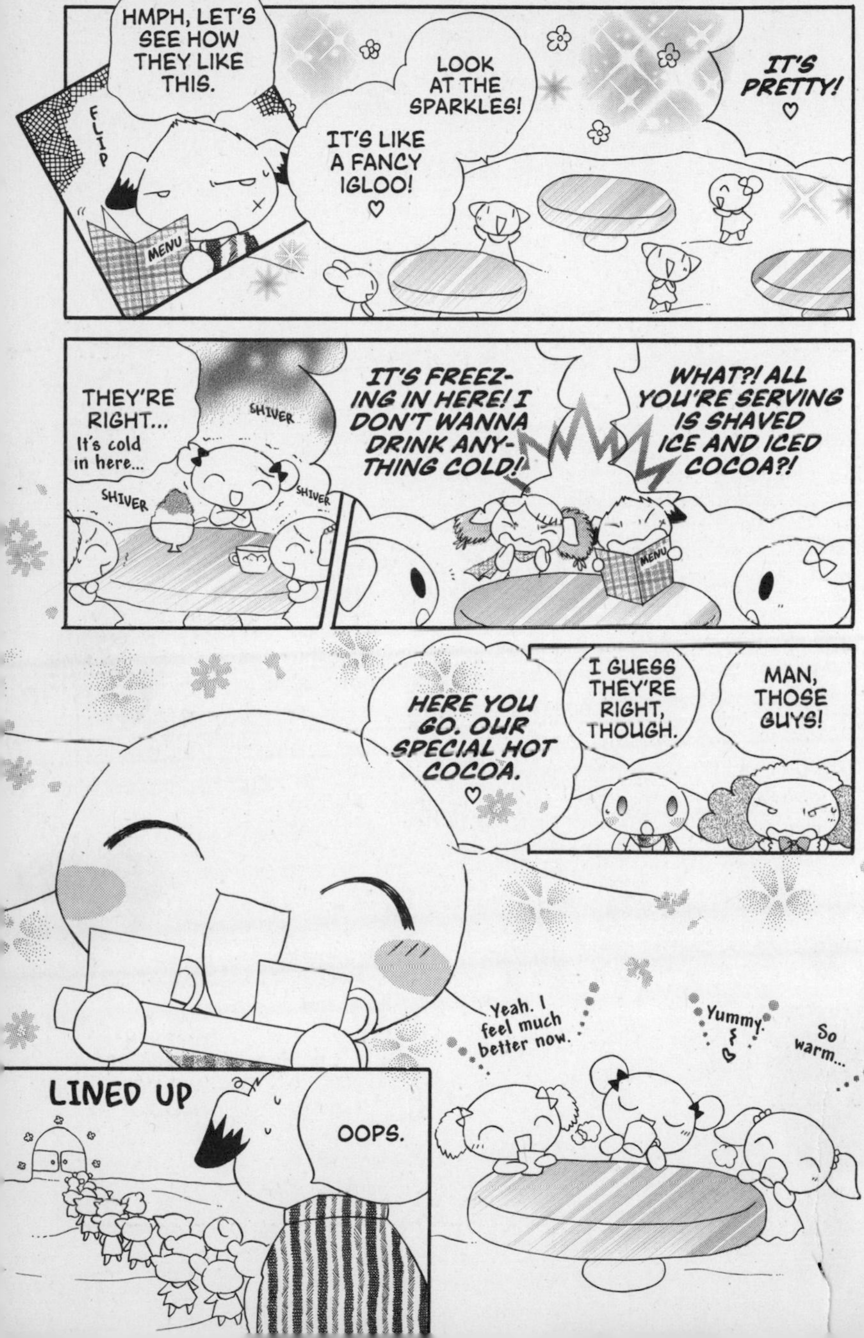
IT'S PRETTY! ♡
LOOK AT THE SPARKLES!
IT'S LIKE A FANCY IGLOO! ♡
HMPH, LET'S SEE HOW THEY LIKE THIS.
FLIP
MENU
WHAT?! ALL YOU'RE SERVING IS SHAVED ICE AND ICED COCOA?!
IT'S FREEZING IN HERE! I DON'T WANNA DRINK ANYTHING COLD!
MENU
THEY'RE RIGHT... It's cold in here...
SHIVER
SHIVER
SHIVER
MAN, THOSE GUYS!
I GUESS THEY'RE RIGHT, THOUGH.
HERE YOU GO. OUR SPECIAL HOT COCOA. ♡
So warm...
Yummy ♡
Yeah. I feel much better now.
LINED UP
OOPS.

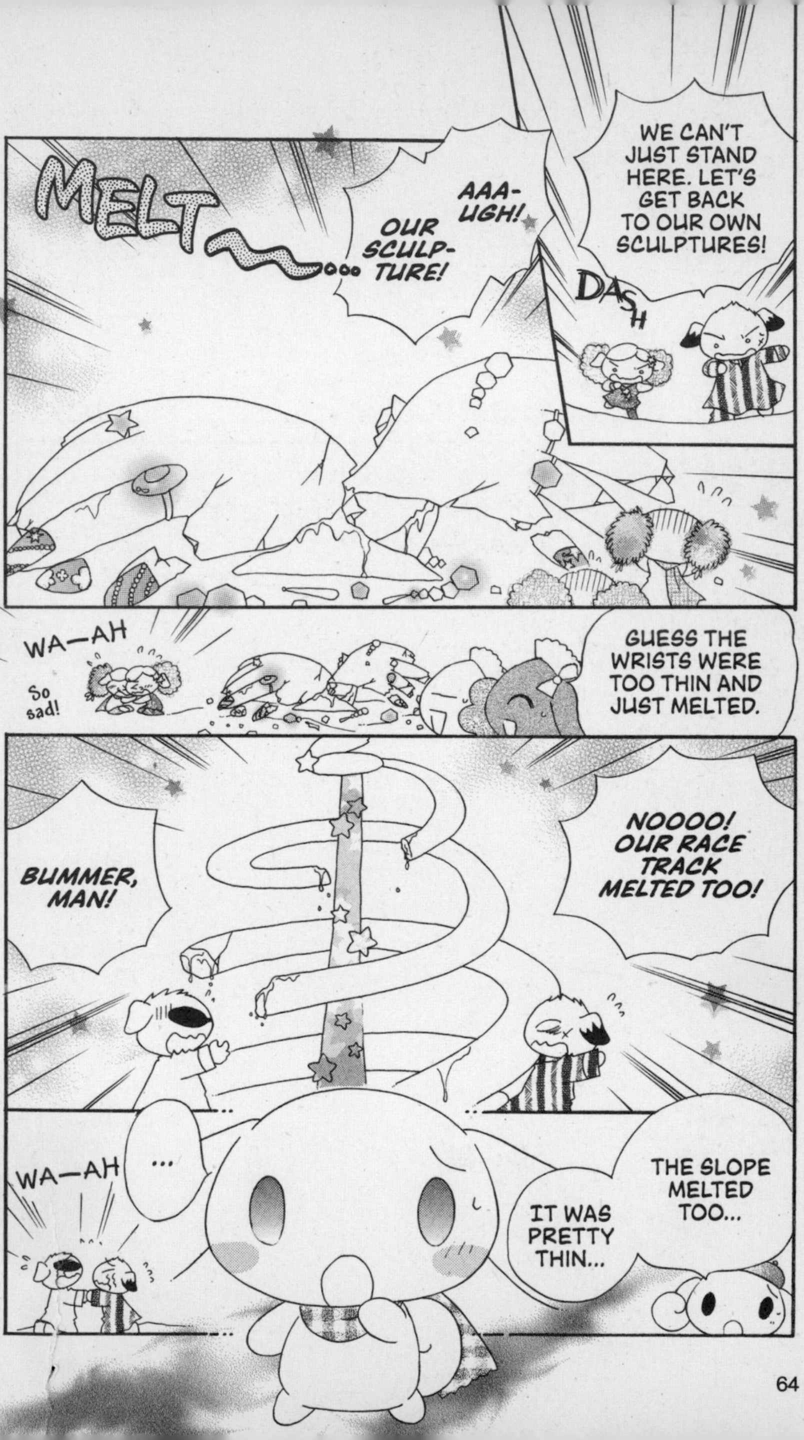
MELT
AAA-UGH!
OUR SCULPTURE!
WE CAN'T JUST STAND HERE. LET'S GET BACK TO OUR OWN SCULPTURES!
DASH
GUESS THE WRISTS WERE TOO THIN AND JUST MELTED.
WA-AH
So sad!
NOOOO! OUR RACE TRACK MELTED TOO!
BUMMER, MAN!
THE SLOPE MELTED TOO...
IT WAS PRETTY THIN...
...
WA-AH

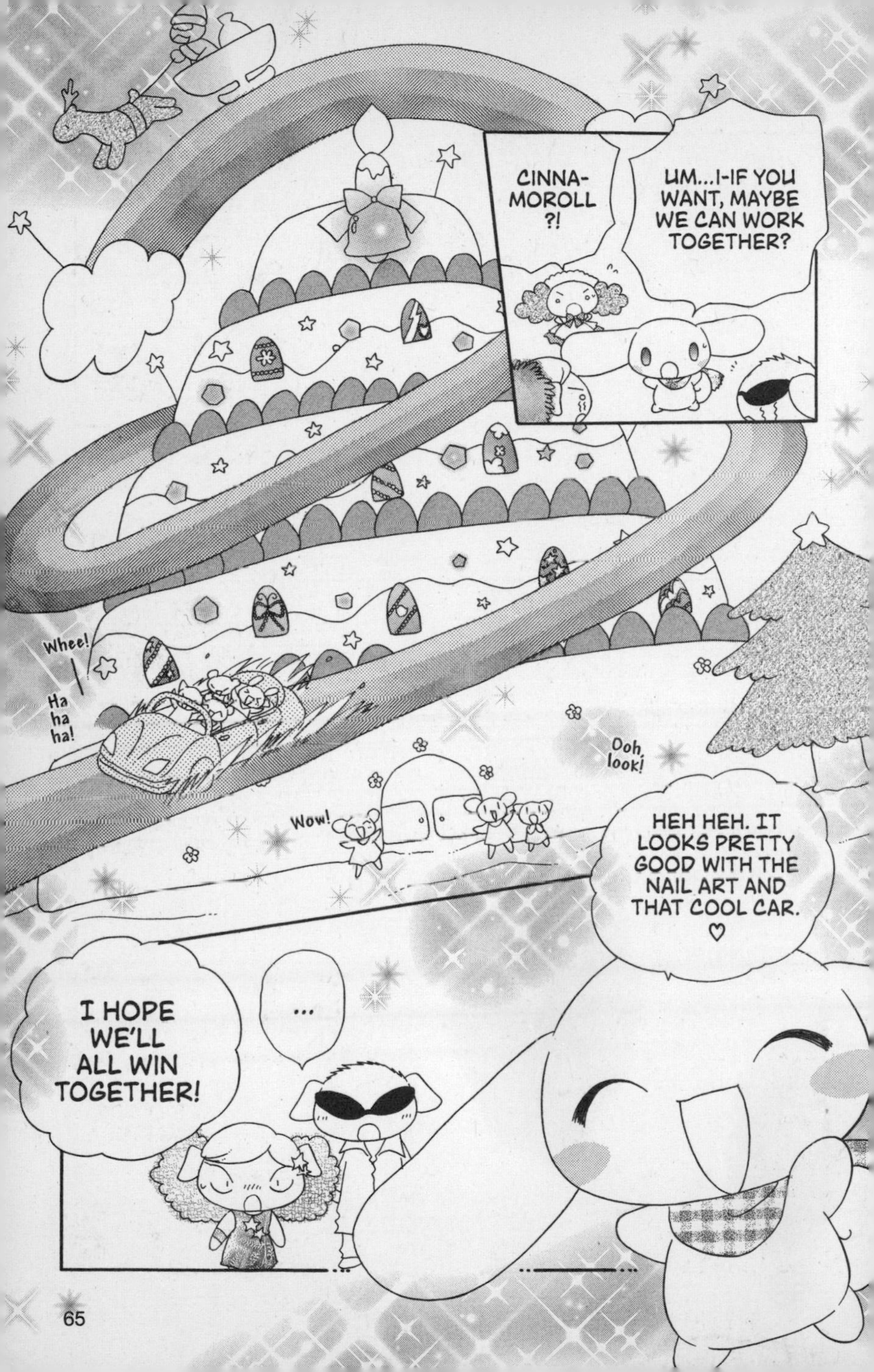
UM...I-IF YOU WANT, MAYBE WE CAN WORK TOGETHER?
CINNA-MOROLL ?!
Whee!
Ha ha ha!
Ooh, look!
Wow!
HEH HEH. IT LOOKS PRETTY GOOD WITH THE NAIL ART AND THAT COOL CAR. ♡
...
I HOPE WE'LL ALL WIN TOGETHER!

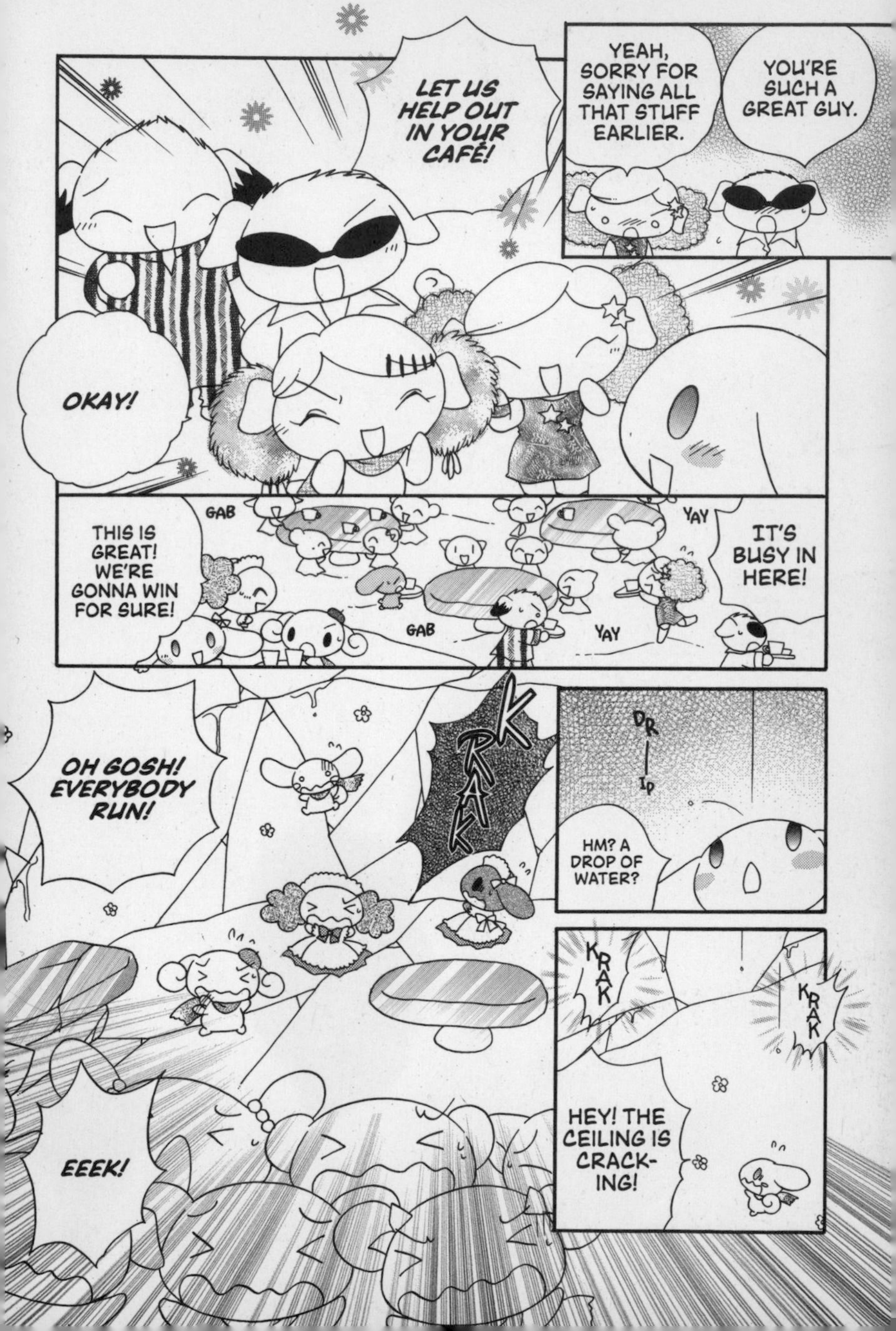
YOU'RE SUCH A GREAT GUY.
YEAH, SORRY FOR SAYING ALL THAT STUFF EARLIER.
LET US HELP OUT IN YOUR CAFÉ!
OKAY!
IT'S BUSY IN HERE!
YAY
YAY
GAB
GAB
THIS IS GREAT! WE'RE GONNA WIN FOR SURE!
DR-IP
HM? A DROP OF WATER?
KRAK
KRAK
HEY! THE CEILING IS CRACK-ING!
KRAK
OH GOSH! EVERYBODY RUN!
EEEK!

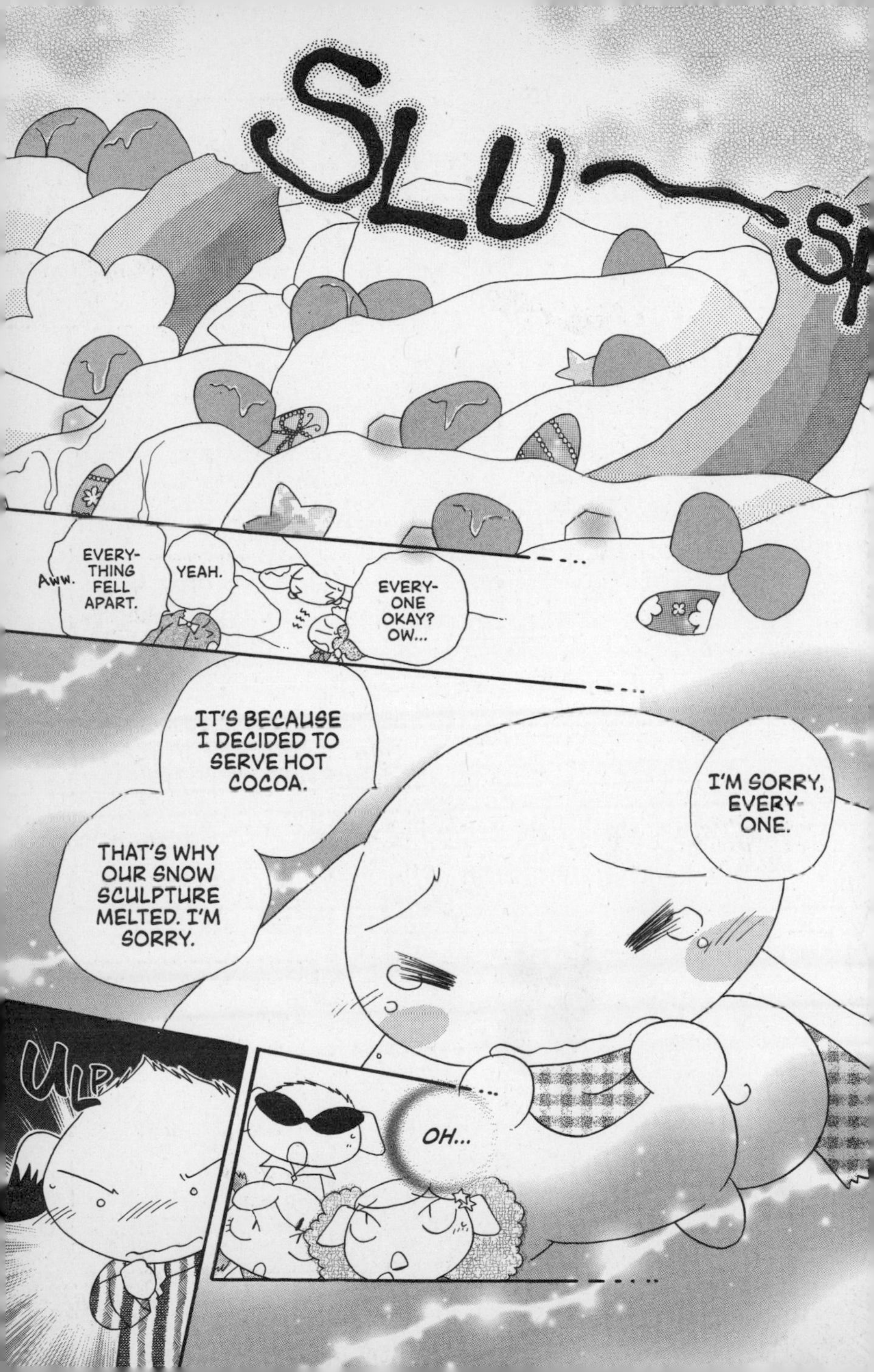
SLU~SH
EVERY-ONE OKAY? OW...
YEAH.
EVERY-THING FELL APART.
Aww.
I'M SORRY, EVERY-ONE.
IT'S BECAUSE I DECIDED TO SERVE HOT COCOA.
THAT'S WHY OUR SNOW SCULPTURE MELTED. I'M SORRY.
OH...
ULP

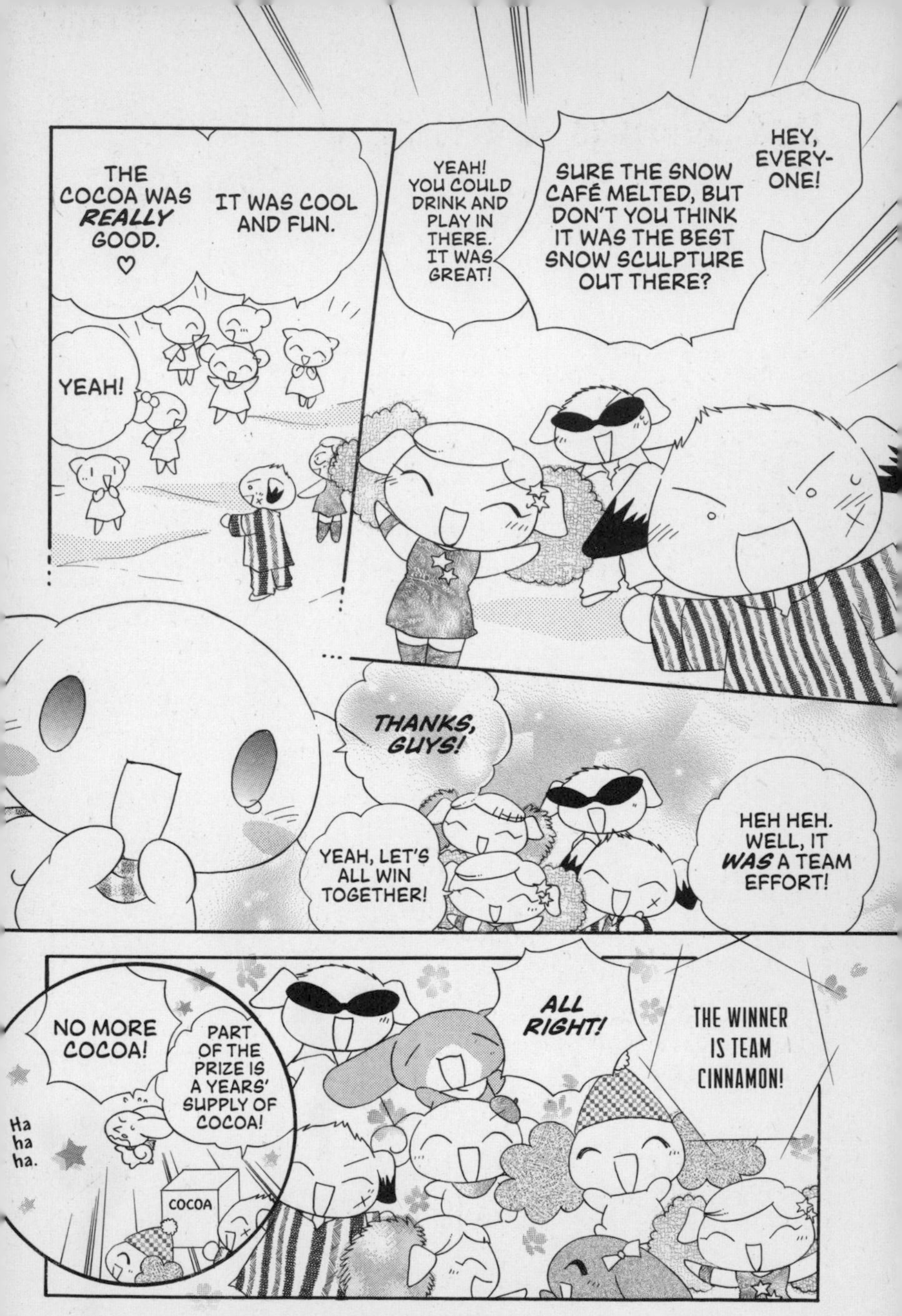
HEY, EVERY-ONE!
SURE THE SNOW CAFÉ MELTED, BUT DON'T YOU THINK IT WAS THE BEST SNOW SCULPTURE OUT THERE?
YEAH! YOU COULD DRINK AND PLAY IN THERE. IT WAS GREAT!
IT WAS COOL AND FUN.
THE COCOA WAS *REALLY* GOOD. ♡
YEAH!
HEH HEH. WELL, IT *WAS* A TEAM EFFORT!
THANKS, GUYS!
YEAH, LET'S ALL WIN TOGETHER!
THE WINNER IS TEAM CINNAMON!
ALL RIGHT!
PART OF THE PRIZE IS A YEARS' SUPPLY OF COCOA!
NO MORE COCOA!
COCOA
Ha ha ha.

Hot Springs Are Nice ♥

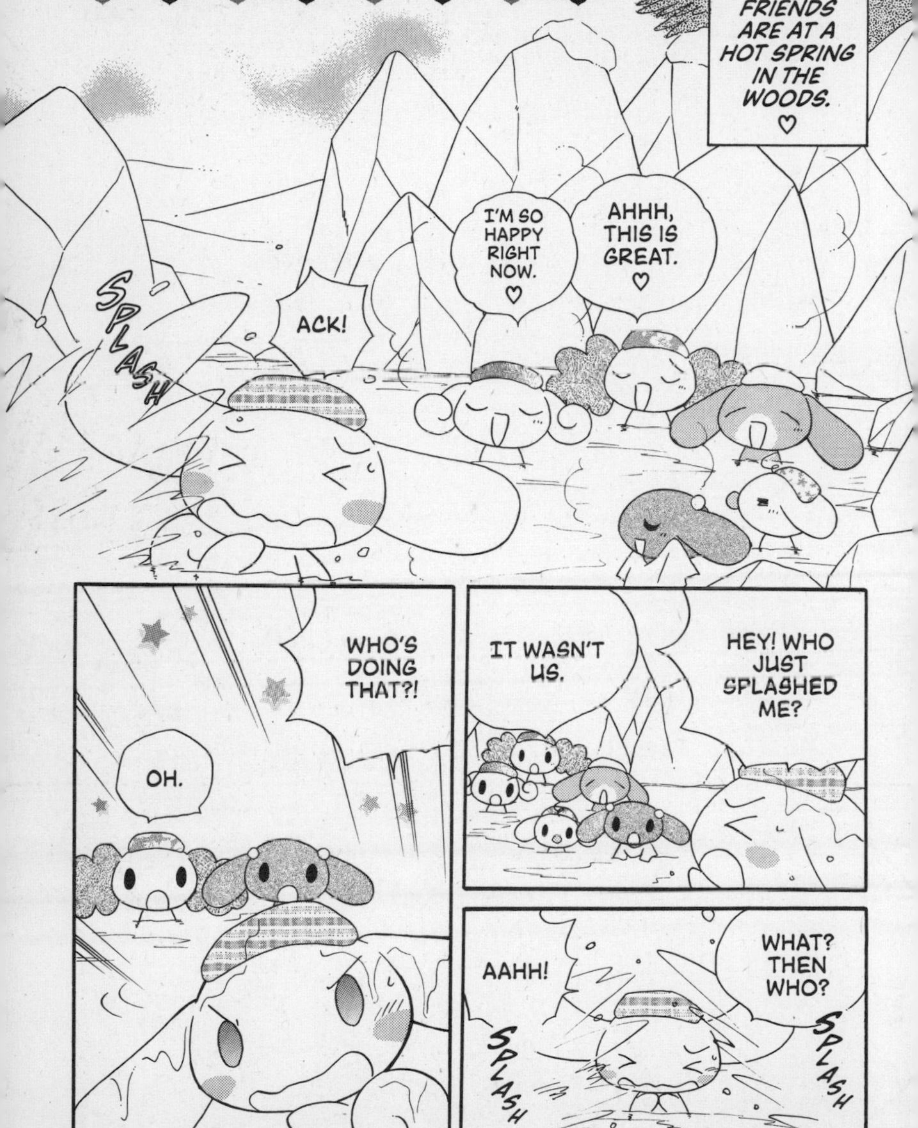
THE FRIENDS ARE AT A HOT SPRING IN THE WOODS. ♡
AHHH, THIS IS GREAT. ♡
I'M SO HAPPY RIGHT NOW. ♡
ACK!
SPLASH
HEY! WHO JUST SPLASHED ME?
IT WASN'T US.
WHAT? THEN WHO?
SPLASH
AAHH!
SPLASH
WHO'S DOING THAT?!
OH.

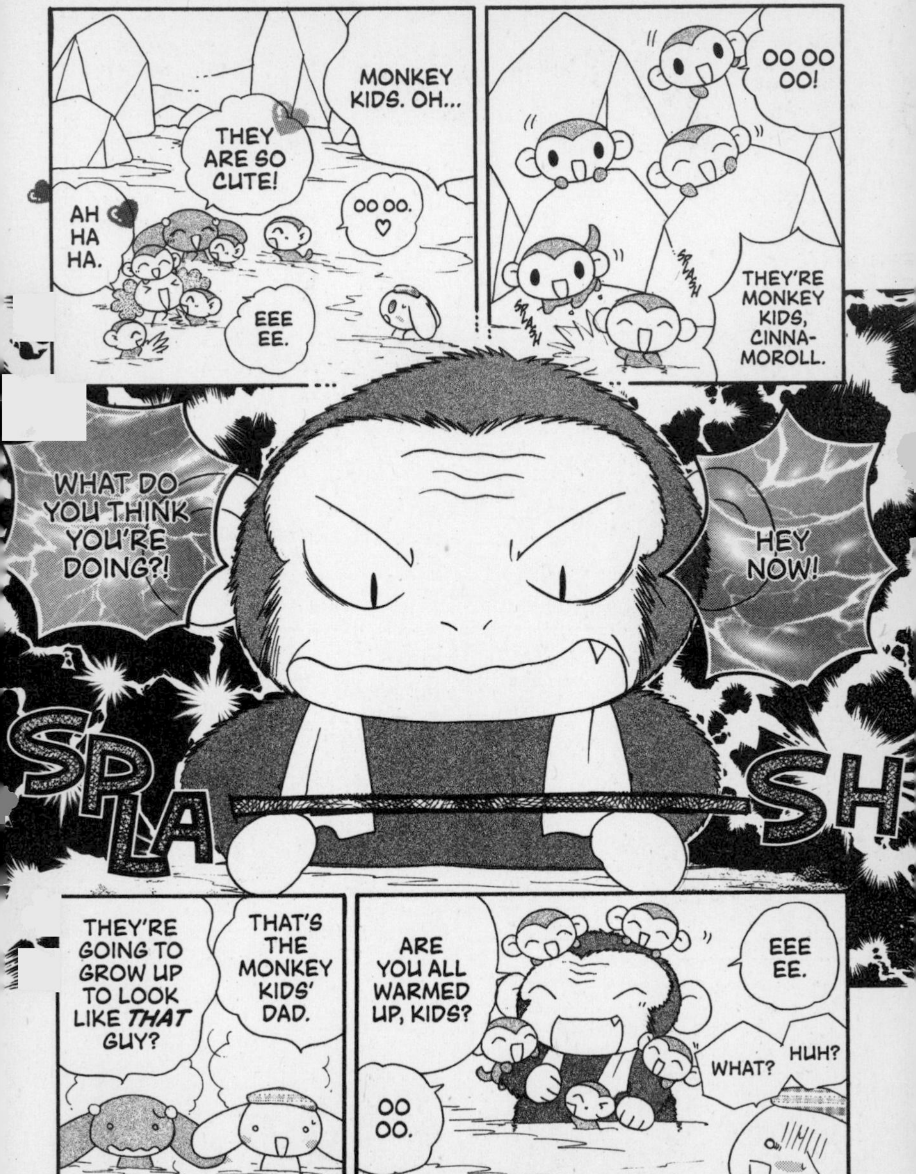
OO OO
OO!
THEY'RE MONKEY KIDS, CINNAMOROLL.
SPLASH
SPLASH
MONKEY KIDS. OH...
THEY ARE SO CUTE!
OO OO. ♡
AH HA HA.
EEE EE.
HEY NOW!
WHAT DO YOU THINK YOU'RE DOING?!
SPLASH
EEE EE.
ARE YOU ALL WARMED UP, KIDS?
HUH?
WHAT?
OO OO.
THAT'S THE MONKEY KIDS' DAD.
THEY'RE GOING TO GROW UP TO LOOK LIKE *THAT* GUY?

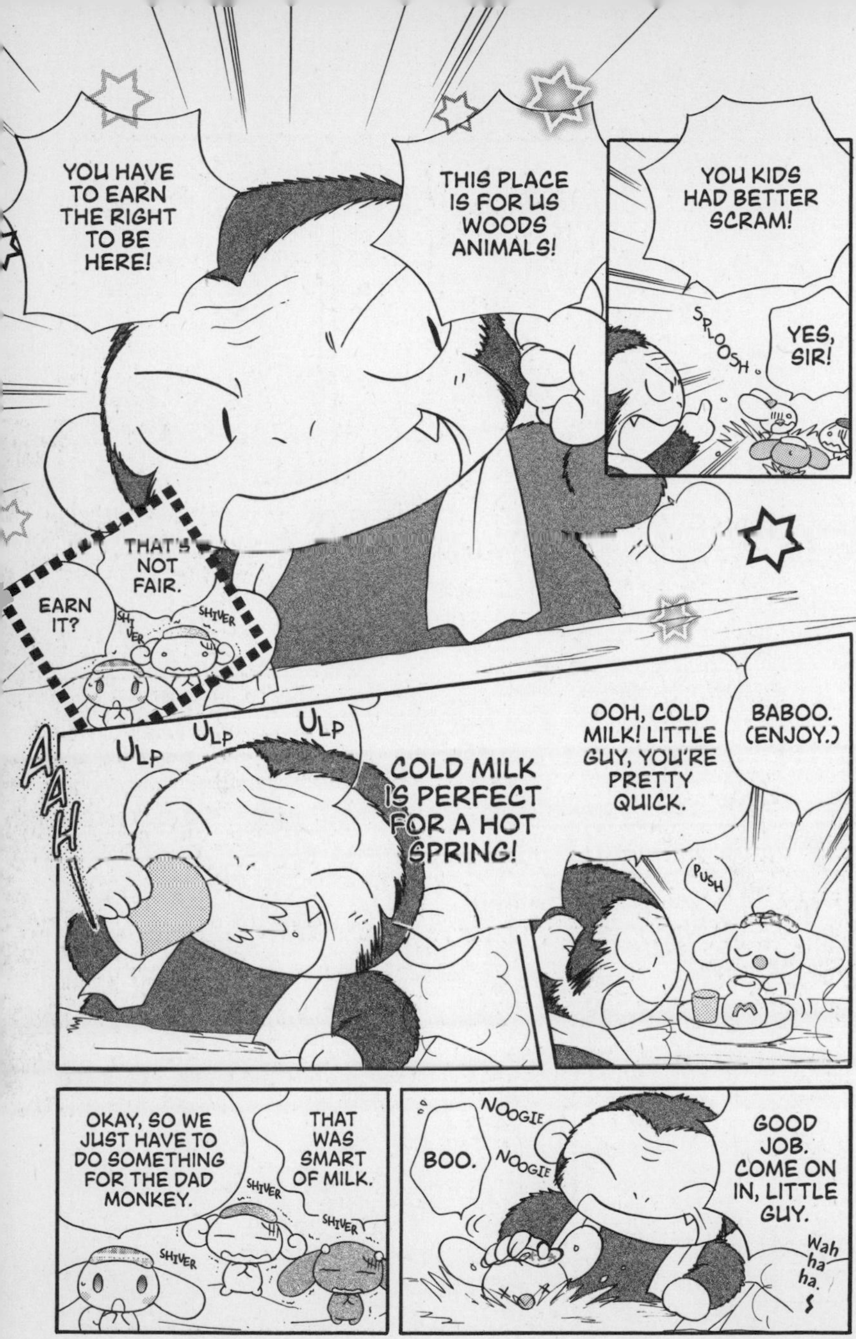
YOU KIDS HAD BETTER SCRAM!
SPLOOSH
YES, SIR!
THIS PLACE IS FOR US WOODS ANIMALS!
YOU HAVE TO EARN THE RIGHT TO BE HERE!
THAT'S NOT FAIR.
EARN IT?
SHIVER
SHIVER
BABOO. (ENJOY.)
OOH, COLD MILK! LITTLE GUY, YOU'RE PRETTY QUICK.
PUSH
COLD MILK IS PERFECT FOR A HOT SPRING!
ULP
ULP
ULP
AAAH
GOOD JOB. COME ON IN, LITTLE GUY.
Wah ha ha.
NOOGIE
NOOGIE
BOO.
THAT WAS SMART OF MILK.
OKAY, SO WE JUST HAVE TO DO SOMETHING FOR THE DAD MONKEY.
SHIVER
SHIVER
SHIVER

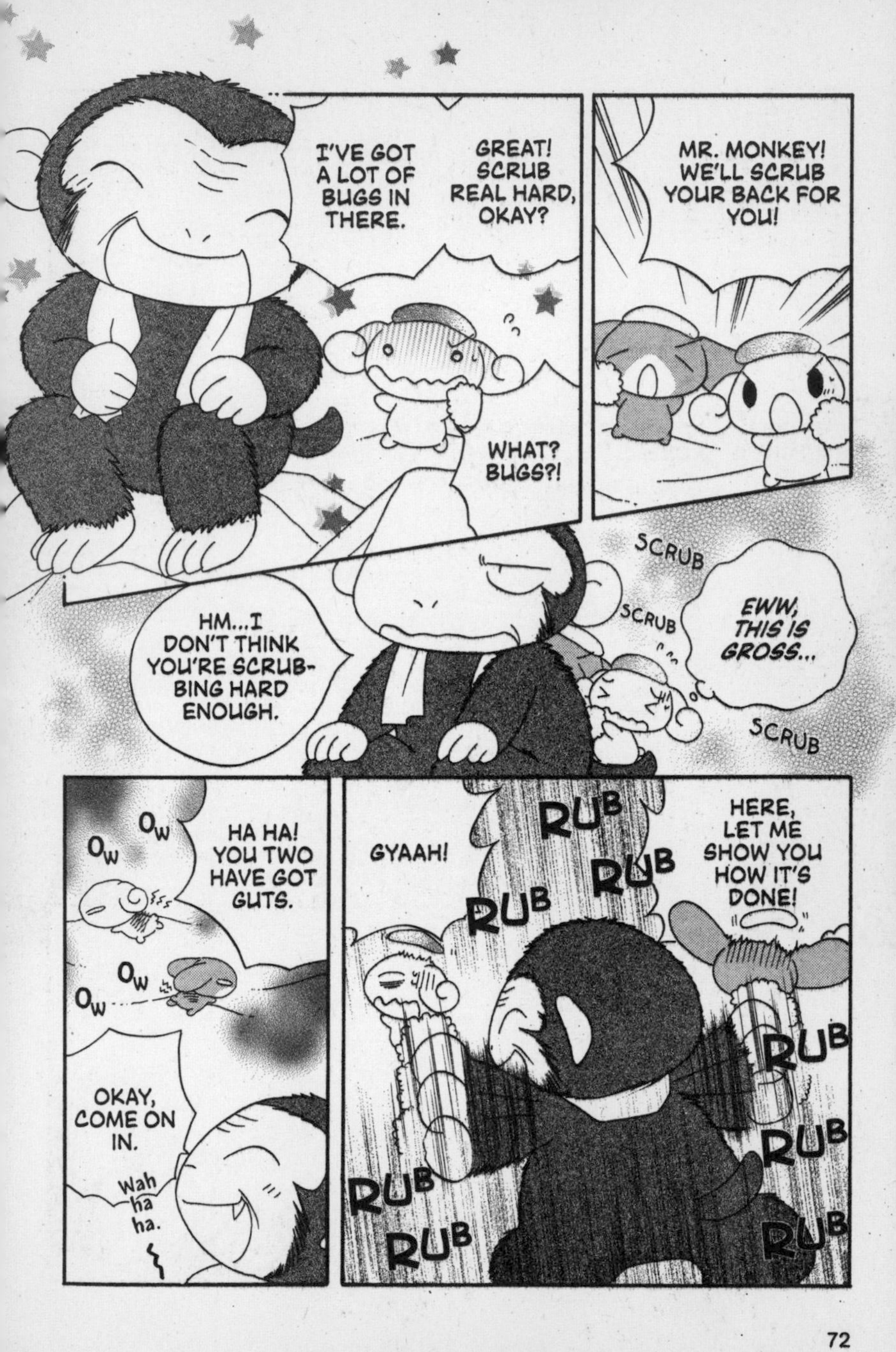
MR. MONKEY! WE'LL SCRUB YOUR BACK FOR YOU!
GREAT! SCRUB REAL HARD, OKAY?
I'VE GOT A LOT OF BUGS IN THERE.
WHAT? BUGS?!
SCRUB
EWW, THIS IS GROSS...
SCRUB
HM...I DON'T THINK YOU'RE SCRUB-BING HARD ENOUGH.
SCRUB
HERE, LET ME SHOW YOU HOW IT'S DONE!
RUB
RUB
RUB
GYAAH!
RUB
RUB
RUB
RUB
RUB
HA HA! YOU TWO HAVE GOT GUTS.
OW
OW
OW
OW
OKAY, COME ON IN.
Wah ha ha.

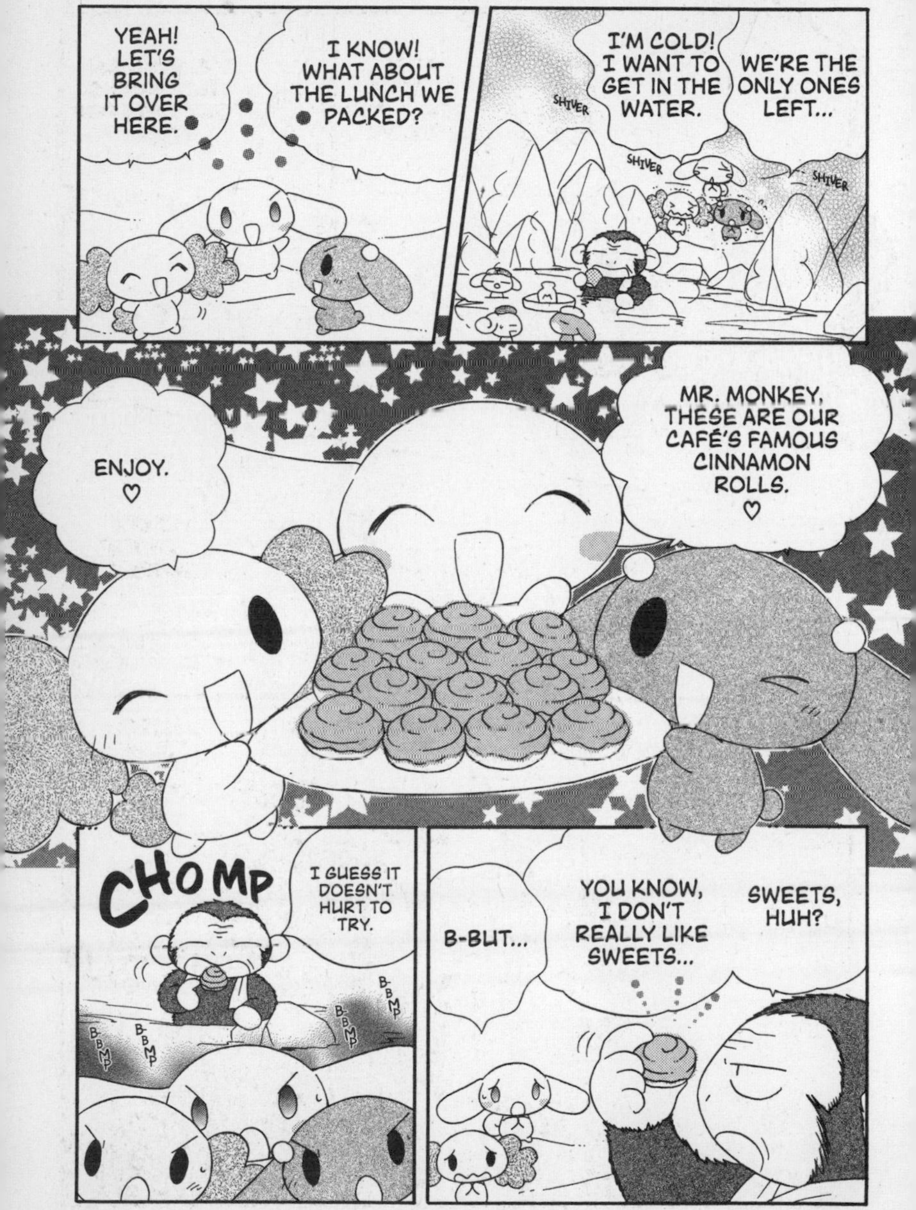
WE'RE THE ONLY ONES LEFT...
I'M COLD! I WANT TO GET IN THE WATER.
SHIVER
SHIVER
SHIVER
I KNOW! WHAT ABOUT THE LUNCH WE PACKED?
YEAH! LET'S BRING IT OVER HERE.
MR. MONKEY, THESE ARE OUR CAFÉ'S FAMOUS CINNAMON ROLLS. ♡
ENJOY. ♡
SWEETS, HUH?
YOU KNOW, I DON'T REALLY LIKE SWEETS...
B-BUT...
I GUESS IT DOESN'T HURT TO TRY.
CHOMP
B-BMP
B-BMP
B-BMP
B-BMP

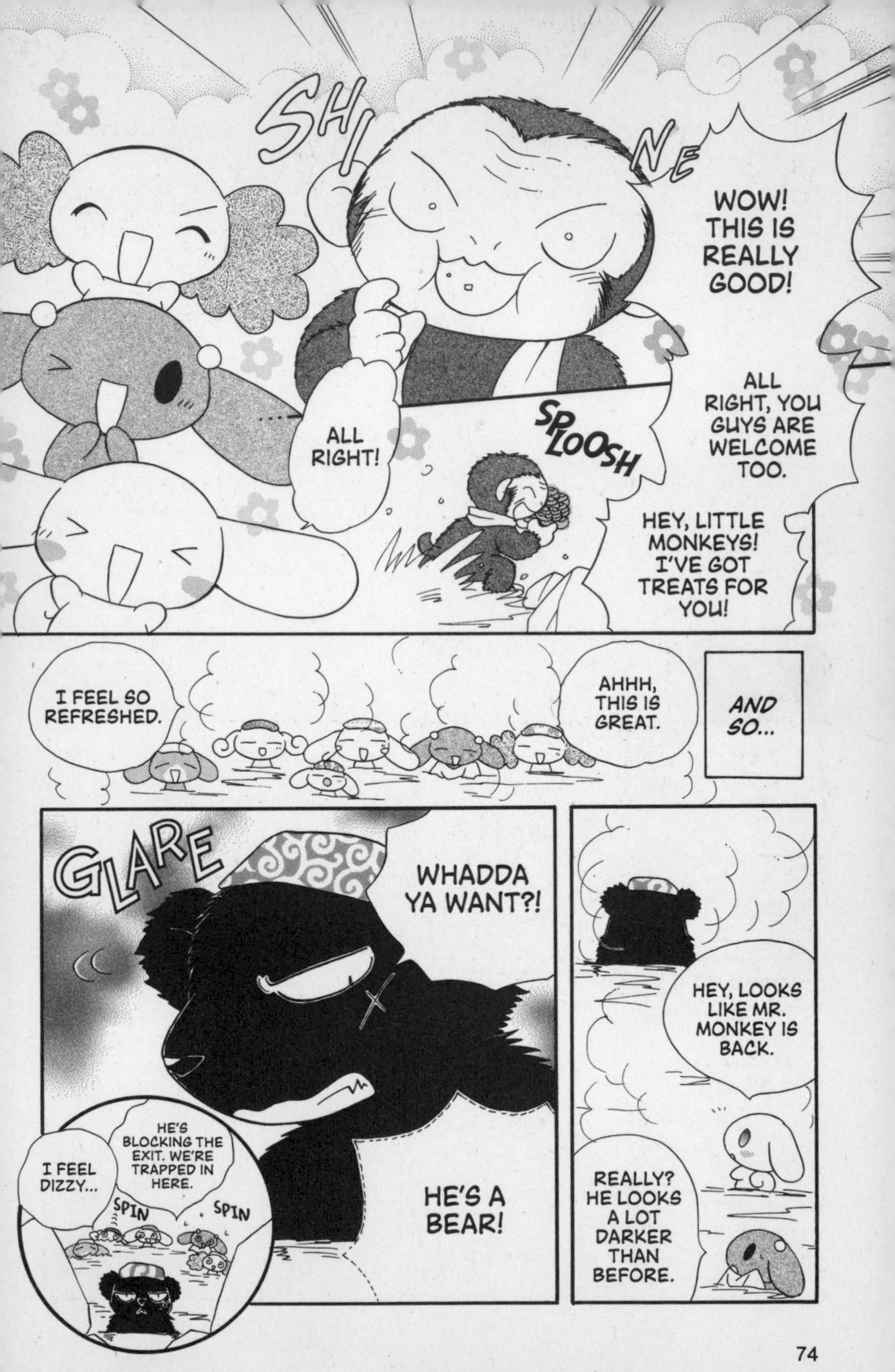
SHINE
WOW! THIS IS REALLY GOOD!
ALL RIGHT, YOU GUYS ARE WELCOME TOO.
HEY, LITTLE MONKEYS! I'VE GOT TREATS FOR YOU!
SPLOOSH
ALL RIGHT!
AND SO...
AHHH, THIS IS GREAT.
I FEEL SO REFRESHED.
HEY, LOOKS LIKE MR. MONKEY IS BACK.
REALLY? HE LOOKS A LOT DARKER THAN BEFORE.
GLARE
WHADDA YA WANT?!
HE'S A BEAR!
HE'S BLOCKING THE EXIT. WE'RE TRAPPED IN HERE.
SPIN
SPIN
I FEEL DIZZY...

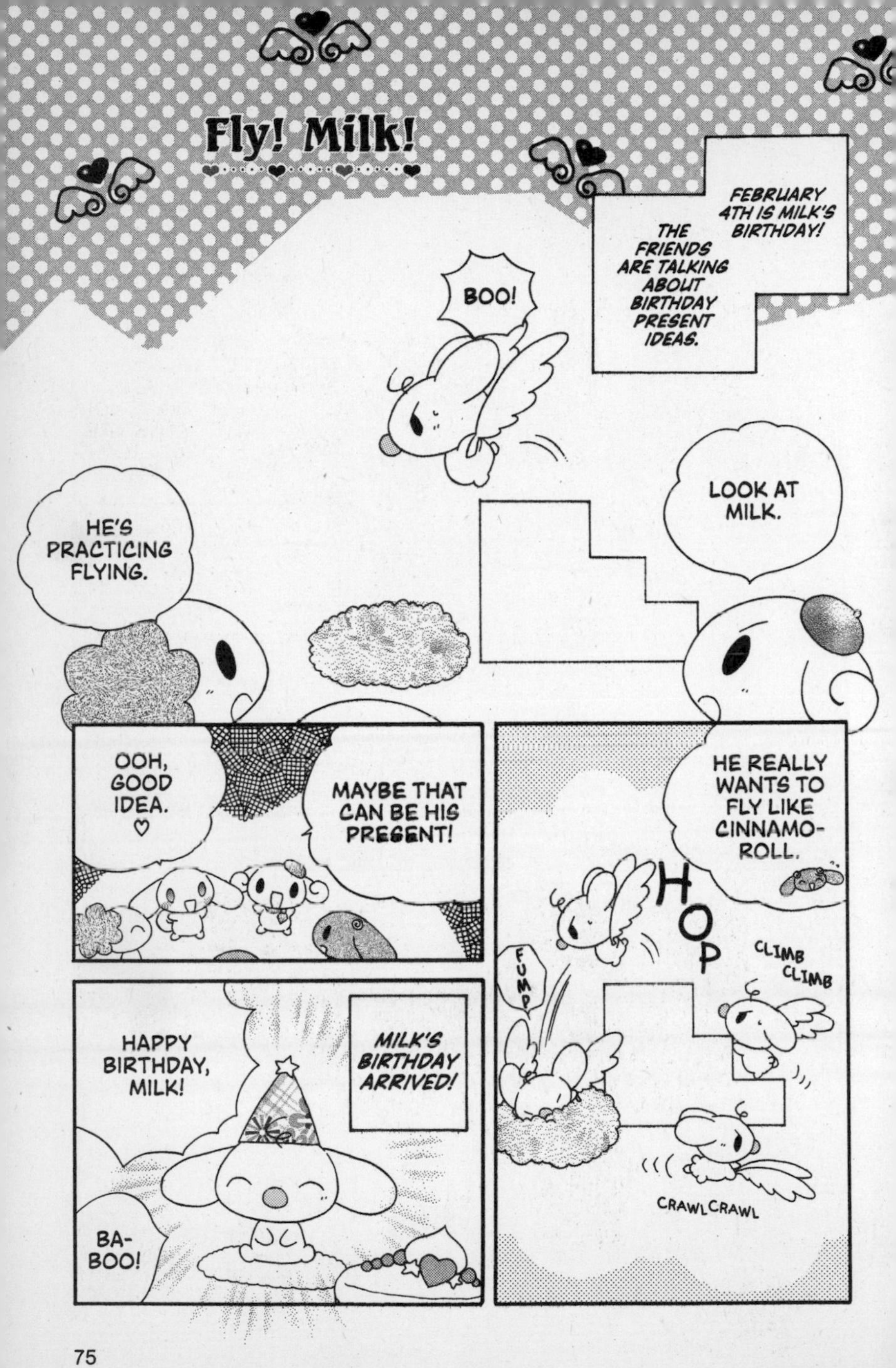
Fly! Milk!
FEBRUARY 4TH IS MILK'S BIRTHDAY!
THE FRIENDS ARE TALKING ABOUT BIRTHDAY PRESENT IDEAS.
BOO!
LOOK AT MILK.
HE'S PRACTICING FLYING.
HE REALLY WANTS TO FLY LIKE CINNAMO-ROLL.
HOP
CLIMB CLIMB
FUMP
CRAWL CRAWL
MAYBE THAT CAN BE HIS PRESENT!
OOH, GOOD IDEA. ♡
MILK'S BIRTHDAY ARRIVED!
HAPPY BIRTHDAY, MILK!
BA-BOO!

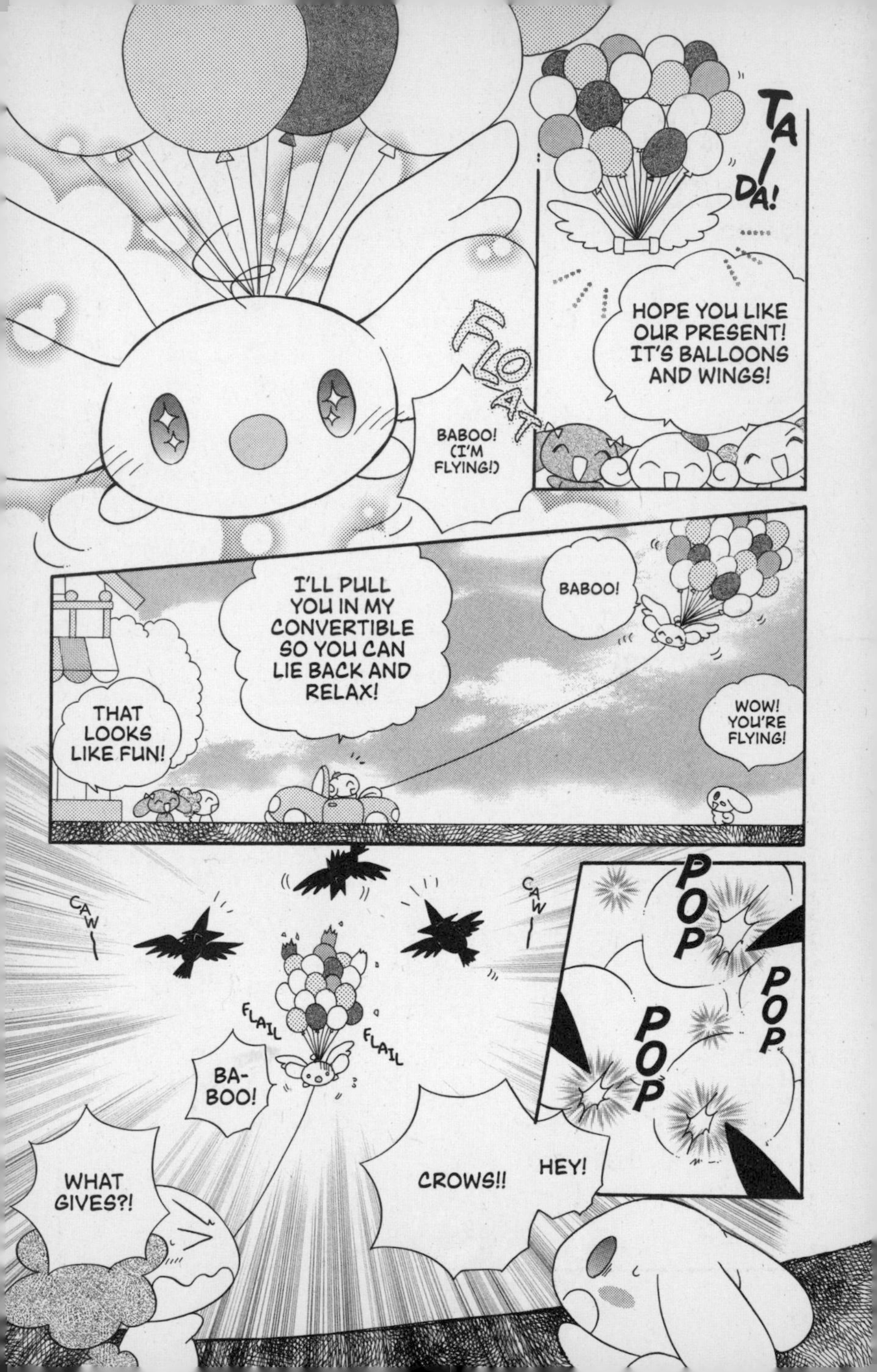
TA-DA!
HOPE YOU LIKE OUR PRESENT! IT'S BALLOONS AND WINGS!
FLOAT
BABOO! (I'M FLYING!)
BABOO!
WOW! YOU'RE FLYING!
I'LL PULL YOU IN MY CONVERTIBLE SO YOU CAN LIE BACK AND RELAX!
THAT LOOKS LIKE FUN!
POP
POP
POP
POP
CAW
CAW
FLAIL
FLAIL
BA-BOO!
HEY!
CROWS!!
WHAT GIVES?!

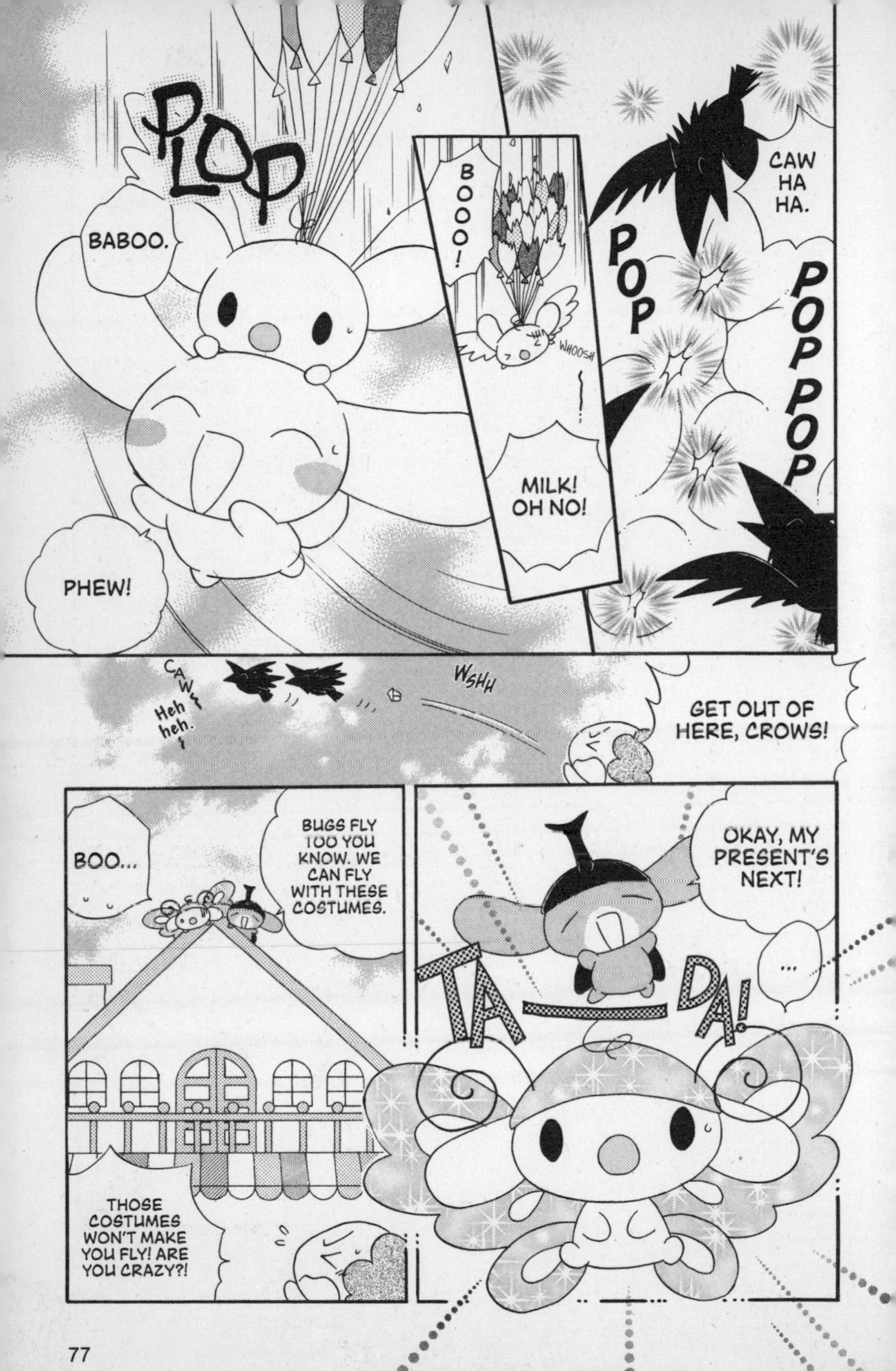
CAW HA HA.
POP
POP POP POP
BOOOO!
WHOOSH
MILK! OH NO!
PLOP
BABOO.
PHEW!
WSHH
GET OUT OF HERE, CROWS!
CAW
Heh heh.
OKAY, MY PRESENT'S NEXT!
TA—DA!
...
BUGS FLY TOO YOU KNOW. WE CAN FLY WITH THESE COSTUMES.
BOO...
THOSE COSTUMES WON'T MAKE YOU FLY! ARE YOU CRAZY?!

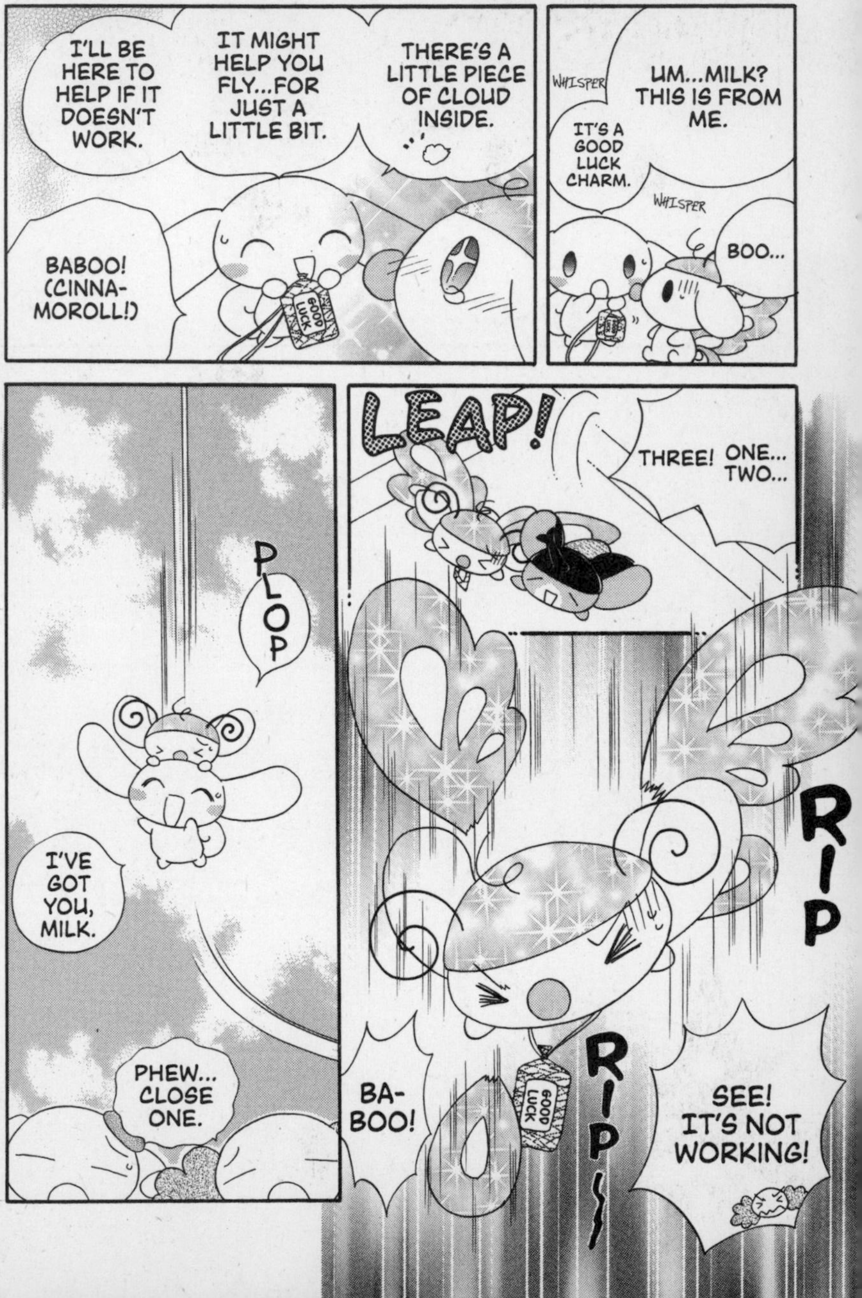
UM...MILK? THIS IS FROM ME.
WHISPER
IT'S A GOOD LUCK CHARM.
WHISPER
BOO...
THERE'S A LITTLE PIECE OF CLOUD INSIDE.
IT MIGHT HELP YOU FLY...FOR JUST A LITTLE BIT.
I'LL BE HERE TO HELP IF IT DOESN'T WORK.
GOOD LUCK
BABOO! (CINNA-MOROLL!)
ONE... TWO...
THREE!
LEAP!
RIP
RIP~
SEE! IT'S NOT WORKING!
BA-BOO!
GOOD LUCK
PLOP
I'VE GOT YOU, MILK.
PHEW... CLOSE ONE.

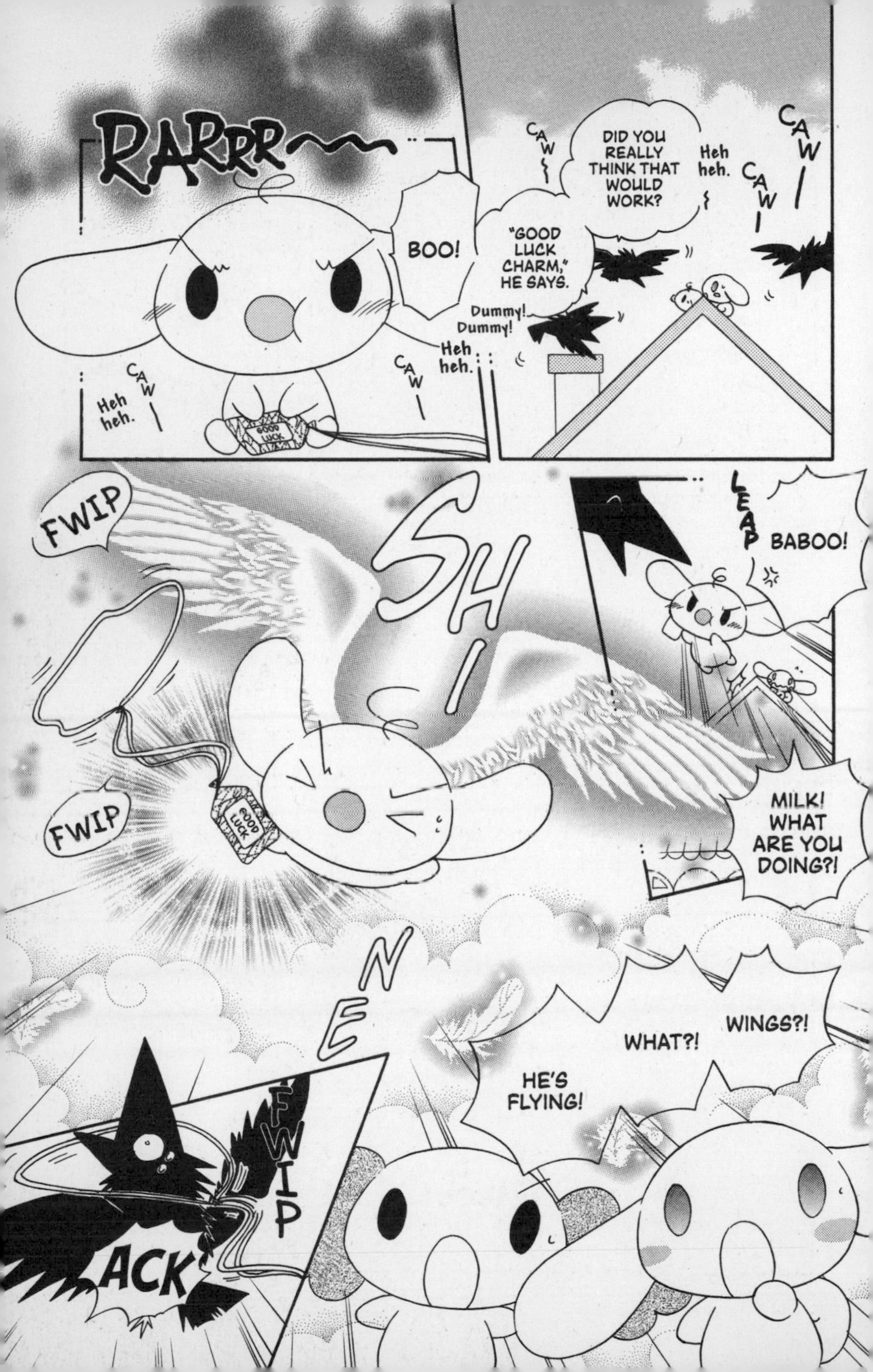
CAW
CAW
DID YOU REALLY THINK THAT WOULD WORK?
Heh heh.
CAW
"GOOD LUCK CHARM," HE SAYS.
Dummy! Dummy!
BOO!
RARRR
Heh heh.
CAW
GOOD LUCK
CAW
Heh heh.
LEAP
BABOO!
MILK! WHAT ARE YOU DOING?!
SHINE
FWIP
GOOD LUCK
FWIP
WINGS?!
WHAT?!
HE'S FLYING!
FWIP
ACK

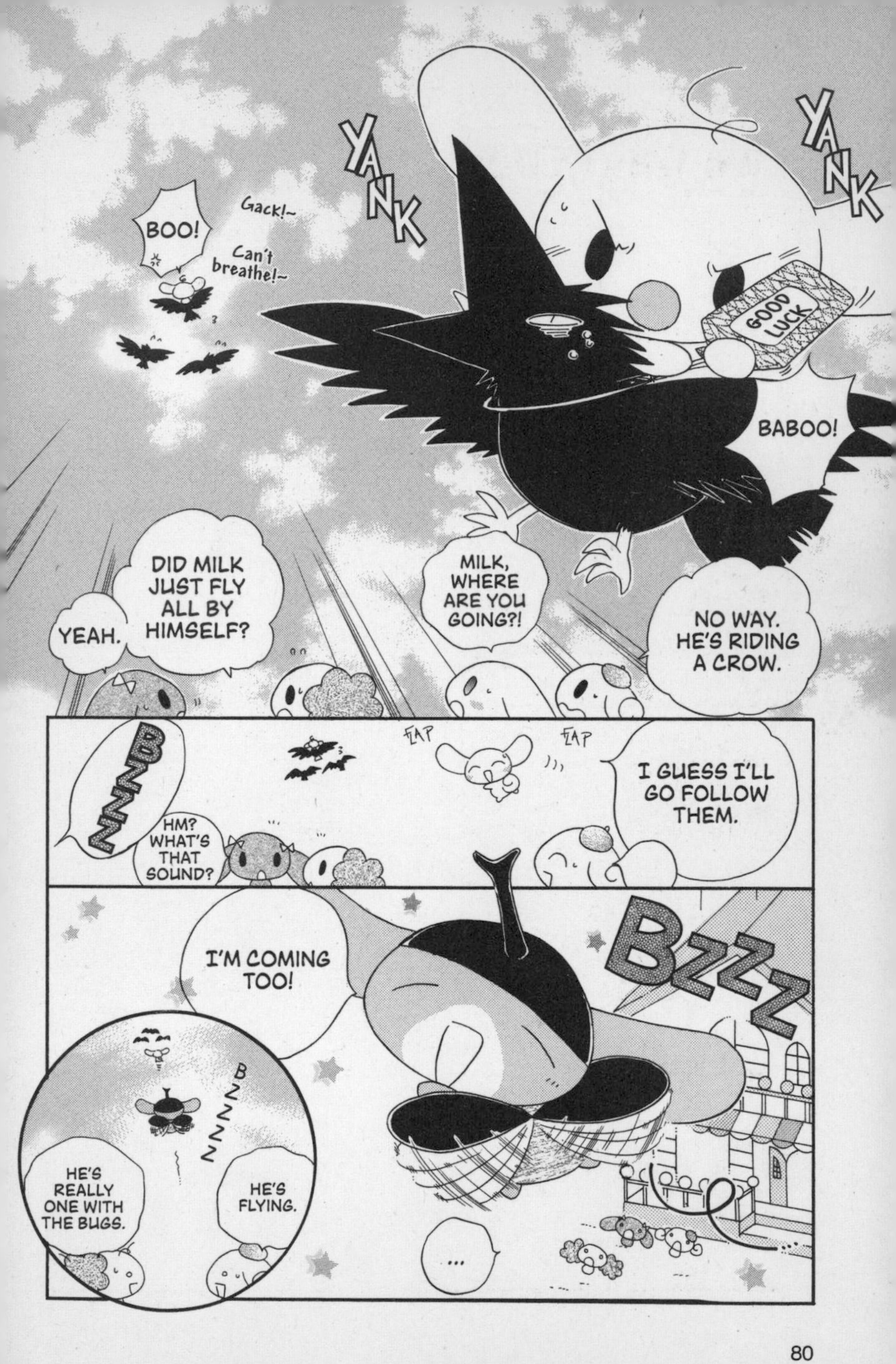

YANK
YANK
GOOD LUCK
BABOO!
Gack!~
Can't breathe!~
BOO!
NO WAY. HE'S RIDING A CROW.
MILK, WHERE ARE YOU GOING?!
DID MILK JUST FLY ALL BY HIMSELF?
YEAH.
I GUESS I'LL GO FOLLOW THEM.
FLAP
FLAP
BZZZZ
HM? WHAT'S THAT SOUND?
BZZZ
I'M COMING TOO!
...
BZZZZ
HE'S FLYING.
HE'S REALLY ONE WITH THE BUGS.

The Cinnamon Friends' Lovey-Dovey Days

We Want Chocolate!

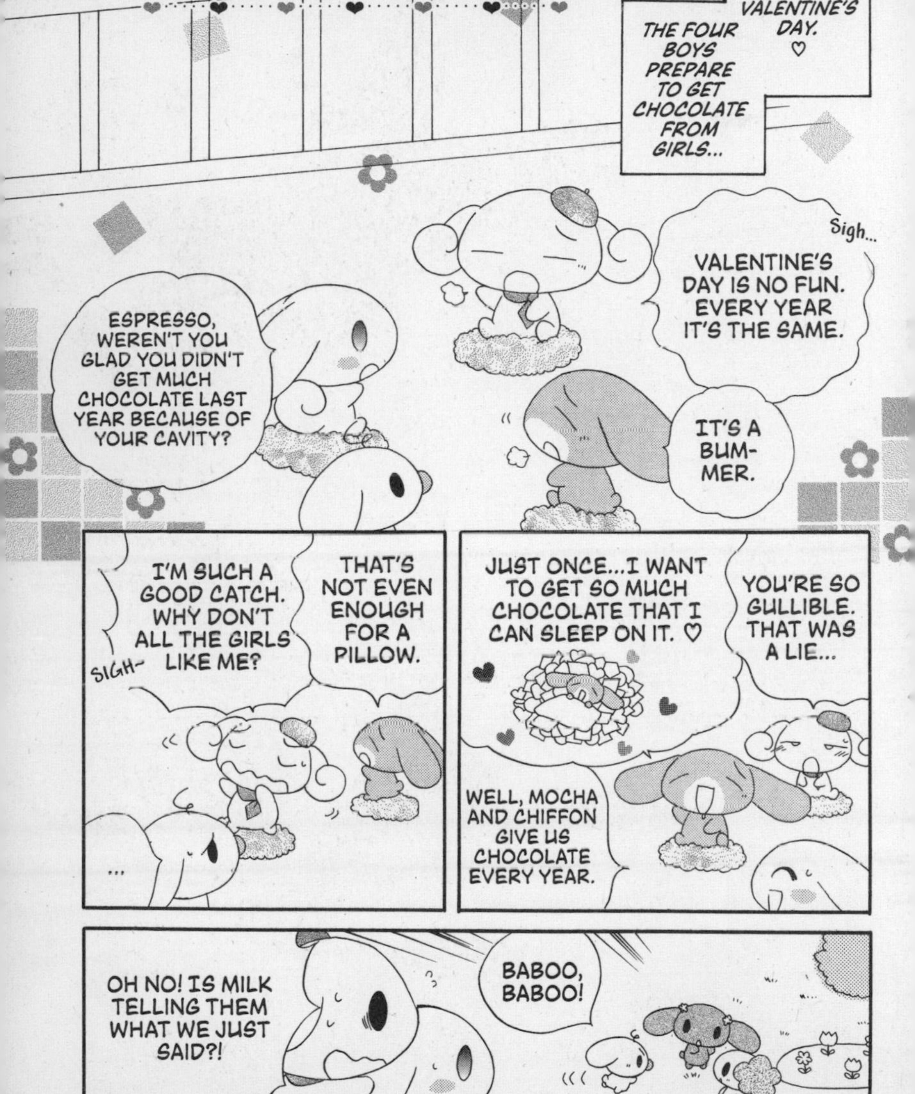
IT'S ALMOST VALENTINE'S DAY. ♡
THE FOUR BOYS PREPARE TO GET CHOCOLATE FROM GIRLS...
Sigh...
VALENTINE'S DAY IS NO FUN. EVERY YEAR IT'S THE SAME.
IT'S A BUMMER.
ESPRESSO, WEREN'T YOU GLAD YOU DIDN'T GET MUCH CHOCOLATE LAST YEAR BECAUSE OF YOUR CAVITY?
YOU'RE SO GULLIBLE. THAT WAS A LIE...
JUST ONCE...I WANT TO GET SO MUCH CHOCOLATE THAT I CAN SLEEP ON IT. ♡
WELL, MOCHA AND CHIFFON GIVE US CHOCOLATE EVERY YEAR.
THAT'S NOT EVEN ENOUGH FOR A PILLOW.
I'M SUCH A GOOD CATCH. WHY DON'T ALL THE GIRLS LIKE ME?
SIGH-
...
BABOO, BABOO!
OH NO! IS MILK TELLING THEM WHAT WE JUST SAID?!

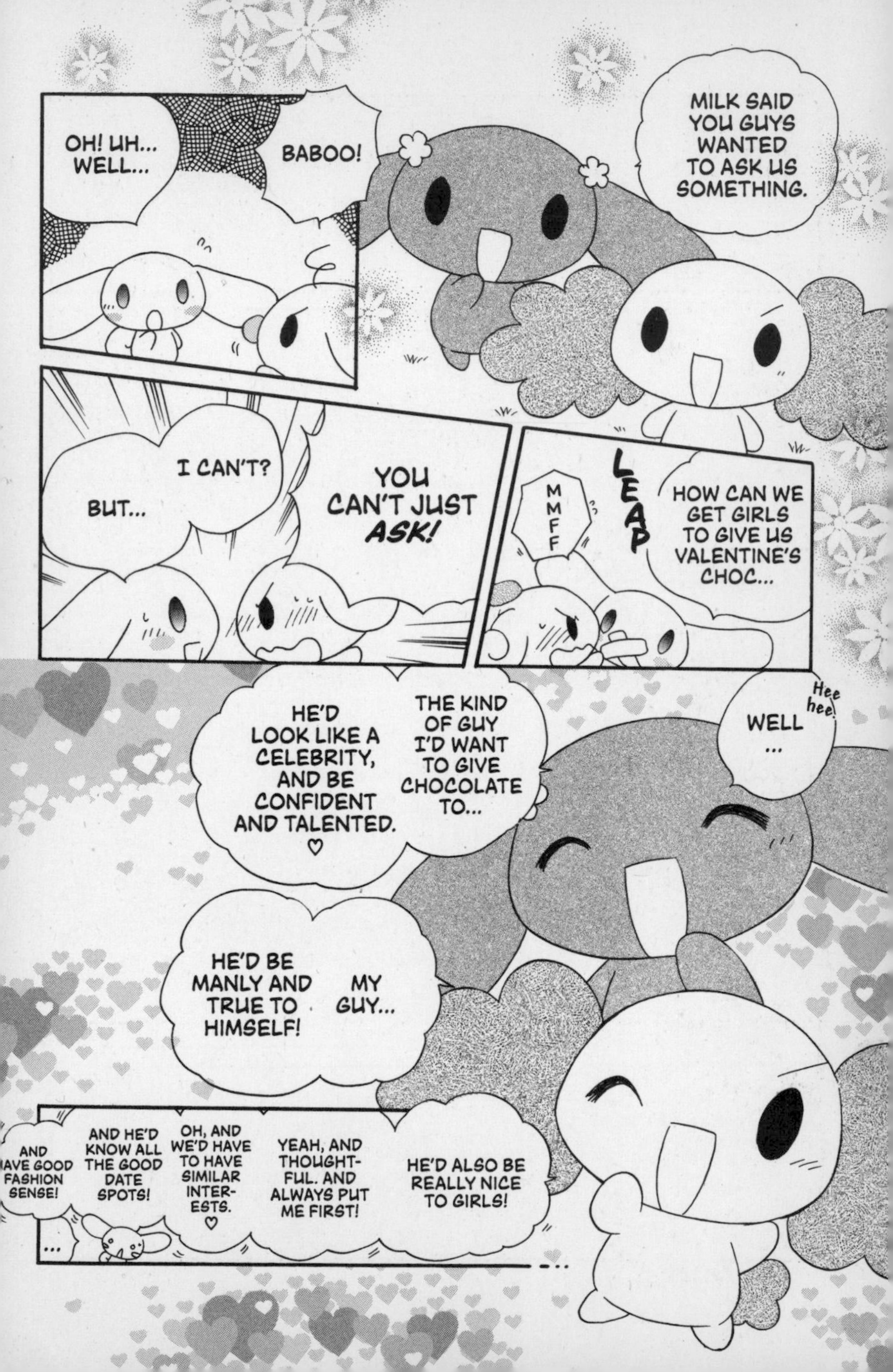
MILK SAID YOU GUYS WANTED TO ASK US SOMETHING.
BABOO!
OH! UH... WELL...
HOW CAN WE GET GIRLS TO GIVE US VALENTINE'S CHOC...
LEAP
MMFF
YOU CAN'T JUST ASK!
I CAN'T?
BUT...
Hee hee!
WELL ...
THE KIND OF GUY I'D WANT TO GIVE CHOCOLATE TO...
HE'D LOOK LIKE A CELEBRITY, AND BE CONFIDENT AND TALENTED. ♡
MY GUY...
HE'D BE MANLY AND TRUE TO HIMSELF!
HE'D ALSO BE REALLY NICE TO GIRLS!
YEAH, AND THOUGHT-FUL. AND ALWAYS PUT ME FIRST!
OH, AND WE'D HAVE TO HAVE SIMILAR INTER-ESTS. ♡
AND HE'D KNOW ALL THE GOOD DATE SPOTS!
AND AVE GOOD FASHION SENSE!
...
...

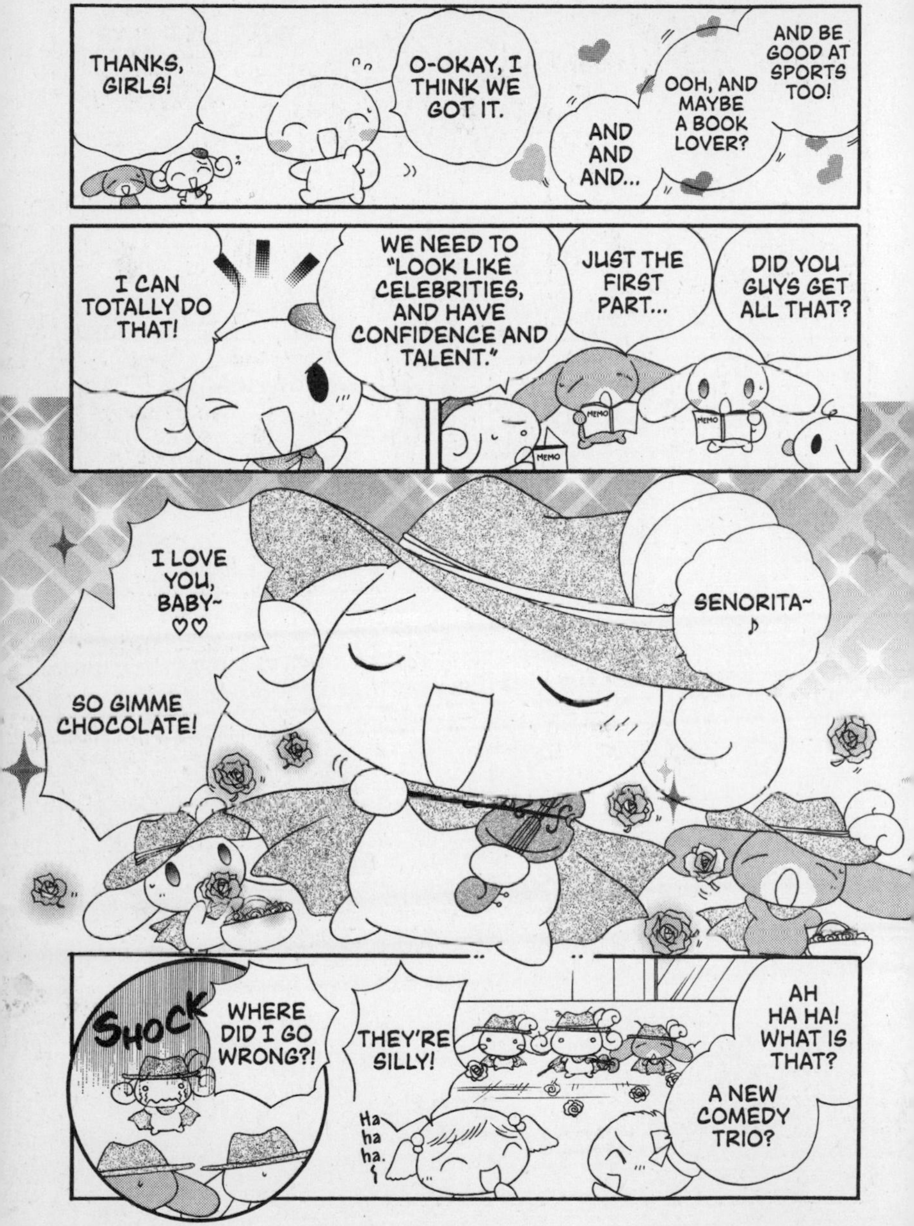
AND BE GOOD AT SPORTS TOO!
OOH, AND MAYBE A BOOK LOVER?
AND AND AND...
O-OKAY, I THINK WE GOT IT.
THANKS, GIRLS!
DID YOU GUYS GET ALL THAT?
JUST THE FIRST PART...
WE NEED TO "LOOK LIKE CELEBRITIES, AND HAVE CONFIDENCE AND TALENT."
I CAN TOTALLY DO THAT!
MEMO
SENORITA~ ♪
I LOVE YOU, BABY~ ♡♡
SO GIMME CHOCOLATE!
AH HA HA! WHAT IS THAT?
A NEW COMEDY TRIO?
Ha ha ha.
THEY'RE SILLY!
WHERE DID I GO WRONG?!
SHOCK

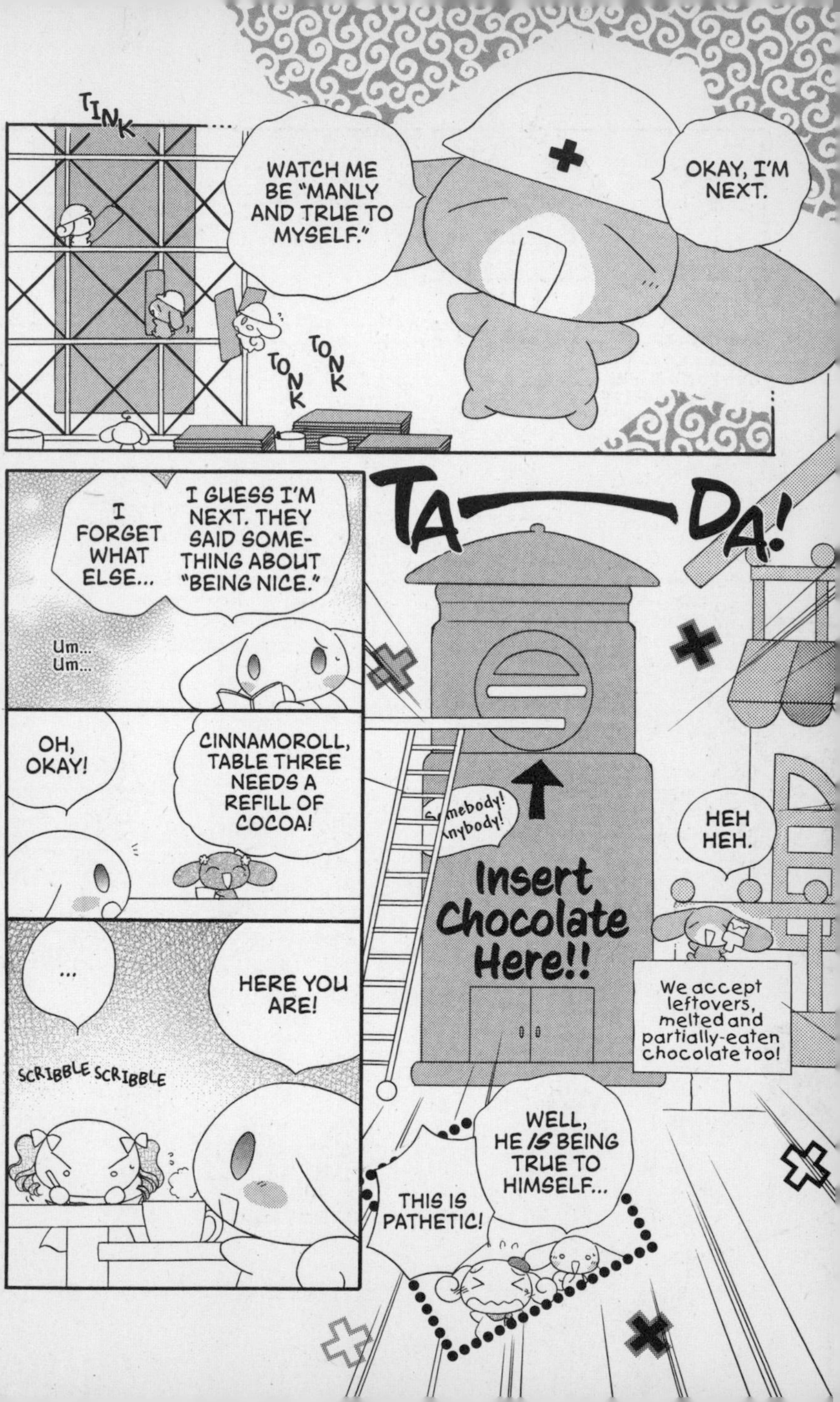
OKAY, I'M NEXT.
WATCH ME BE "MANLY AND TRUE TO MYSELF."
TINK...
TONK TONK
TA—DA!
Insert Chocolate Here!!
Somebody! Anybody!
HEH HEH.
We accept leftovers, melted and partially-eaten chocolate too!
WELL, HE IS BEING TRUE TO HIMSELF...
THIS IS PATHETIC!
I GUESS I'M NEXT. THEY SAID SOME-THING ABOUT "BEING NICE."
I FORGET WHAT ELSE...
Um... Um...
CINNAMOROLL, TABLE THREE NEEDS A REFILL OF COCOA!
OH, OKAY!
HERE YOU ARE!
...
SCRIBBLE SCRIBBLE

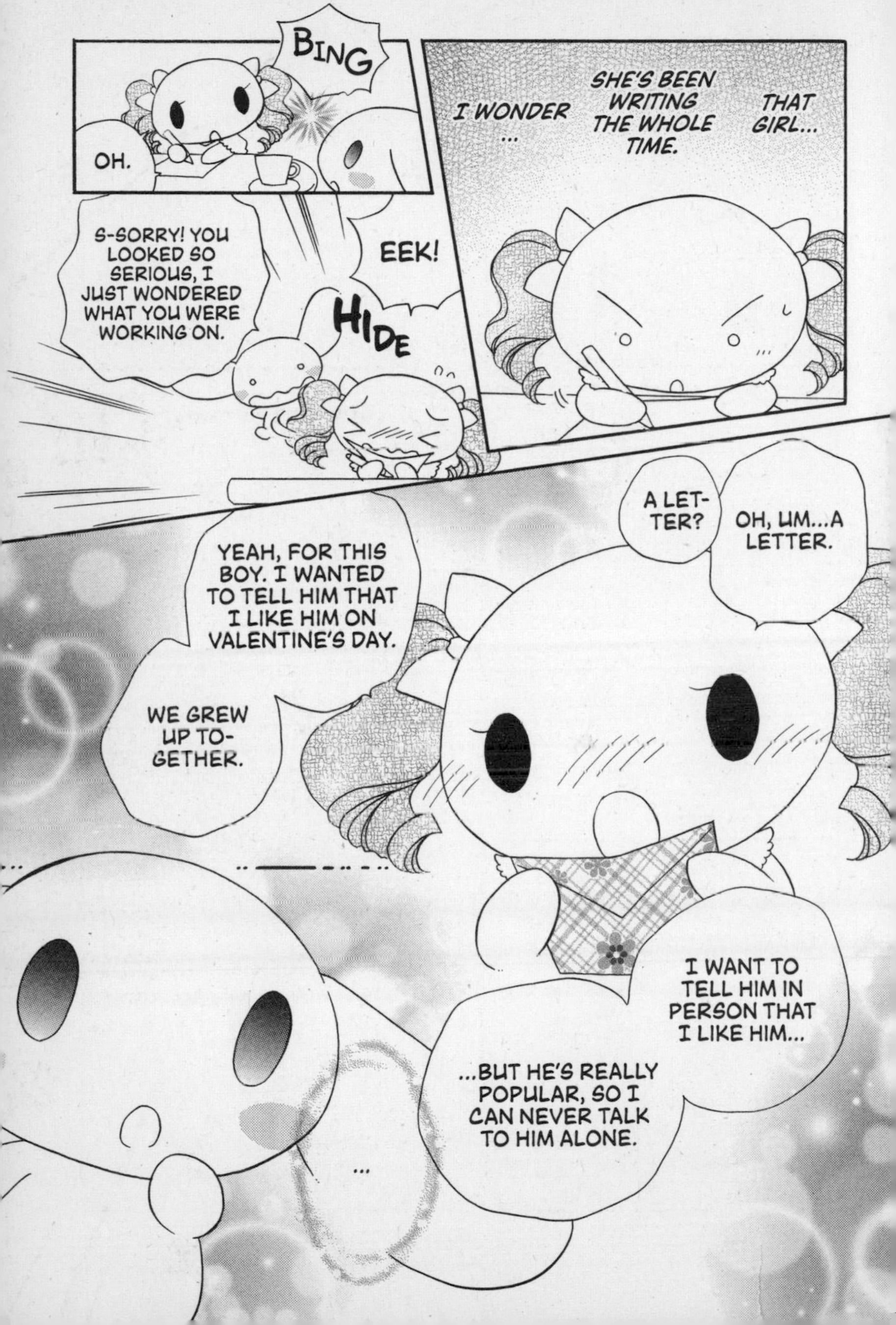
THAT GIRL...
SHE'S BEEN WRITING THE WHOLE TIME.
I WONDER ...
BING
OH.
EEK!
HIDE
S-SORRY! YOU LOOKED SO SERIOUS, I JUST WONDERED WHAT YOU WERE WORKING ON.
OH, UM...A LETTER.
A LET-TER?
YEAH, FOR THIS BOY. I WANTED TO TELL HIM THAT I LIKE HIM ON VALENTINE'S DAY.
WE GREW UP TO-GETHER.
I WANT TO TELL HIM IN PERSON THAT I LIKE HIM...
...BUT HE'S REALLY POPULAR, SO I CAN NEVER TALK TO HIM ALONE.
...

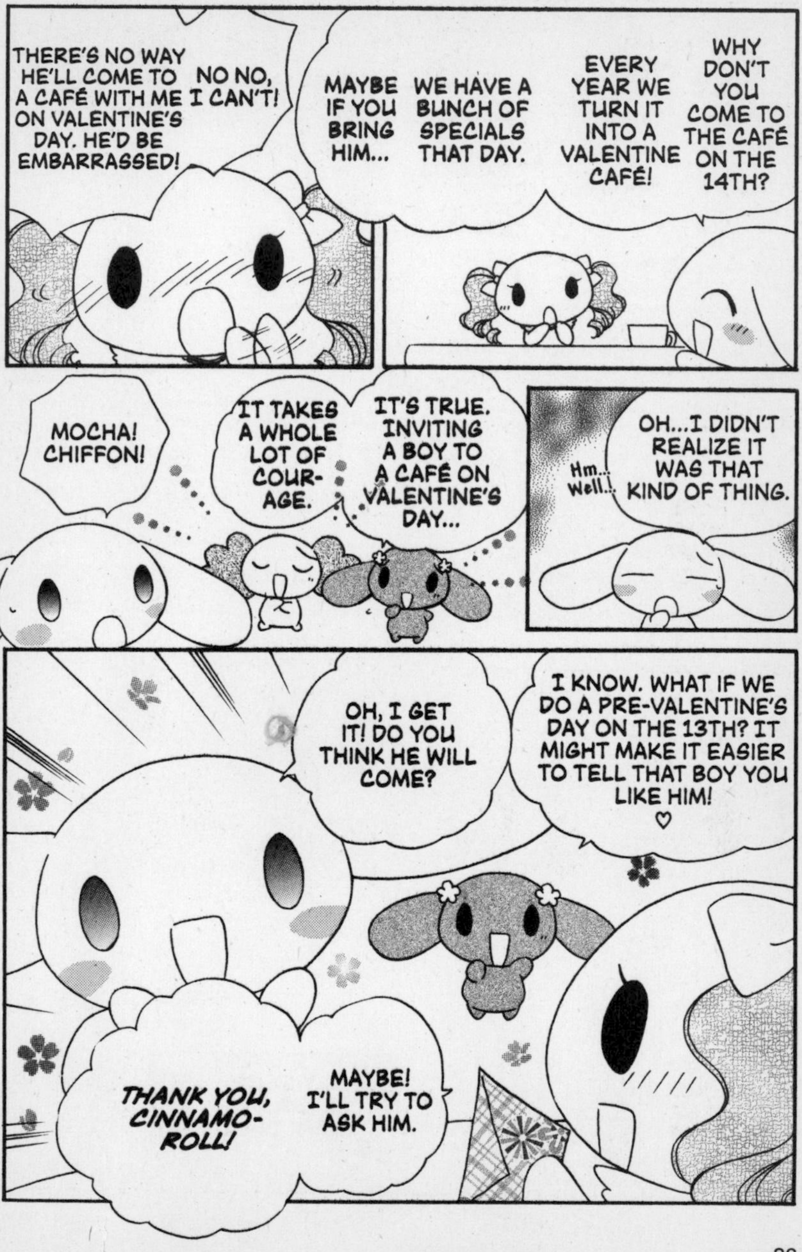
WHY DON'T YOU COME TO THE CAFÉ ON THE 14TH?
EVERY YEAR WE TURN IT INTO A VALENTINE CAFÉ!
WE HAVE A BUNCH OF SPECIALS THAT DAY.
MAYBE IF YOU BRING HIM...
NO NO, I CAN'T!
THERE'S NO WAY HE'LL COME TO A CAFÉ WITH ME ON VALENTINE'S DAY. HE'D BE EMBARRASSED!
OH...I DIDN'T REALIZE IT WAS THAT KIND OF THING.
Hm... Well..!
IT'S TRUE. INVITING A BOY TO A CAFÉ ON VALENTINE'S DAY...
IT TAKES A WHOLE LOT OF COURAGE.
MOCHA! CHIFFON!
I KNOW. WHAT IF WE DO A PRE-VALENTINE'S DAY ON THE 13TH? IT MIGHT MAKE IT EASIER TO TELL THAT BOY YOU LIKE HIM! ♡
OH, I GET IT! DO YOU THINK HE WILL COME?
MAYBE! I'LL TRY TO ASK HIM.
THANK YOU, CINNAMOROLL!

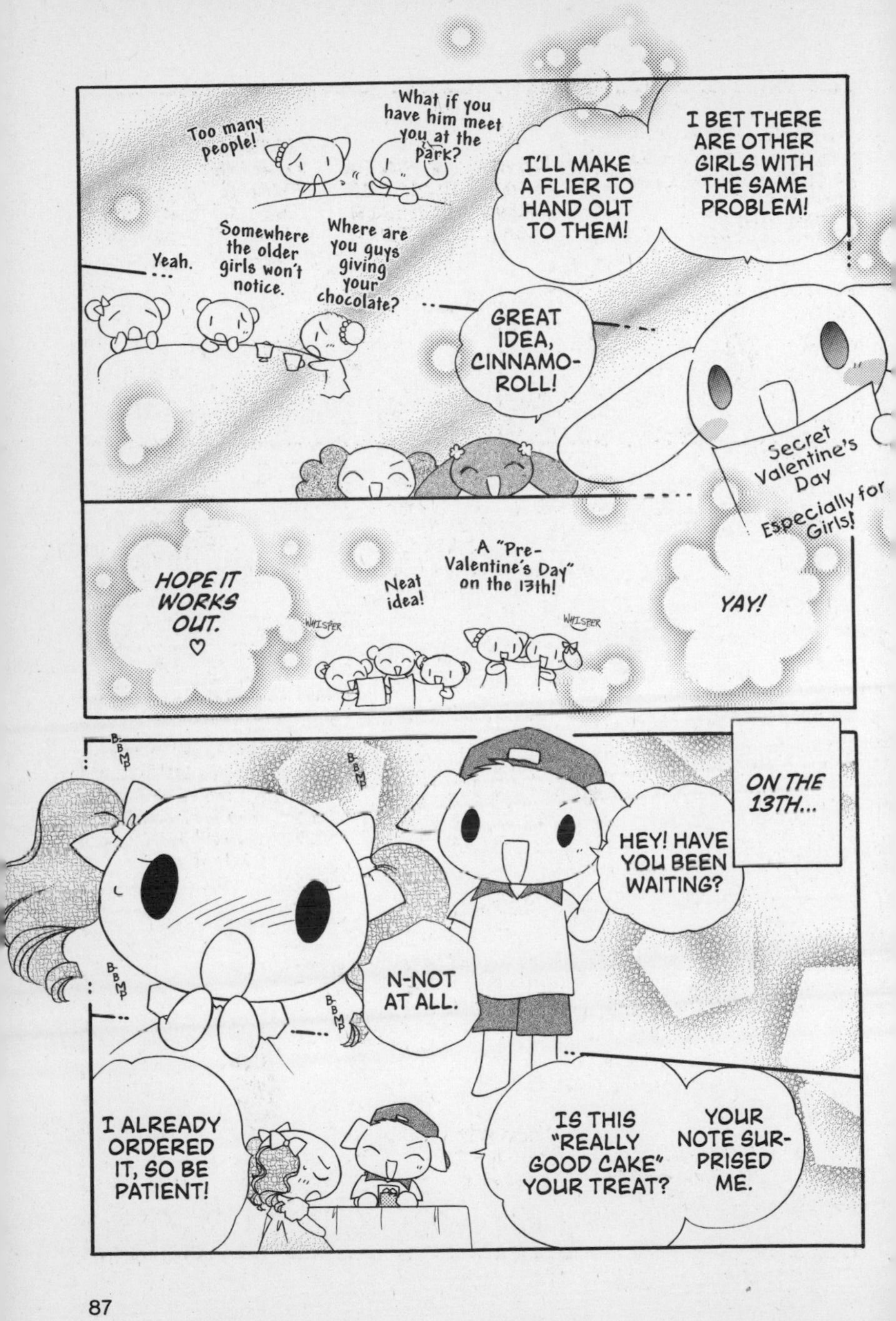
I BET THERE ARE OTHER GIRLS WITH THE SAME PROBLEM!
I'LL MAKE A FLIER TO HAND OUT TO THEM!
What if you have him meet you at the park?
Too many people!
Where are you guys giving your chocolate?
Somewhere the older girls won't notice.
Yeah.
GREAT IDEA, CINNAMOROLL!
Secret Valentine's Day
Especially for Girls!
YAY!
A "Pre-Valentine's Day" on the 13th!
WHISPER
Neat idea!
WHISPER
HOPE IT WORKS OUT. ♡
ON THE 13TH...
HEY! HAVE YOU BEEN WAITING?
B-BMP
B-BMP
N-NOT AT ALL.
B-BMP
B-BMP
YOUR NOTE SURPRISED ME.
IS THIS "REALLY GOOD CAKE" YOUR TREAT?
I ALREADY ORDERED IT, SO BE PATIENT!

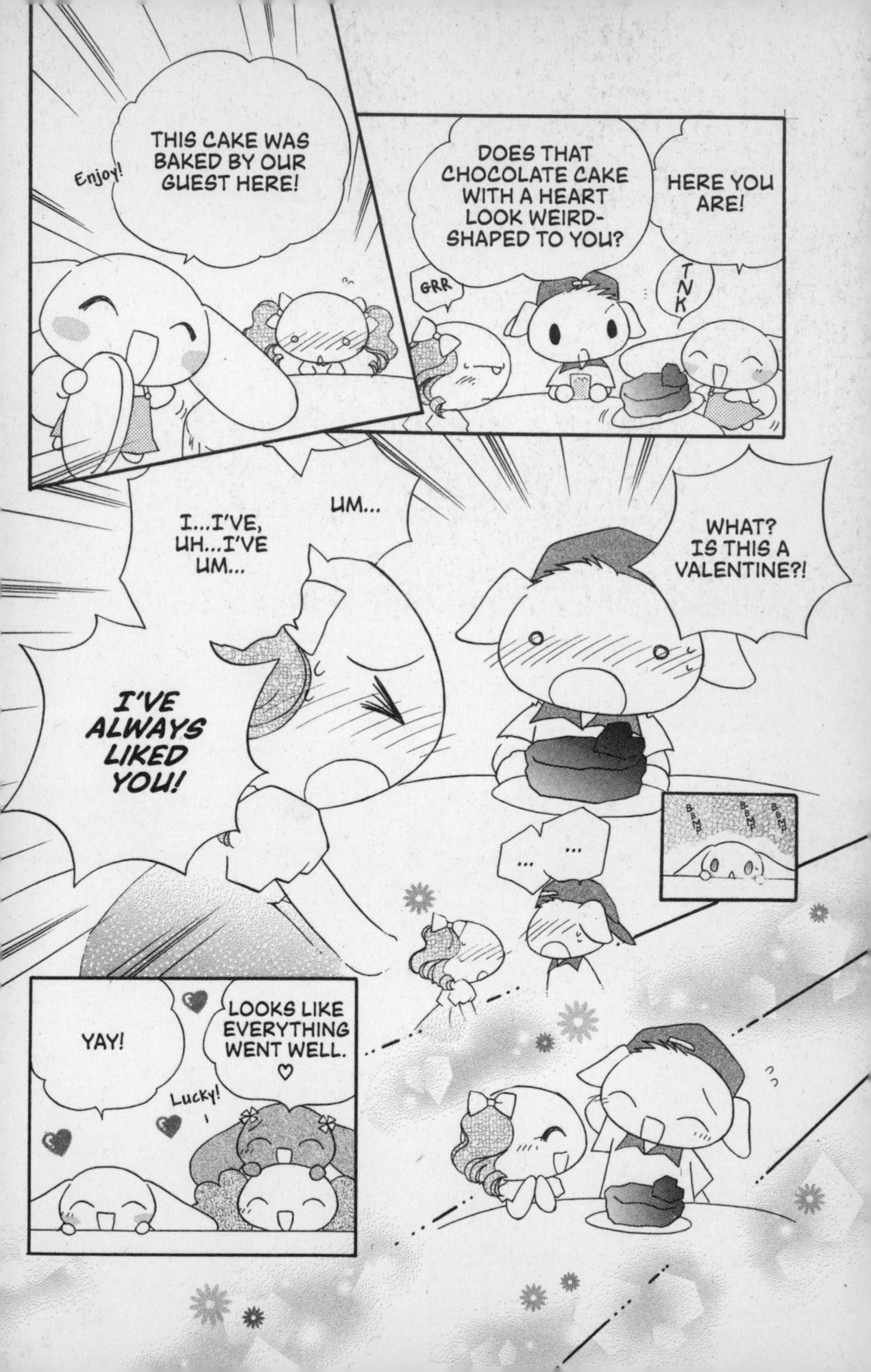
HERE YOU ARE!
DOES THAT CHOCOLATE CAKE WITH A HEART LOOK WEIRD-SHAPED TO YOU?
TNK
GRR
THIS CAKE WAS BAKED BY OUR GUEST HERE!
Enjoy!
WHAT? IS THIS A VALENTINE?!
UM...
I...I'VE, UH...I'VE UM...
I'VE ALWAYS LIKED YOU!
BBMP
BBMP
BBMP
...
...
LOOKS LIKE EVERYTHING WENT WELL. ♡
YAY!
Lucky!

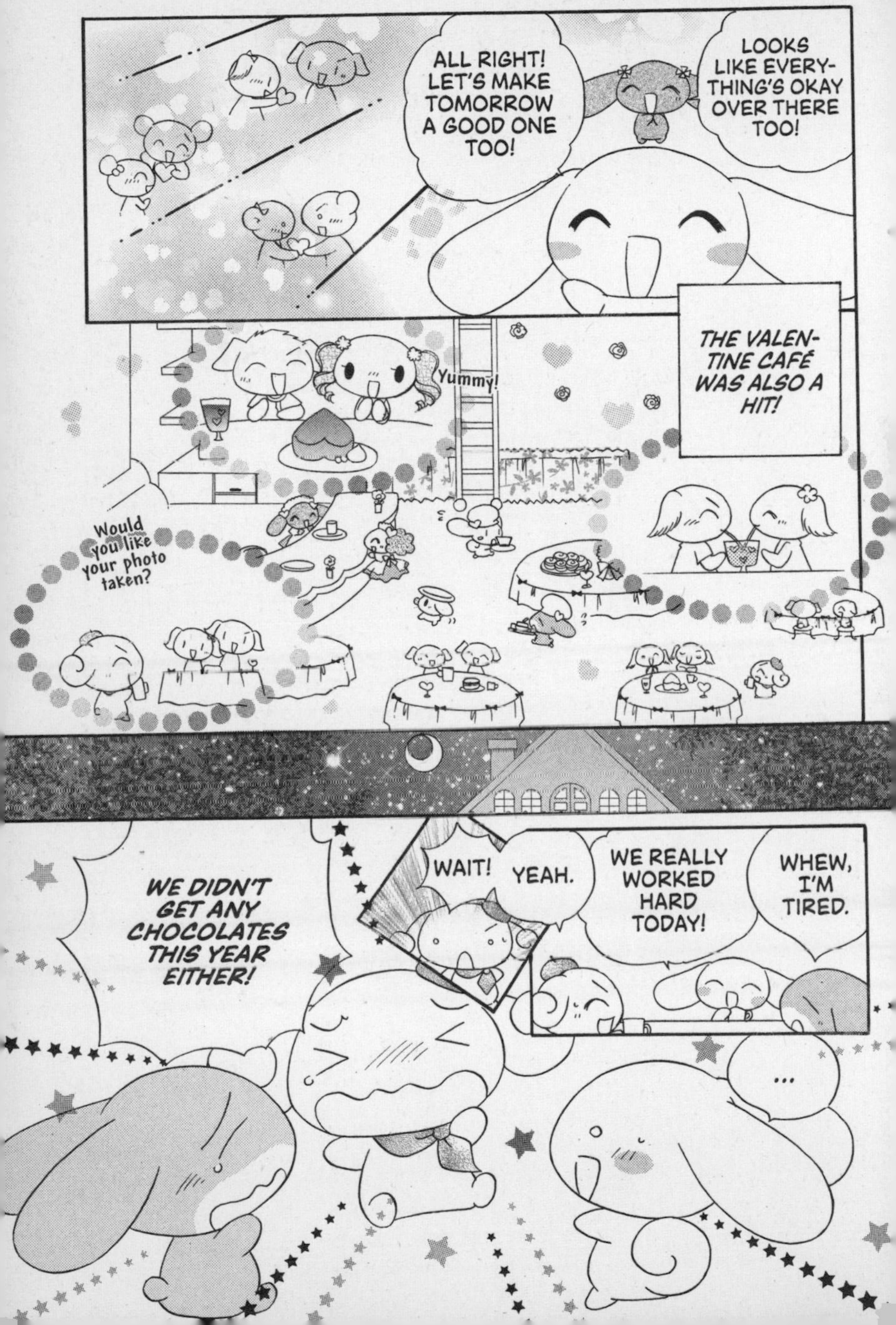
LOOKS LIKE EVERY-THING'S OKAY OVER THERE TOO!
ALL RIGHT! LET'S MAKE TOMORROW A GOOD ONE TOO!
THE VALEN-TINE CAFÉ WAS ALSO A HIT!
Yummy!
Would you like your photo taken?
WHEW, I'M TIRED.
WE REALLY WORKED HARD TODAY!
YEAH.
WAIT!
...
WE DIDN'T GET ANY CHOCOLATES THIS YEAR EITHER!

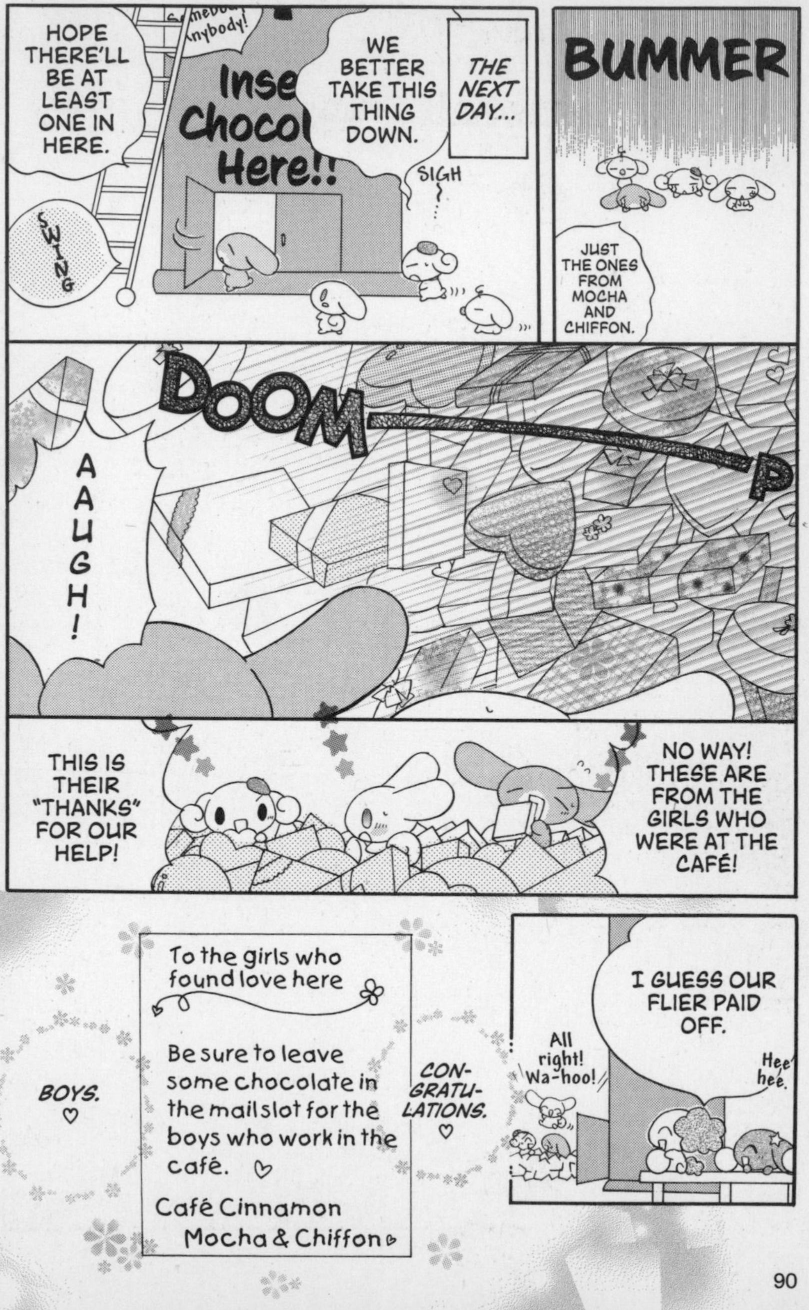
BUMMER
JUST THE ONES FROM MOCHA AND CHIFFON.
THE NEXT DAY...
WE BETTER TAKE THIS THING DOWN.
SIGH
Somebod
nybody!
Inse
Chocol
Here!!
HOPE THERE'LL BE AT LEAST ONE IN HERE.
SWING
DOOM
P
AAUGH!
NO WAY! THESE ARE FROM THE GIRLS WHO WERE AT THE CAFÉ!
THIS IS THEIR "THANKS" FOR OUR HELP!
I GUESS OUR FLIER PAID OFF.
Hee hee.
All right! Wa-hoo!
CONGRATULATIONS. ♡
To the girls who found love here
Be sure to leave some chocolate in the mailslot for the boys who work in the café. ♡
Café Cinnamon
Mocha & Chiffon
BOYS. ♡

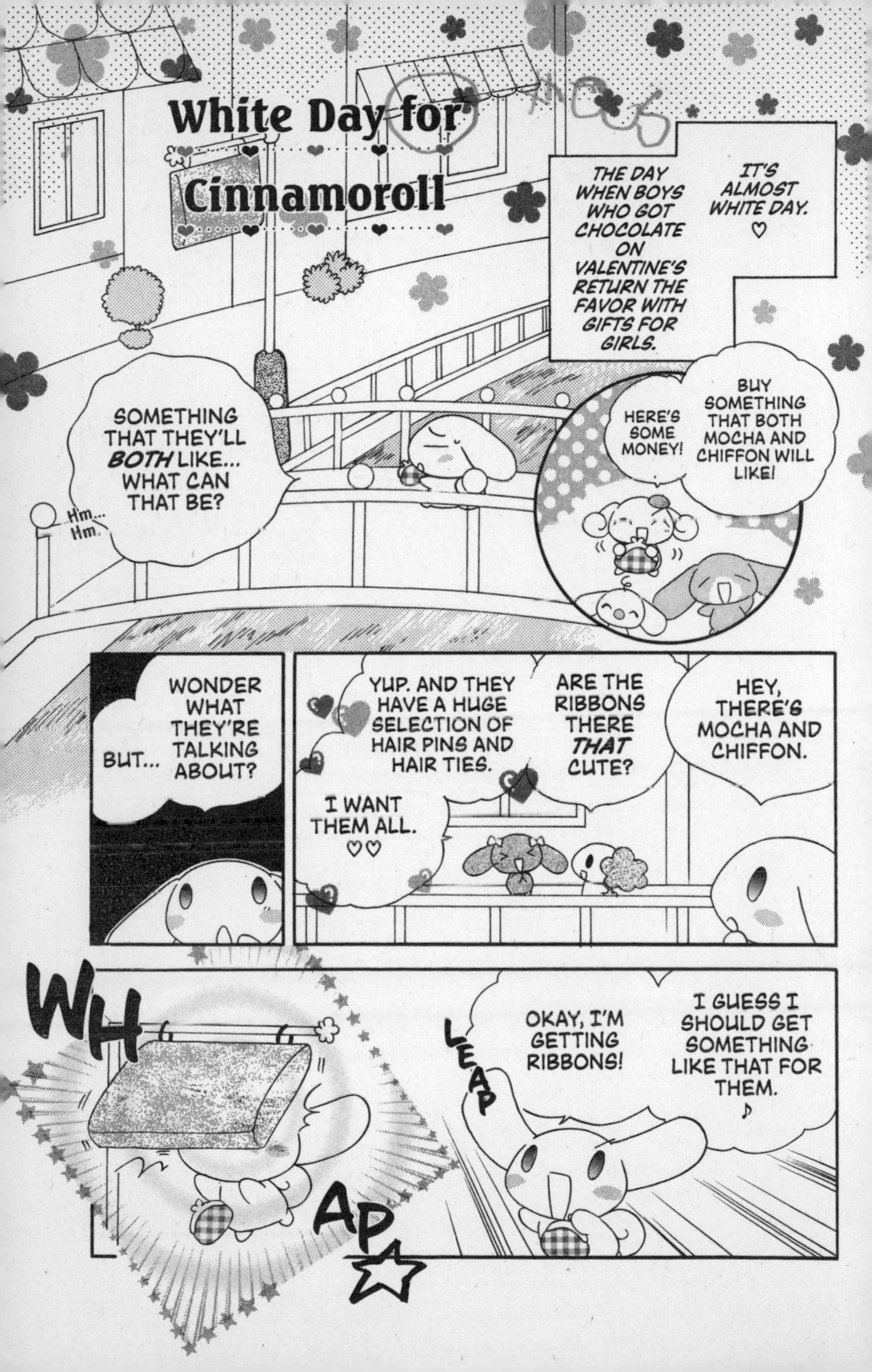
White Day for Cinnamoroll
IT'S ALMOST WHITE DAY. ♡
THE DAY WHEN BOYS WHO GOT CHOCOLATE ON VALENTINE'S RETURN THE FAVOR WITH GIFTS FOR GIRLS.
BUY SOMETHING THAT BOTH MOCHA AND CHIFFON WILL LIKE!
HERE'S SOME MONEY!
SOMETHING THAT THEY'LL *BOTH* LIKE... WHAT CAN THAT BE?
Hm... Hm.
HEY, THERE'S MOCHA AND CHIFFON.
ARE THE RIBBONS THERE *THAT* CUTE?
YUP. AND THEY HAVE A HUGE SELECTION OF HAIR PINS AND HAIR TIES.
I WANT THEM ALL. ♡♡
WONDER WHAT THEY'RE TALKING ABOUT?
BUT...
I GUESS I SHOULD GET SOMETHING LIKE THAT FOR THEM. ♪
OKAY, I'M GETTING RIBBONS!
LEAP
WHAP

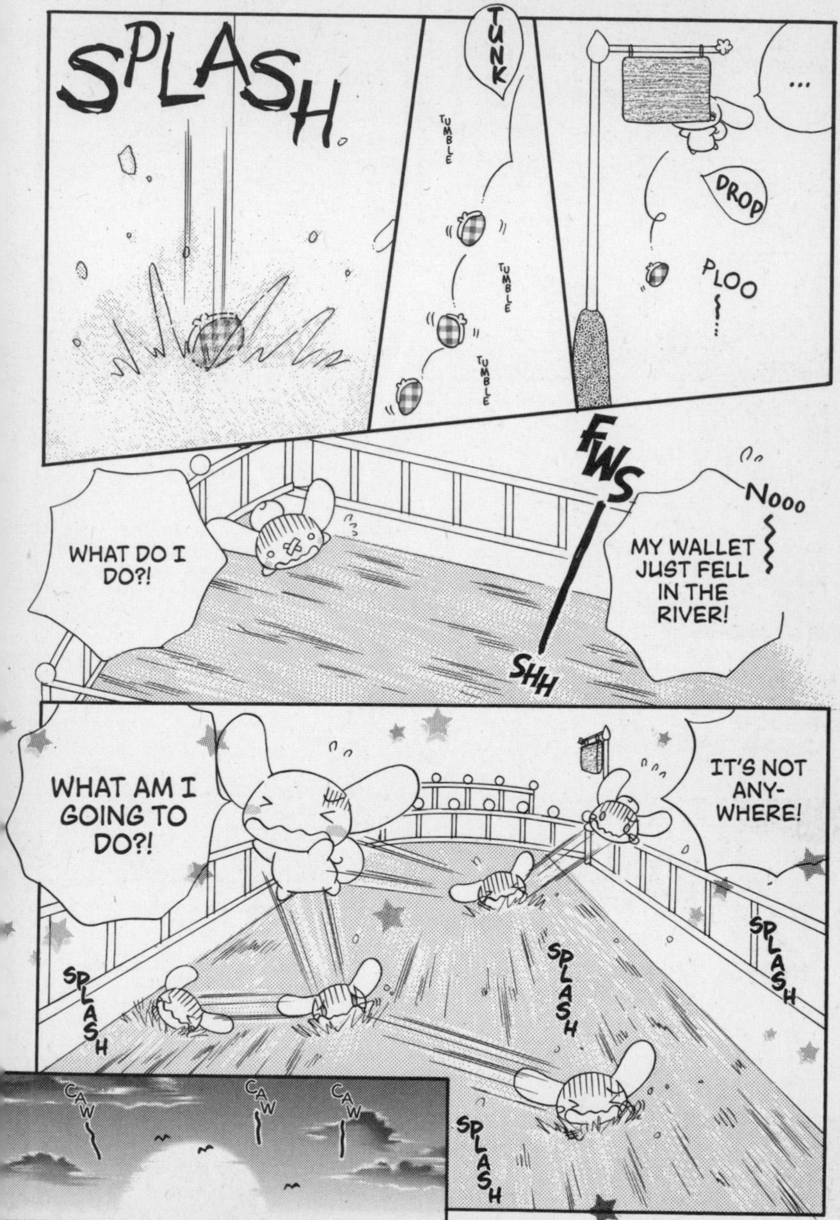
...
DROP
PLOO~...
TUNK
TUMBLE
TUMBLE
TUMBLE
SPLASH
Nooo~
MY WALLET JUST FELL IN THE RIVER!
FWS
SHH
WHAT DO I DO?!
IT'S NOT ANY-WHERE!
WHAT AM I GOING TO DO?!
SPLASH
SPLASH
SPLASH
SPLASH
CAW~
CAW~
CAW~

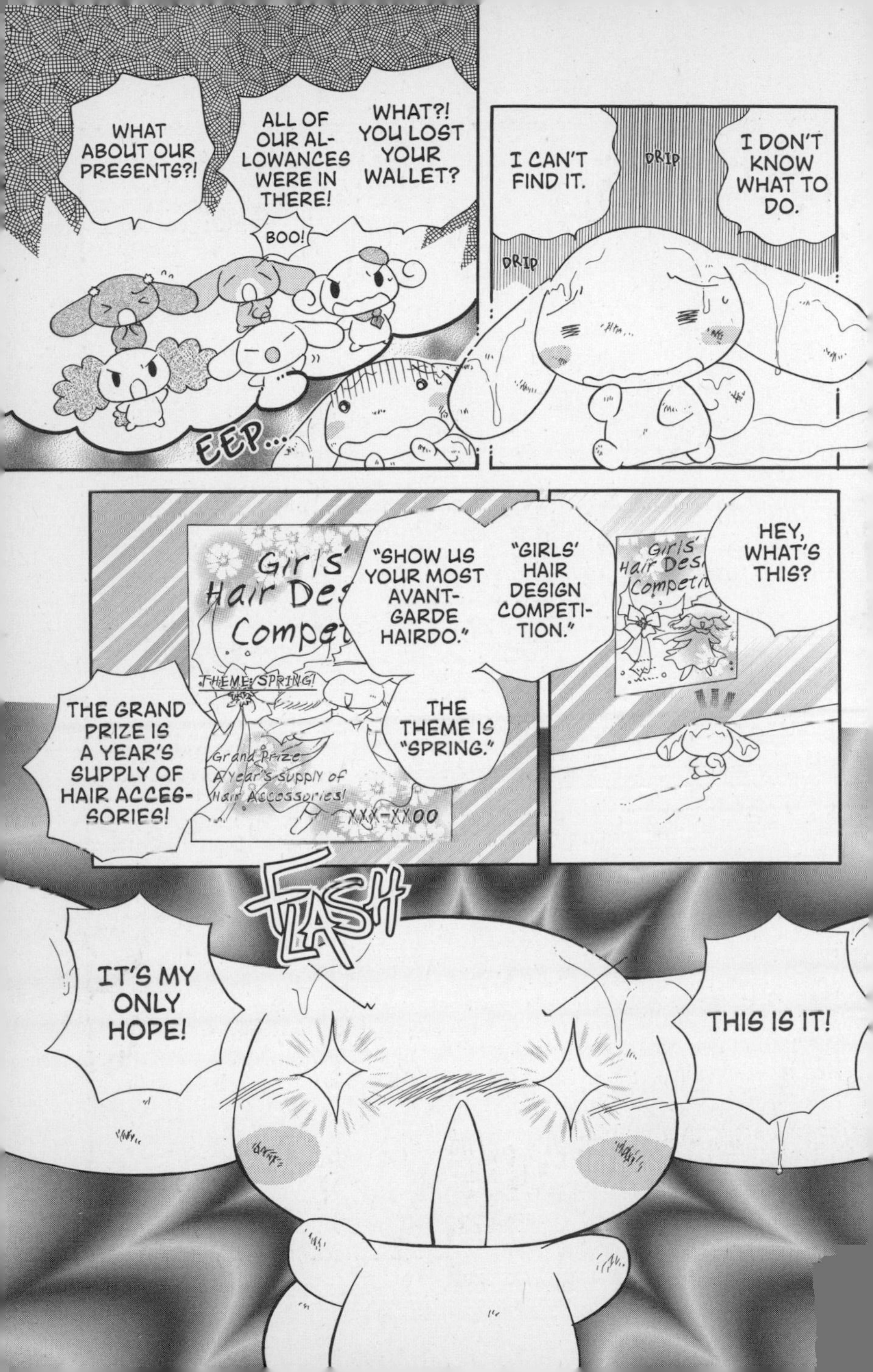
I DON'T KNOW WHAT TO DO.
DRIP
I CAN'T FIND IT.
DRIP
WHAT?! YOU LOST YOUR WALLET?
ALL OF OUR AL-LOWANCES WERE IN THERE!
WHAT ABOUT OUR PRESENTS?!
BOO!
EEP...
HEY, WHAT'S THIS?
"GIRLS' HAIR DESIGN COMPETI-TION."
"SHOW US YOUR MOST AVANT-GARDE HAIRDO."
THE THEME IS "SPRING."
THEME: SPRING!
Grand Prize A Year's supply of Hair Accessories!
XXX-XXOO
THE GRAND PRIZE IS A YEAR'S SUPPLY OF HAIR ACCES-SORIES!
FLASH
THIS IS IT!
IT'S MY ONLY HOPE!

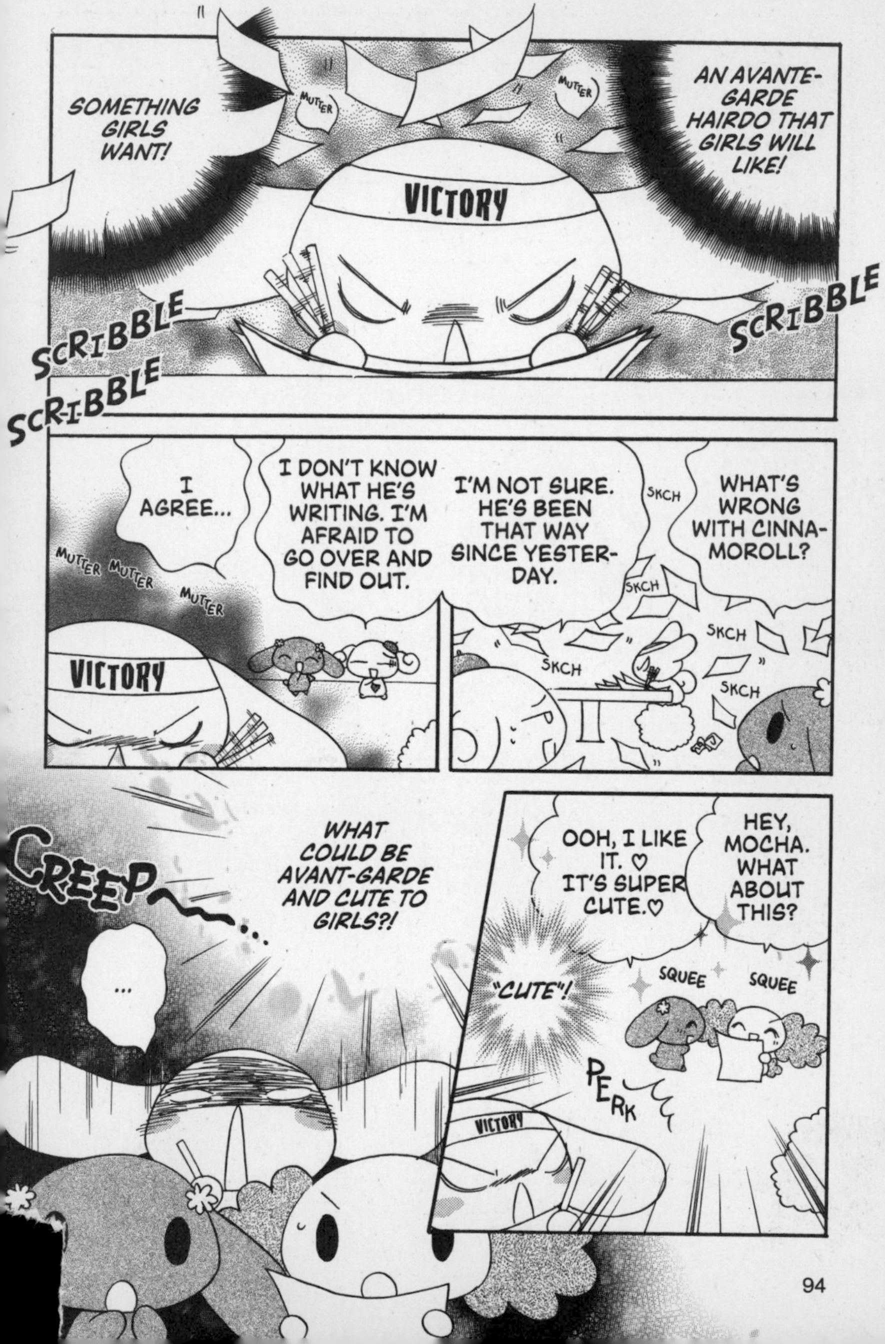
AN AVANTE-GARDE HAIRDO THAT GIRLS WILL LIKE!
MUTTER
MUTTER
SOMETHING GIRLS WANT!
VICTORY
SCRIBBLE
SCRIBBLE
SCRIBBLE
WHAT'S WRONG WITH CINNA-MOROLL?
I'M NOT SURE. HE'S BEEN THAT WAY SINCE YESTER-DAY.
SKCH
SKCH
SKCH
SKCH
SKCH
I DON'T KNOW WHAT HE'S WRITING. I'M AFRAID TO GO OVER AND FIND OUT.
I AGREE...
MUTTER MUTTER MUTTER
VICTORY
HEY, MOCHA. WHAT ABOUT THIS?
OOH, I LIKE IT. ♡ IT'S SUPER CUTE.♡
SQUEE
SQUEE
"CUTE"!
PERK
VICTORY
WHAT COULD BE AVANT-GARDE AND CUTE TO GIRLS?!
CREEP~...
...

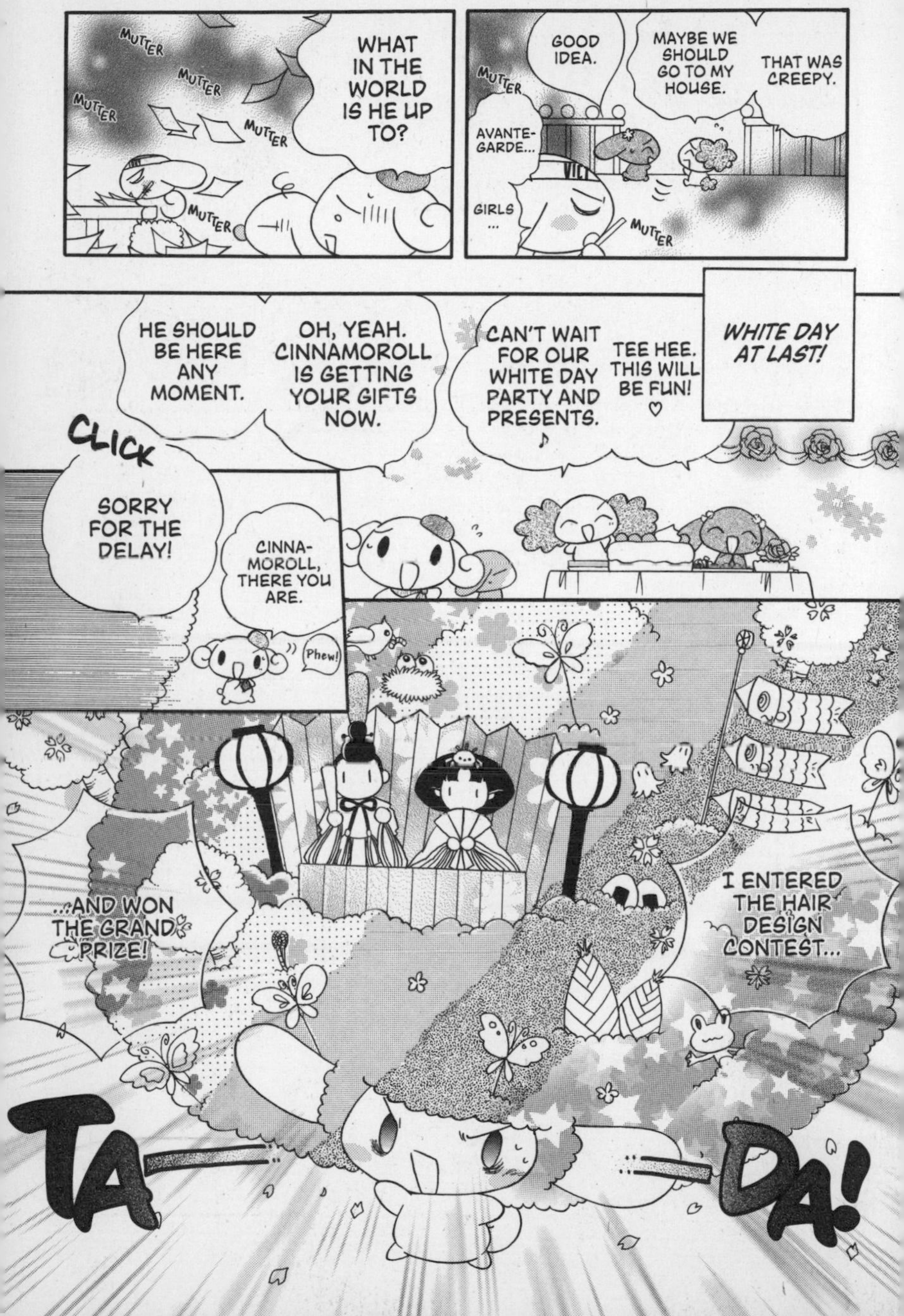
THAT WAS CREEPY.
MAYBE WE SHOULD GO TO MY HOUSE.
GOOD IDEA.
MUTTER
AVANTE-GARDE...
GIRLS ...
MUTTER
WHAT IN THE WORLD IS HE UP TO?
MUTTER
MUTTER
MUTTER
MUTTER
MUTTER
WHITE DAY AT LAST!
TEE HEE. THIS WILL BE FUN! ♡
CAN'T WAIT FOR OUR WHITE DAY PARTY AND PRESENTS. ♪
OH, YEAH. CINNAMOROLL IS GETTING YOUR GIFTS NOW.
HE SHOULD BE HERE ANY MOMENT.
CLICK
SORRY FOR THE DELAY!
CINNA-MOROLL, THERE YOU ARE.
Phew!
I ENTERED THE HAIR DESIGN CONTEST...
...AND WON THE GRAND PRIZE!
TA——DA!

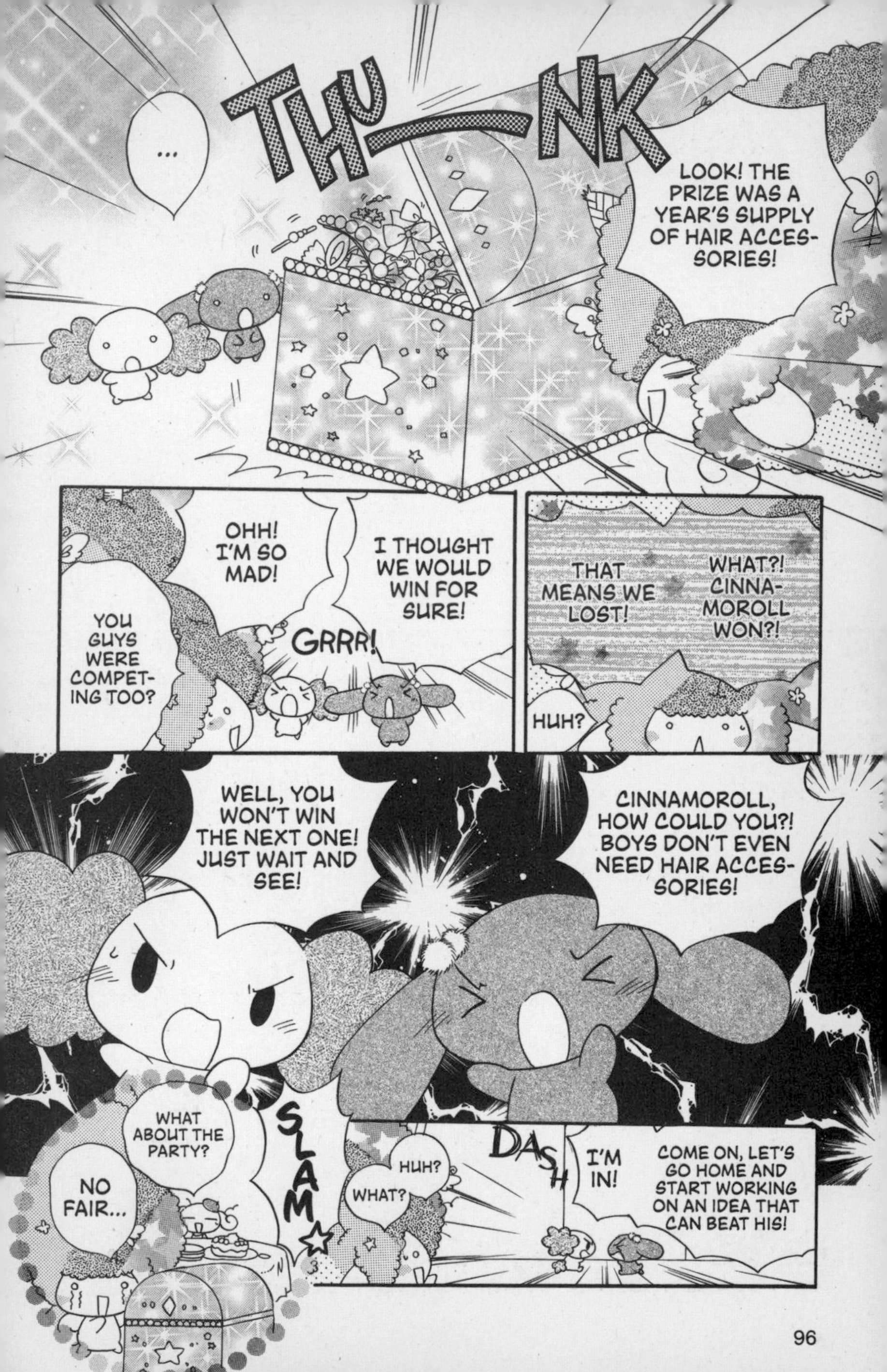
THU—NK
LOOK! THE PRIZE WAS A YEAR'S SUPPLY OF HAIR ACCES-SORIES!
...
WHAT?! CINNA-MOROLL WON?!
THAT MEANS WE LOST!
HUH?
I THOUGHT WE WOULD WIN FOR SURE!
OHH! I'M SO MAD!
GRRR!
YOU GUYS WERE COMPET-ING TOO?
CINNAMOROLL, HOW COULD YOU?! BOYS DON'T EVEN NEED HAIR ACCES-SORIES!
WELL, YOU WON'T WIN THE NEXT ONE! JUST WAIT AND SEE!
COME ON, LET'S GO HOME AND START WORKING ON AN IDEA THAT CAN BEAT HIS!
I'M IN!
DASH
HUH?
WHAT?
SLAM
WHAT ABOUT THE PARTY?
NO FAIR...

Espresso's Crush

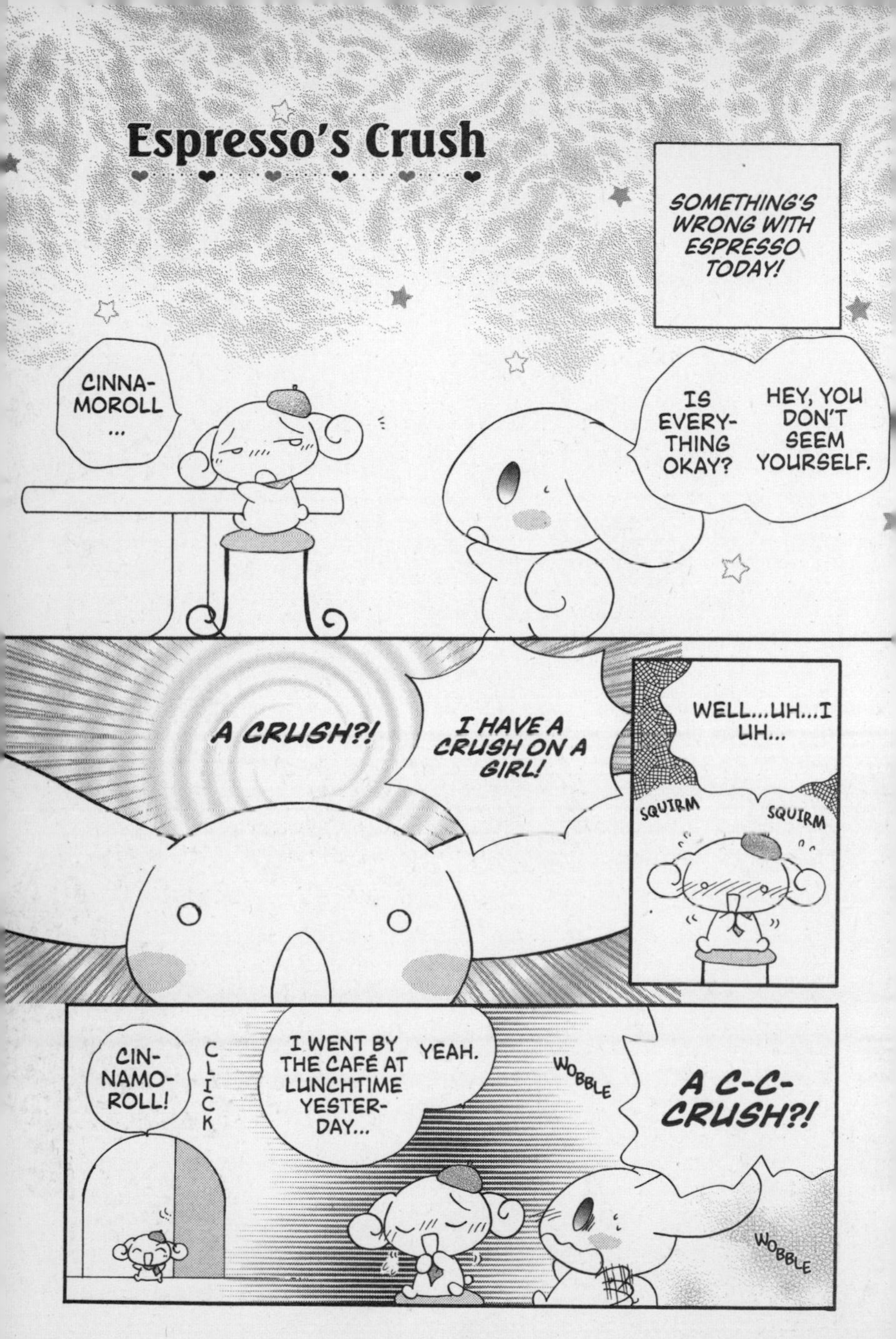

SOMETHING'S WRONG WITH ESPRESSO TODAY!
HEY, YOU DON'T SEEM YOURSELF. IS EVERYTHING OKAY?
CINNAMOROLL ...
WELL...UH...I UH...
SQUIRM
SQUIRM
I HAVE A CRUSH ON A GIRL!
A CRUSH?!
A C-C-CRUSH?!
WOBBLE
WOBBLE
YEAH.
I WENT BY THE CAFÉ AT LUNCHTIME YESTERDAY...
CLICK
CINNAMOROLL!

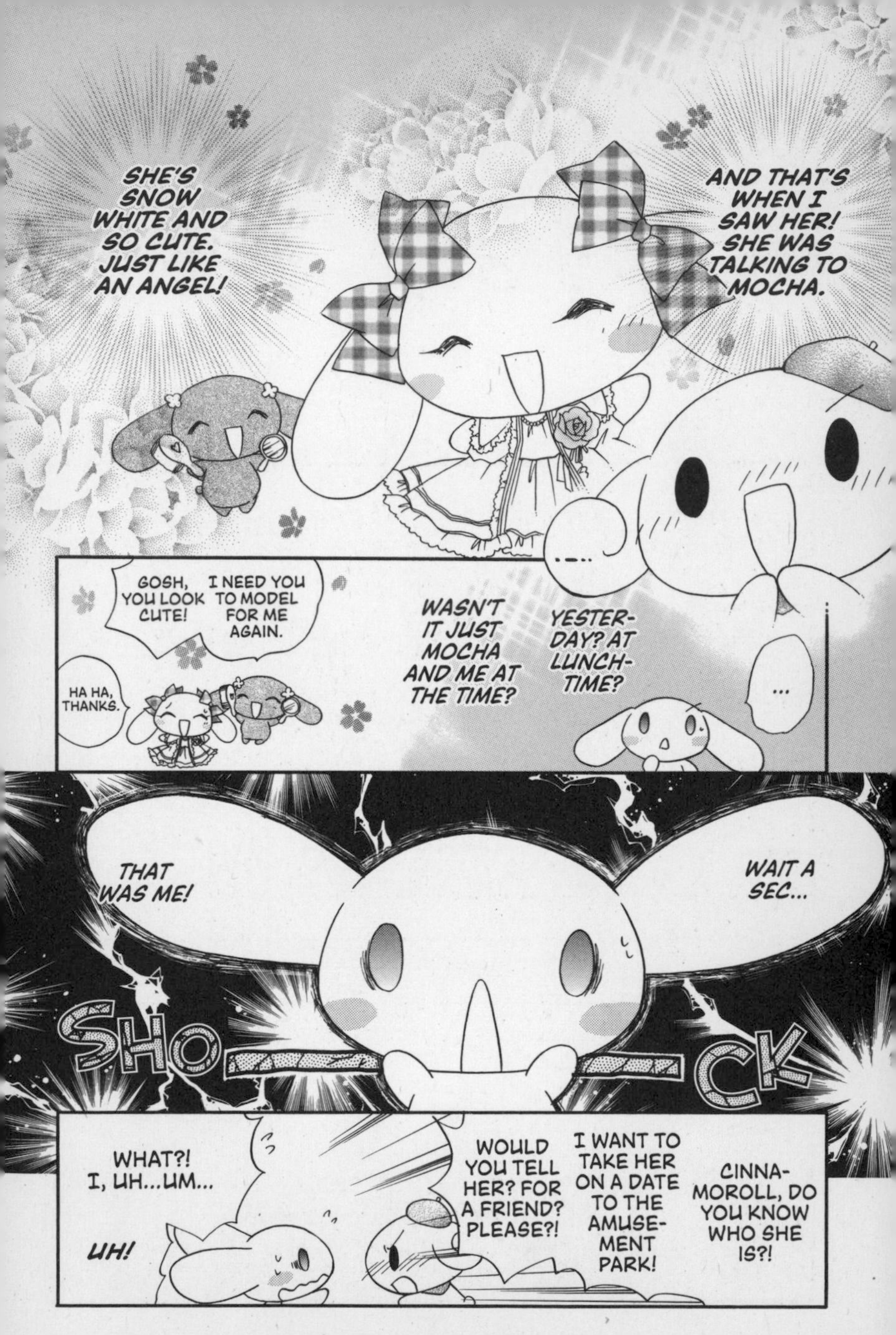
AND THAT'S WHEN I SAW HER! SHE WAS TALKING TO MOCHA.
SHE'S SNOW WHITE AND SO CUTE. JUST LIKE AN ANGEL!
-...
...
YESTER-DAY? AT LUNCH-TIME?
WASN'T IT JUST MOCHA AND ME AT THE TIME?
GOSH, YOU LOOK CUTE! I NEED YOU TO MODEL FOR ME AGAIN.
HA HA, THANKS.
WAIT A SEC...
THAT WAS ME!
SHO—CK
CINNA-MOROLL, DO YOU KNOW WHO SHE IS?!
I WANT TO TAKE HER ON A DATE TO THE AMUSE-MENT PARK!
WOULD YOU TELL HER? FOR A FRIEND? PLEASE?!
WHAT?! I, UH...UM...
UH!

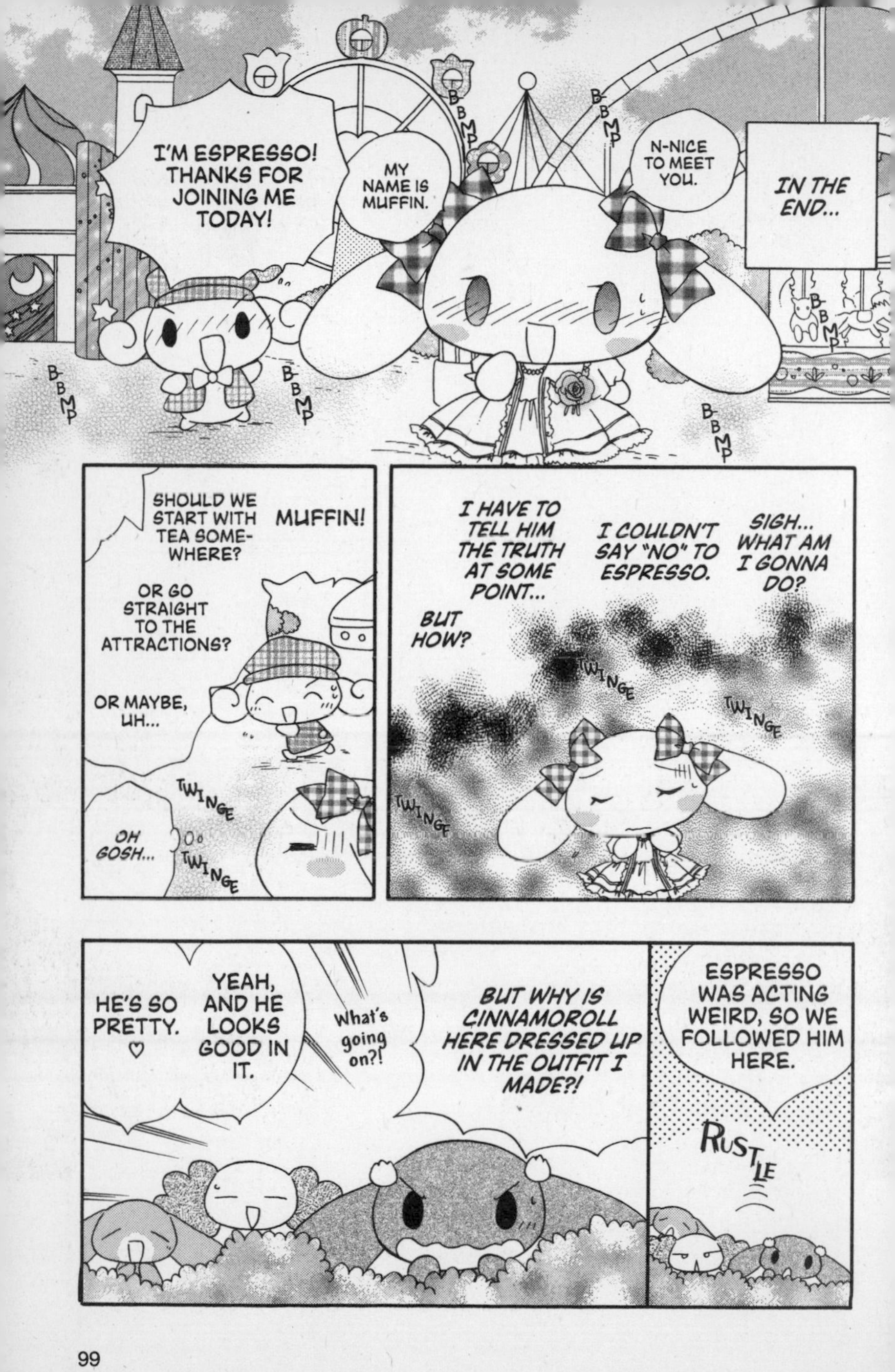
IN THE END...
N-NICE TO MEET YOU.
B-B-BMP
MY NAME IS MUFFIN.
B-B-BMP
I'M ESPRESSO! THANKS FOR JOINING ME TODAY!
B-B-BMP
B-B-BMP
B-B-BMP
B-B-BMP
SIGH... WHAT AM I GONNA DO?
I COULDN'T SAY "NO" TO ESPRESSO.
I HAVE TO TELL HIM THE TRUTH AT SOME POINT...
BUT HOW?
TWINGE
TWINGE
TWINGE
MUFFIN!
SHOULD WE START WITH TEA SOME-WHERE?
OR GO STRAIGHT TO THE ATTRACTIONS?
OR MAYBE, UH...
TWINGE
OH GOSH...
TWINGE
ESPRESSO WAS ACTING WEIRD, SO WE FOLLOWED HIM HERE.
RUSTLE
BUT WHY IS CINNAMOROLL HERE DRESSED UP IN THE OUTFIT I MADE?!
What's going on?!
YEAH, AND HE LOOKS GOOD IN IT.
HE'S SO PRETTY. ♡

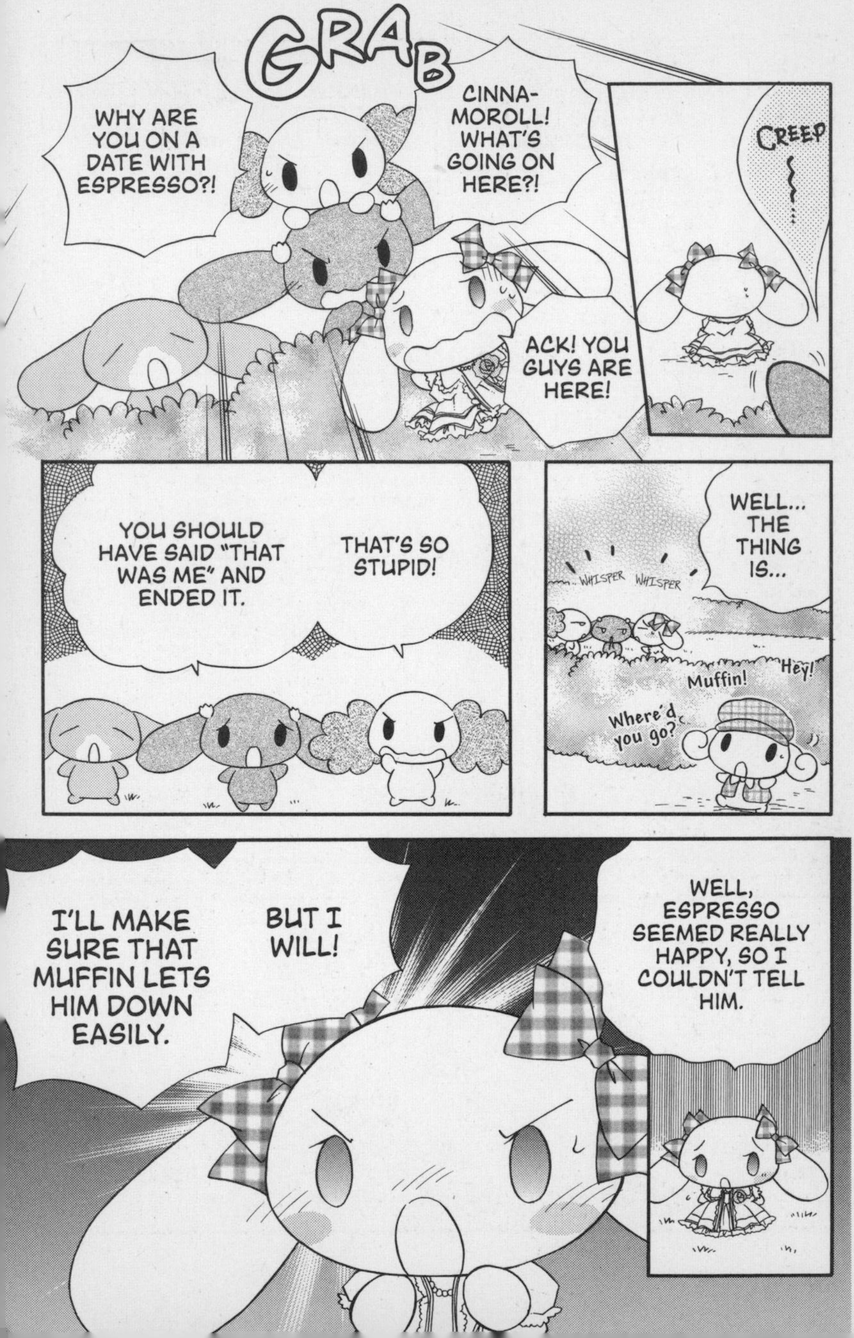
CREEP...
GRAB
CINNA-MOROLL! WHAT'S GOING ON HERE?!
WHY ARE YOU ON A DATE WITH ESPRESSO?!
ACK! YOU GUYS ARE HERE!
WELL... THE THING IS...
WHISPER WHISPER
Hey!
Muffin!
Where'd you go?
THAT'S SO STUPID!
YOU SHOULD HAVE SAID "THAT WAS ME" AND ENDED IT.
WELL, ESPRESSO SEEMED REALLY HAPPY, SO I COULDN'T TELL HIM.
BUT I WILL!
I'LL MAKE SURE THAT MUFFIN LETS HIM DOWN EASILY.

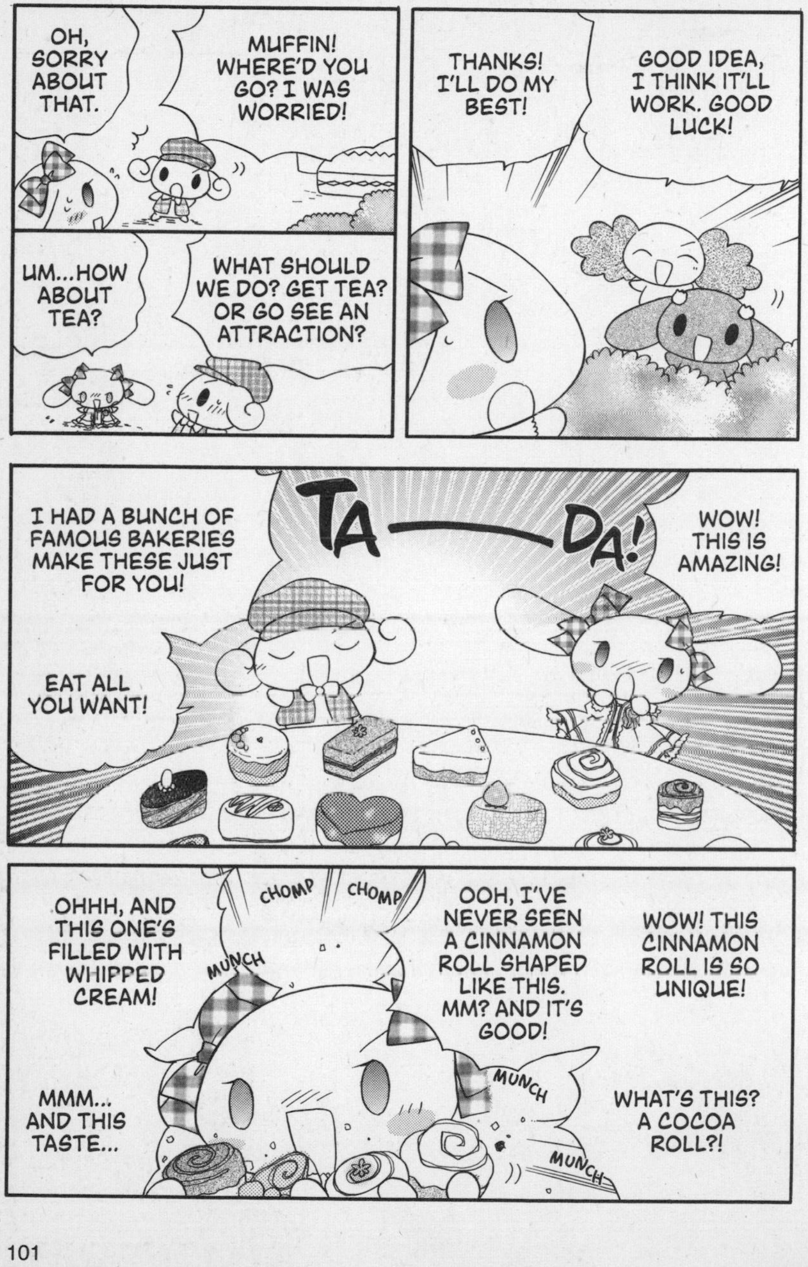
GOOD IDEA, I THINK IT'LL WORK. GOOD LUCK!
THANKS! I'LL DO MY BEST!
MUFFIN! WHERE'D YOU GO? I WAS WORRIED!
OH, SORRY ABOUT THAT.
WHAT SHOULD WE DO? GET TEA? OR GO SEE AN ATTRACTION?
UM...HOW ABOUT TEA?
WOW! THIS IS AMAZING!
TA—DA!
I HAD A BUNCH OF FAMOUS BAKERIES MAKE THESE JUST FOR YOU!
EAT ALL YOU WANT!
WOW! THIS CINNAMON ROLL IS SO UNIQUE!
CHOMP CHOMP
OOH, I'VE NEVER SEEN A CINNAMON ROLL SHAPED LIKE THIS. MM? AND IT'S GOOD!
MUNCH
OHHH, AND THIS ONE'S FILLED WITH WHIPPED CREAM!
WHAT'S THIS? A COCOA ROLL?!
MUNCH
MUNCH
MMM... AND THIS TASTE...

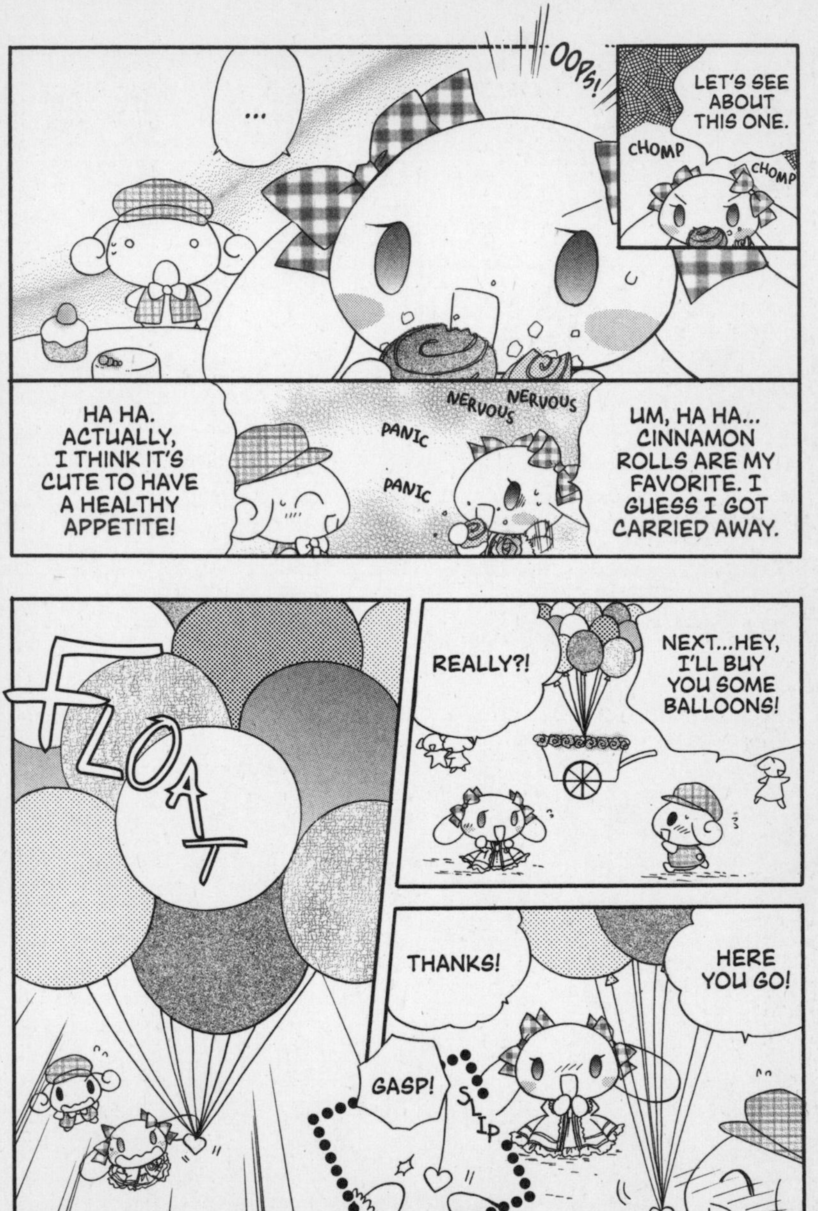
LET'S SEE ABOUT THIS ONE.
CHOMP
CHOMP
OOPS!
...
UM, HA HA... CINNAMON ROLLS ARE MY FAVORITE. I GUESS I GOT CARRIED AWAY.
NERVOUS
NERVOUS
PANIC
PANIC
HA HA. ACTUALLY, I THINK IT'S CUTE TO HAVE A HEALTHY APPETITE!
NEXT...HEY, I'LL BUY YOU SOME BALLOONS!
REALLY?!
HERE YOU GO!
THANKS!
SLIP
GASP!
FLOAT

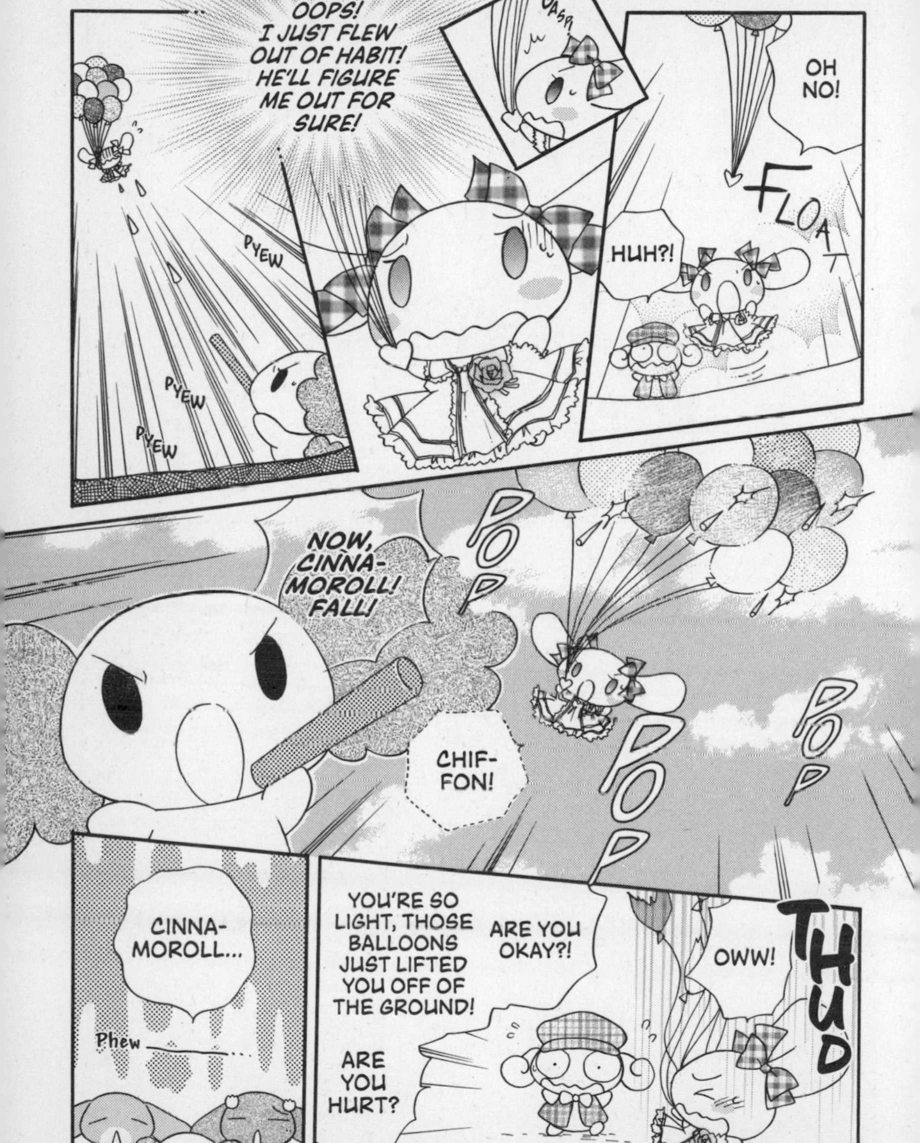
OH NO!
FLOAT
HUH?!
GASP!
OOPS! I JUST FLEW OUT OF HABIT! HE'LL FIGURE ME OUT FOR SURE!
PYEW
PYEW
PYEW
POP
POP
POP
POP
NOW, CINNA-MOROLL! FALL!
CHIF-FON!
THUD
OWW!
ARE YOU OKAY?!
YOU'RE SO LIGHT, THOSE BALLOONS JUST LIFTED YOU OFF OF THE GROUND!
ARE YOU HURT?
CINNA-MOROLL...
Phew

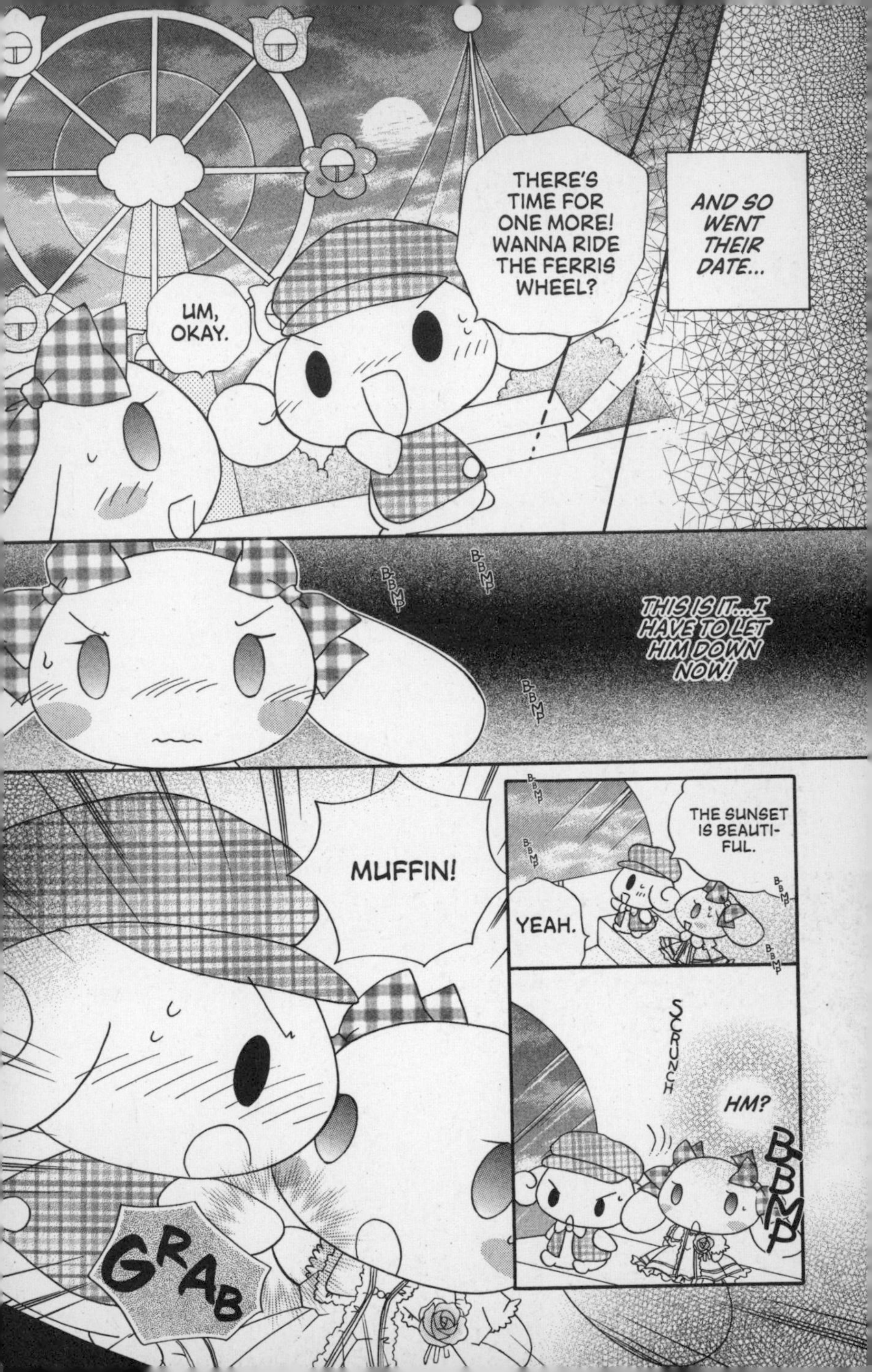
AND SO WENT THEIR DATE...
THERE'S TIME FOR ONE MORE! WANNA RIDE THE FERRIS WHEEL?
UM, OKAY.
THIS IS IT...I HAVE TO LET HIM DOWN NOW!
B-BMP
B-BMP
B-BMP
B-BMP
B-BMP
THE SUNSET IS BEAUTI-FUL.
YEAH.
B-BMP
B-BMP
SCRUNCH
HM?
BBMP
MUFFIN!
GRAB

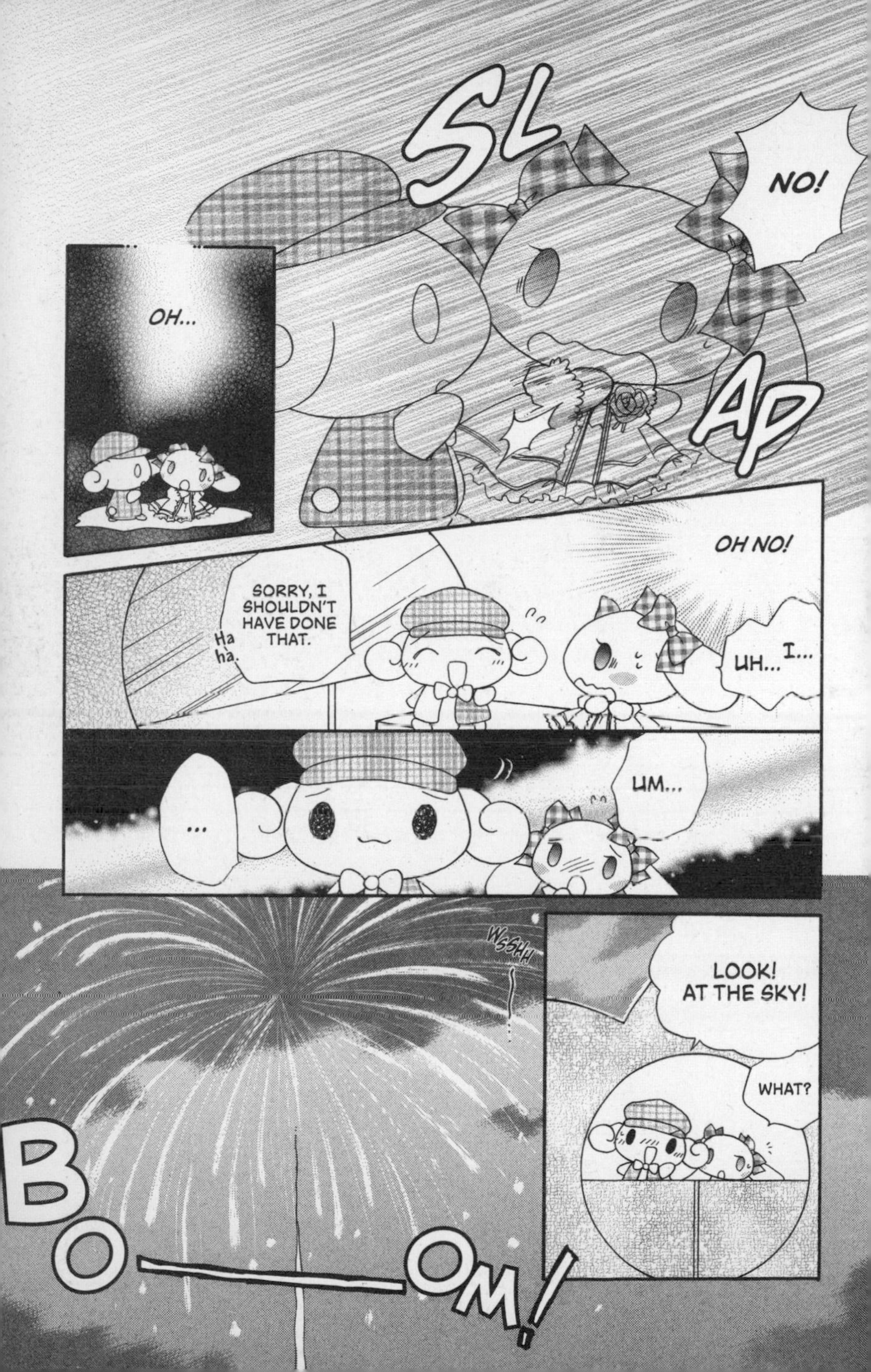
SLAP
NO!
OH...
OH NO!
UH... I...
SORRY, I SHOULDN'T HAVE DONE THAT.
Ha ha.
UM...
...
LOOK! AT THE SKY!
WHAT?
WSSHH
BO—OM!

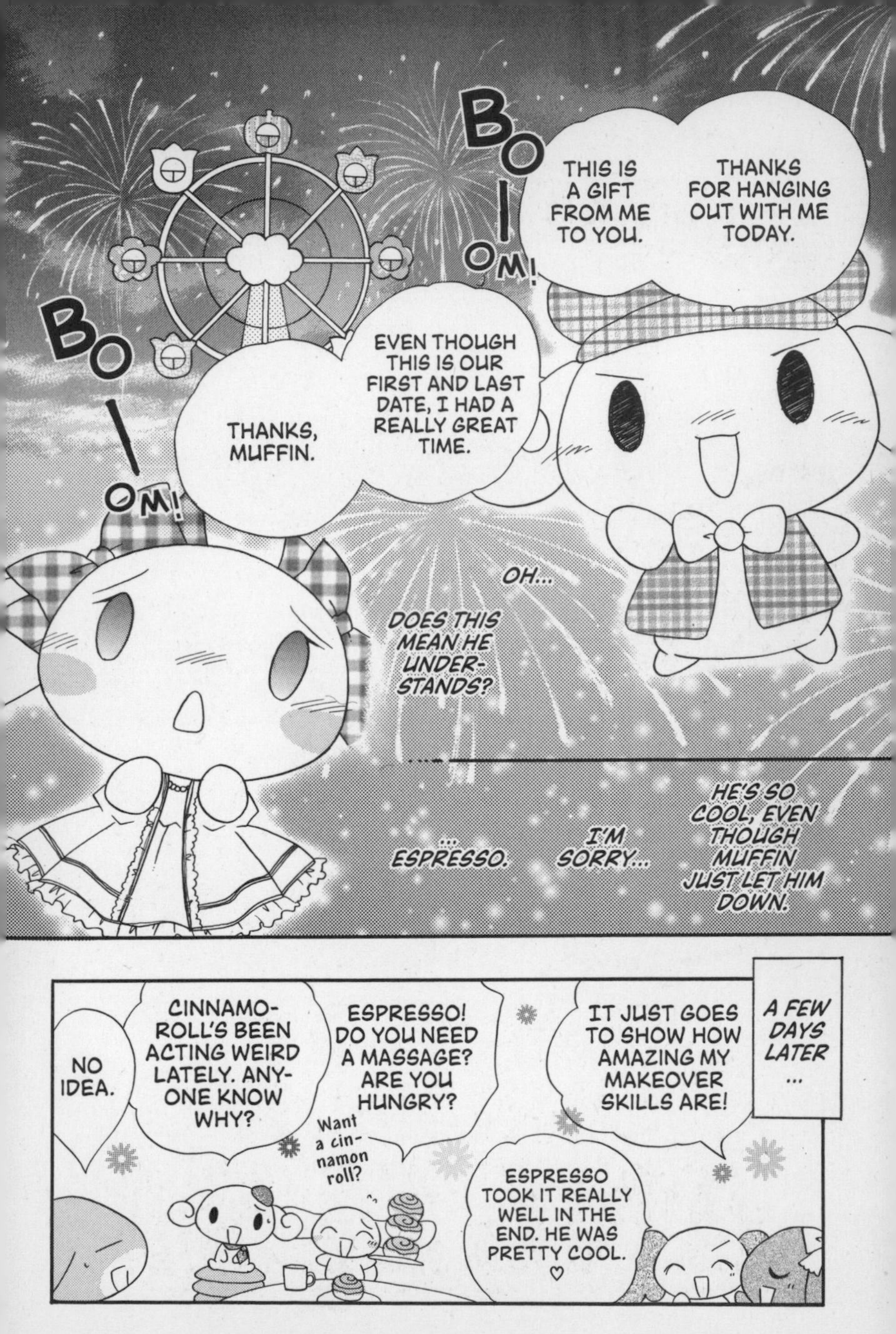
BOOM!
THANKS FOR HANGING OUT WITH ME TODAY.
THIS IS A GIFT FROM ME TO YOU.
EVEN THOUGH THIS IS OUR FIRST AND LAST DATE, I HAD A REALLY GREAT TIME.
THANKS, MUFFIN.
BOOM!
OH...
DOES THIS MEAN HE UNDERSTANDS?
HE'S SO COOL, EVEN THOUGH MUFFIN JUST LET HIM DOWN.
I'M SORRY...
...ESPRESSO.
A FEW DAYS LATER...
IT JUST GOES TO SHOW HOW AMAZING MY MAKEOVER SKILLS ARE!
ESPRESSO TOOK IT REALLY WELL IN THE END. HE WAS PRETTY COOL. ♡
ESPRESSO! DO YOU NEED A MASSAGE? ARE YOU HUNGRY?
Want a cinnamon roll?
CINNAMOROLL'S BEEN ACTING WEIRD LATELY. ANYONE KNOW WHY?
NO IDEA.

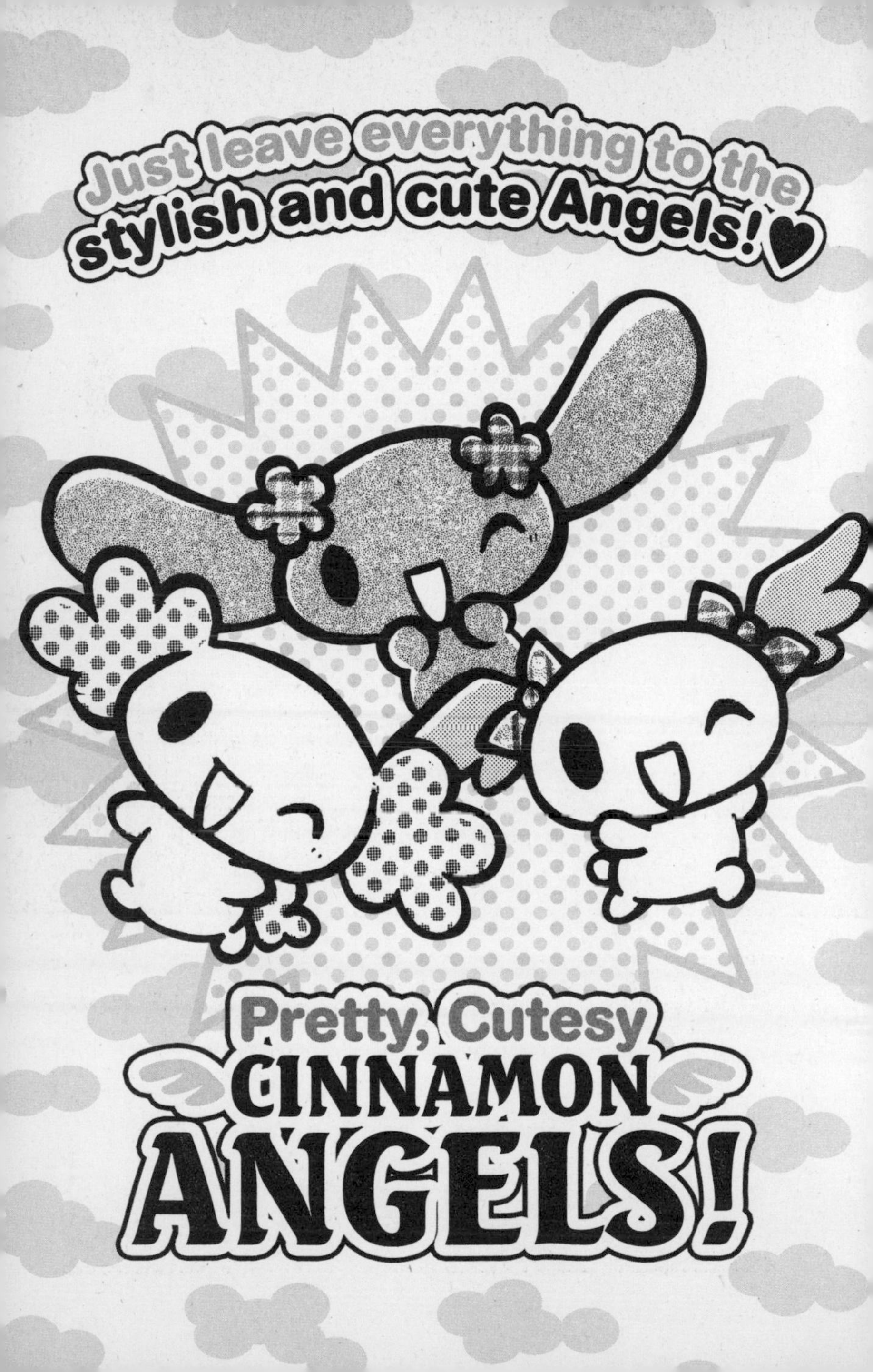
Just leave everything to the stylish and cute Angels! ♥
Pretty, Cutesy
CINNAMON
ANGELS!

The Cinnamon Angels' Biggest Secrets!

The three Angels are always full of energy. They've each shared a little about what they think of each other—is it what you expected?

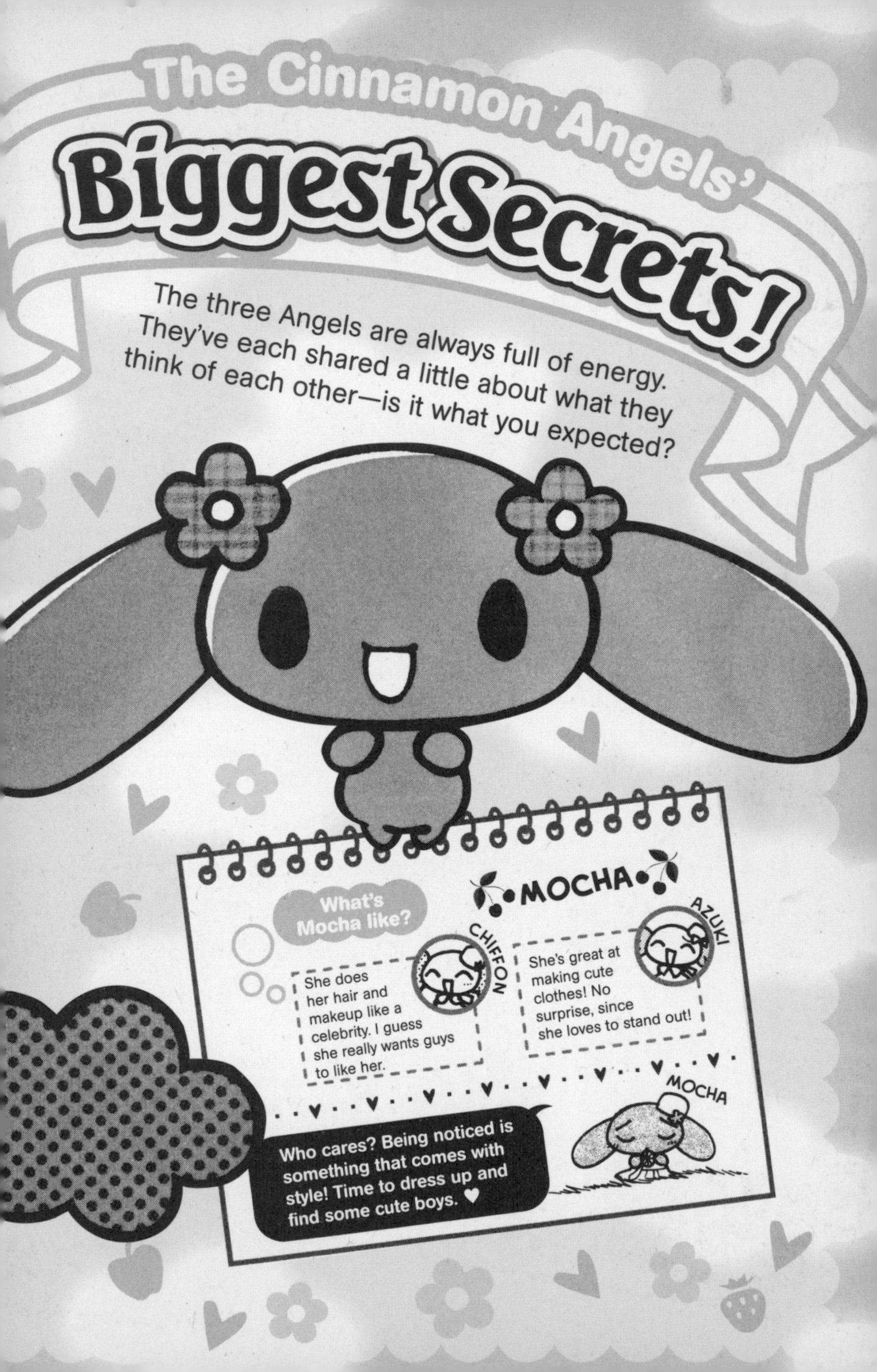
MOCHA
What's Mocha like?
CHIFFON
She does her hair and makeup like a celebrity. I guess she really wants guys to like her.
AZUKI
She's great at making cute clothes! No surprise, since she loves to stand out!
MOCHA
Who cares? Being noticed is something that comes with style! Time to dress up and find some cute boys. ♥

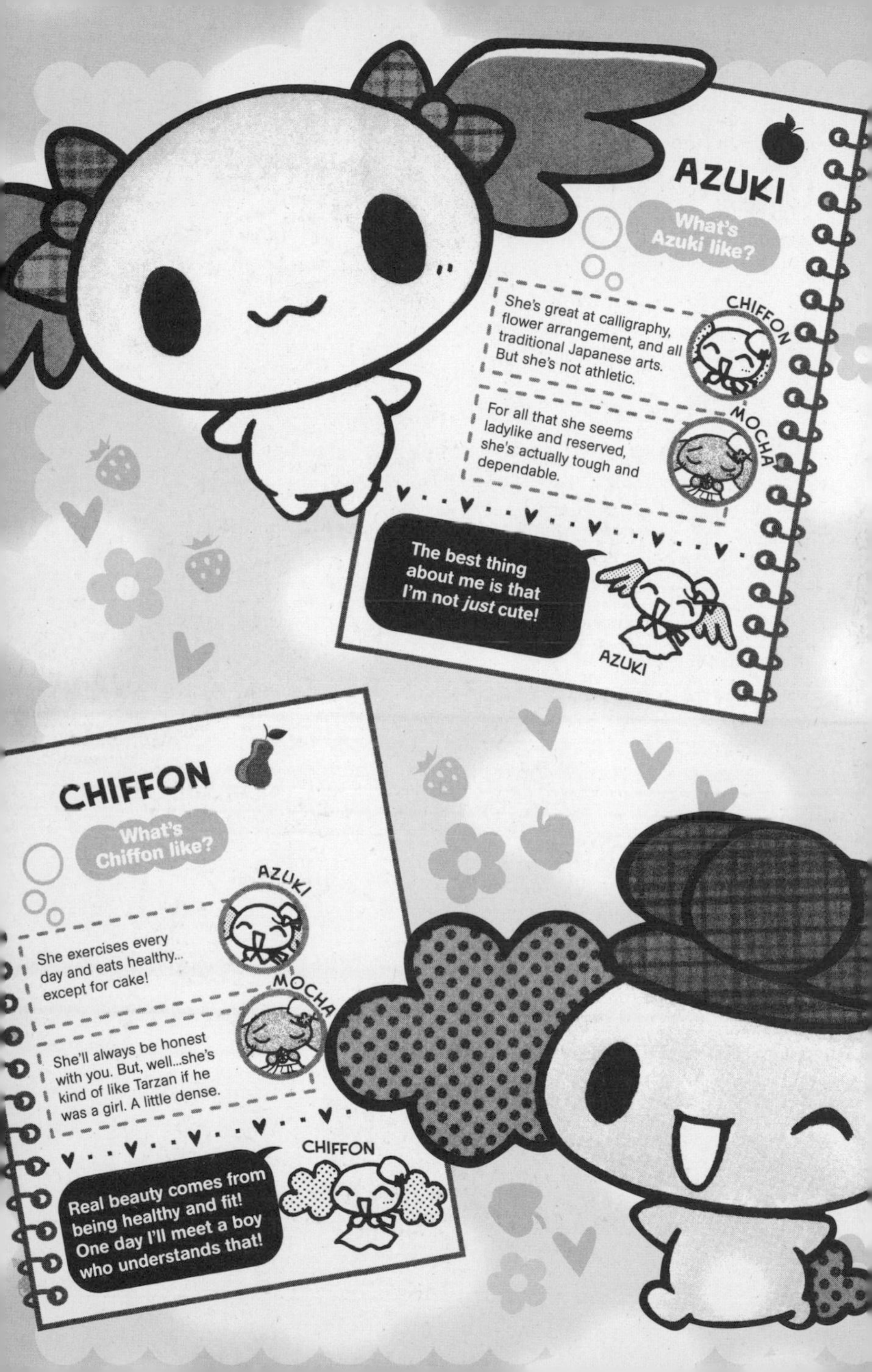
AZUKI
What's Azuki like?
CHIFFON
She's great at calligraphy, flower arrangement, and all traditional Japanese arts. But she's not athletic.
MOCHA
For all that she seems ladylike and reserved, she's actually tough and dependable.
The best thing about me is that I'm not *just* cute!
AZUKI
CHIFFON
What's Chiffon like?
AZUKI
She exercises every day and eats healthy... except for cake!
MOCHA
She'll always be honest with you. But, well...she's kind of like Tarzan if he was a girl. A little dense.
CHIFFON
Real beauty comes from being healthy and fit! One day I'll meet a boy who understands that!

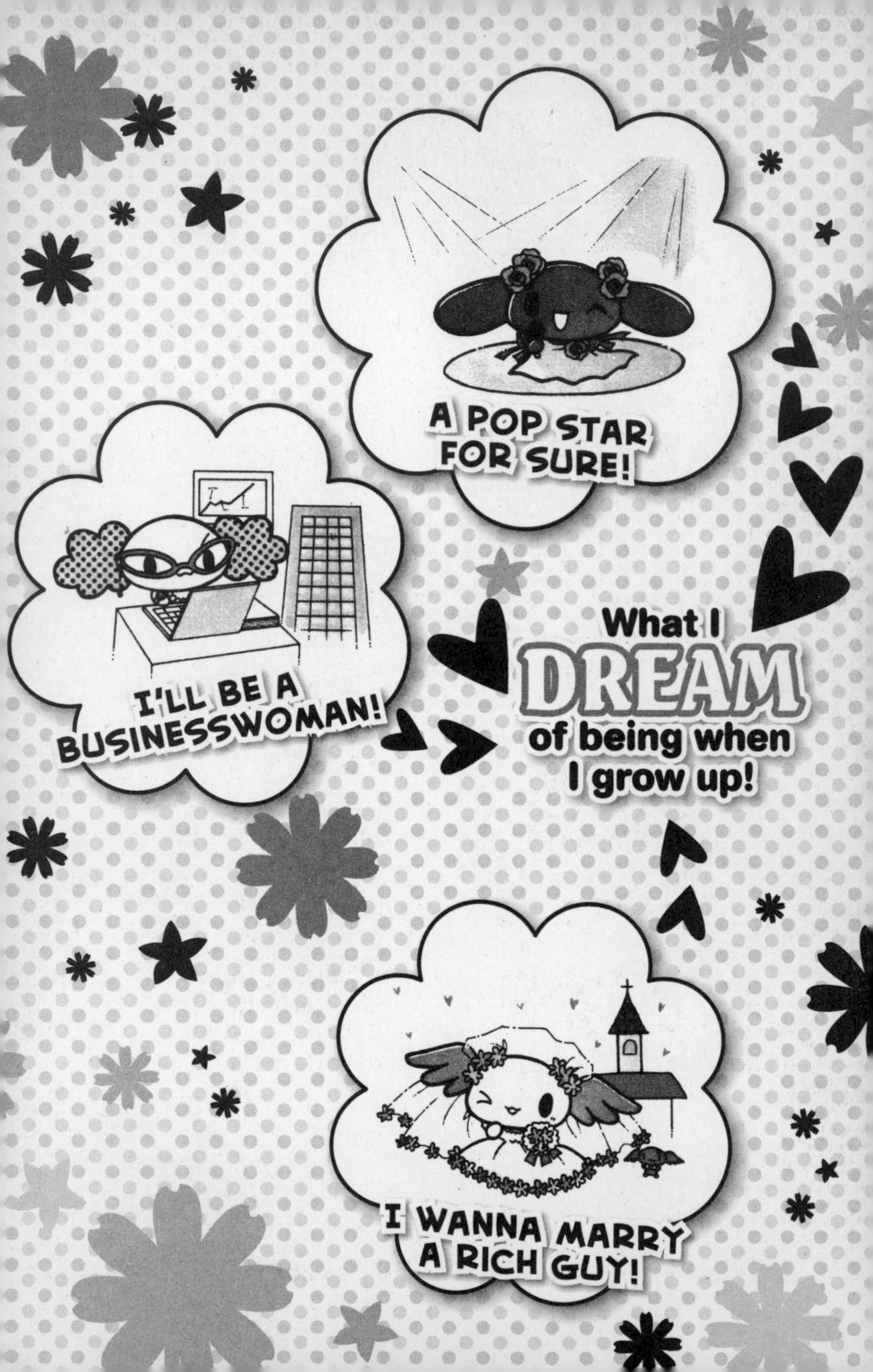
A POP STAR FOR SURE!
What I DREAM of being when I grow up!
I'LL BE A BUSINESSWOMAN!
I WANNA MARRY A RICH GUY!

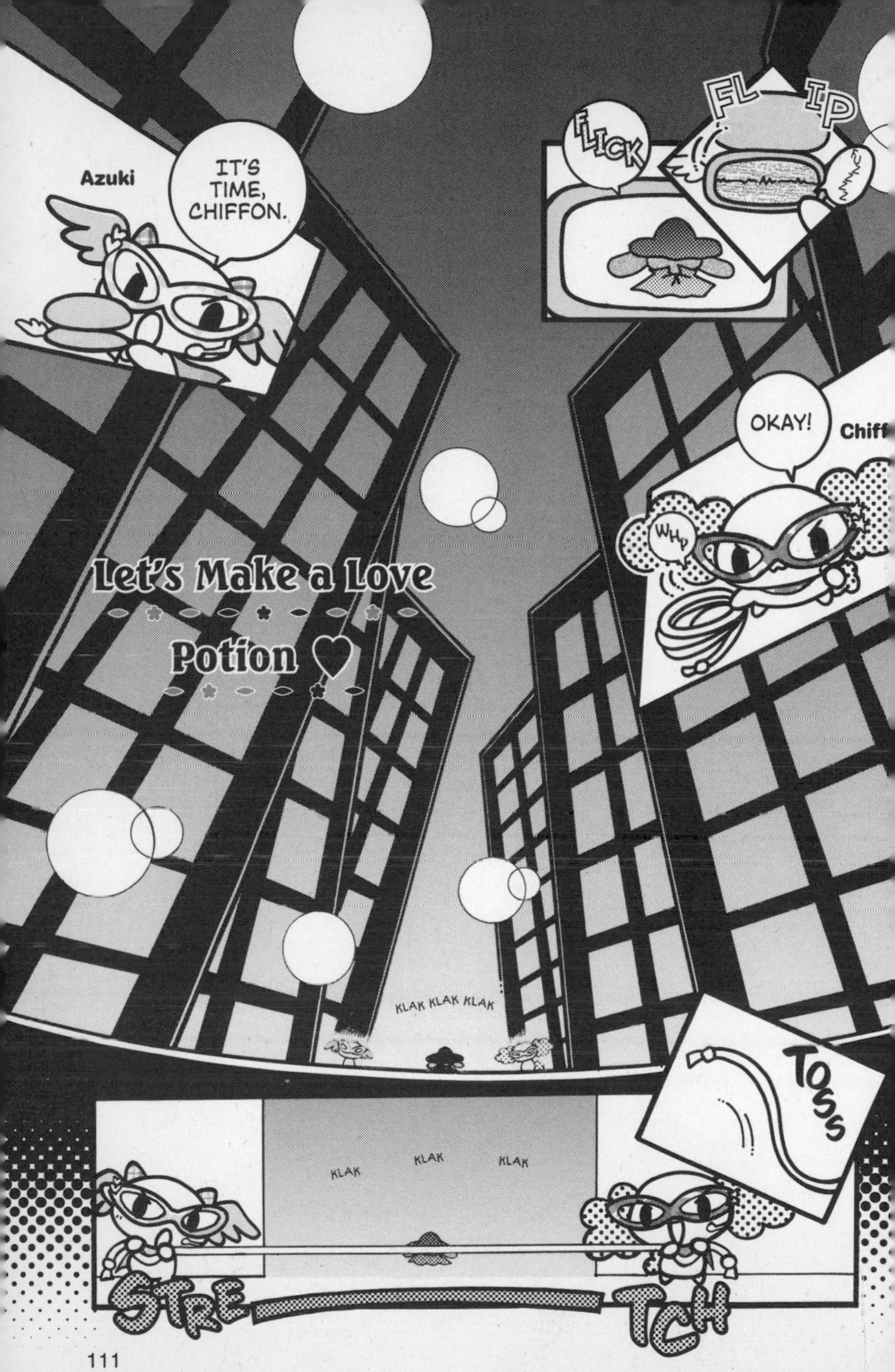
FL IP
FUZZZZ
FLICK
Azuki
IT'S TIME, CHIFFON.
Chiff
OKAY!
WHP
Let's Make a Love Potion ♥
KLAK KLAK KLAK
TOSS
KLAK
KLAK
KLAK
STRE——TCH

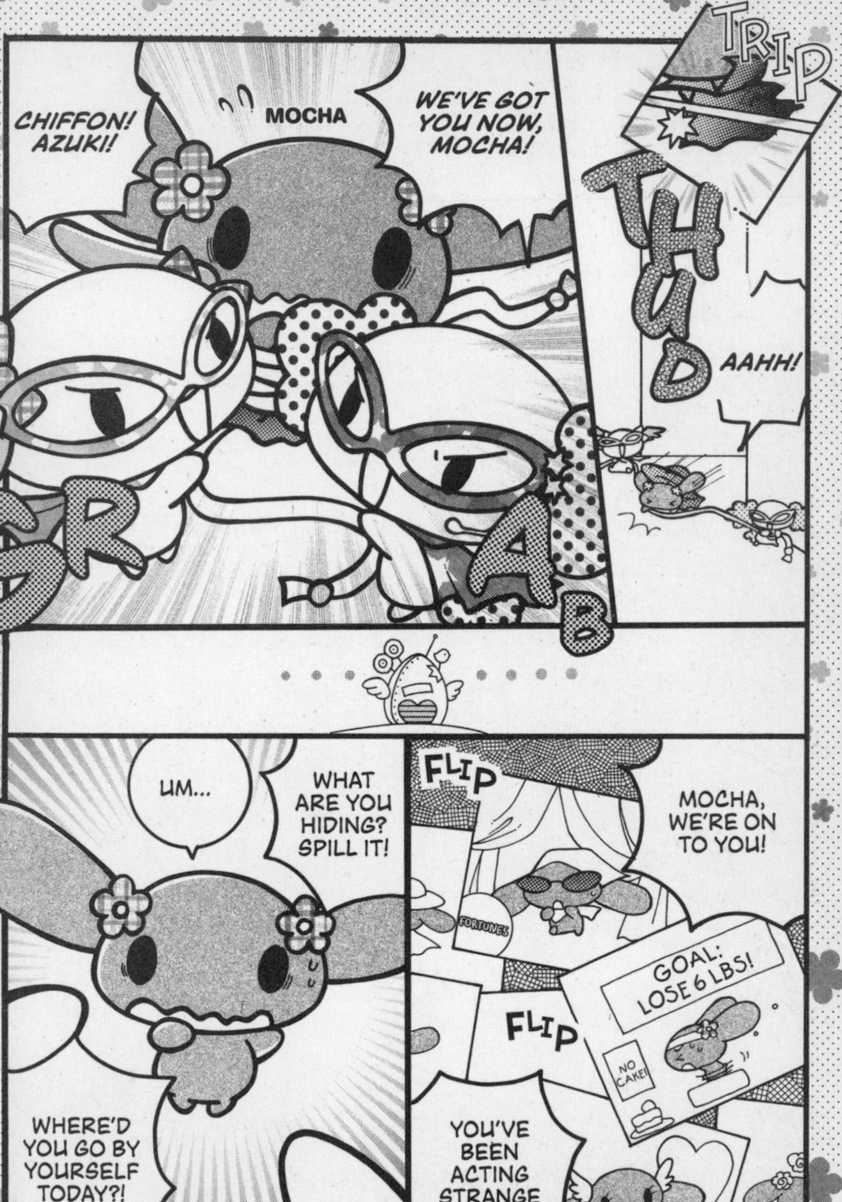
TRIP
THUD
AAHH!
WE'VE GOT YOU NOW, MOCHA!
MOCHA
CHIFFON! AZUKI!
GRAB
FLIP
MOCHA, WE'RE ON TO YOU!
FORTUNES
GOAL: LOSE 6 LBS!
FLIP
NO CAKE!
YOU'VE BEEN ACTING STRANGE LATELY!
WHAT ARE YOU HIDING? SPILL IT!
UM...
WHERE'D YOU GO BY YOURSELF TODAY?!

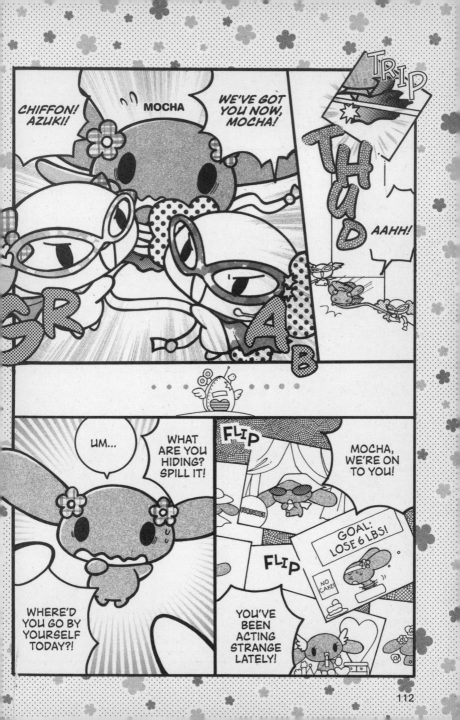

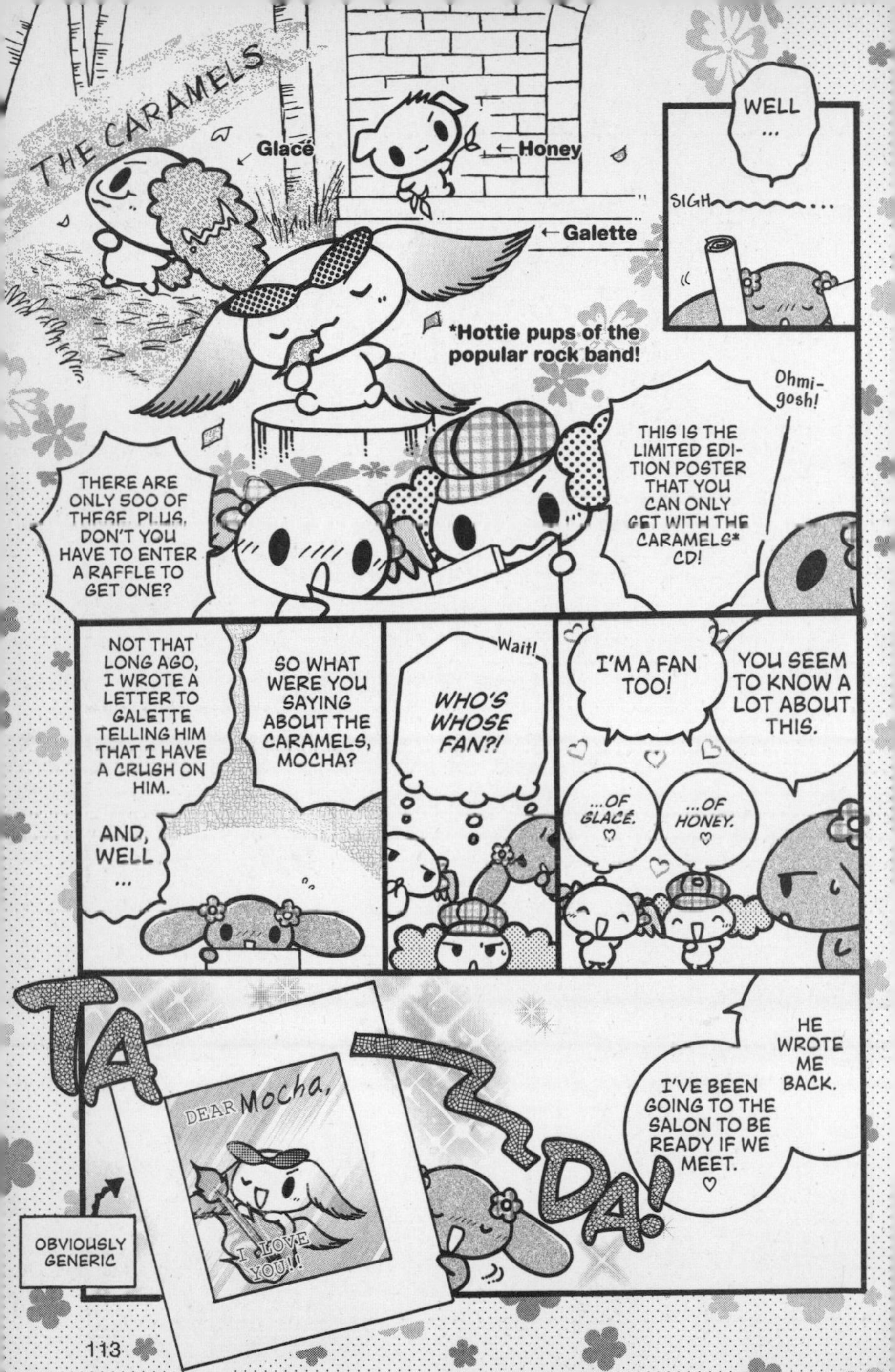
WELL ...
SIGH...
THE CARAMELS
Glacé
Honey
Galette
*Hottie pups of the popular rock band!
Ohmi-gosh!
THIS IS THE LIMITED EDI-TION POSTER THAT YOU CAN ONLY GET WITH THE CARAMELS* CD!
THERE ARE ONLY 500 OF THESE. PLUS, DON'T YOU HAVE TO ENTER A RAFFLE TO GET ONE?
YOU SEEM TO KNOW A LOT ABOUT THIS.
I'M A FAN TOO!
...OF HONEY. ♡
...OF GLACÉ. ♡
Wait!
WHO'S WHOSE FAN?!
SO WHAT WERE YOU SAYING ABOUT THE CARAMELS, MOCHA?
NOT THAT LONG AGO, I WROTE A LETTER TO GALETTE TELLING HIM THAT I HAVE A CRUSH ON HIM.
AND, WELL ...
HE WROTE ME BACK.
I'VE BEEN GOING TO THE SALON TO BE READY IF WE MEET. ♡
TA-DA!
DEAR Mocha,
I LOVE YOU!!
OBVIOUSLY GENERIC

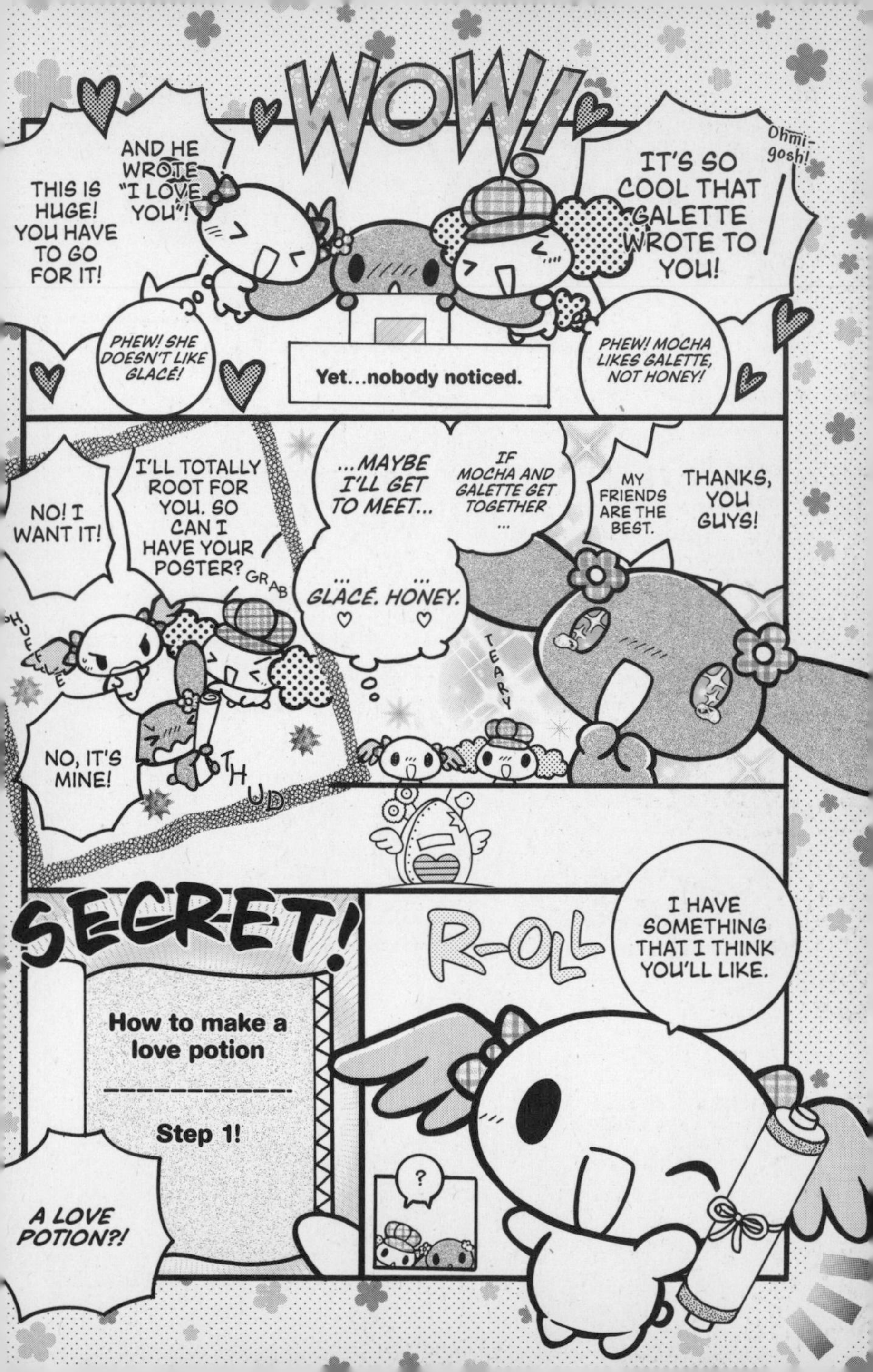
Ohmi-gosh!
IT'S SO COOL THAT GALETTE WROTE TO YOU!
WOW!
AND HE WROTE "I LOVE YOU"!
THIS IS HUGE! YOU HAVE TO GO FOR IT!
PHEW! MOCHA LIKES GALETTE, NOT HONEY!
Yet…nobody noticed.
PHEW! SHE DOESN'T LIKE GLACÉ!
THANKS, YOU GUYS!
MY FRIENDS ARE THE BEST.
TEARY
IF MOCHA AND GALETTE GET TOGETHER …
…MAYBE I'LL GET TO MEET…
… GLACÉ. … HONEY.
I'LL TOTALLY ROOT FOR YOU. SO CAN I HAVE YOUR POSTER?
GRAB
NO! I WANT IT!
SHUFFLE
NO, IT'S MINE!
THUD
I HAVE SOMETHING THAT I THINK YOU'LL LIKE.
R-OLL
?
SECRET!
How to make a love potion
Step 1!
A LOVE POTION?!

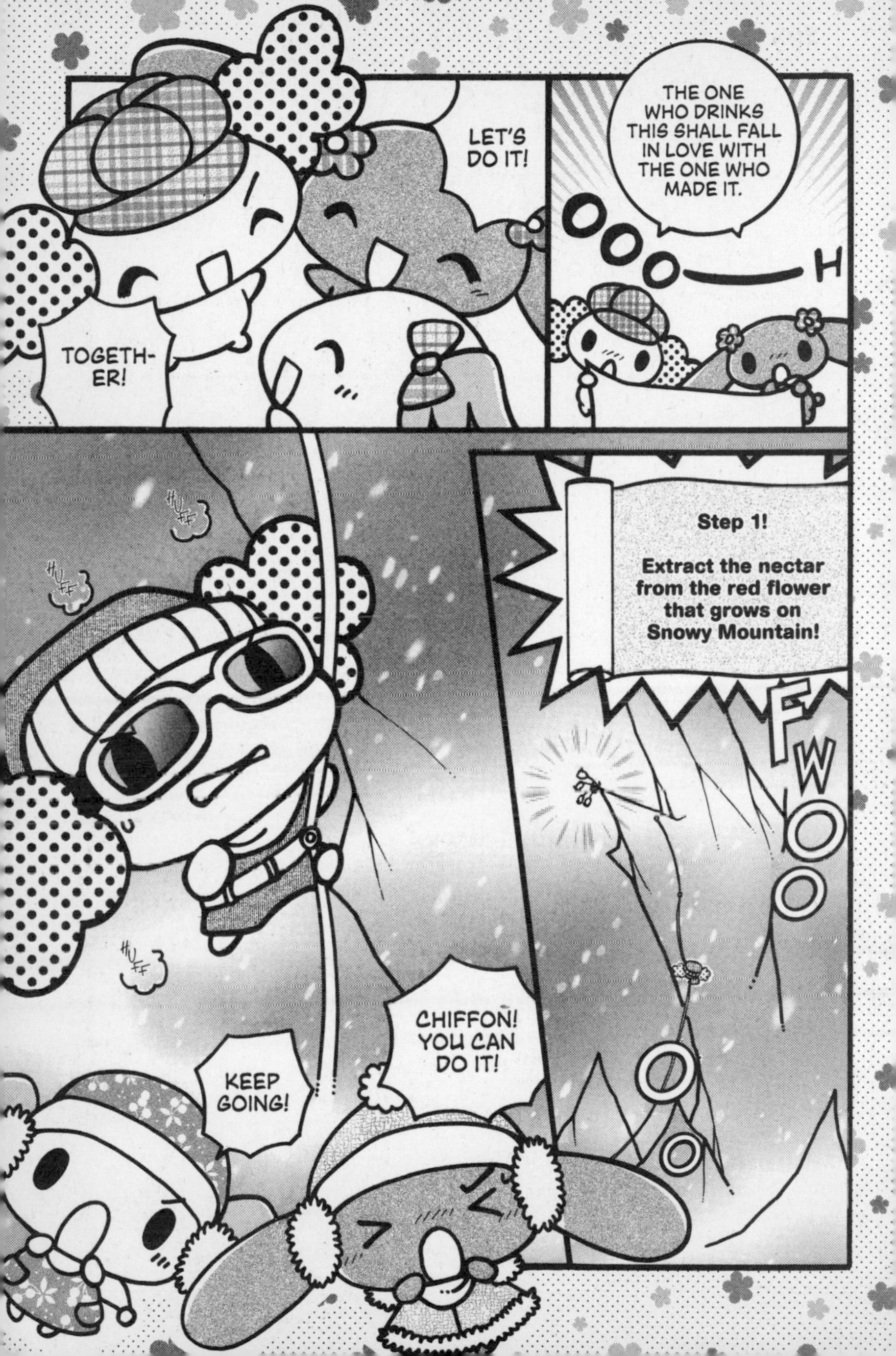
THE ONE WHO DRINKS THIS SHALL FALL IN LOVE WITH THE ONE WHO MADE IT.
OOO——H
LET'S DO IT!
TOGETH-ER!
Step 1!
Extract the nectar from the red flower that grows on Snowy Mountain!
FWOOO
HUFF
HUFF
HUFF
CHIFFON! YOU CAN DO IT!
KEEP GOING!

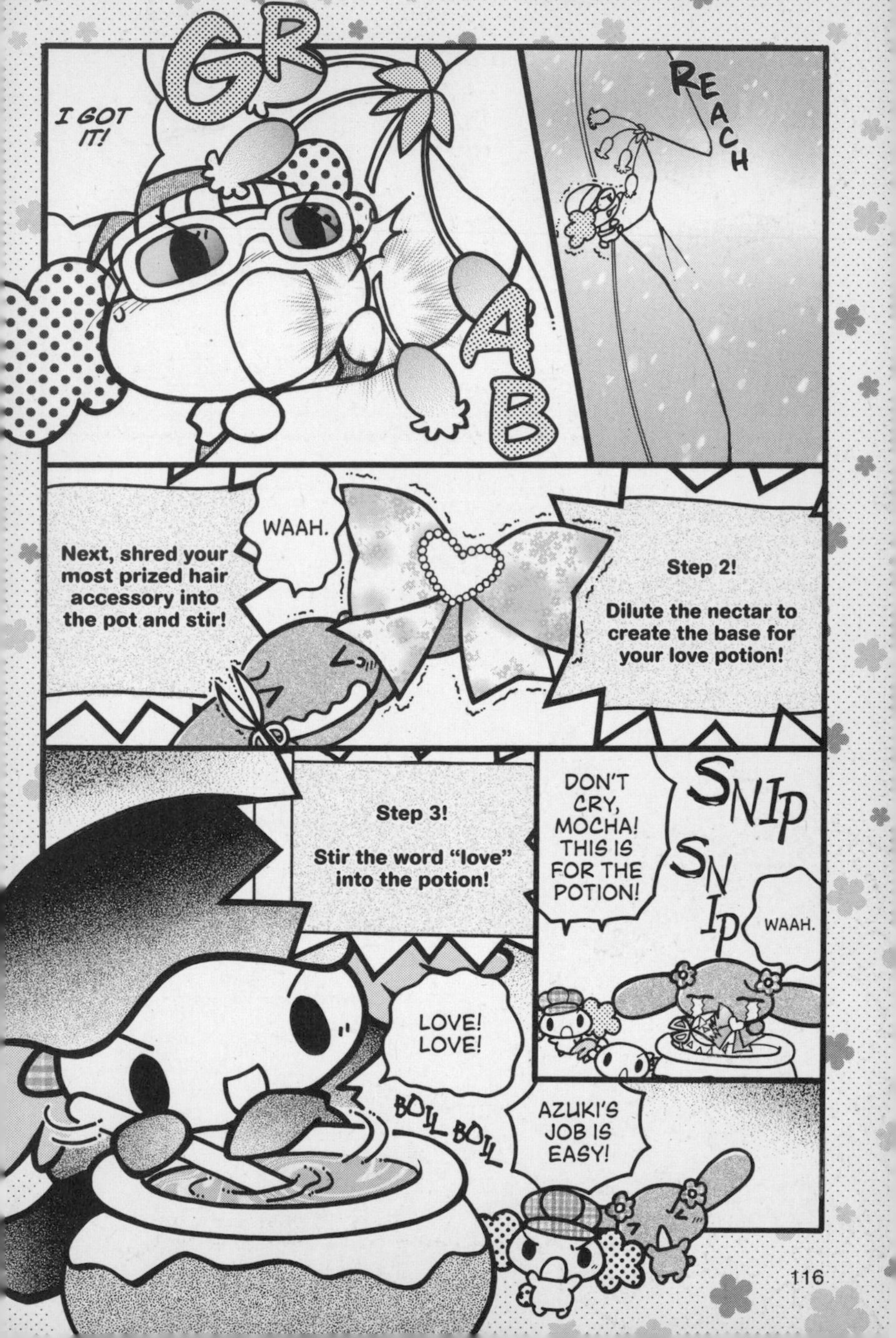
REACH
GRAB
I GOT IT!
Step 2!
Dilute the nectar to create the base for your love potion!
WAAH.
Next, shred your most prized hair accessory into the pot and stir!
SNIP
SNIP
DON'T CRY, MOCHA! THIS IS FOR THE POTION!
WAAH.
Step 3!
Stir the word "love" into the potion!
LOVE! LOVE!
BOIL BOIL
AZUKI'S JOB IS EASY!

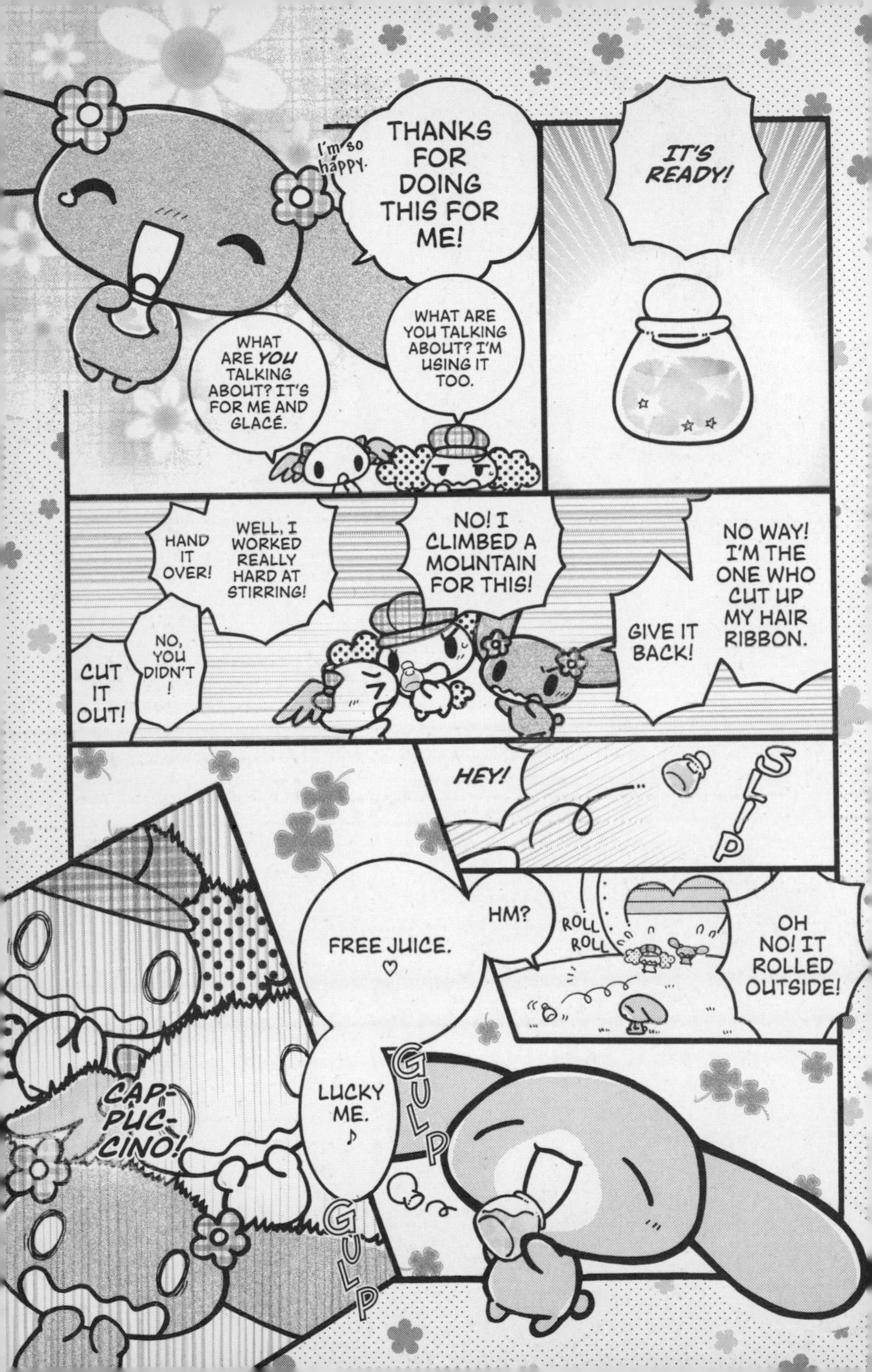
IT'S READY!
I'm so happy.
THANKS FOR DOING THIS FOR ME!
WHAT ARE YOU TALKING ABOUT? I'M USING IT TOO.
WHAT ARE *YOU* TALKING ABOUT? IT'S FOR ME AND GLACÉ.
NO WAY! I'M THE ONE WHO CUT UP MY HAIR RIBBON.
GIVE IT BACK!
NO! I CLIMBED A MOUNTAIN FOR THIS!
WELL, I WORKED REALLY HARD AT STIRRING!
HAND IT OVER!
NO, YOU DIDN'T!
CUT IT OUT!
SLIP
HEY!
OH NO! IT ROLLED OUTSIDE!
ROLL ROLL
HM?
FREE JUICE. ♡
LUCKY ME. ♪
GULP
GULP
CAP-PUC-CINO!

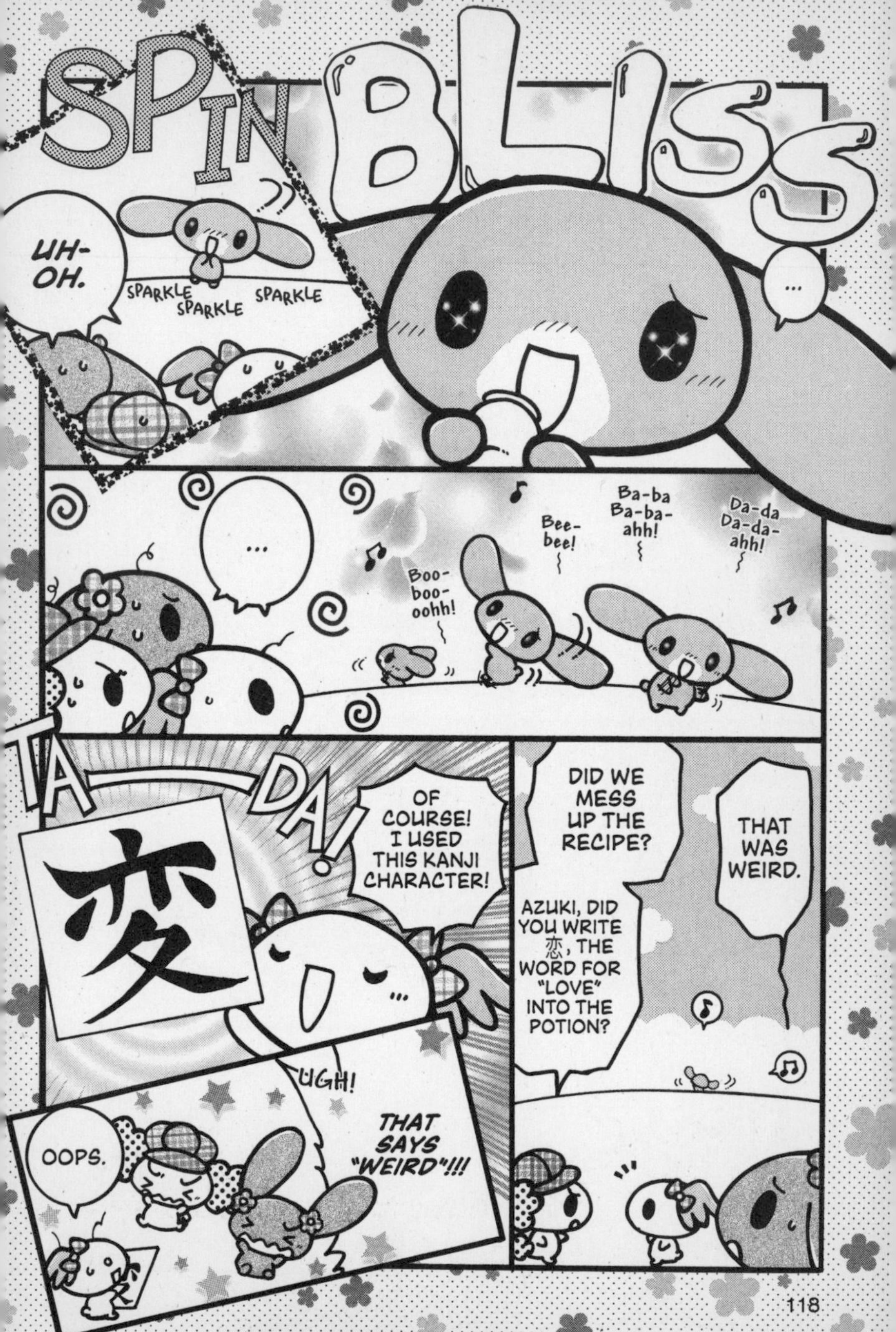
SPIN BLISS
...
UH-OH.
SPARKLE SPARKLE SPARKLE
Da-da Da-da-ahh!
Ba-ba Ba-ba-ahh!
Bee-bee!
Boo-boo-oohh!
...
THAT WAS WEIRD.
DID WE MESS UP THE RECIPE?
AZUKI, DID YOU WRITE 恋, THE WORD FOR "LOVE" INTO THE POTION?
TA—DA!
OF COURSE! I USED THIS KANJI CHARACTER!
変
UGH!
THAT SAYS "WEIRD"!!!
OOPS.

★ Fluffy, Fluffy ♥ Cinnamoroll ★

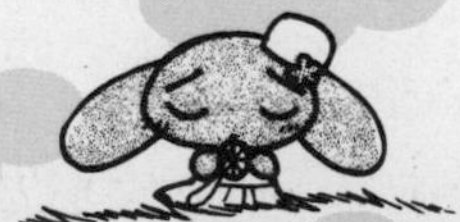

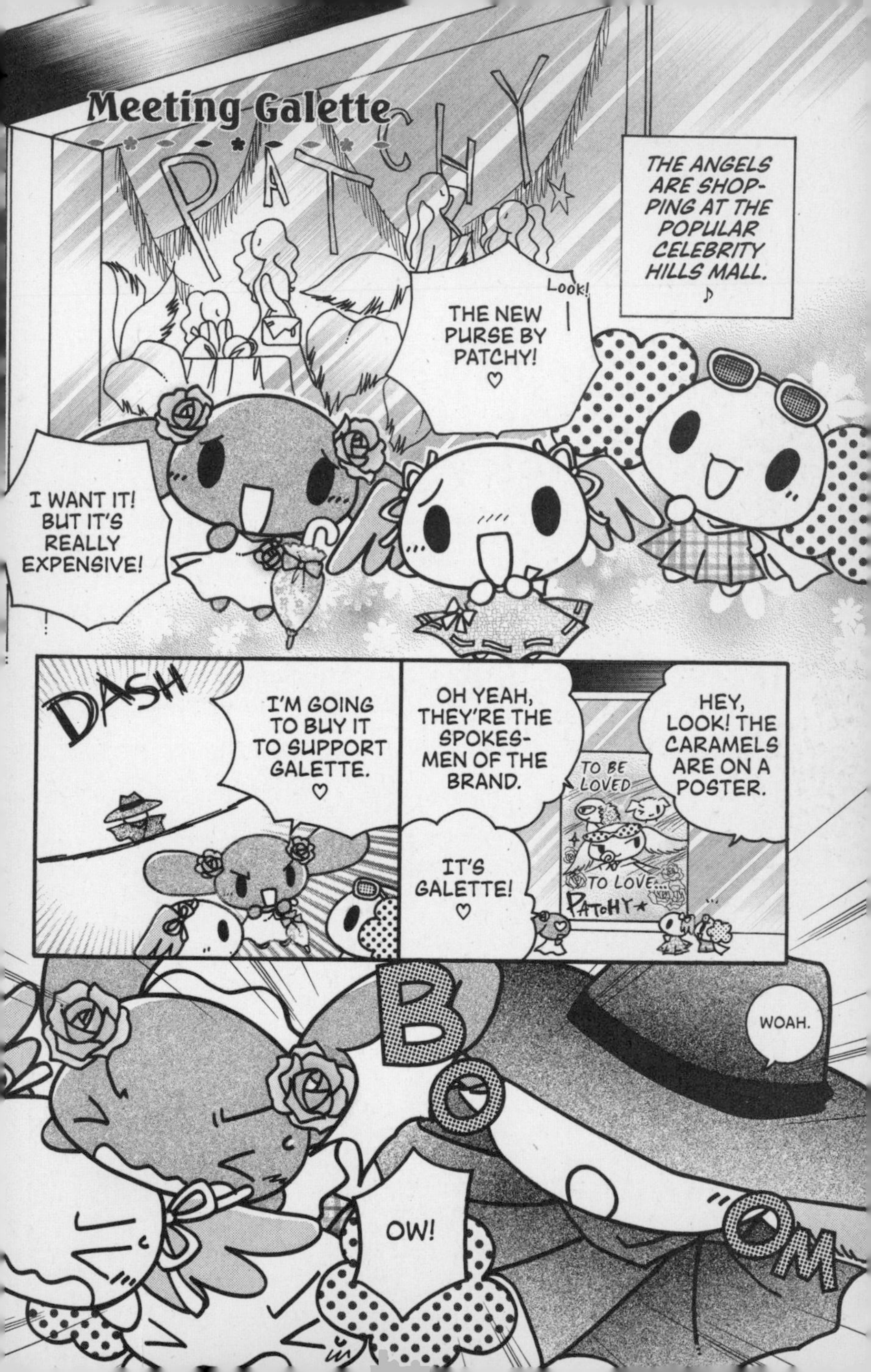

Meeting Galette
THE ANGELS ARE SHOPPING AT THE POPULAR CELEBRITY HILLS MALL. ♪
PATCHY
Look!
THE NEW PURSE BY PATCHY! ♡
I WANT IT! BUT IT'S REALLY EXPENSIVE!
HEY, LOOK! THE CARAMELS ARE ON A POSTER.
OH YEAH, THEY'RE THE SPOKESMEN OF THE BRAND.
TO BE LOVED
TO LOVE...
PATCHY★
IT'S GALETTE! ♡
I'M GOING TO BUY IT TO SUPPORT GALETTE. ♡
DASH
WOAH.
BOOM
OW!

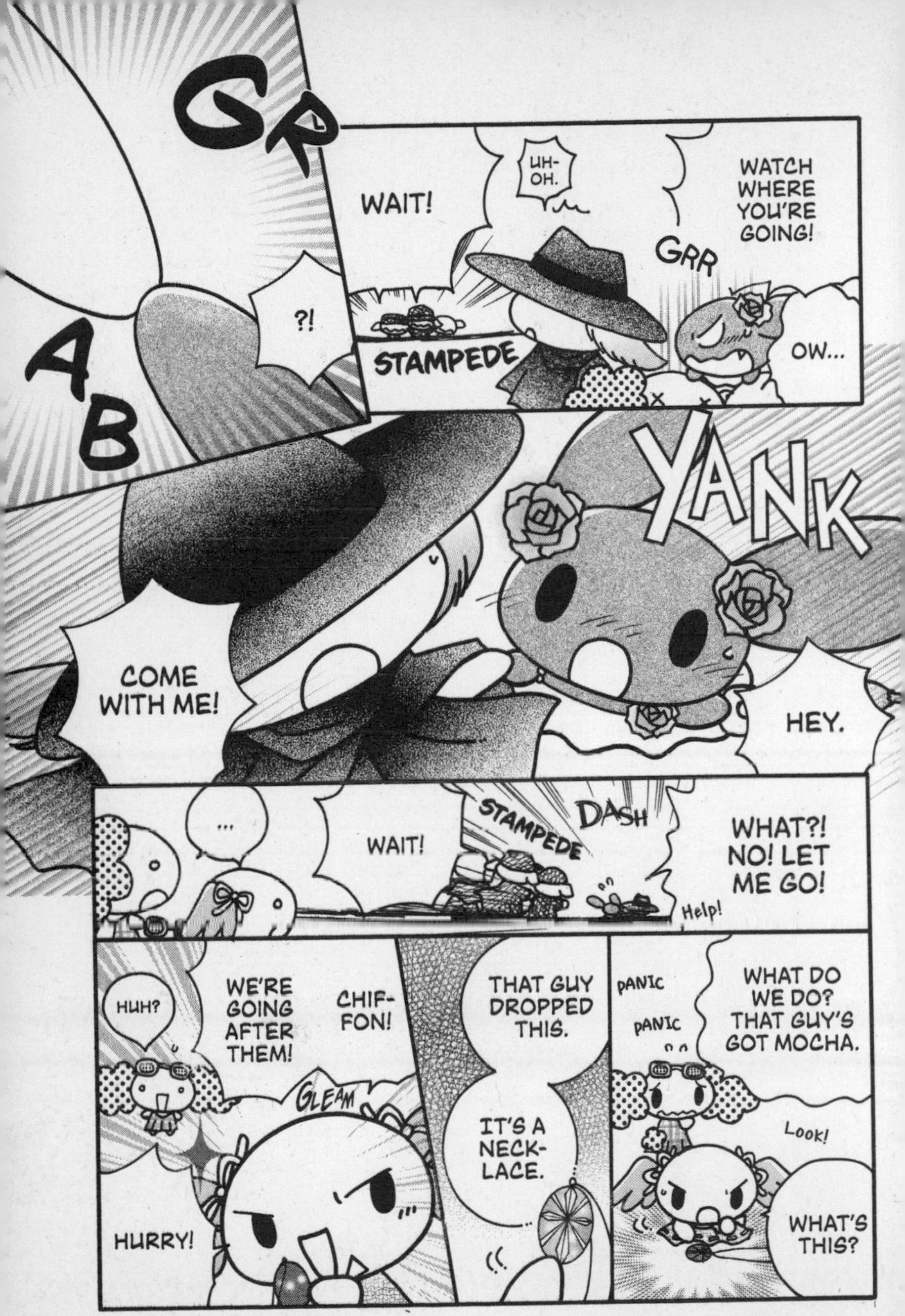
WATCH WHERE YOU'RE GOING!
GRR
UH-OH.
WAIT!
OW...
STAMPEDE
GRAB
?!
YANK
HEY.
COME WITH ME!
WHAT?! NO! LET ME GO!
Help!
DASH
STAMPEDE
WAIT!
...
WHAT DO WE DO? THAT GUY'S GOT MOCHA.
PANIC
PANIC
Look!
WHAT'S THIS?
THAT GUY DROPPED THIS.
IT'S A NECK-LACE.
CHIF-FON!
WE'RE GOING AFTER THEM!
HUH?
GLEAM
HURRY!

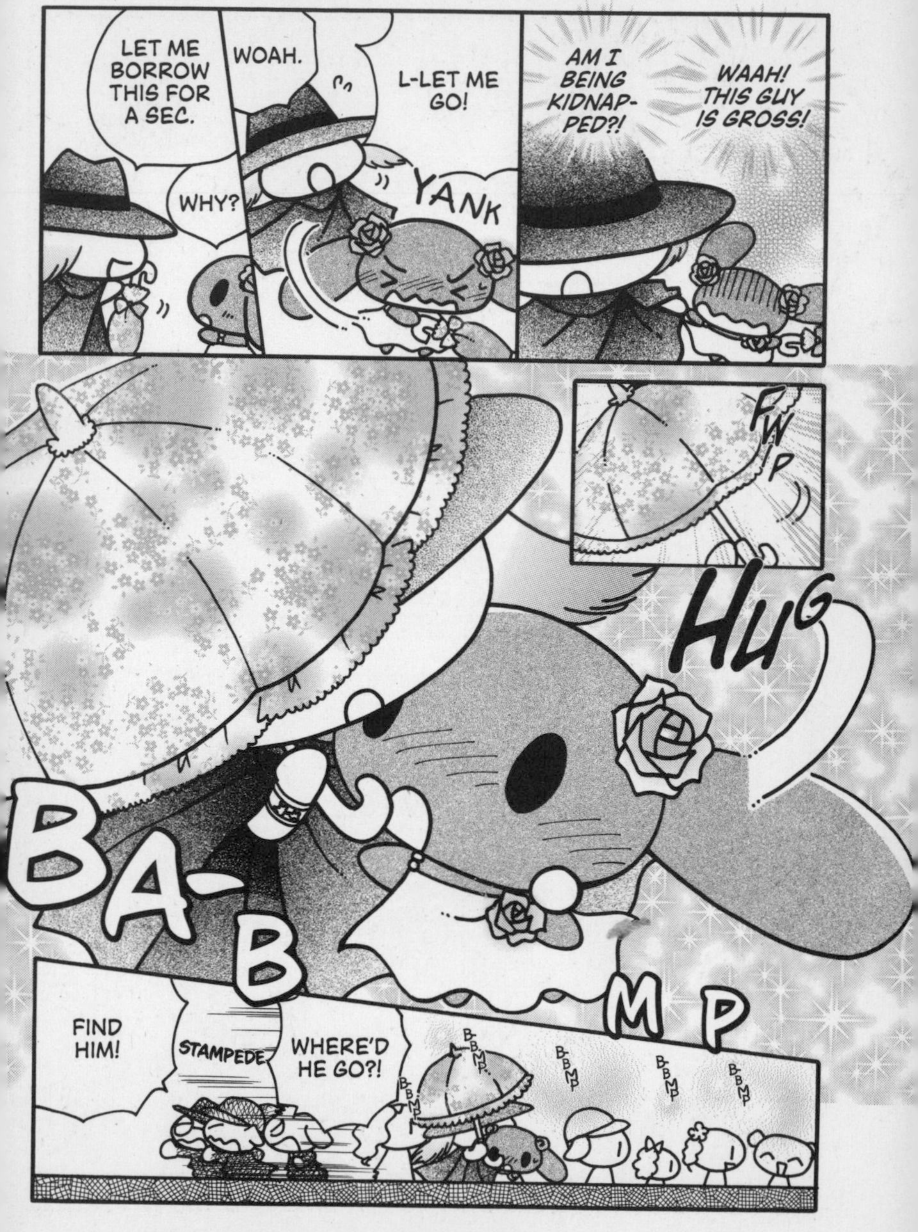

WAAH! THIS GUY IS GROSS!
AM I BEING KIDNAP-PED?!
L-LET ME GO!
WOAH.
YANK
LET ME BORROW THIS FOR A SEC.
WHY?
FWP
HUG
BA-BMP
B-BMP
B-BMP
B-BMP
B-BMP
B-BMP
WHERE'D HE GO?!
STAMPEDE
FIND HIM!

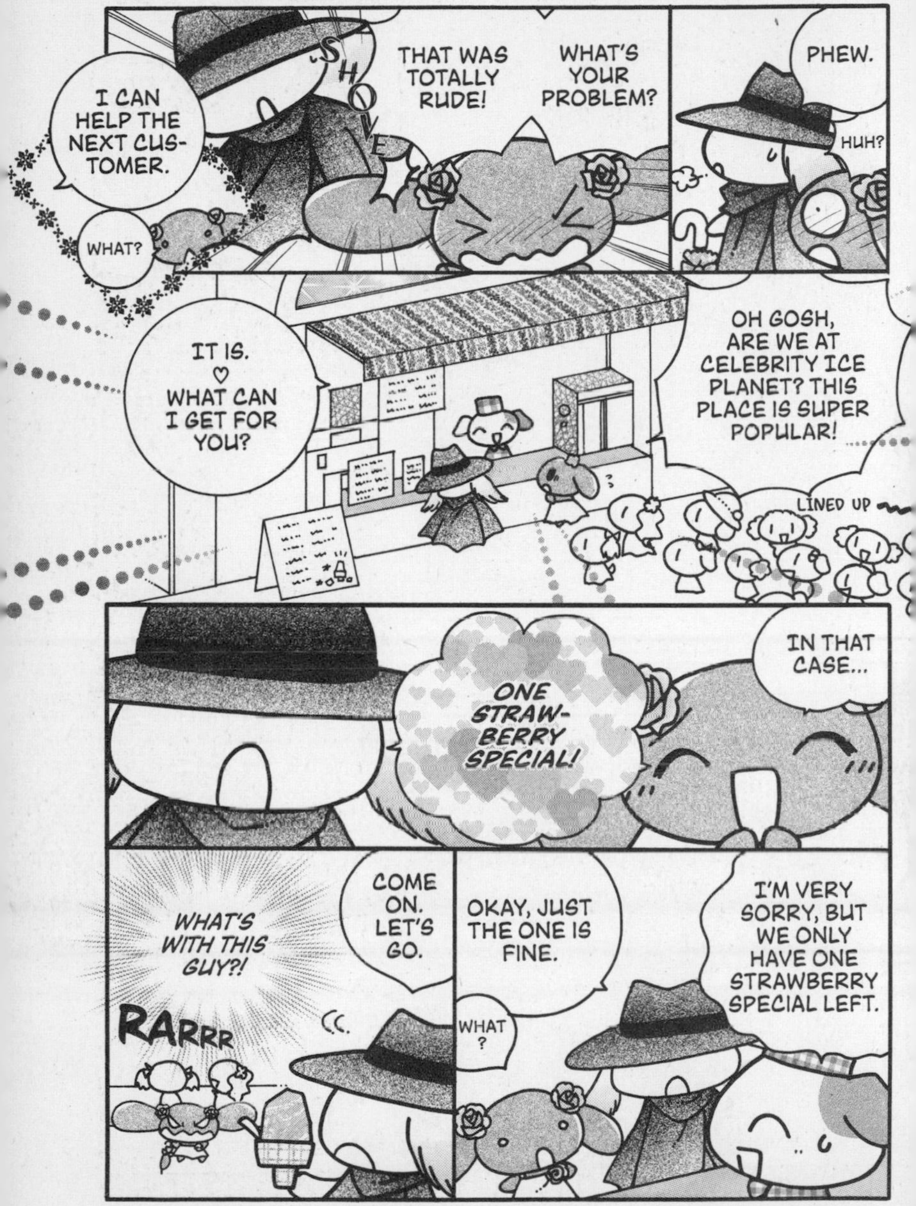
PHEW.
HUH?
WHAT'S YOUR PROBLEM?
THAT WAS TOTALLY RUDE!
SHOVE
I CAN HELP THE NEXT CUS-TOMER.
WHAT?
OH GOSH, ARE WE AT CELEBRITY ICE PLANET? THIS PLACE IS SUPER POPULAR!
LINED UP
IT IS. ♡ WHAT CAN I GET FOR YOU?
IN THAT CASE...
ONE STRAW-BERRY SPECIAL!
I'M VERY SORRY, BUT WE ONLY HAVE ONE STRAWBERRY SPECIAL LEFT.
OKAY, JUST THE ONE IS FINE.
WHAT?
COME ON. LET'S GO.
WHAT'S WITH THIS GUY?!
RARRR

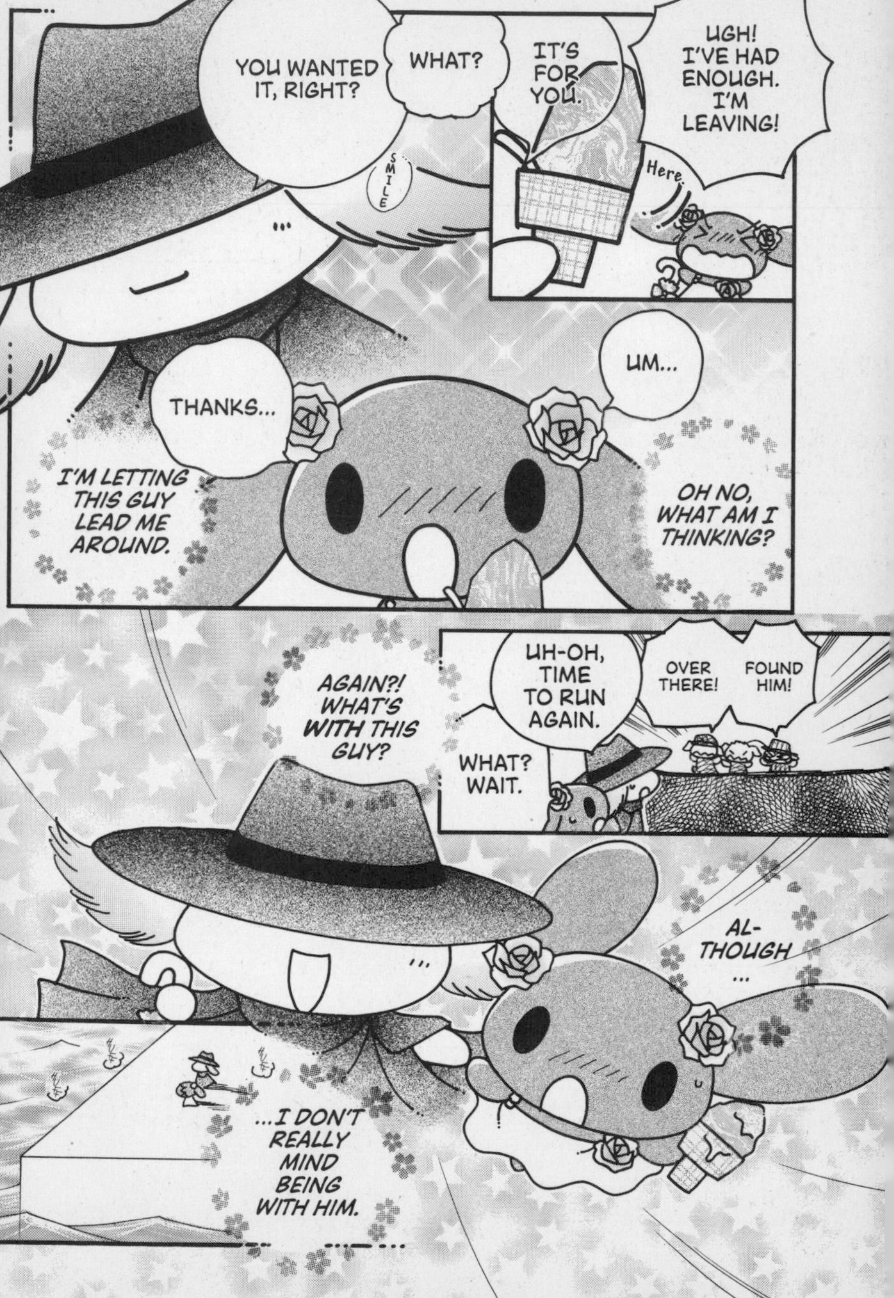
UGH! I'VE HAD ENOUGH. I'M LEAVING!
Here.
IT'S FOR YOU.
WHAT?
YOU WANTED IT, RIGHT?
SMILE
...
UM...
THANKS...
OH NO, WHAT AM I THINKING?
I'M LETTING THIS GUY LEAD ME AROUND.
FOUND HIM!
OVER THERE!
UH-OH, TIME TO RUN AGAIN.
WHAT? WAIT.
AGAIN?! WHAT'S WITH THIS GUY?
...
AL-THOUGH ...
...I DON'T REALLY MIND BEING WITH HIM.

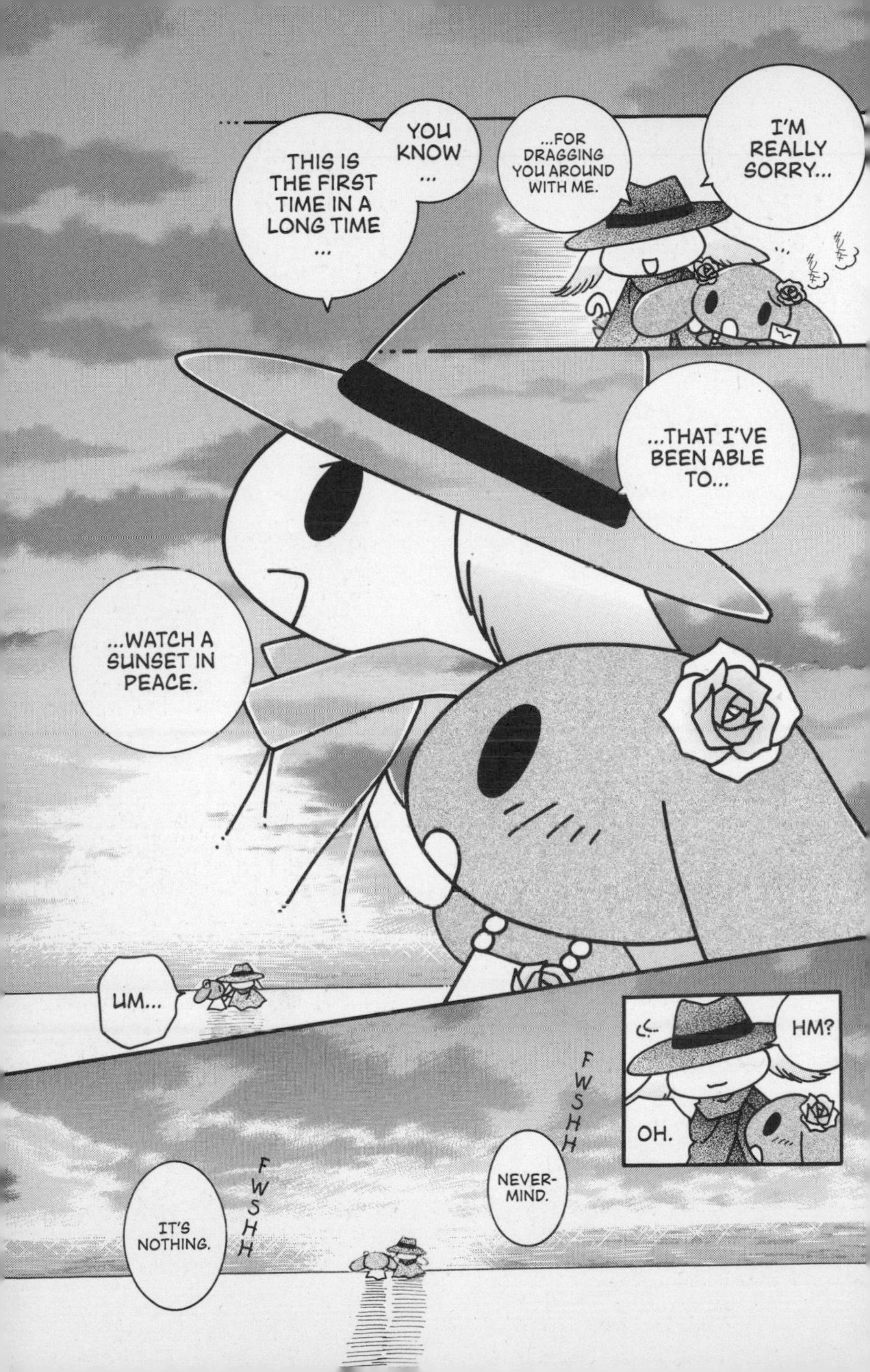
I'M REALLY SORRY...
...FOR DRAGGING YOU AROUND WITH ME.
YOU KNOW ...
THIS IS THE FIRST TIME IN A LONG TIME ...
...THAT I'VE BEEN ABLE TO...
...WATCH A SUNSET IN PEACE.
UM...
HM?
OH.
FWSHH
NEVER-MIND.
FWSHH
IT'S NOTHING.

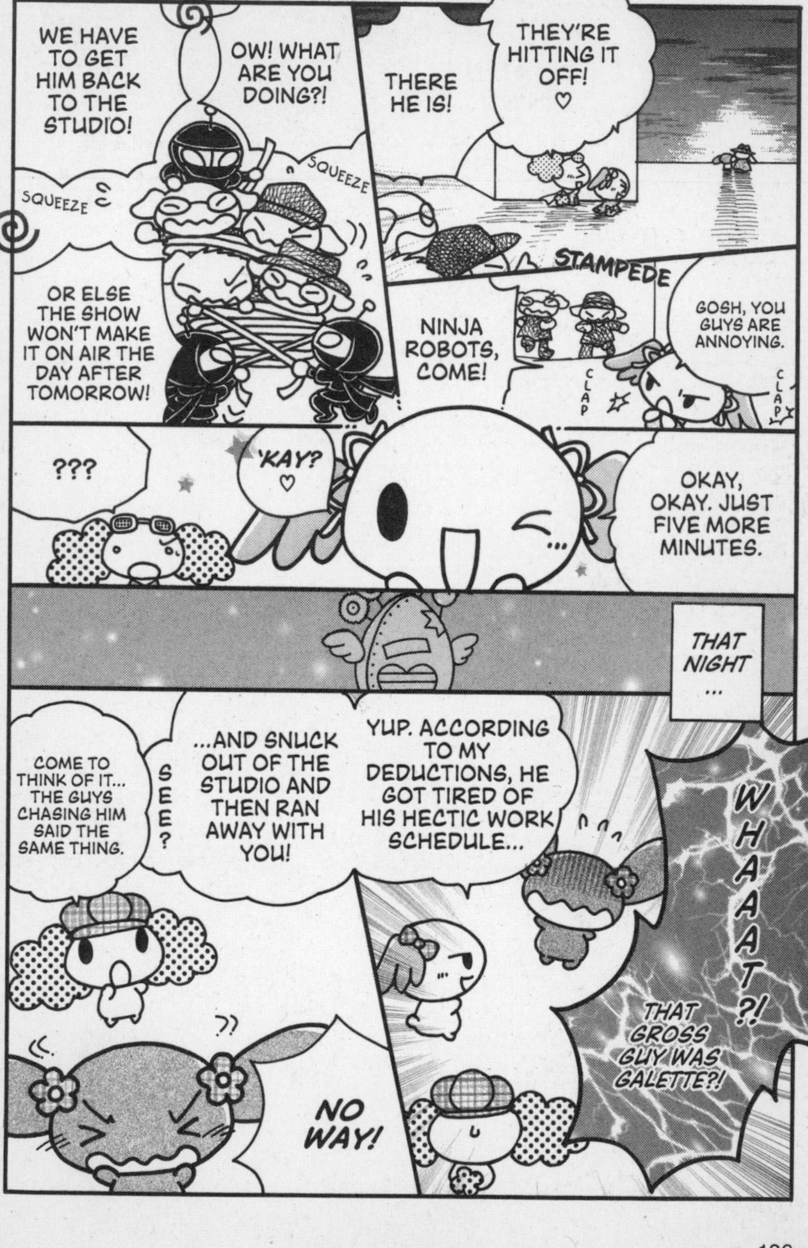
THEY'RE HITTING IT OFF! ♡
THERE HE IS!
STAMPEDE
GOSH, YOU GUYS ARE ANNOYING.
CLAP
CLAP
NINJA ROBOTS, COME!
OW! WHAT ARE YOU DOING?!
WE HAVE TO GET HIM BACK TO THE STUDIO!
SQUEEZE
SQUEEZE
OR ELSE THE SHOW WON'T MAKE IT ON AIR THE DAY AFTER TOMORROW!
OKAY, OKAY. JUST FIVE MORE MINUTES.
'KAY? ♡
???
THAT NIGHT...
YUP. ACCORDING TO MY DEDUCTIONS, HE GOT TIRED OF HIS HECTIC WORK SCHEDULE...
...AND SNUCK OUT OF THE STUDIO AND THEN RAN AWAY WITH YOU!
SEE?
COME TO THINK OF IT... THE GUYS CHASING HIM SAID THE SAME THING.
WHAAAAT?!
THAT GROSS GUY WAS GALETTE?!
NO WAY!

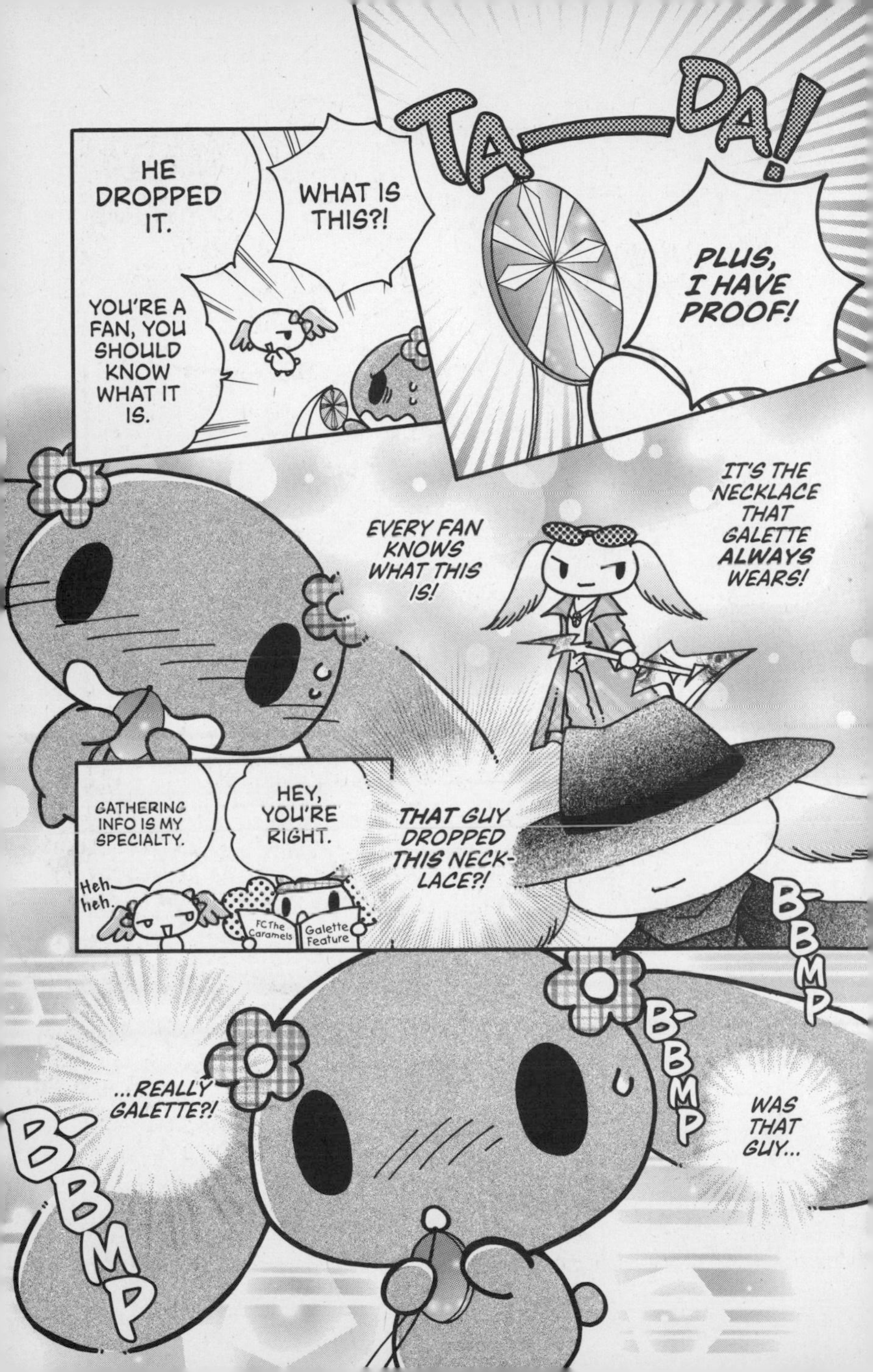
TA—DA!
PLUS, I HAVE PROOF!
WHAT IS THIS?!
HE DROPPED IT.
YOU'RE A FAN, YOU SHOULD KNOW WHAT IT IS.
IT'S THE NECKLACE THAT GALETTE ALWAYS WEARS!
EVERY FAN KNOWS WHAT THIS IS!
THAT GUY DROPPED THIS NECK-LACE?!
B-BMP
HEY, YOU'RE RIGHT.
GATHERING INFO IS MY SPECIALTY.
Heh heh.
FC The Caramels
Galette Feature
B-BMP
WAS THAT GUY...
...REALLY GALETTE?!
B-BMP

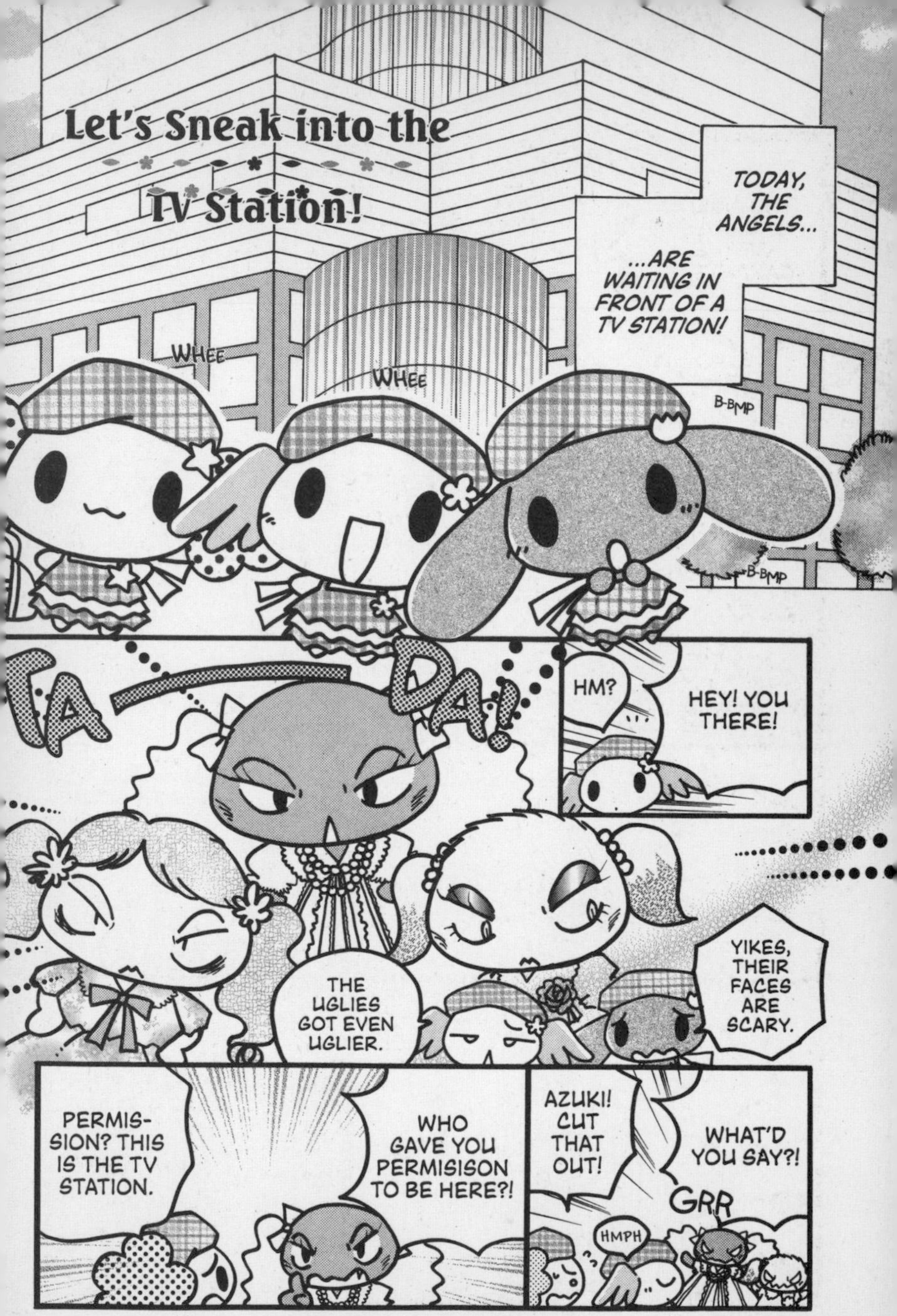
Let's Sneak into the TV Station!
TODAY, THE ANGELS...
...ARE WAITING IN FRONT OF A TV STATION!
B-BMP
WHEE
WHEE
B-BMP
HEY! YOU THERE!
HM?
TA-DA!
YIKES, THEIR FACES ARE SCARY.
THE UGLIES GOT EVEN UGLIER.
WHAT'D YOU SAY?!
AZUKI! CUT THAT OUT!
GRR
HMPH
WHO GAVE YOU PERMISISON TO BE HERE?!
PERMIS-SION? THIS IS THE TV STATION.

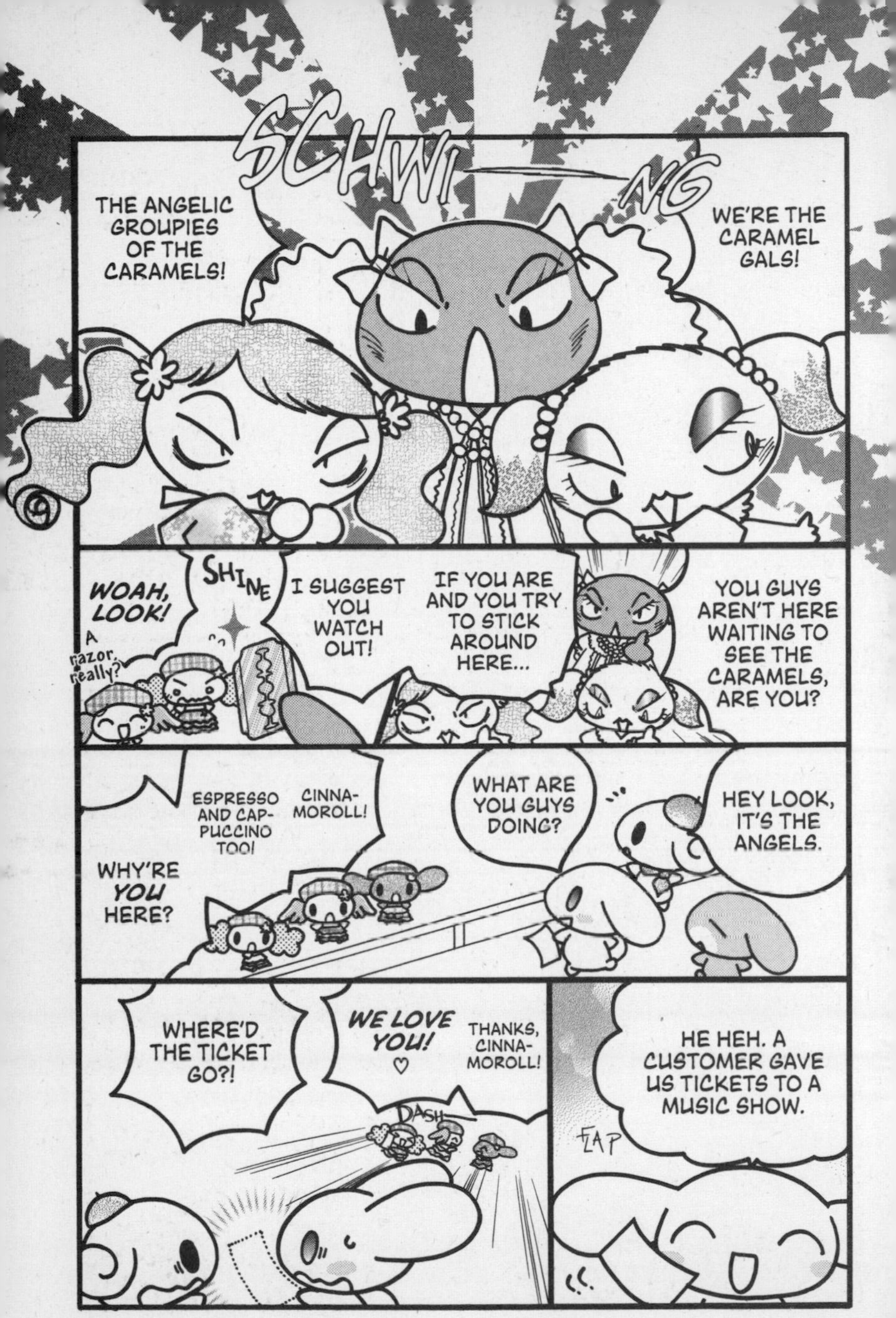
SCHWI—NG
WE'RE THE CARAMEL GALS!
THE ANGELIC GROUPIES OF THE CARAMELS!
YOU GUYS AREN'T HERE WAITING TO SEE THE CARAMELS, ARE YOU?
IF YOU ARE AND YOU TRY TO STICK AROUND HERE...
I SUGGEST YOU WATCH OUT!
SHINE
WOAH, LOOK!
A razor, really?
HEY LOOK, IT'S THE ANGELS.
WHAT ARE YOU GUYS DOING?
CINNA-MOROLL!
ESPRESSO AND CAP-PUCCINO TOO!
WHY'RE *YOU* HERE?
HE HEH. A CUSTOMER GAVE US TICKETS TO A MUSIC SHOW.
FLAP
THANKS, CINNA-MOROLL!
WE LOVE YOU! ♡
WHERE'D THE TICKET GO?!
DASH

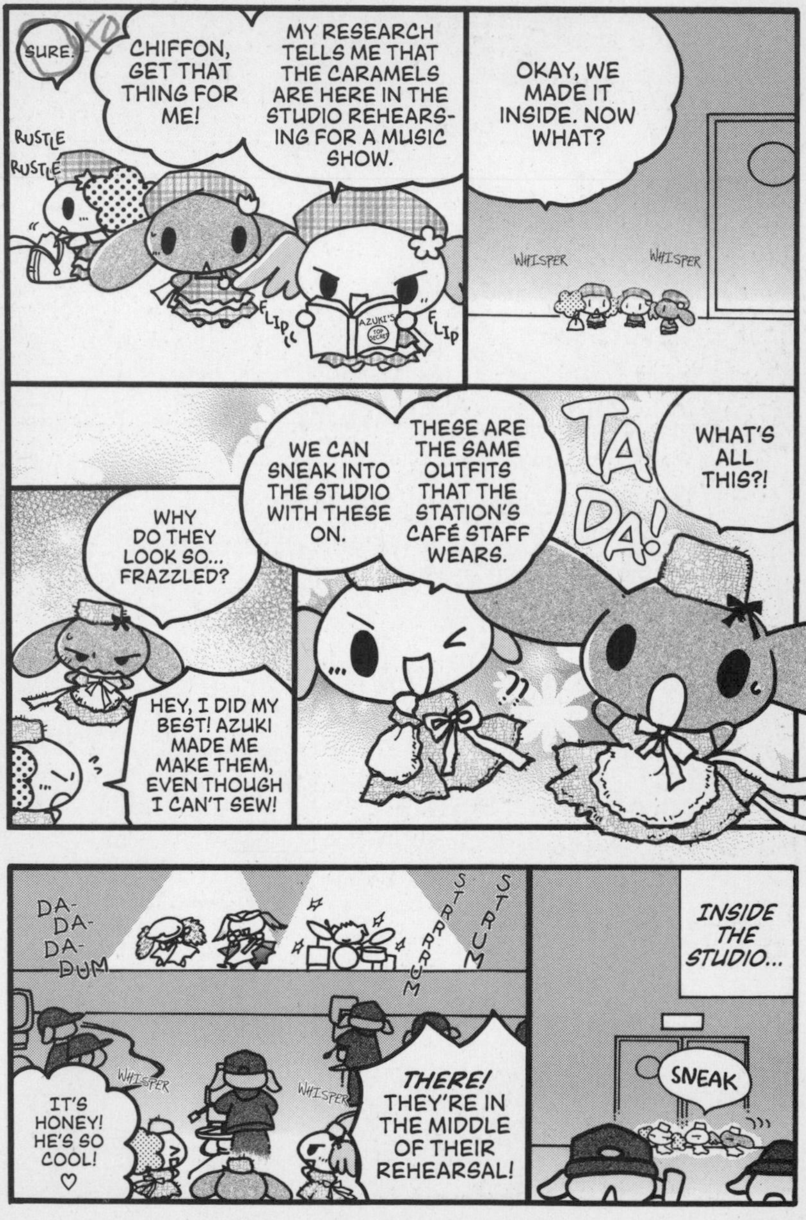
OKAY, WE MADE IT INSIDE. NOW WHAT?
WHISPER
WHISPER
MY RESEARCH TELLS ME THAT THE CARAMELS ARE HERE IN THE STUDIO REHEARS-ING FOR A MUSIC SHOW.
CHIFFON, GET THAT THING FOR ME!
SURE.
RUSTLE
RUSTLE
FLIP
FLIP
AZUKI'S
TOP SECRET
WHAT'S ALL THIS?!
TA DA!
THESE ARE THE SAME OUTFITS THAT THE STATION'S CAFÉ STAFF WEARS.
WE CAN SNEAK INTO THE STUDIO WITH THESE ON.
WHY DO THEY LOOK SO... FRAZZLED?
HEY, I DID MY BEST! AZUKI MADE ME MAKE THEM, EVEN THOUGH I CAN'T SEW!
INSIDE THE STUDIO...
SNEAK
STRUM
STRRRUM
DA-DA-DA-DUM
THERE! THEY'RE IN THE MIDDLE OF THEIR REHEARSAL!
WHISPER
WHISPER
IT'S HONEY! HE'S SO COOL! ♡

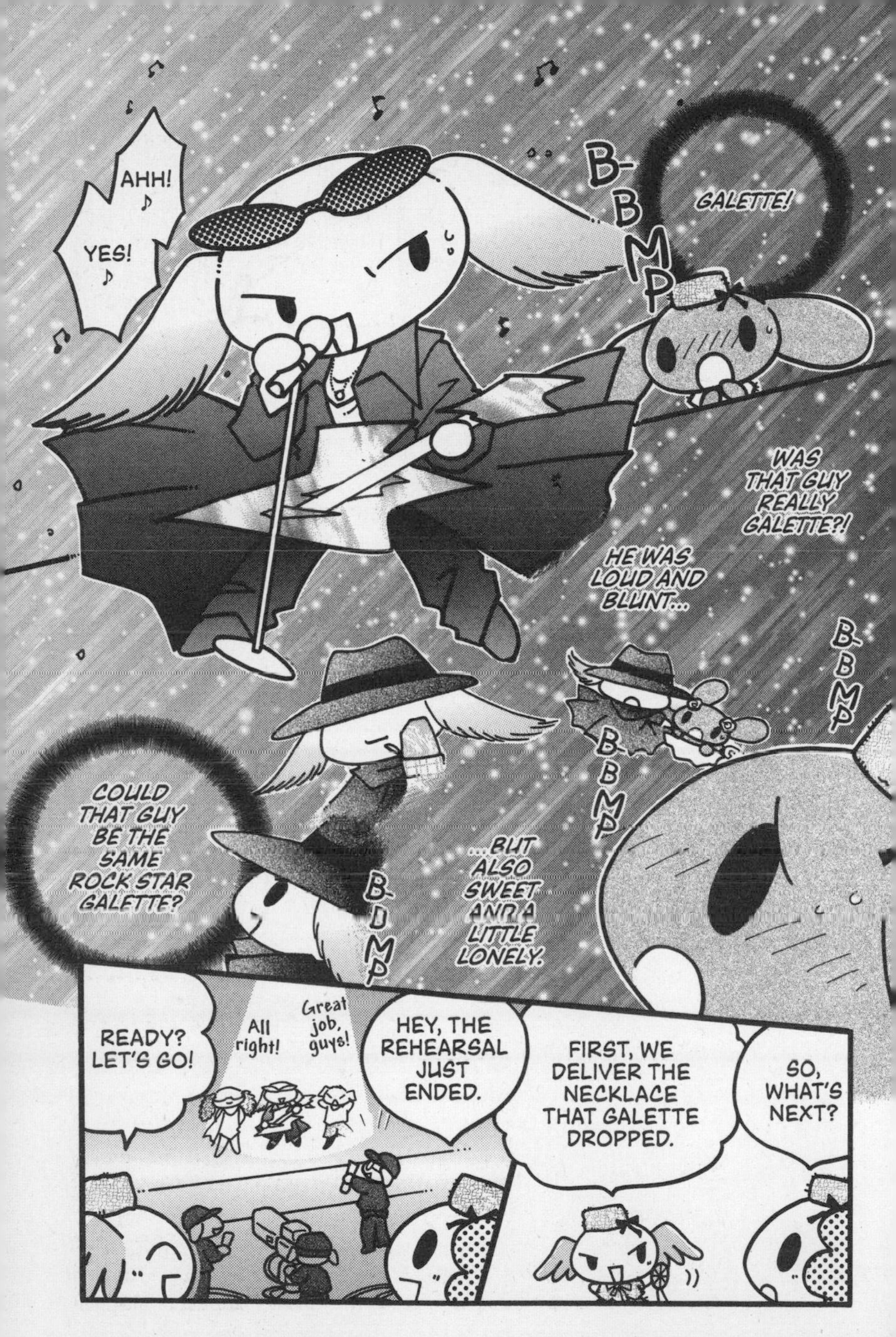
B-BMP
GALETTE!
AHH! ♪
YES! ♪
WAS THAT GUY REALLY GALETTE?!
HE WAS LOUD AND BLUNT...
B-BMP
B-BMP
...BUT ALSO SWEET AND A LITTLE LONELY.
B-BMP
COULD THAT GUY BE THE SAME ROCK STAR GALETTE?
SO, WHAT'S NEXT?
FIRST, WE DELIVER THE NECKLACE THAT GALETTE DROPPED.
HEY, THE REHEARSAL JUST ENDED.
Great job, guys!
All right!
READY? LET'S GO!

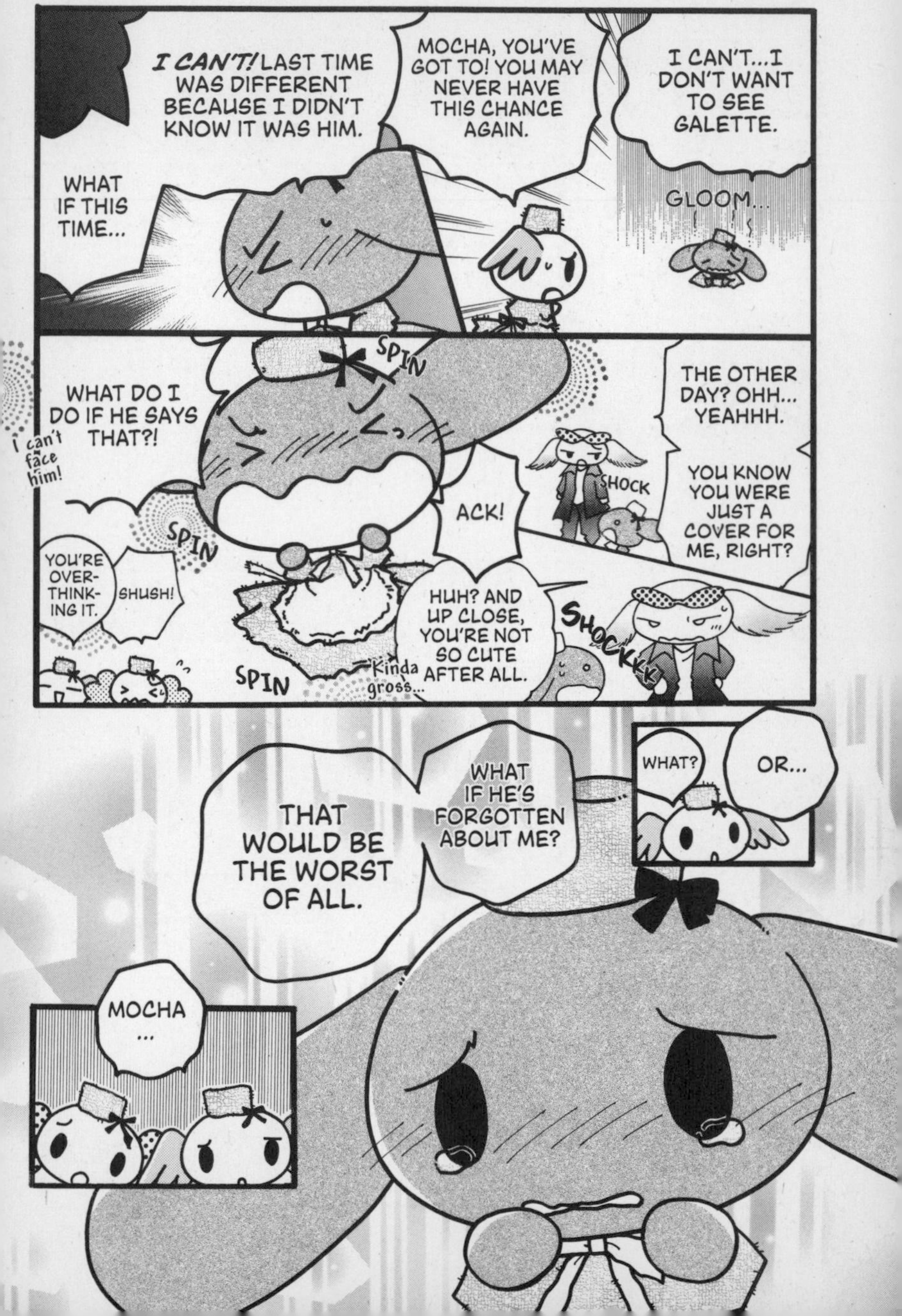
I CAN'T...I DON'T WANT TO SEE GALETTE.
GLOOM...
MOCHA, YOU'VE GOT TO! YOU MAY NEVER HAVE THIS CHANCE AGAIN.
I CAN'T! LAST TIME WAS DIFFERENT BECAUSE I DIDN'T KNOW IT WAS HIM.
WHAT IF THIS TIME...
THE OTHER DAY? OHH... YEAHHH.
YOU KNOW YOU WERE JUST A COVER FOR ME, RIGHT?
SHOCK
ACK!
HUH? AND UP CLOSE, YOU'RE NOT SO CUTE AFTER ALL.
SHOCKKK
Kinda gross...
SPIN
WHAT DO I DO IF HE SAYS THAT?!
I can't face him!
SPIN
SHUSH!
YOU'RE OVER-THINKING IT.
SPIN
OR...
WHAT?
WHAT IF HE'S FORGOTTEN ABOUT ME?
THAT WOULD BE THE WORST OF ALL.
MOCHA ...

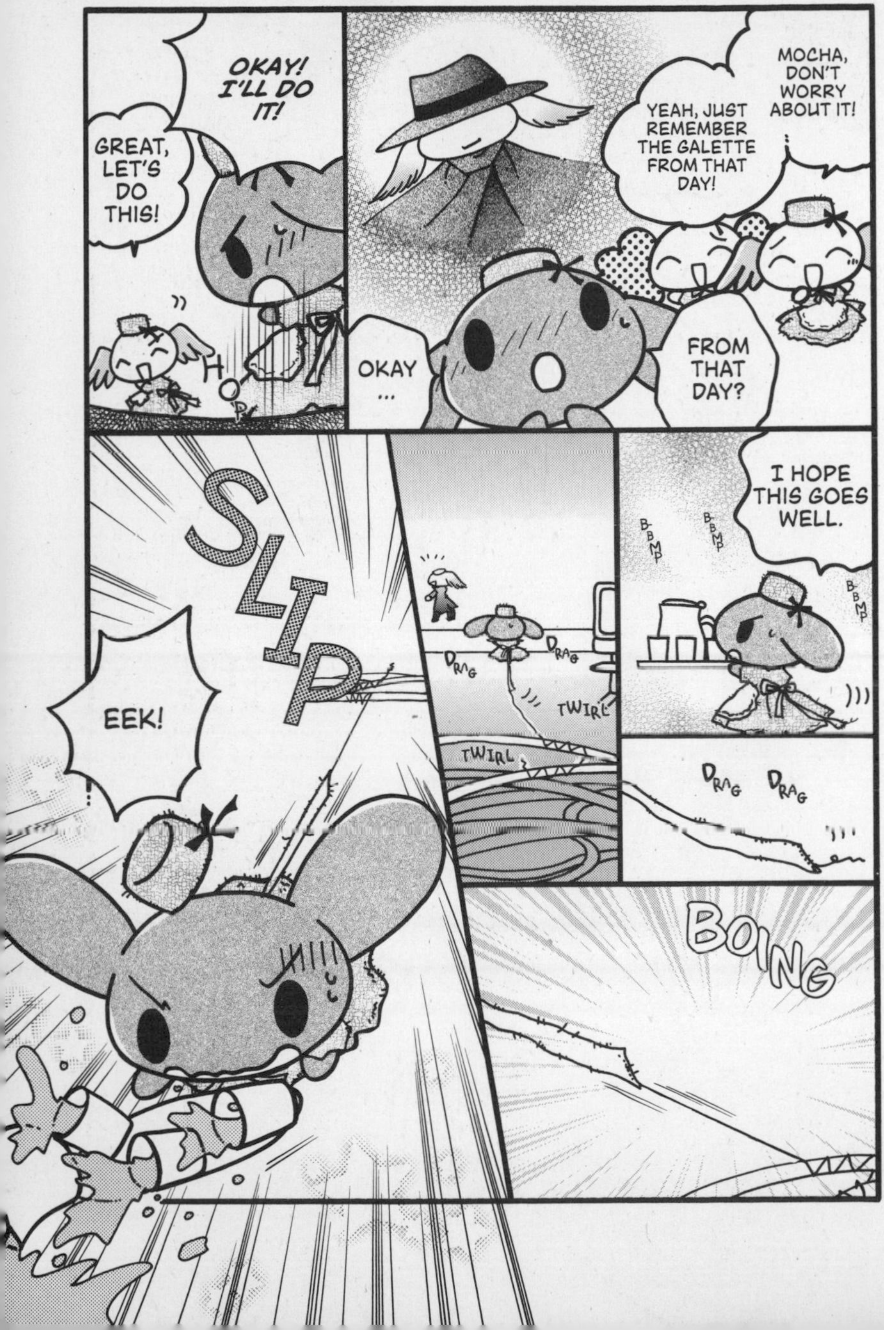
MOCHA, DON'T WORRY ABOUT IT!
YEAH, JUST REMEMBER THE GALETTE FROM THAT DAY!
FROM THAT DAY?
OKAY ...
OKAY! I'LL DO IT!
GREAT, LET'S DO THIS!
HOP
I HOPE THIS GOES WELL.
B-BMP
B-BMP
B-BMP
DRAG
DRAG
DRAG
DRAG
TWIRL
TWIRL
BOING
SLIP
EEK!

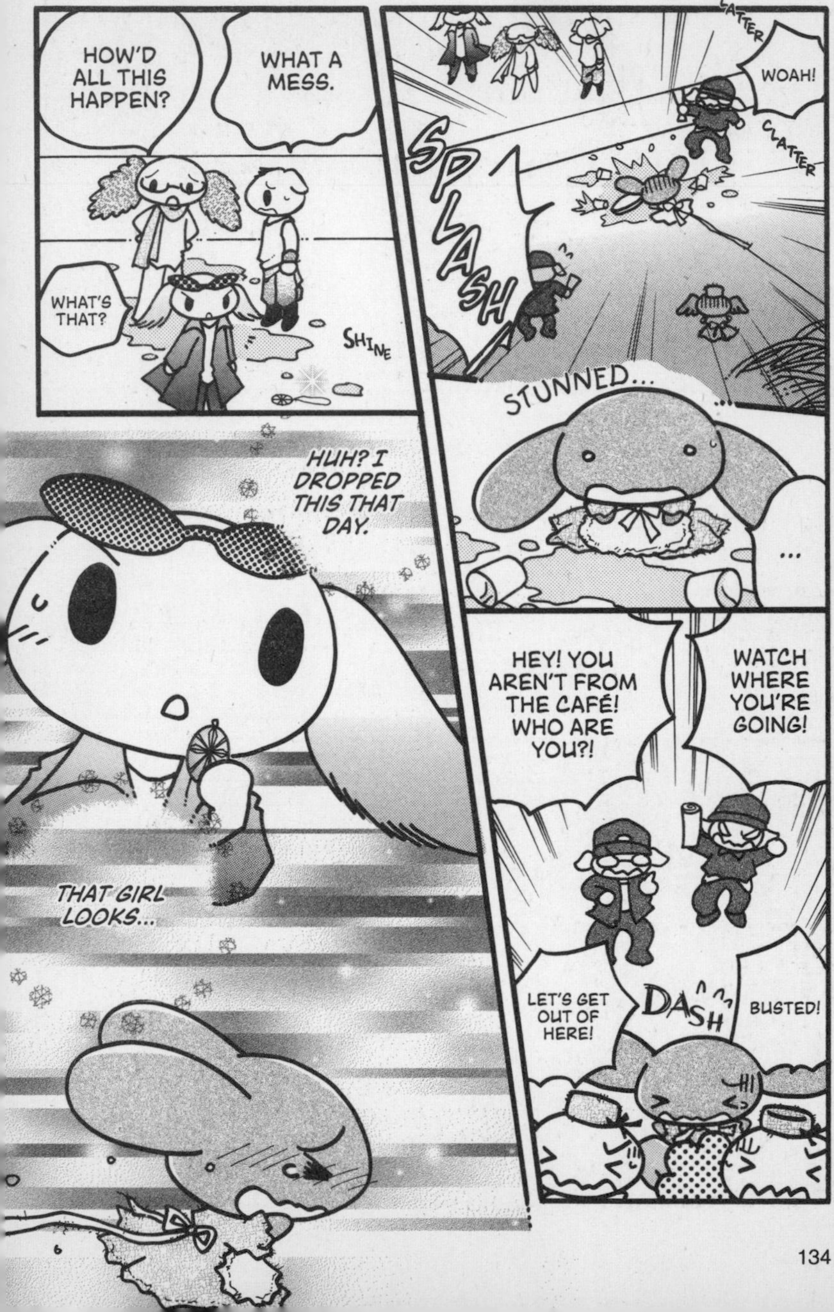
CLATTER
WOAH!
CLATTER
SPLASH
STUNNED...
...
WATCH WHERE YOU'RE GOING!
HEY! YOU AREN'T FROM THE CAFÉ! WHO ARE YOU?!
BUSTED!
DASH
LET'S GET OUT OF HERE!
WHAT A MESS.
HOW'D ALL THIS HAPPEN?
SHINE
WHAT'S THAT?
HUH? I DROPPED THIS THAT DAY.
THAT GIRL LOOKS...

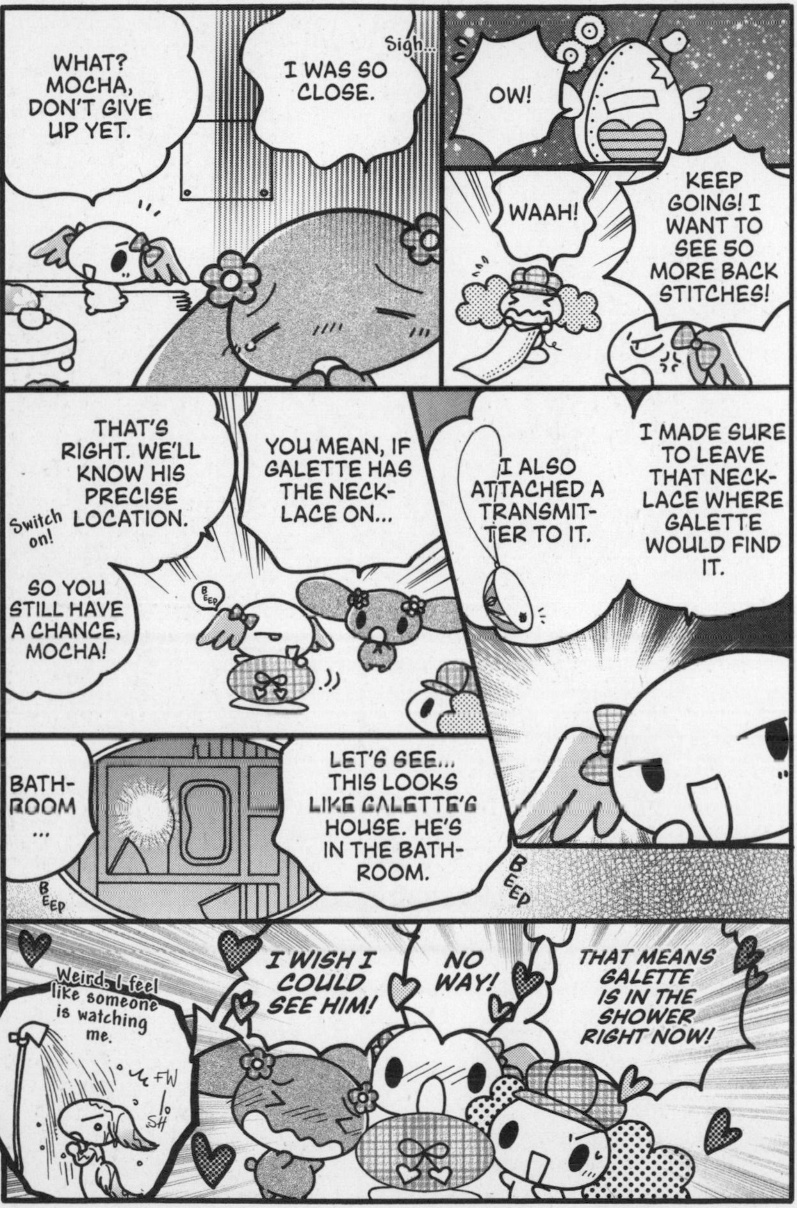
OW!
KEEP GOING! I WANT TO SEE 50 MORE BACK STITCHES!
WAAH!
Sigh...
I WAS SO CLOSE.
WHAT? MOCHA, DON'T GIVE UP YET.
I MADE SURE TO LEAVE THAT NECKLACE WHERE GALETTE WOULD FIND IT.
I ALSO ATTACHED A TRANSMITTER TO IT.
YOU MEAN, IF GALETTE HAS THE NECKLACE ON...
THAT'S RIGHT. WE'LL KNOW HIS PRECISE LOCATION.
Switch on!
BEEP
SO YOU STILL HAVE A CHANCE, MOCHA!
BEEP
LET'S SEE... THIS LOOKS LIKE GALETTE'S HOUSE. HE'S IN THE BATHROOM.
BATHROOM ...
BEEP
THAT MEANS GALETTE IS IN THE SHOWER RIGHT NOW!
NO WAY!
I WISH I COULD SEE HIM!
Weird. I feel like someone is watching me.
FW
SH

Following the Band!

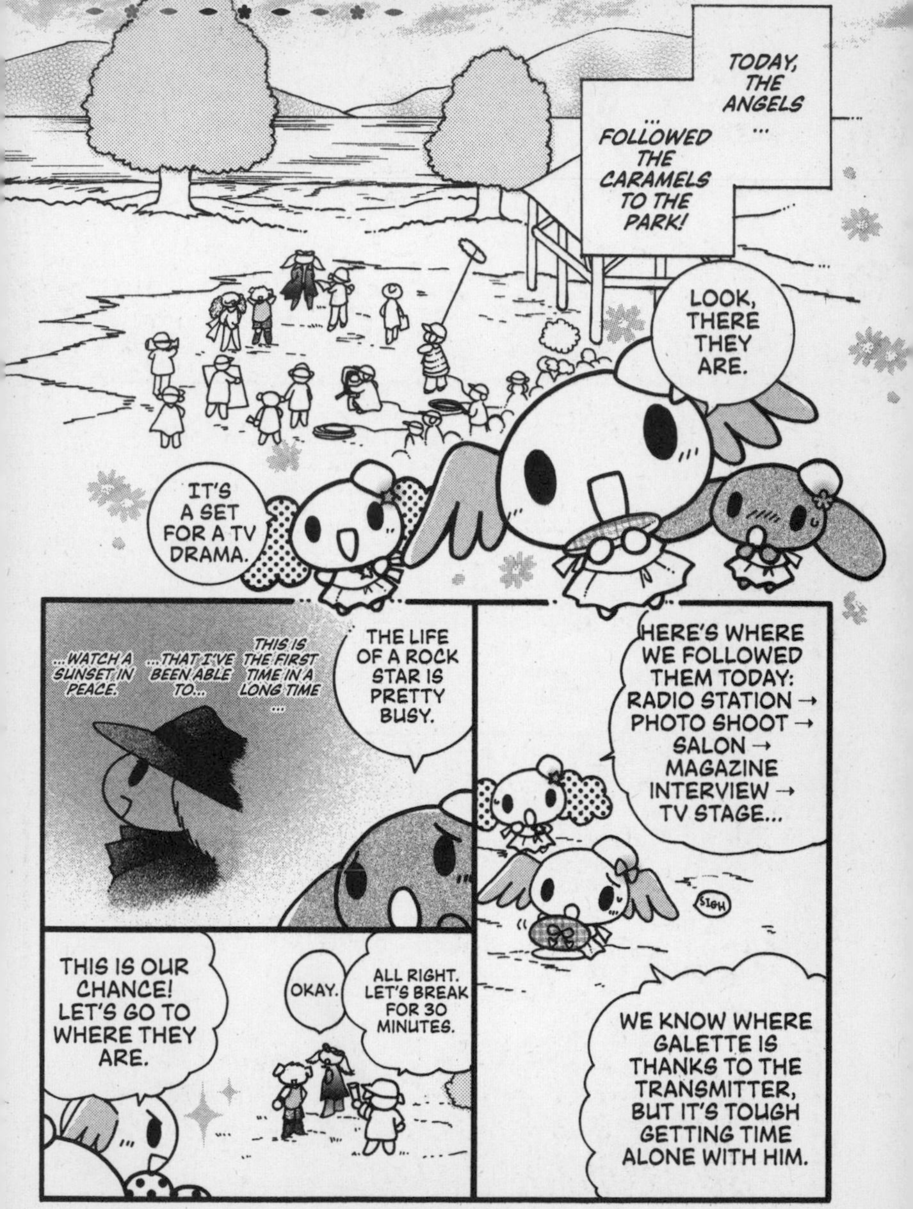
TODAY, THE ANGELS ...
... FOLLOWED THE CARAMELS TO THE PARK!
LOOK, THERE THEY ARE.
IT'S A SET FOR A TV DRAMA.
HERE'S WHERE WE FOLLOWED THEM TODAY: RADIO STATION → PHOTO SHOOT → SALON → MAGAZINE INTERVIEW → TV STAGE...
SIGH
THE LIFE OF A ROCK STAR IS PRETTY BUSY.
THIS IS THE FIRST TIME IN A LONG TIME ...
...THAT I'VE BEEN ABLE TO...
...WATCH A SUNSET IN PEACE.
WE KNOW WHERE GALETTE IS THANKS TO THE TRANSMITTER, BUT IT'S TOUGH GETTING TIME ALONE WITH HIM.
ALL RIGHT. LET'S BREAK FOR 30 MINUTES.
OKAY.
THIS IS OUR CHANCE! LET'S GO TO WHERE THEY ARE.
...

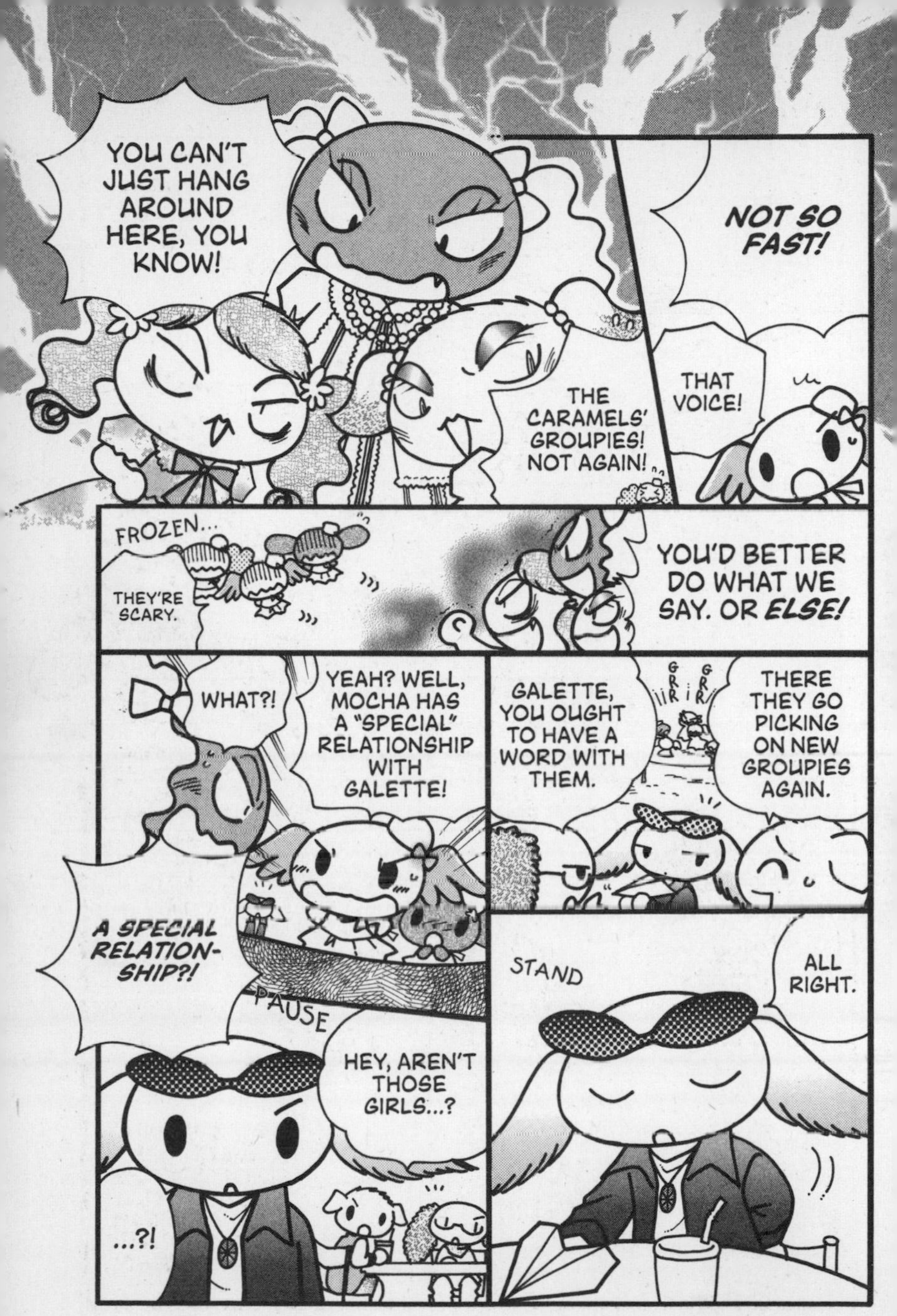
NOT SO FAST!
THAT VOICE!
YOU CAN'T JUST HANG AROUND HERE, YOU KNOW!
THE CARAMELS' GROUPIES! NOT AGAIN!
YOU'D BETTER DO WHAT WE SAY. OR ELSE!
FROZEN...
THEY'RE SCARY.
THERE THEY GO PICKING ON NEW GROUPIES AGAIN.
GRR GRR
GALETTE, YOU OUGHT TO HAVE A WORD WITH THEM.
ALL RIGHT.
STAND
YEAH? WELL, MOCHA HAS A "SPECIAL" RELATIONSHIP WITH GALETTE!
WHAT?!
A SPECIAL RELATIONSHIP?!
PAUSE
HEY, AREN'T THOSE GIRLS...?
...?!

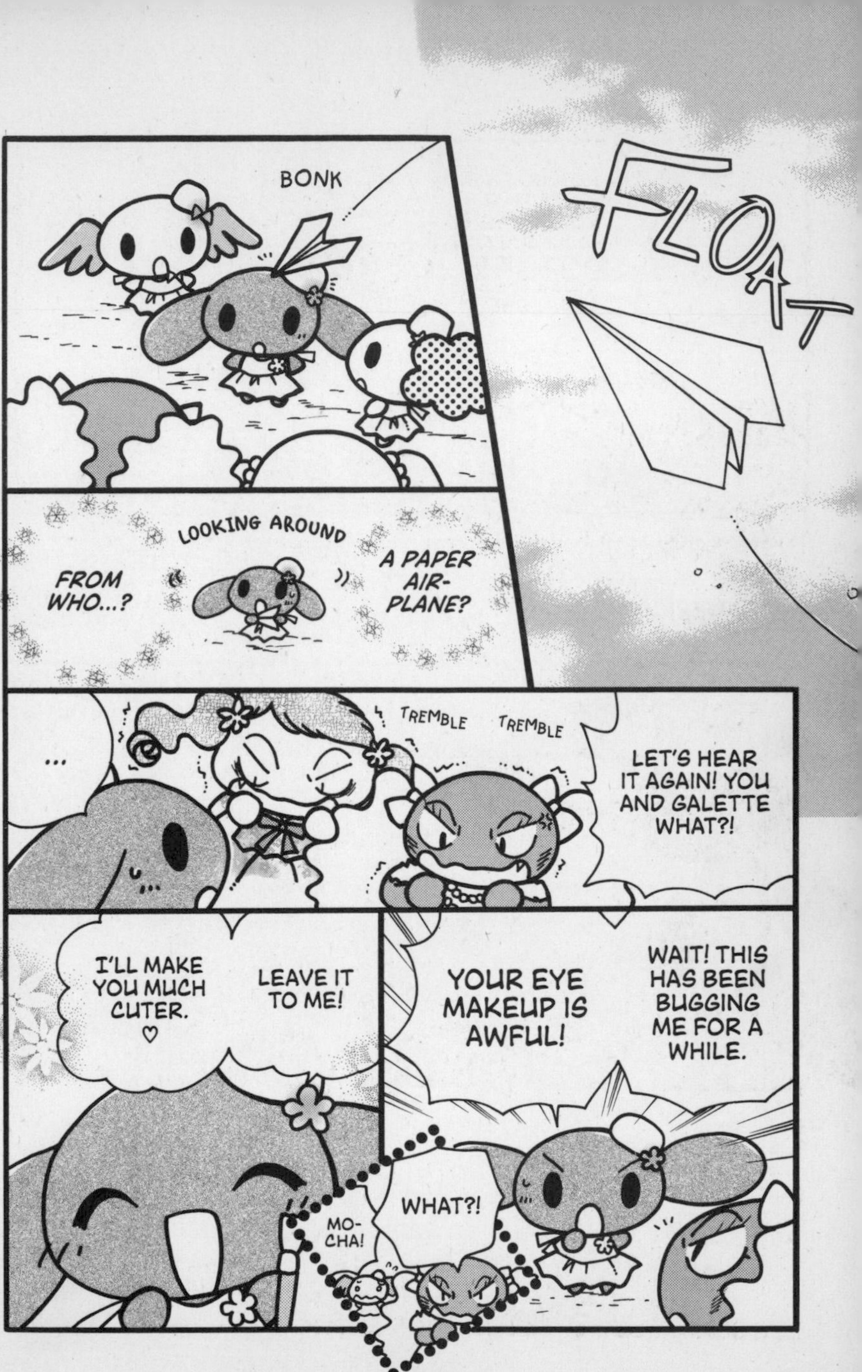
FLOAT
BONK
A PAPER AIR-PLANE?
LOOKING AROUND
FROM WHO...?
LET'S HEAR IT AGAIN! YOU AND GALETTE WHAT?!
TREMBLE TREMBLE
...
WAIT! THIS HAS BEEN BUGGING ME FOR A WHILE.
YOUR EYE MAKEUP IS AWFUL!
WHAT?!
MO-CHA!
LEAVE IT TO ME!
I'LL MAKE YOU MUCH CUTER. ♡

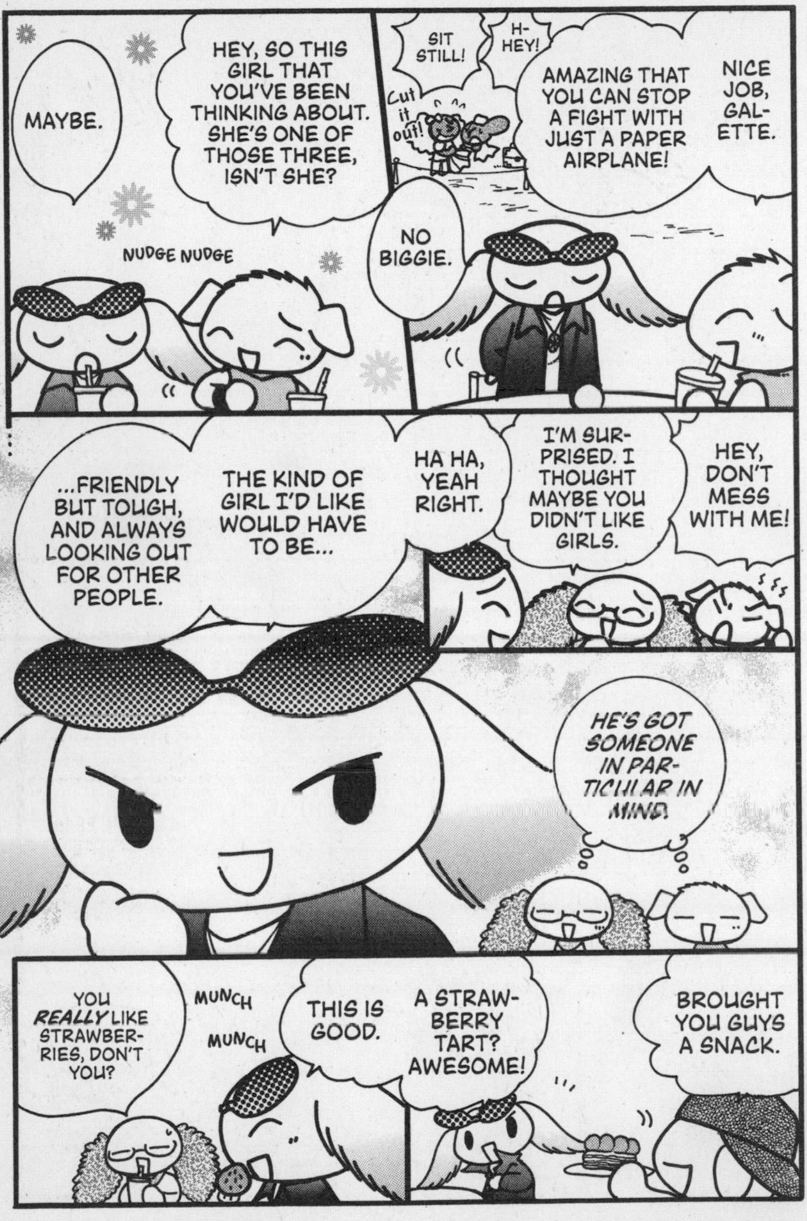
NICE JOB, GALETTE.
AMAZING THAT YOU CAN STOP A FIGHT WITH JUST A PAPER AIRPLANE!
H-HEY!
SIT STILL!
Cut it out!
NO BIGGIE.
HEY, SO THIS GIRL THAT YOU'VE BEEN THINKING ABOUT. SHE'S ONE OF THOSE THREE, ISN'T SHE?
MAYBE.
NUDGE NUDGE
HEY, DON'T MESS WITH ME!
I'M SURPRISED. I THOUGHT MAYBE YOU DIDN'T LIKE GIRLS.
HA HA, YEAH RIGHT.
HE'S GOT SOMEONE IN PARTICULAR IN MIND.
THE KIND OF GIRL I'D LIKE WOULD HAVE TO BE...
...FRIENDLY BUT TOUGH, AND ALWAYS LOOKING OUT FOR OTHER PEOPLE.
BROUGHT YOU GUYS A SNACK.
A STRAWBERRY TART? AWESOME!
THIS IS GOOD.
MUNCH
MUNCH
YOU *REALLY* LIKE STRAWBERRIES, DON'T YOU?

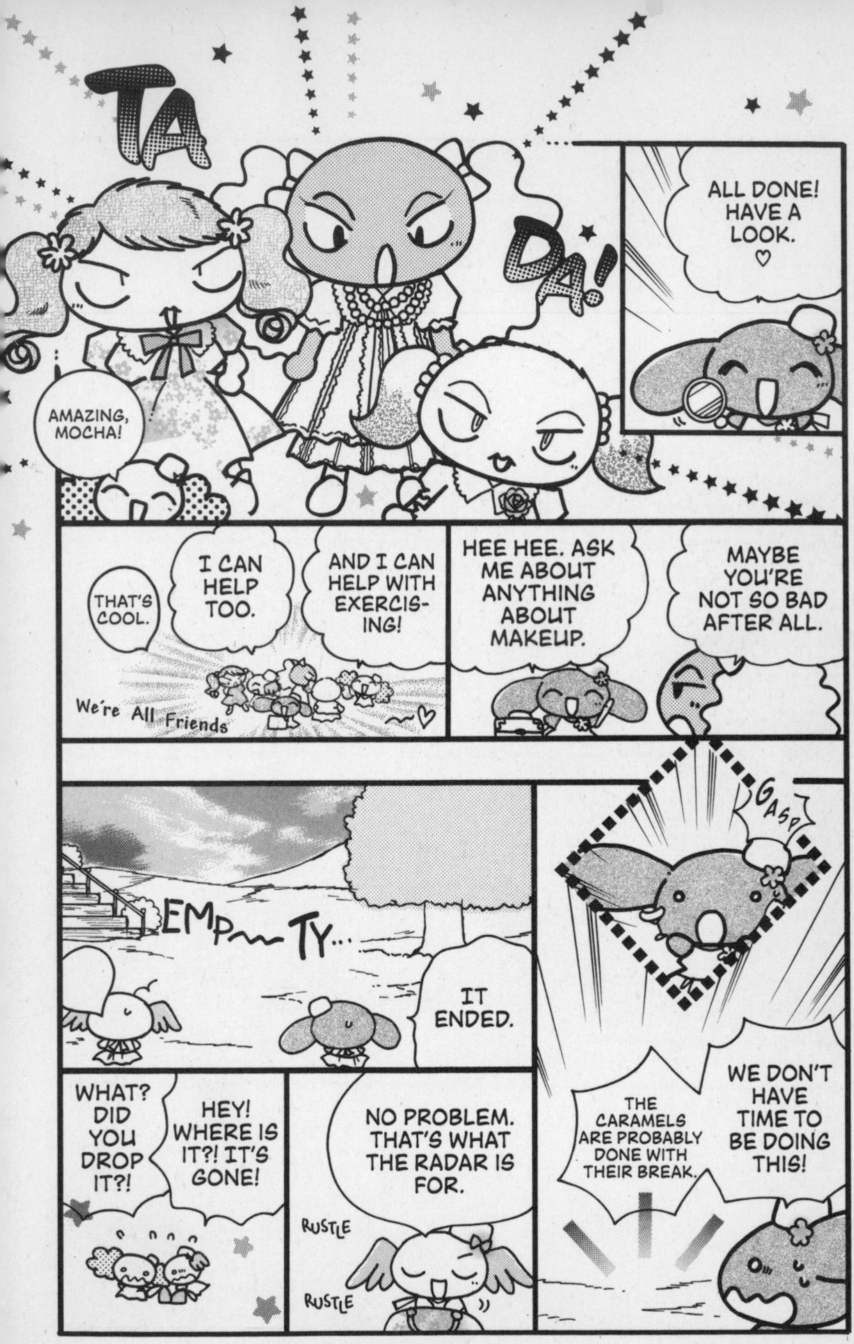
ALL DONE! HAVE A LOOK. ♡
TA DA!
AMAZING, MOCHA!
MAYBE YOU'RE NOT SO BAD AFTER ALL.
HEE HEE. ASK ME ABOUT ANYTHING ABOUT MAKEUP.
AND I CAN HELP WITH EXERCISING!
I CAN HELP TOO.
THAT'S COOL.
We're All Friends ~♡
GASP
WE DON'T HAVE TIME TO BE DOING THIS!
THE CARAMELS ARE PROBABLY DONE WITH THEIR BREAK.
EMP~~TY...
IT ENDED.
NO PROBLEM. THAT'S WHAT THE RADAR IS FOR.
RUSTLE
RUSTLE
HEY! WHERE IS IT?! IT'S GONE!
WHAT? DID YOU DROP IT?!

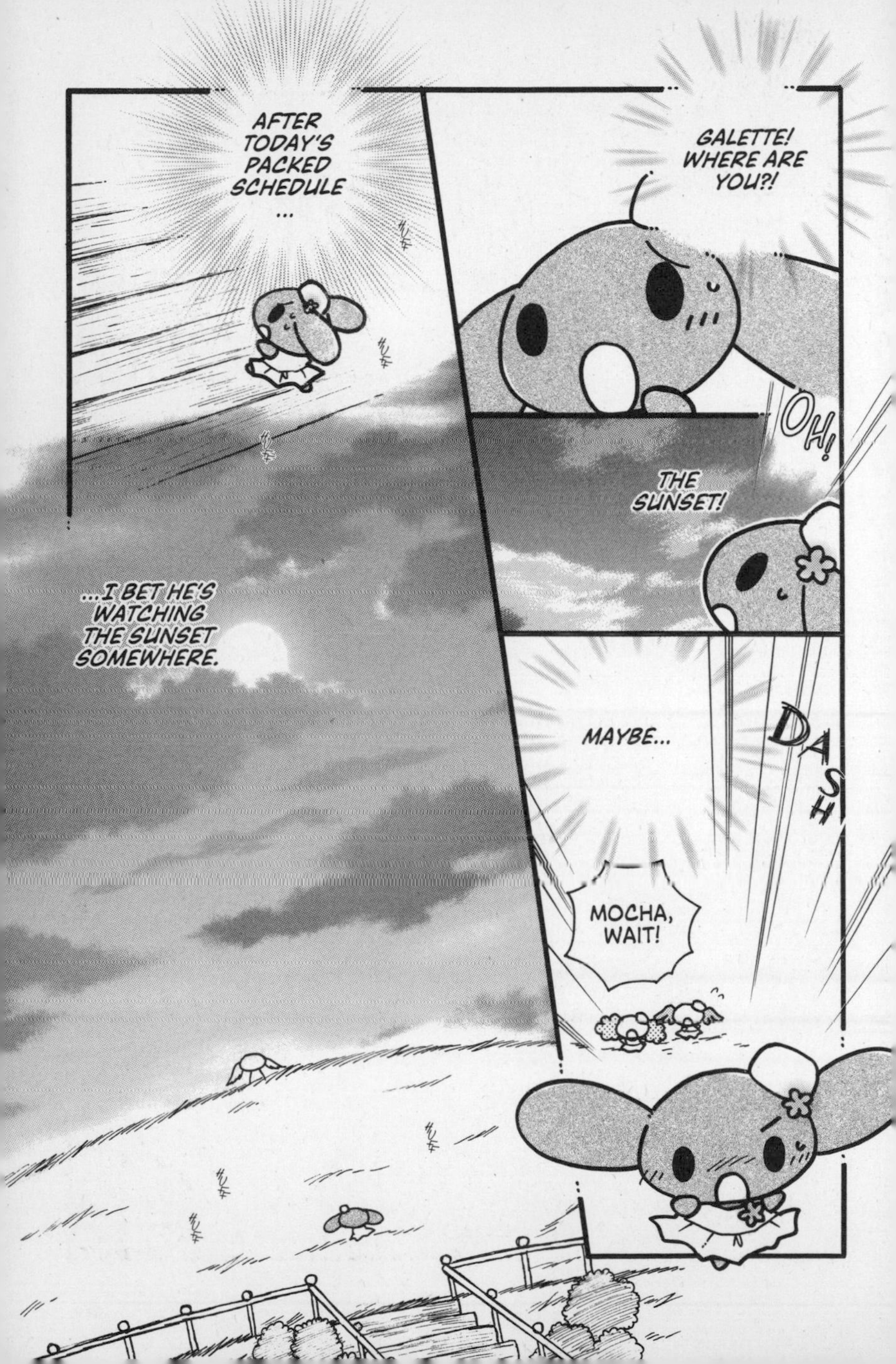
GALETTE! WHERE ARE YOU?!
OH!
THE SUNSET!
MAYBE...
DASH
MOCHA, WAIT!
AFTER TODAY'S PACKED SCHEDULE...
...I BET HE'S WATCHING THE SUNSET SOMEWHERE.

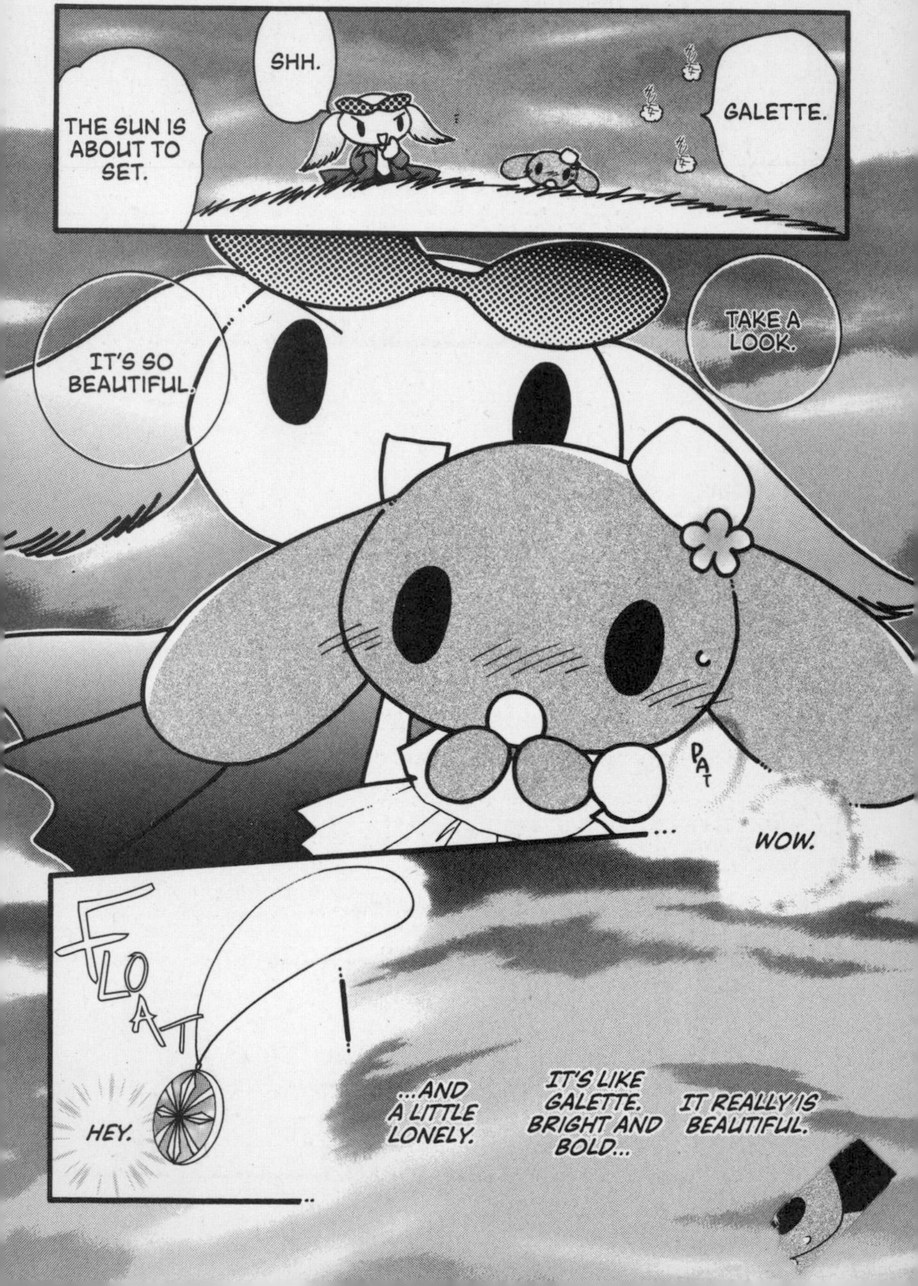
GALETTE.
SHH.
THE SUN IS ABOUT TO SET.
TAKE A LOOK.
IT'S SO BEAUTIFUL.
PAT
WOW.
IT REALLY IS BEAUTIFUL.
IT'S LIKE GALETTE. BRIGHT AND BOLD...
...AND A LITTLE LONELY.
FLOAT
HEY.

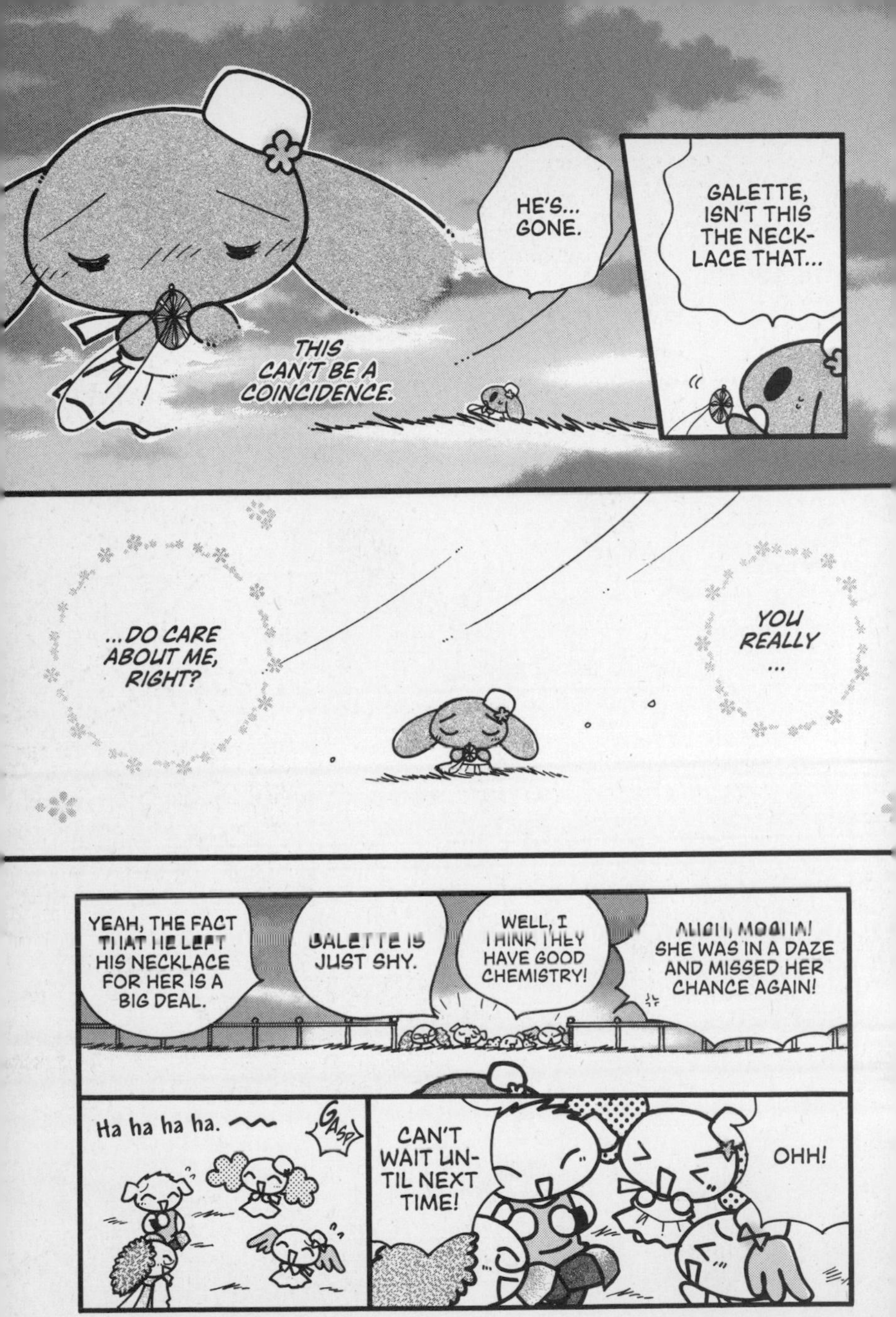
GALETTE, ISN'T THIS THE NECKLACE THAT...
HE'S... GONE.
THIS CAN'T BE A COINCIDENCE.
YOU REALLY...
...DO CARE ABOUT ME, RIGHT?
AUGH, MOCHA! SHE WAS IN A DAZE AND MISSED HER CHANCE AGAIN!
WELL, I THINK THEY HAVE GOOD CHEMISTRY!
GALETTE IS JUST SHY.
YEAH, THE FACT THAT HE LEFT HIS NECKLACE FOR HER IS A BIG DEAL.
OHH!
CAN'T WAIT UNTIL NEXT TIME!
GASP
Ha ha ha ha.

Galette's So Cold

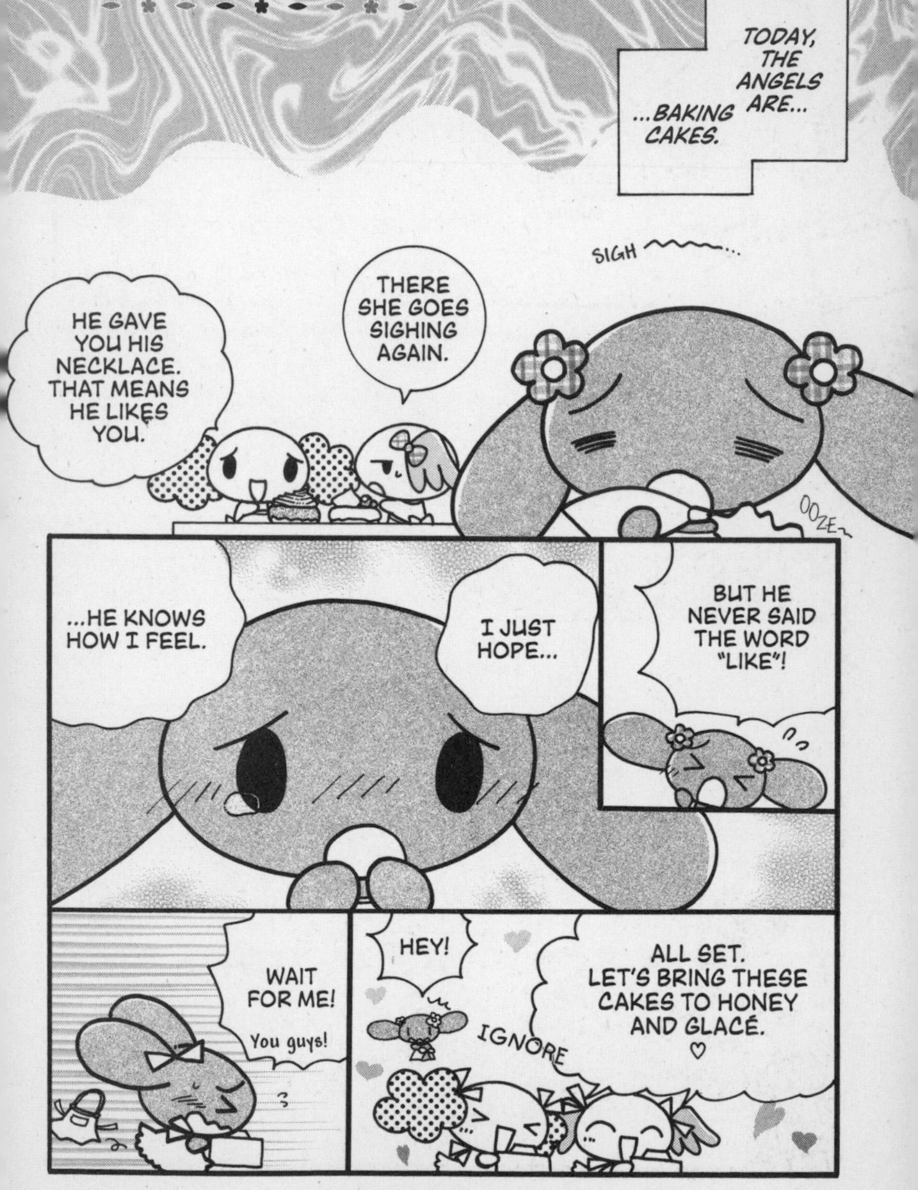
TODAY, THE ANGELS ARE... ...BAKING CAKES.
SIGH...
THERE SHE GOES SIGHING AGAIN.
HE GAVE YOU HIS NECKLACE. THAT MEANS HE LIKES YOU.
OOZE
BUT HE NEVER SAID THE WORD "LIKE"!
I JUST HOPE...
...HE KNOWS HOW I FEEL.
ALL SET. LET'S BRING THESE CAKES TO HONEY AND GLACÉ.
HEY!
IGNORE
WAIT FOR ME!
You guys!

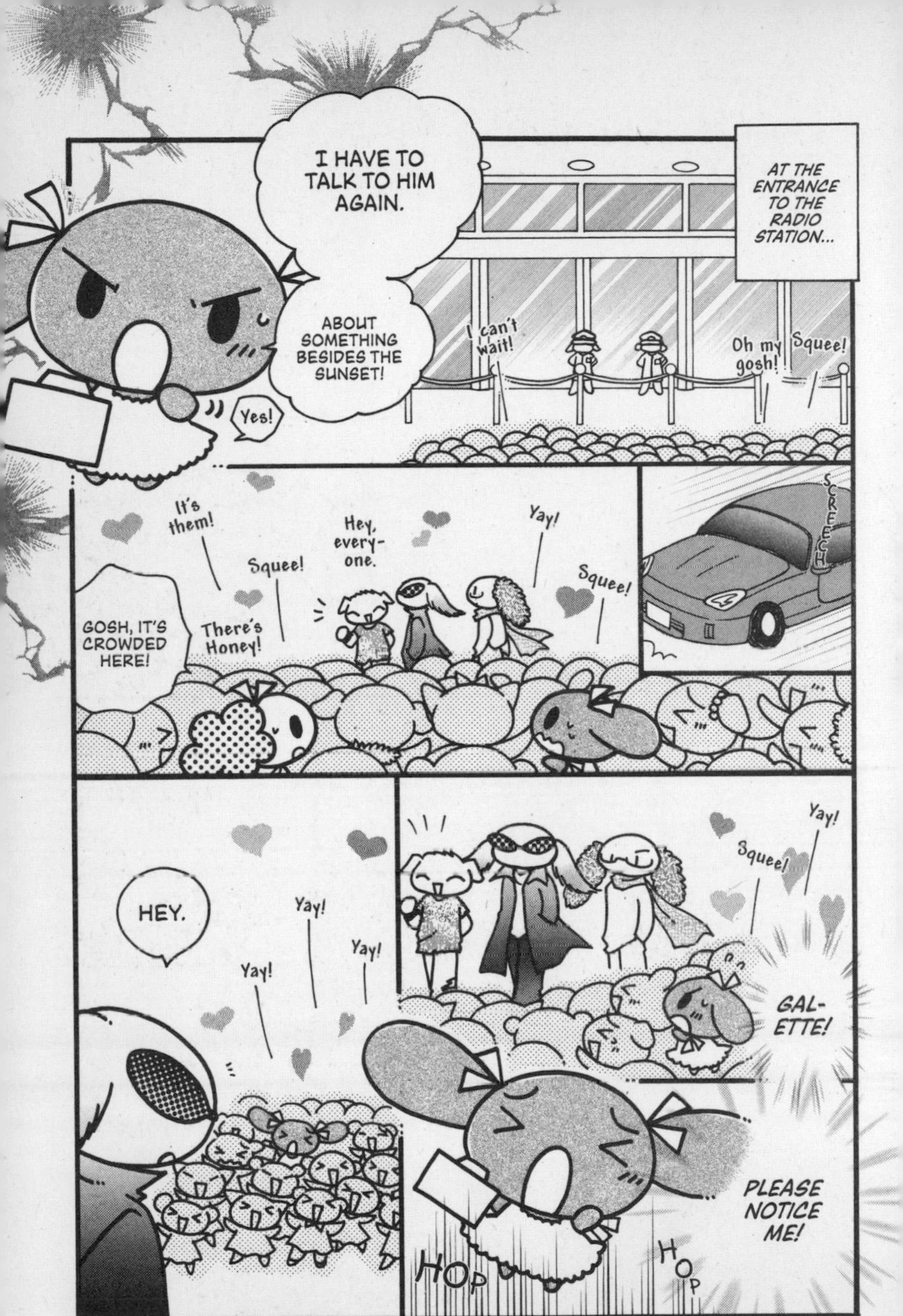
AT THE ENTRANCE TO THE RADIO STATION...
Squee!
Oh my gosh!
I can't wait!
I HAVE TO TALK TO HIM AGAIN.
ABOUT SOMETHING BESIDES THE SUNSET!
Yes!
SCREECH
Squee!
Yay!
Hey, every- one.
Squee!
It's them!
There's Honey!
GOSH, IT'S CROWDED HERE!
Yay!
Squee!
GAL- ETTE!
PLEASE NOTICE ME!
HOP
HOP
HEY.
Yay!
Yay!
Yay!

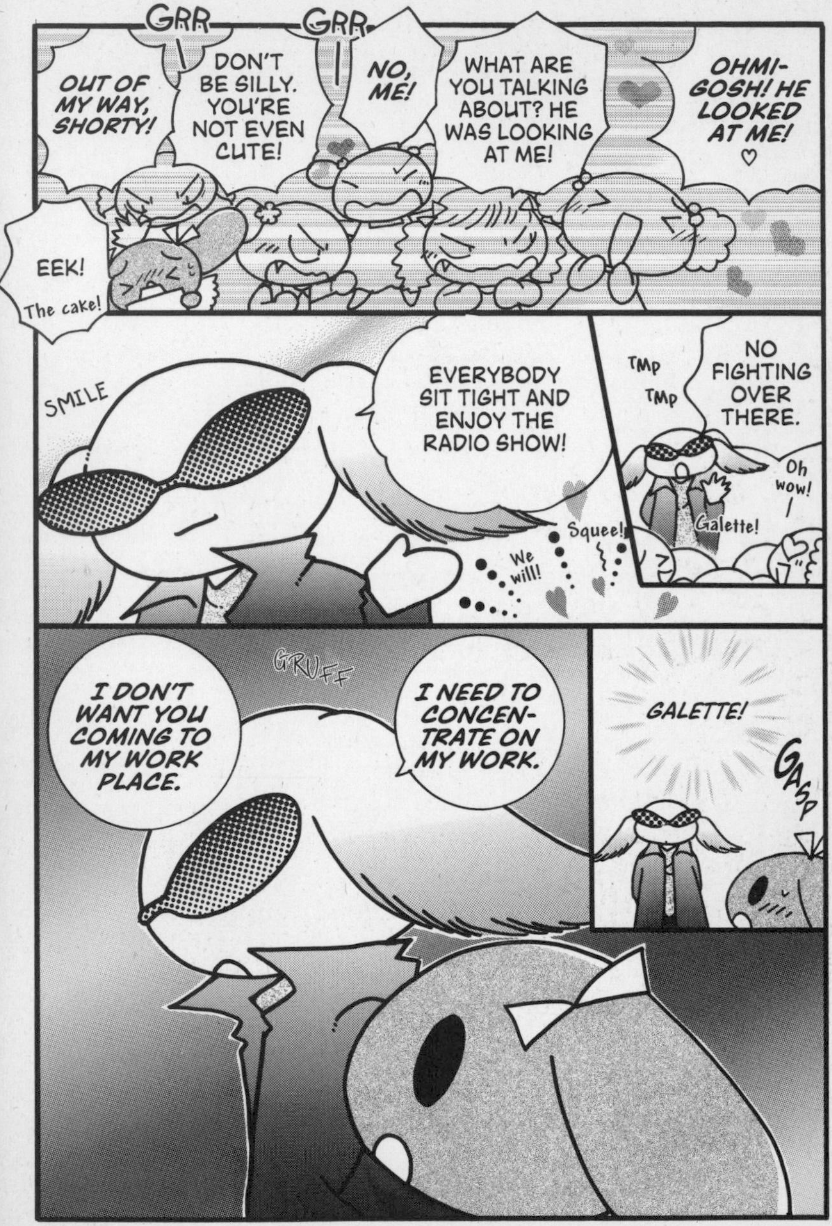
OHMI-GOSH! HE LOOKED AT ME! ♡
WHAT ARE YOU TALKING ABOUT? HE WAS LOOKING AT ME!
NO, ME!
GRR
DON'T BE SILLY. YOU'RE NOT EVEN CUTE!
GRR
OUT OF MY WAY, SHORTY!
EEK!
The cake!
NO FIGHTING OVER THERE.
TMp TMp
Oh wow!
Galette!
EVERYBODY SIT TIGHT AND ENJOY THE RADIO SHOW!
SMILE
Squee!
We will!
GALETTE!
GASP
I NEED TO CONCENTRATE ON MY WORK.
GRUFF
I DON'T WANT YOU COMING TO MY WORK PLACE.

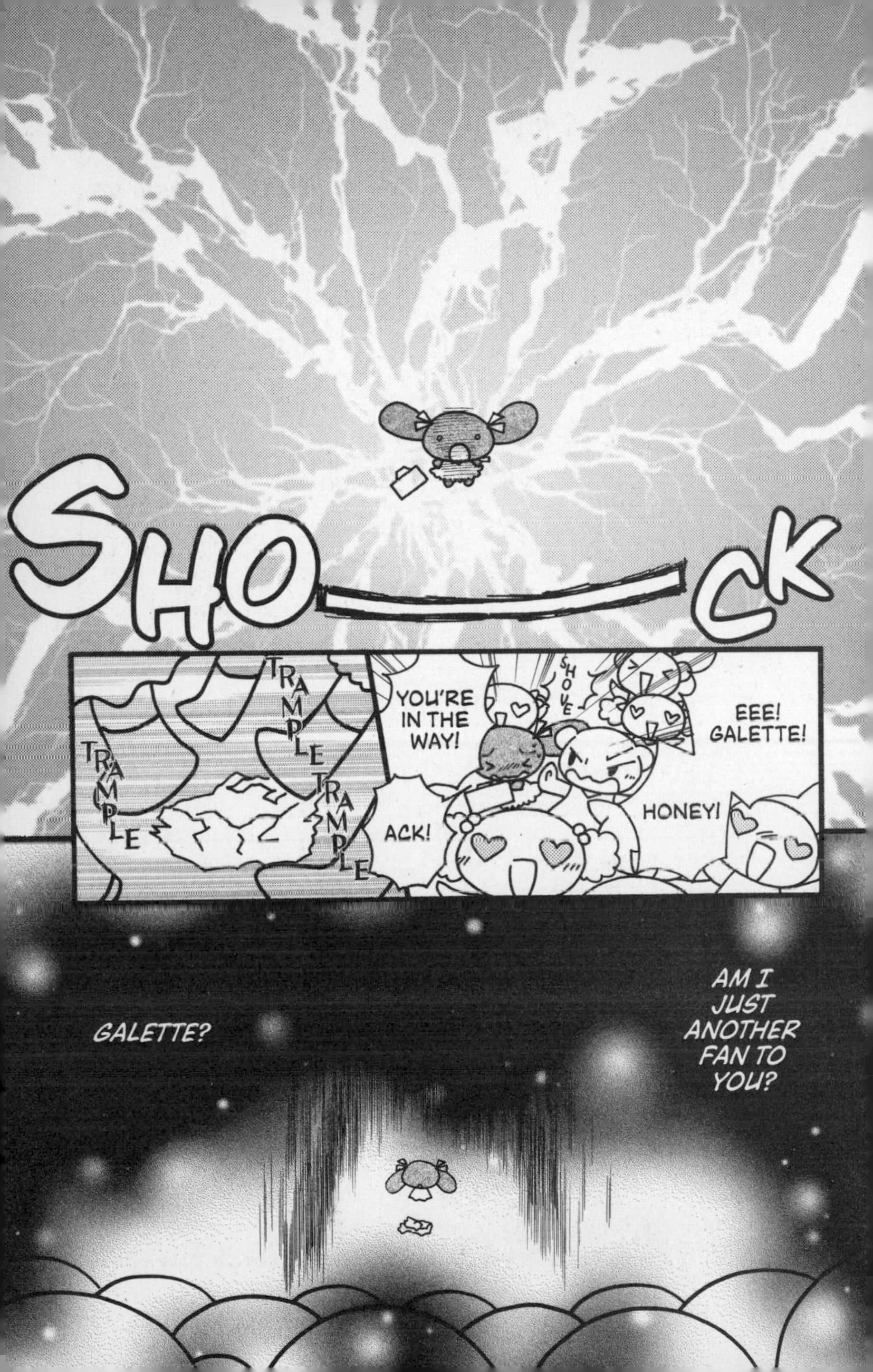
SHO—CK
EEE! GALETTE!
SHOVE
YOU'RE IN THE WAY!
HONEY!
ACK!
TRAMPLE
TRAMPLE
TRAMPLE
TRAMPLE
AM I JUST ANOTHER FAN TO YOU?
GALETTE?

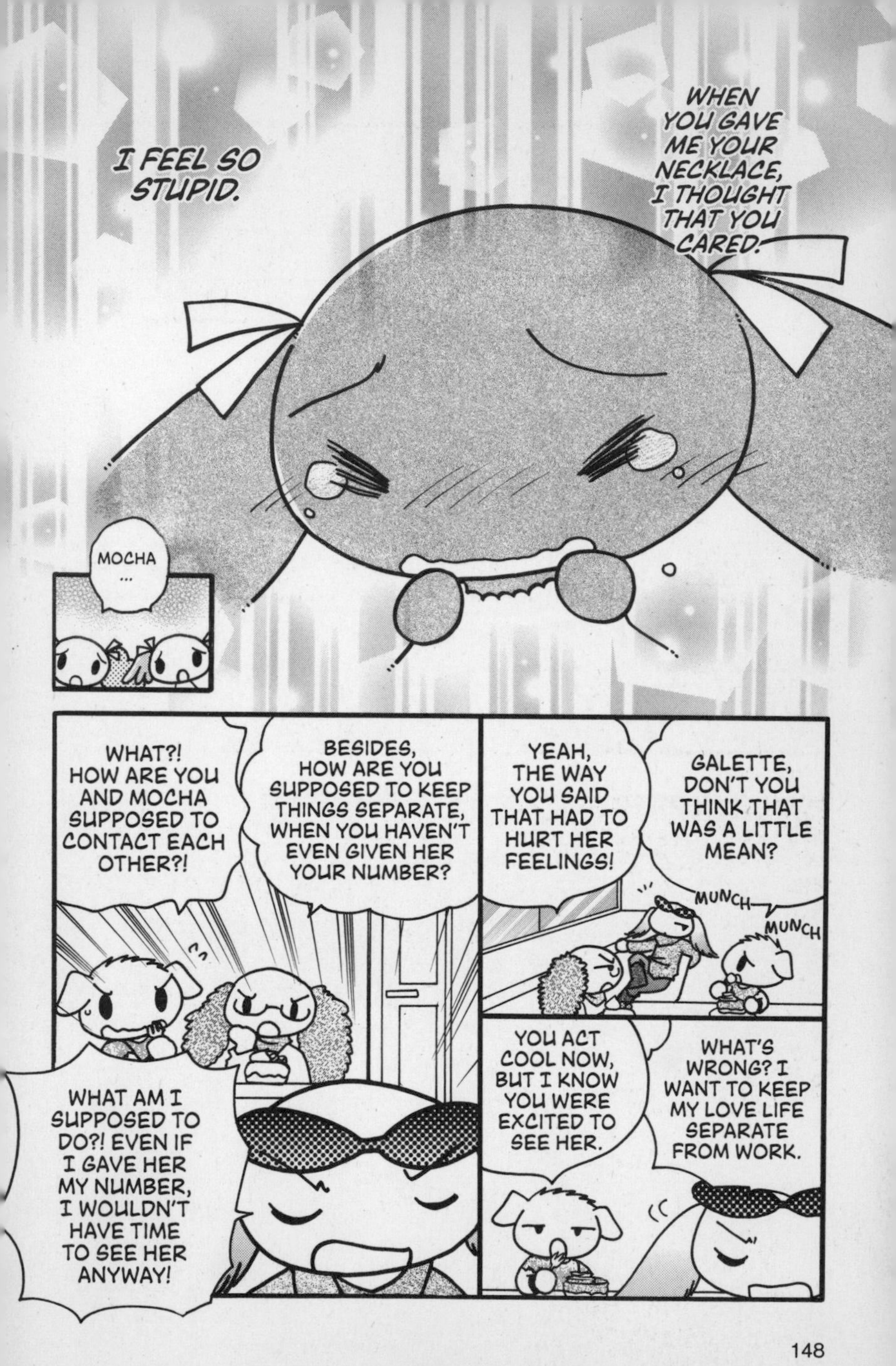
WHEN YOU GAVE ME YOUR NECKLACE, I THOUGHT THAT YOU CARED.
I FEEL SO STUPID.
MOCHA ...
GALETTE, DON'T YOU THINK THAT WAS A LITTLE MEAN?
YEAH, THE WAY YOU SAID THAT HAD TO HURT HER FEELINGS!
MUNCH
MUNCH
WHAT'S WRONG? I WANT TO KEEP MY LOVE LIFE SEPARATE FROM WORK.
YOU ACT COOL NOW, BUT I KNOW YOU WERE EXCITED TO SEE HER.
BESIDES, HOW ARE YOU SUPPOSED TO KEEP THINGS SEPARATE, WHEN YOU HAVEN'T EVEN GIVEN HER YOUR NUMBER?
WHAT?! HOW ARE YOU AND MOCHA SUPPOSED TO CONTACT EACH OTHER?!
WHAT AM I SUPPOSED TO DO?! EVEN IF I GAVE HER MY NUMBER, I WOULDN'T HAVE TIME TO SEE HER ANYWAY!

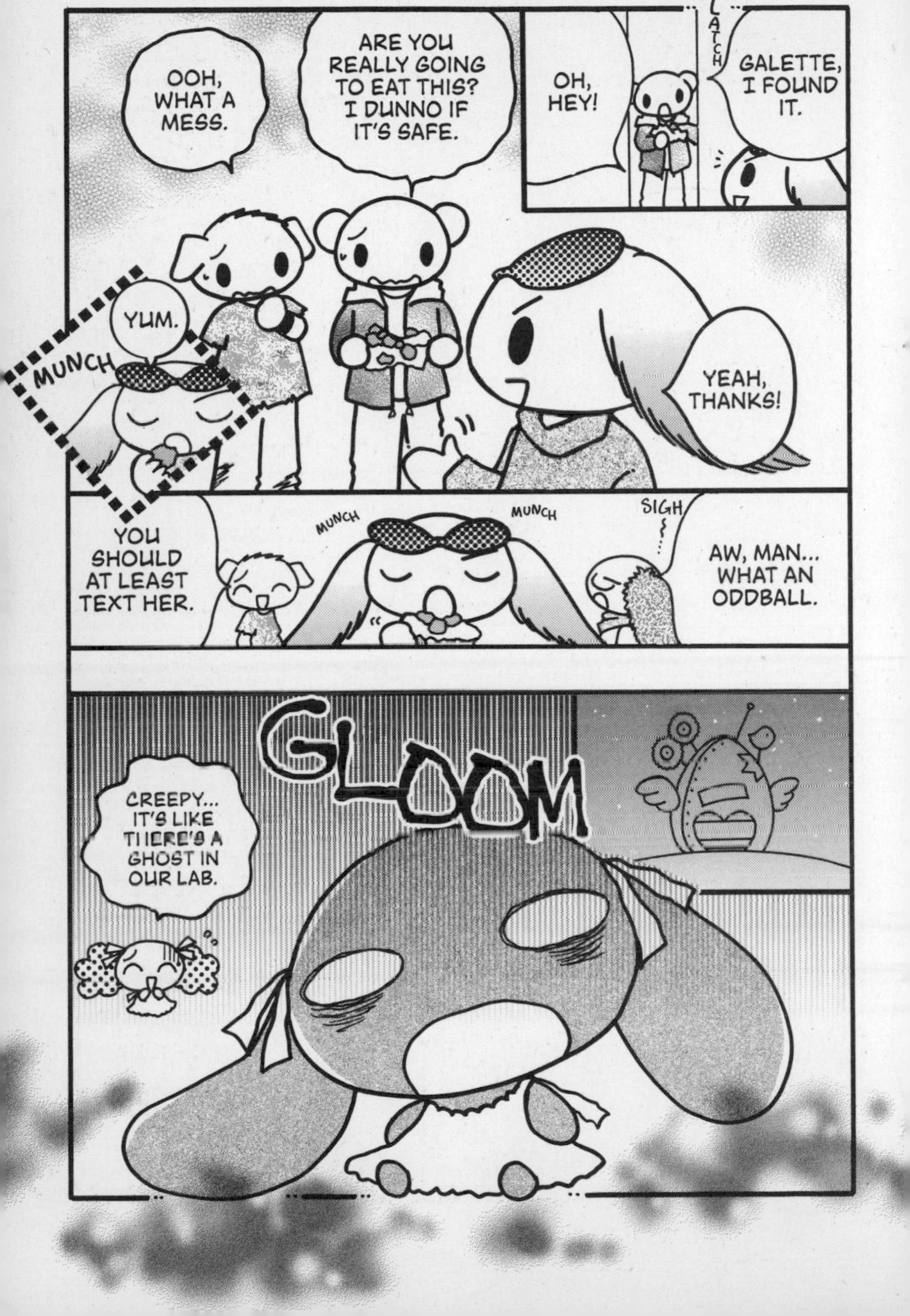
KLATCH
GALETTE, I FOUND IT.
OH, HEY!
YEAH, THANKS!
ARE YOU REALLY GOING TO EAT THIS? I DUNNO IF IT'S SAFE.
OOH, WHAT A MESS.
MUNCH
YUM.
SIGH
AW, MAN... WHAT AN ODDBALL.
MUNCH
MUNCH
YOU SHOULD AT LEAST TEXT HER.
GLOOM
CREEPY... IT'S LIKE THERE'S A GHOST IN OUR LAB.

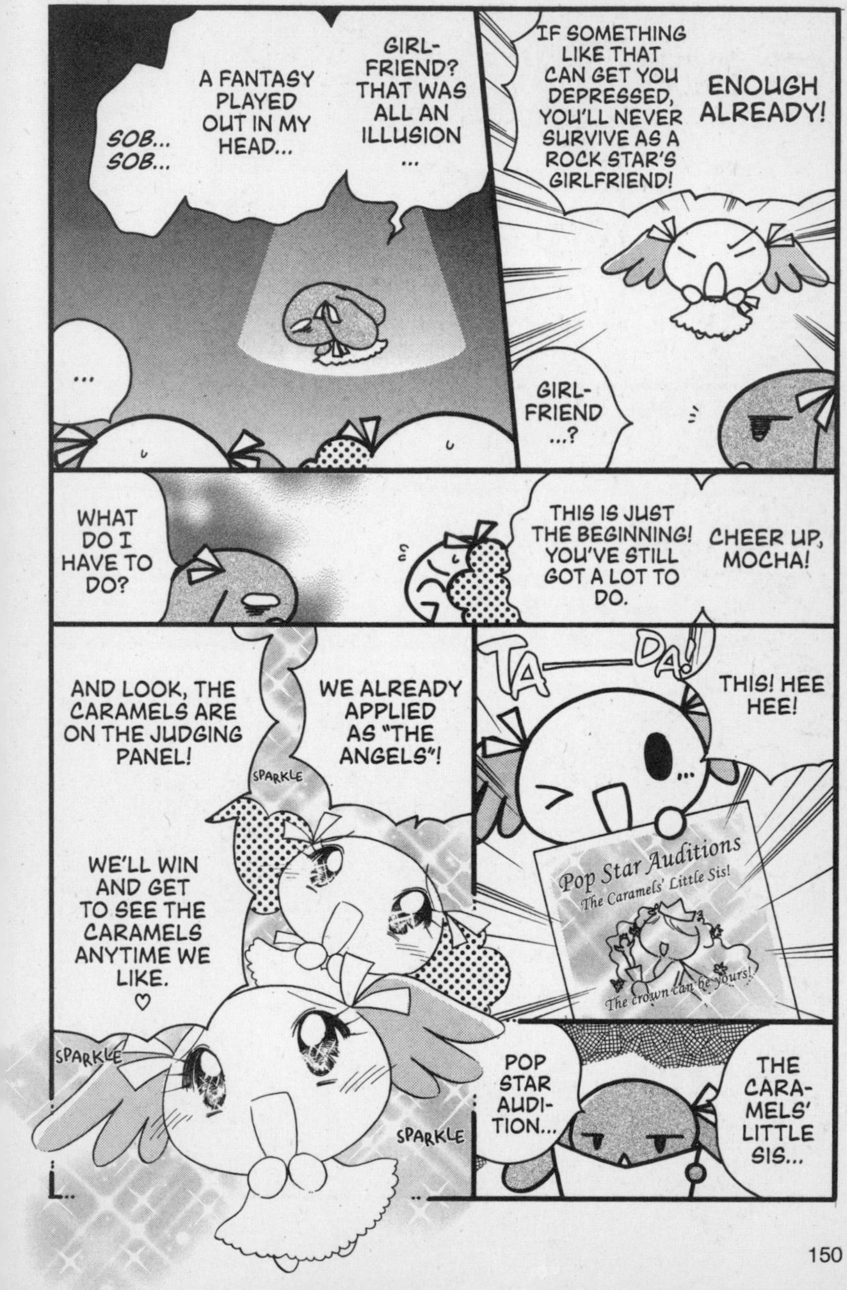
ENOUGH ALREADY!
IF SOMETHING LIKE THAT CAN GET YOU DEPRESSED, YOU'LL NEVER SURVIVE AS A ROCK STAR'S GIRLFRIEND!
GIRL-FRIEND ...?
GIRL-FRIEND? THAT WAS ALL AN ILLUSION ...
A FANTASY PLAYED OUT IN MY HEAD...
SOB... SOB...
...
CHEER UP, MOCHA!
THIS IS JUST THE BEGINNING! YOU'VE STILL GOT A LOT TO DO.
WHAT DO I HAVE TO DO?
TA—DA!
THIS! HEE HEE!
...
Pop Star Auditions
The Caramels' Little Sis!
The crown can be yours!
THE CARA-MELS' LITTLE SIS...
POP STAR AUDI-TION...
WE ALREADY APPLIED AS "THE ANGELS"!
AND LOOK, THE CARAMELS ARE ON THE JUDGING PANEL!
SPARKLE
WE'LL WIN AND GET TO SEE THE CARAMELS ANYTIME WE LIKE. ♡
SPARKLE
SPARKLE

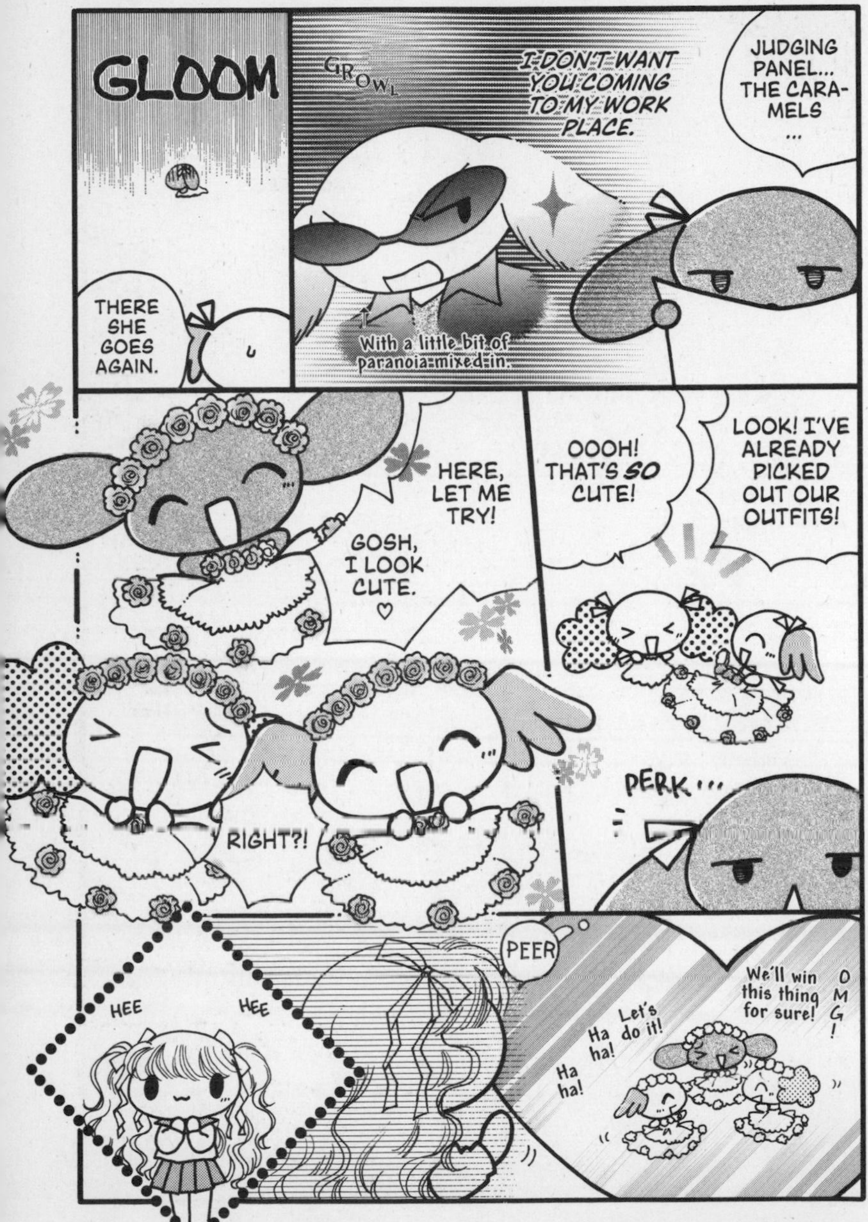
JUDGING PANEL... THE CARAMELS ...
GROWL
I DON'T WANT YOU COMING TO MY WORK PLACE.
With a little bit of paranoia mixed in.
GLOOM
THERE SHE GOES AGAIN.
LOOK! I'VE ALREADY PICKED OUT OUR OUTFITS!
OOOH! THAT'S *SO* CUTE!
HERE, LET ME TRY!
GOSH, I LOOK CUTE. ♡
RIGHT?!
PERK...
PEER
O M G !
We'll win this thing for sure!
Let's do it!
Ha ha!
Ha ha!
HEE
HEE

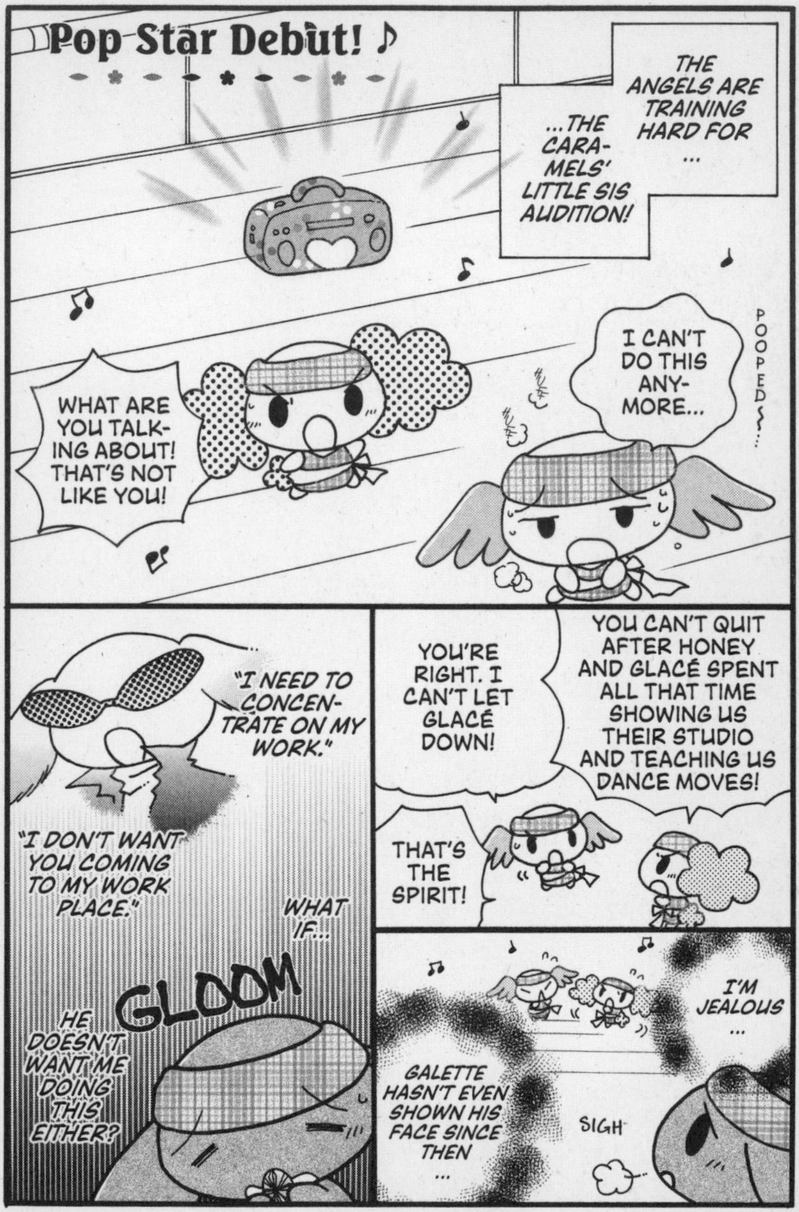
Pop Star Debut! ♪
THE ANGELS ARE TRAINING HARD FOR ...
...THE CARAMELS' LITTLE SIS AUDITION!
I CAN'T DO THIS ANYMORE...
POOPED~...
WHAT ARE YOU TALKING ABOUT! THAT'S NOT LIKE YOU!
YOU CAN'T QUIT AFTER HONEY AND GLACÉ SPENT ALL THAT TIME SHOWING US THEIR STUDIO AND TEACHING US DANCE MOVES!
YOU'RE RIGHT. I CAN'T LET GLACÉ DOWN!
THAT'S THE SPIRIT!
I'M JEALOUS ...
SIGH
GALETTE HASN'T EVEN SHOWN HIS FACE SINCE THEN ...
"I NEED TO CONCENTRATE ON MY WORK."
"I DON'T WANT YOU COMING TO MY WORK PLACE."
WHAT IF...
GLOOM
HE DOESN'T WANT ME DOING THIS EITHER?

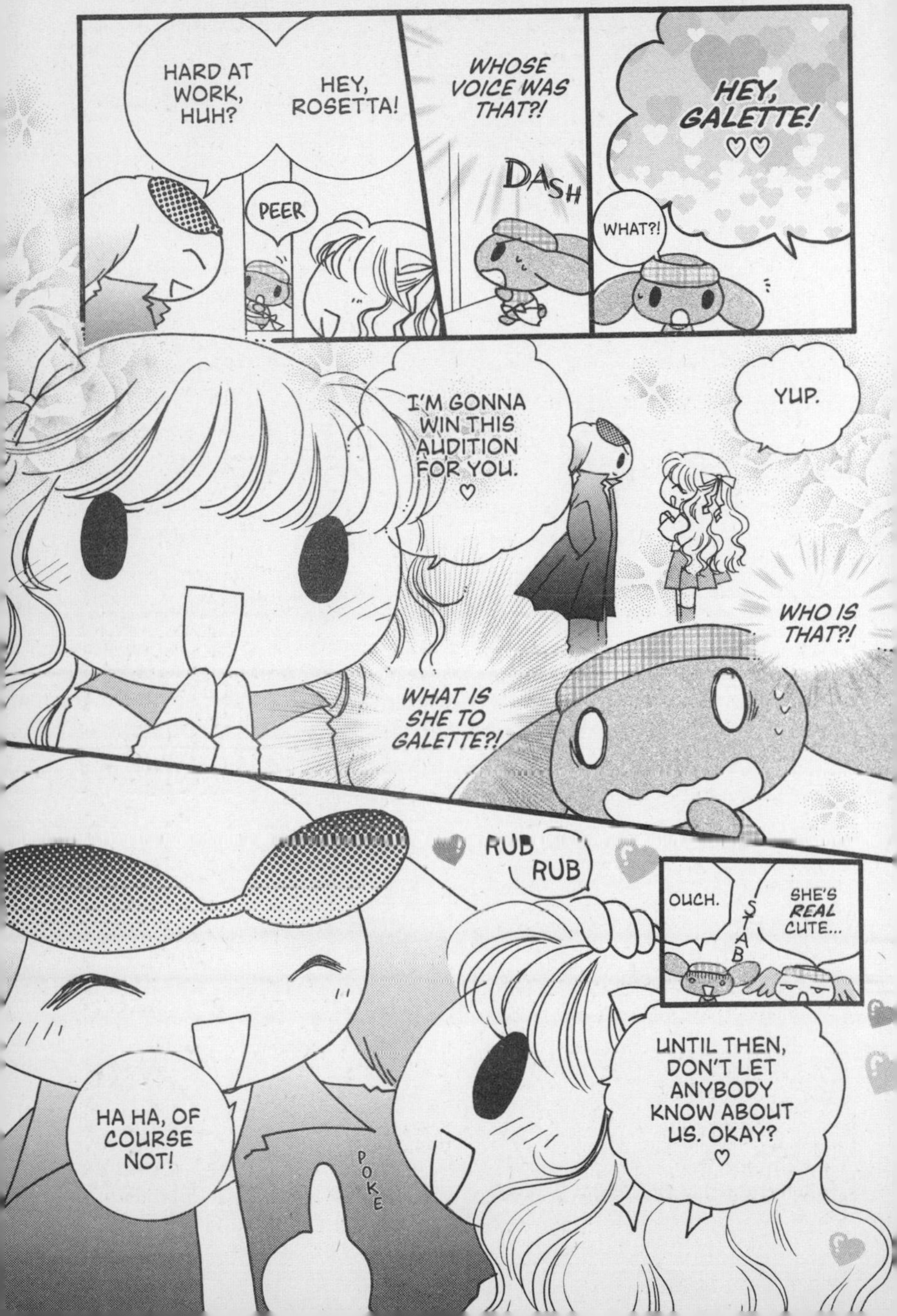
HEY, GALETTE! ♡♡
WHAT?!
WHOSE VOICE WAS THAT?!
DASH
HEY, ROSETTA!
HARD AT WORK, HUH?
PEER
YUP.
I'M GONNA WIN THIS AUDITION FOR YOU. ♡
WHO IS THAT?!
WHAT IS SHE TO GALETTE?!
SHE'S **REAL** CUTE...
STAB
OUCH.
RUB RUB
UNTIL THEN, DON'T LET ANYBODY KNOW ABOUT US. OKAY? ♡
HA HA, OF COURSE NOT!
POKE

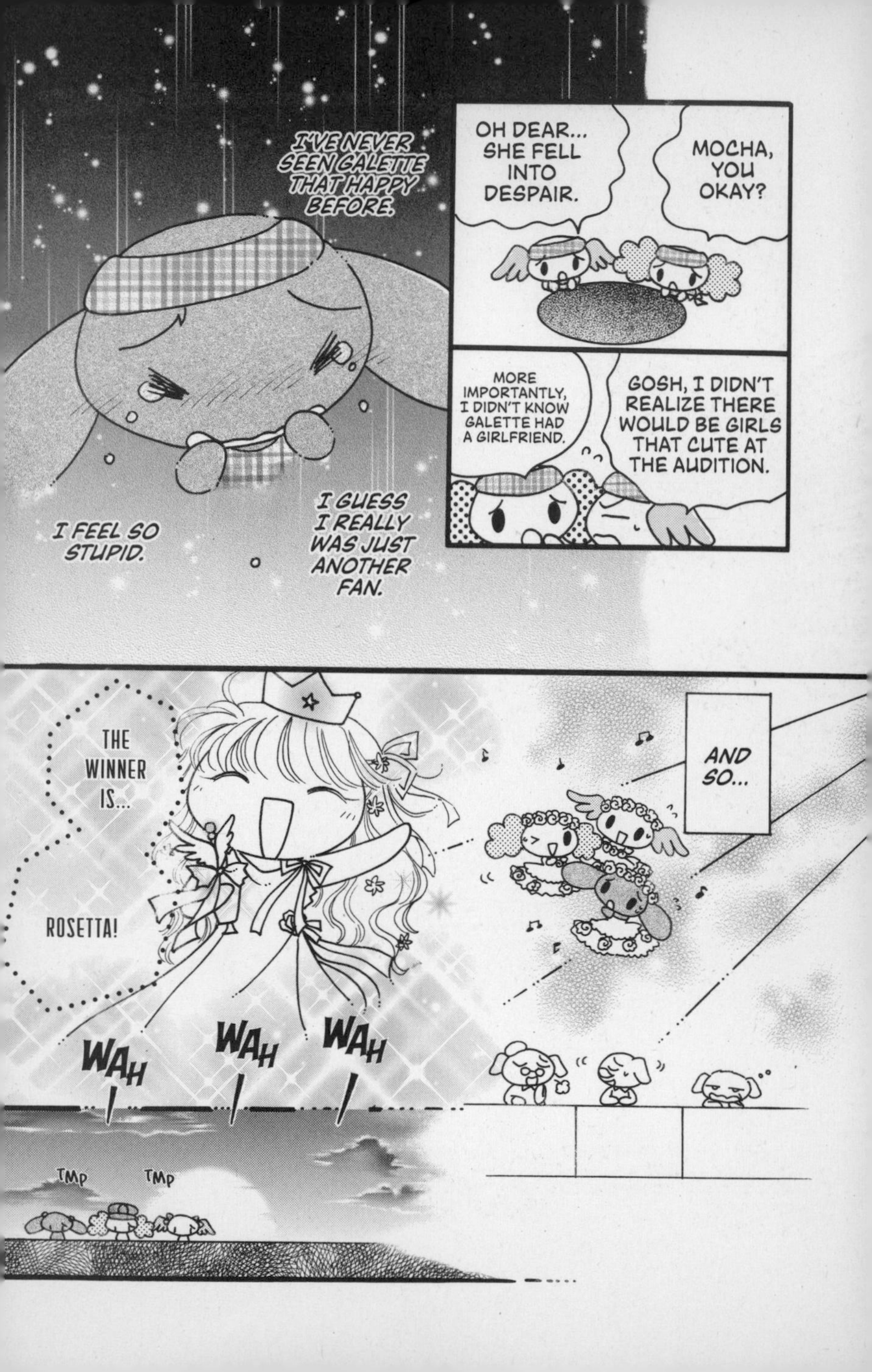
MOCHA, YOU OKAY?
OH DEAR... SHE FELL INTO DESPAIR.
GOSH, I DIDN'T REALIZE THERE WOULD BE GIRLS THAT CUTE AT THE AUDITION.
MORE IMPORTANTLY, I DIDN'T KNOW GALETTE HAD A GIRLFRIEND.
I'VE NEVER SEEN GALETTE THAT HAPPY BEFORE.
I GUESS I REALLY WAS JUST ANOTHER FAN.
I FEEL SO STUPID.
AND SO...
THE WINNER IS...
ROSETTA!
WAH
WAH
WAH
TMP
TMP

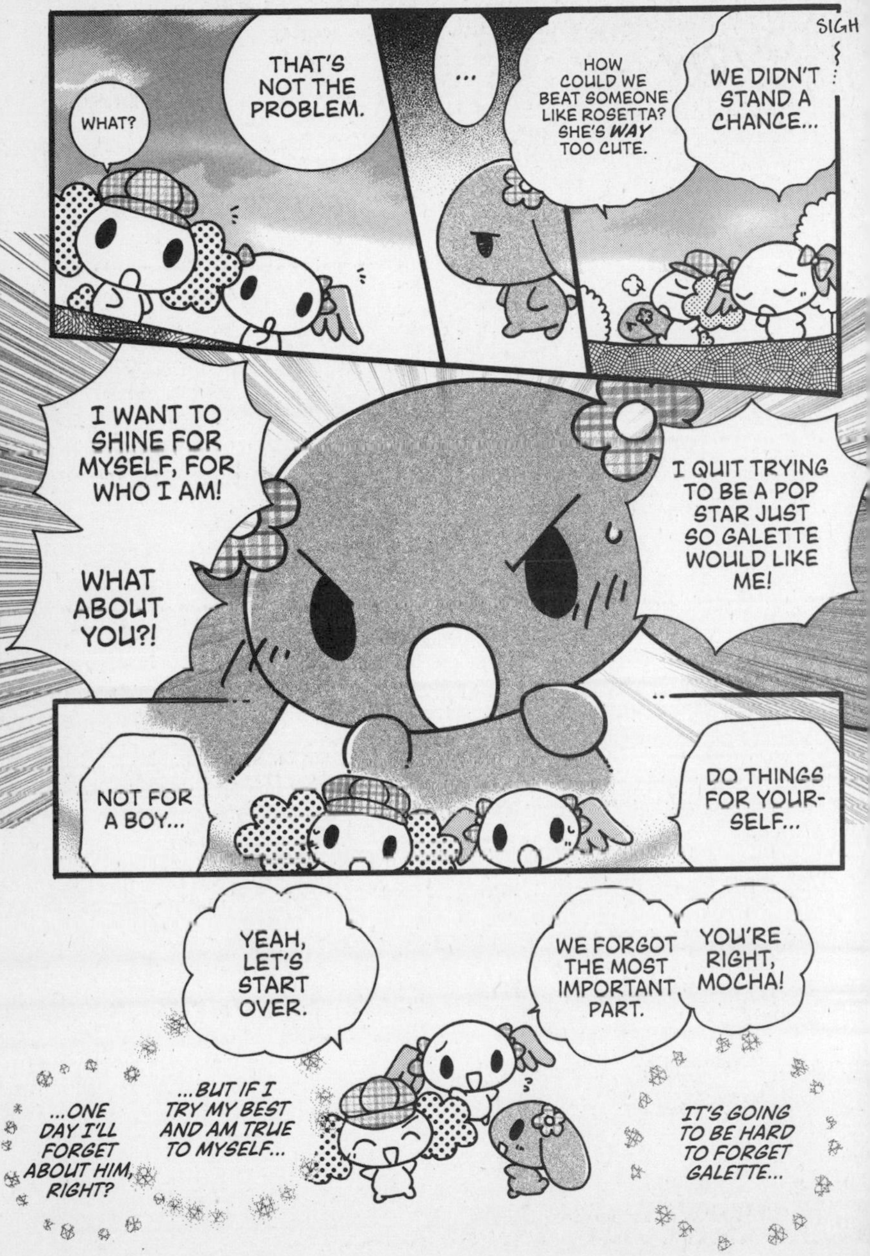
SIGH
WE DIDN'T STAND A CHANCE...
HOW COULD WE BEAT SOMEONE LIKE ROSETTA? SHE'S *WAY* TOO CUTE.
...
THAT'S NOT THE PROBLEM.
WHAT?
I QUIT TRYING TO BE A POP STAR JUST SO GALETTE WOULD LIKE ME!
I WANT TO SHINE FOR MYSELF, FOR WHO I AM!
WHAT ABOUT YOU?!
DO THINGS FOR YOUR-SELF...
NOT FOR A BOY...
YOU'RE RIGHT, MOCHA!
WE FORGOT THE MOST IMPORTANT PART.
YEAH, LET'S START OVER.
IT'S GOING TO BE HARD TO FORGET GALETTE...
...BUT IF I TRY MY BEST AND AM TRUE TO MYSELF...
...ONE DAY I'LL FORGET ABOUT HIM, RIGHT?

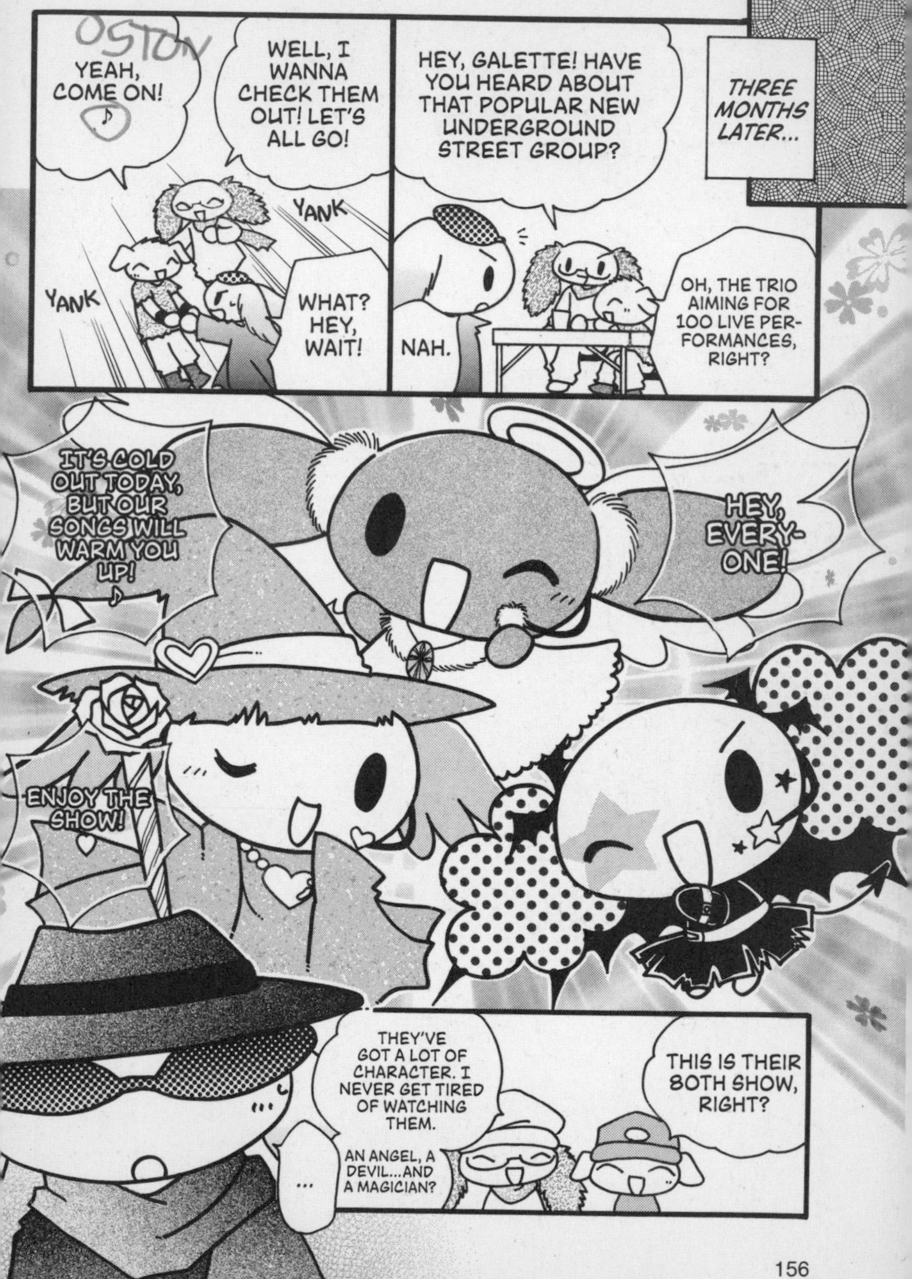
THREE MONTHS LATER...
HEY, GALETTE! HAVE YOU HEARD ABOUT THAT POPULAR NEW UNDERGROUND STREET GROUP?
NAH.
OH, THE TRIO AIMING FOR 100 LIVE PERFORMANCES, RIGHT?
WELL, I WANNA CHECK THEM OUT! LET'S ALL GO!
YEAH, COME ON! ♪
YANK
WHAT? HEY, WAIT!
YANK
HEY, EVERYONE!
IT'S COLD OUT TODAY, BUT OUR SONGS WILL WARM YOU UP! ♪
ENJOY THE SHOW!
THIS IS THEIR 80TH SHOW, RIGHT?
THEY'VE GOT A LOT OF CHARACTER. I NEVER GET TIRED OF WATCHING THEM.
AN ANGEL, A DEVIL...AND A MAGICIAN?
...

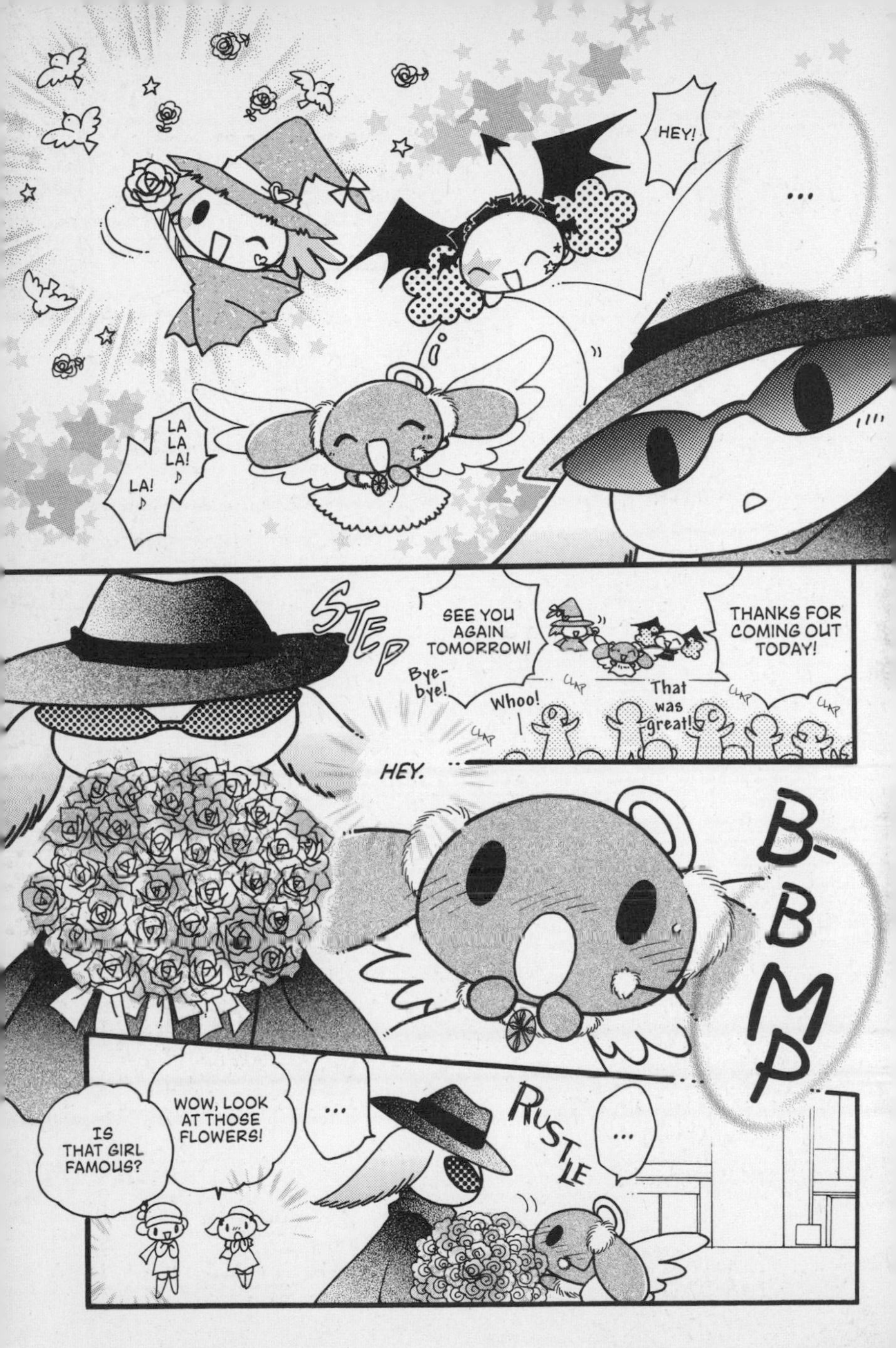
HEY!
...
LA LA LA! ♪
LA! ♪
THANKS FOR COMING OUT TODAY!
SEE YOU AGAIN TOMORROW!
CLAP
That was great!
CLAP
Whoo!
CLAP
Bye-bye!
STEP
HEY.
B-B-BMP
...
RUSTLE
...
WOW, LOOK AT THOSE FLOWERS!
IS THAT GIRL FAMOUS?

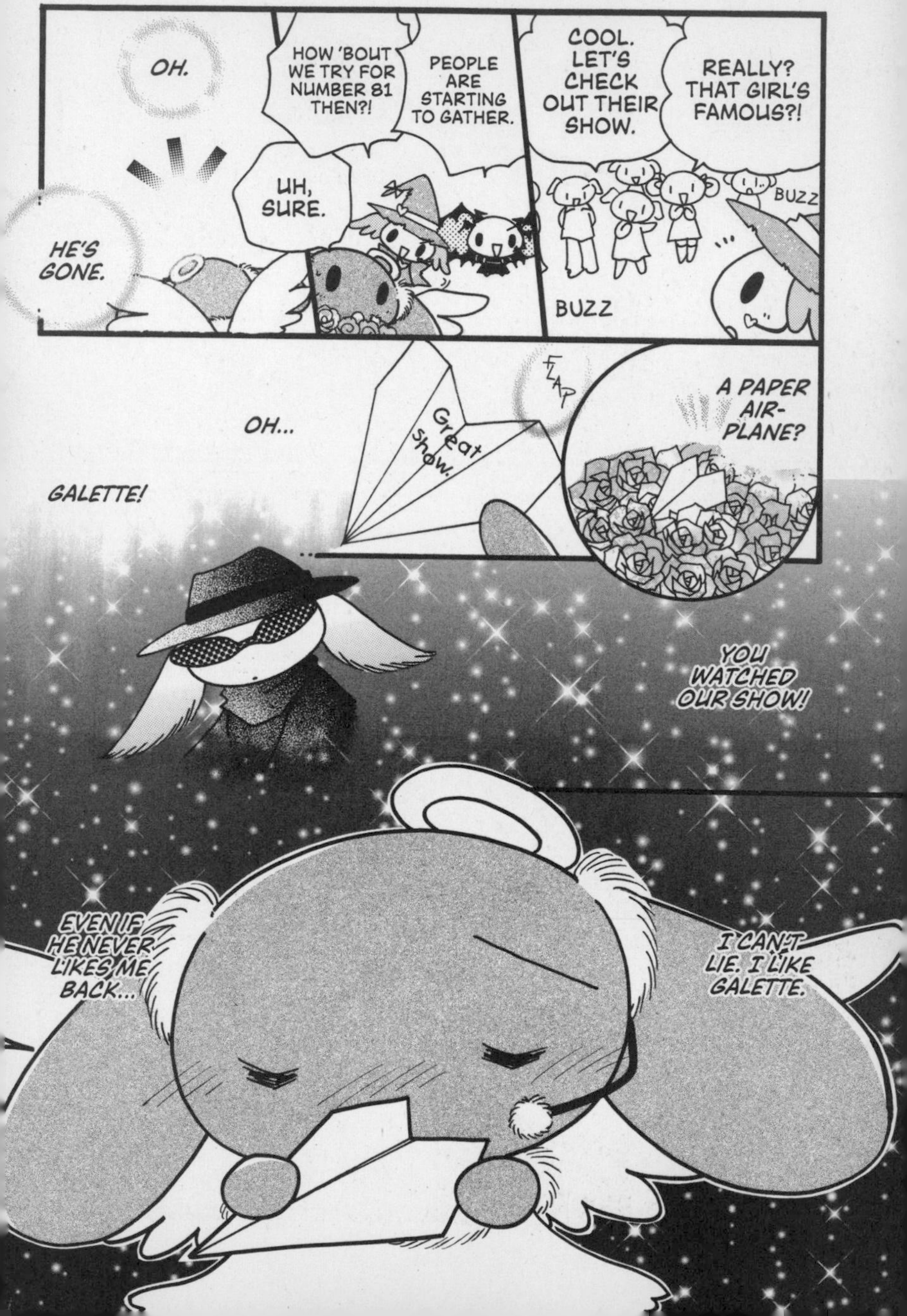
REALLY? THAT GIRL'S FAMOUS?!
COOL. LET'S CHECK OUT THEIR SHOW.
BUZZ
BUZZ
PEOPLE ARE STARTING TO GATHER.
HOW 'BOUT WE TRY FOR NUMBER 81 THEN?!
UH, SURE.
OH.
HE'S GONE.
A PAPER AIR-PLANE?
FLAP
Great show.
OH...
GALETTE!
YOU WATCHED OUR SHOW!
I CAN'T LIE. I LIKE GALETTE.
EVEN IF HE NEVER LIKES ME BACK...

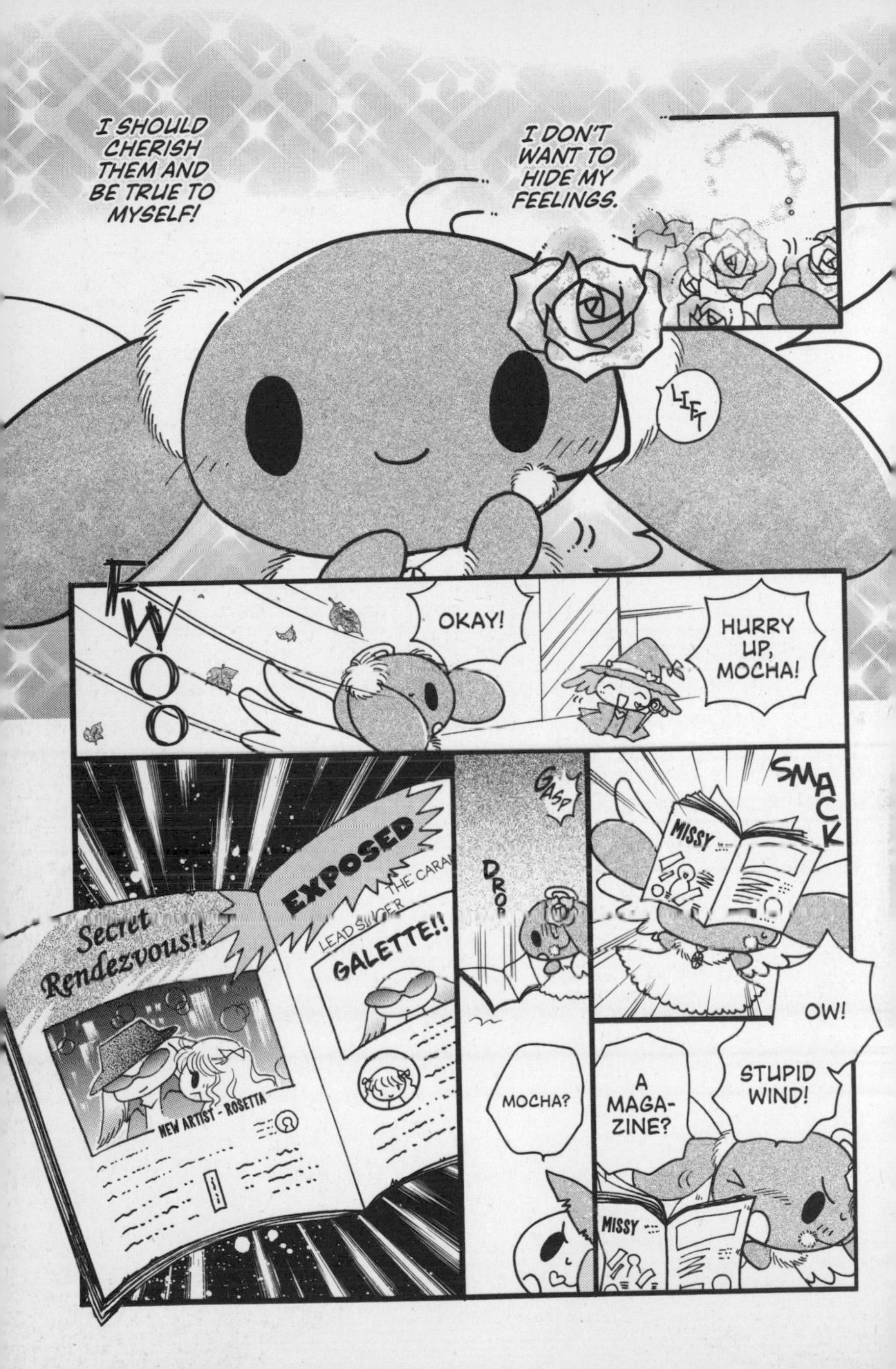
I DON'T WANT TO HIDE MY FEELINGS.
I SHOULD CHERISH THEM AND BE TRUE TO MYSELF!
LIFT
HURRY UP, MOCHA!
OKAY!
FWOOO
SMACK
MISSY
OW!
STUPID WIND!
A MAGA-ZINE?
MISSY
MOCHA?
GASP
DROP
EXPOSED
THE CARA
LEAD SINGER
GALETTE!!
Secret Rendezvous!!
NEW ARTIST - ROSETTA

Time to Move On

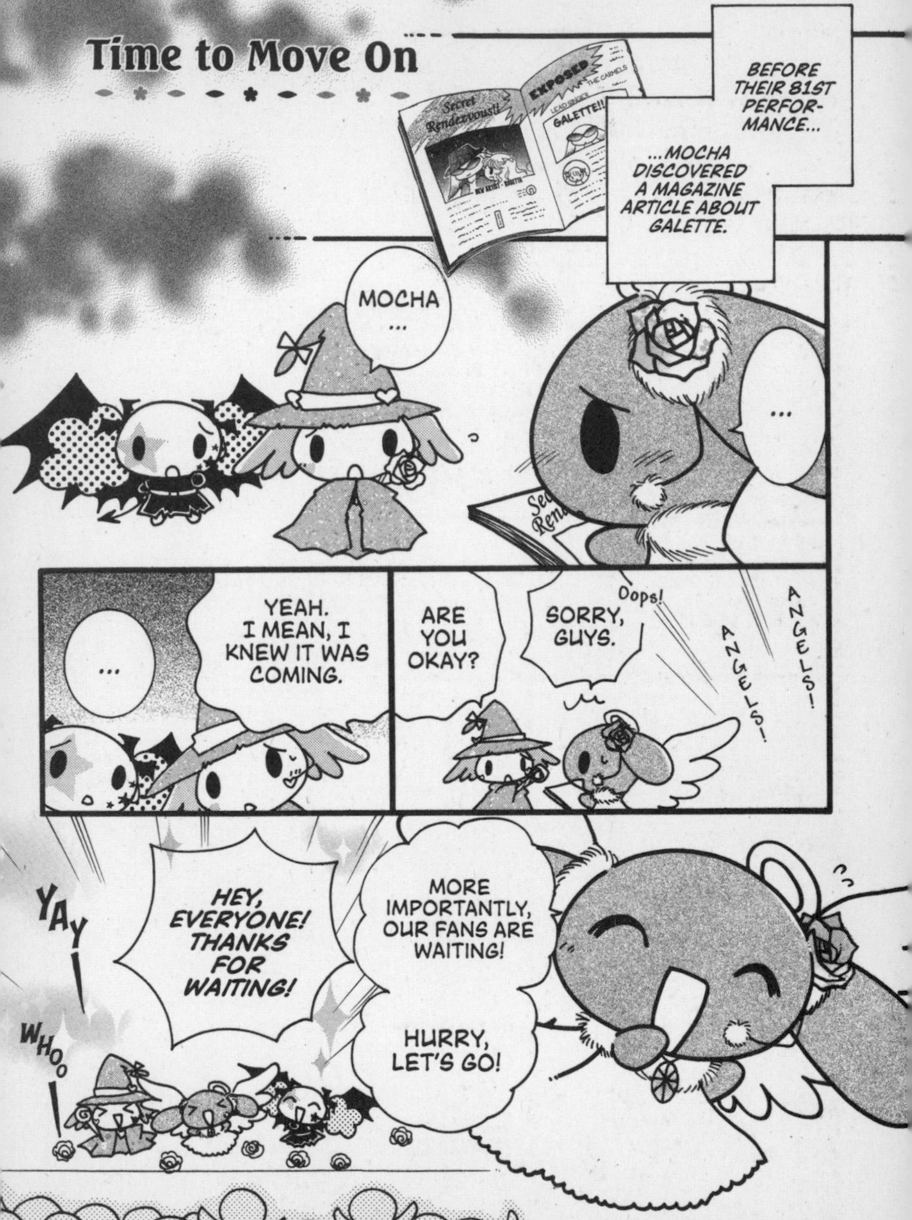

BEFORE THEIR 81ST PERFORMANCE...
...MOCHA DISCOVERED A MAGAZINE ARTICLE ABOUT GALETTE.
Secret Rendezvous!!
EXPOSED
GALETTE!!
...
MOCHA ...
ANGELS!
ANGELS!
Oops!
SORRY, GUYS.
ARE YOU OKAY?
YEAH. I MEAN, I KNEW IT WAS COMING.
...
MORE IMPORTANTLY, OUR FANS ARE WAITING!
HURRY, LET'S GO!
HEY, EVERYONE! THANKS FOR WAITING!
YAY
WHOO

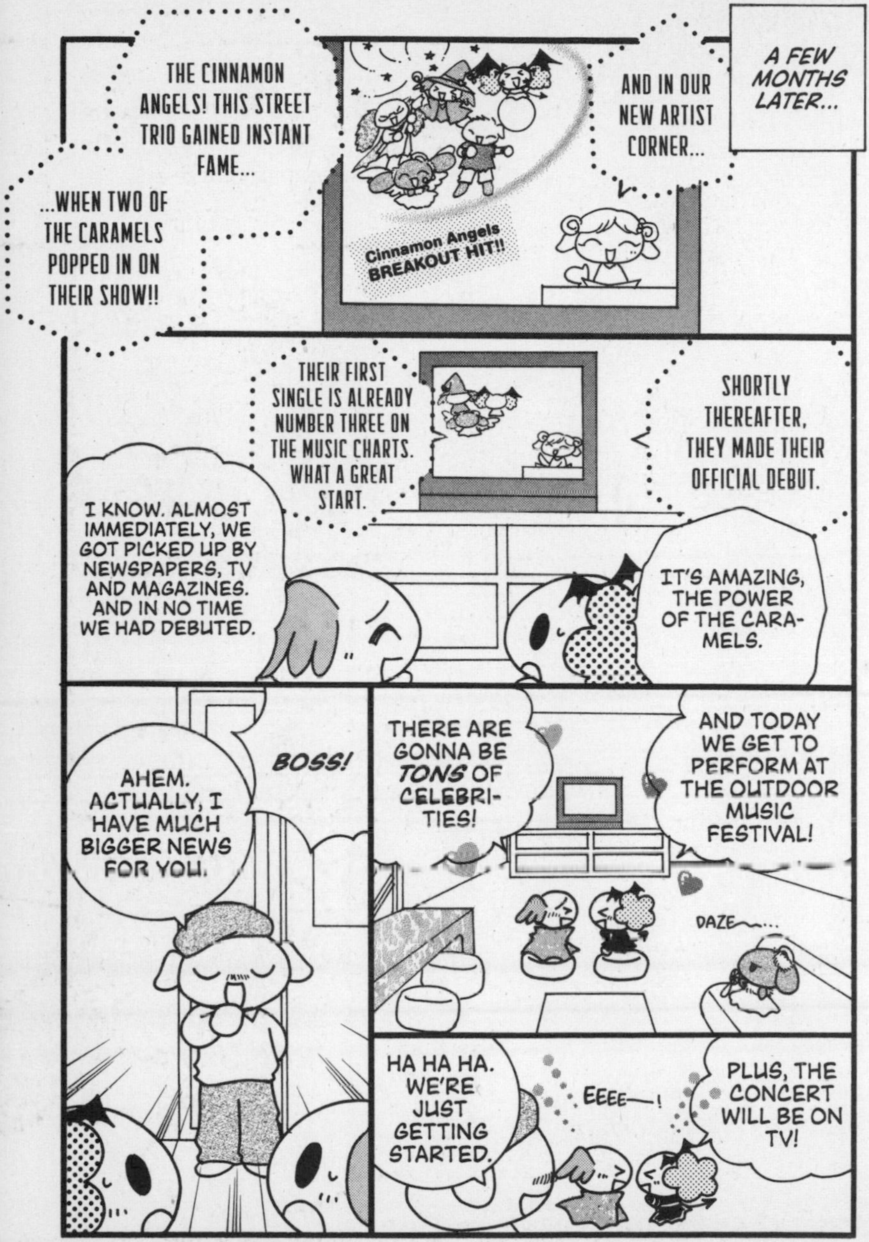
A FEW MONTHS LATER...
AND IN OUR NEW ARTIST CORNER...
THE CINNAMON ANGELS! THIS STREET TRIO GAINED INSTANT FAME...
...WHEN TWO OF THE CARAMELS POPPED IN ON THEIR SHOW!!
Cinnamon Angels BREAKOUT HIT!!
SHORTLY THEREAFTER, THEY MADE THEIR OFFICIAL DEBUT.
THEIR FIRST SINGLE IS ALREADY NUMBER THREE ON THE MUSIC CHARTS. WHAT A GREAT START.
IT'S AMAZING, THE POWER OF THE CARA-MELS.
I KNOW. ALMOST IMMEDIATELY, WE GOT PICKED UP BY NEWSPAPERS, TV AND MAGAZINES. AND IN NO TIME WE HAD DEBUTED.
AND TODAY WE GET TO PERFORM AT THE OUTDOOR MUSIC FESTIVAL!
THERE ARE GONNA BE *TONS* OF CELEBRI-TIES!
DAZE~...
PLUS, THE CONCERT WILL BE ON TV!
EEEE—!
HA HA HA. WE'RE JUST GETTING STARTED.
BOSS!
AHEM. ACTUALLY, I HAVE MUCH BIGGER NEWS FOR YOU.

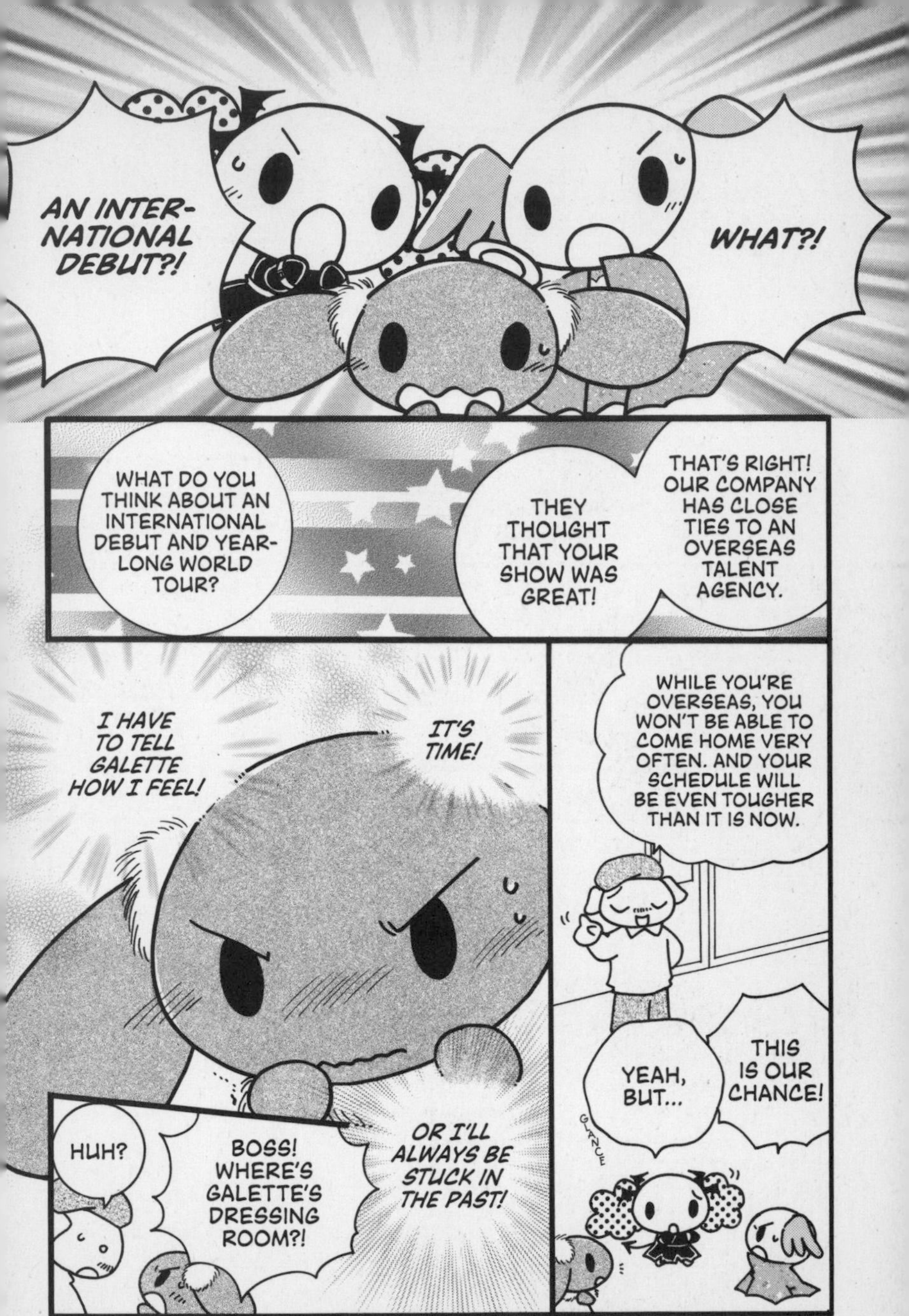
WHAT?!
AN INTER-NATIONAL DEBUT?!
THAT'S RIGHT! OUR COMPANY HAS CLOSE TIES TO AN OVERSEAS TALENT AGENCY.
THEY THOUGHT THAT YOUR SHOW WAS GREAT!
WHAT DO YOU THINK ABOUT AN INTERNATIONAL DEBUT AND YEAR-LONG WORLD TOUR?
WHILE YOU'RE OVERSEAS, YOU WON'T BE ABLE TO COME HOME VERY OFTEN. AND YOUR SCHEDULE WILL BE EVEN TOUGHER THAN IT IS NOW.
THIS IS OUR CHANCE!
YEAH, BUT...
GLANCE
IT'S TIME!
I HAVE TO TELL GALETTE HOW I FEEL!
OR I'LL ALWAYS BE STUCK IN THE PAST!
BOSS! WHERE'S GALETTE'S DRESSING ROOM?!
HUH?

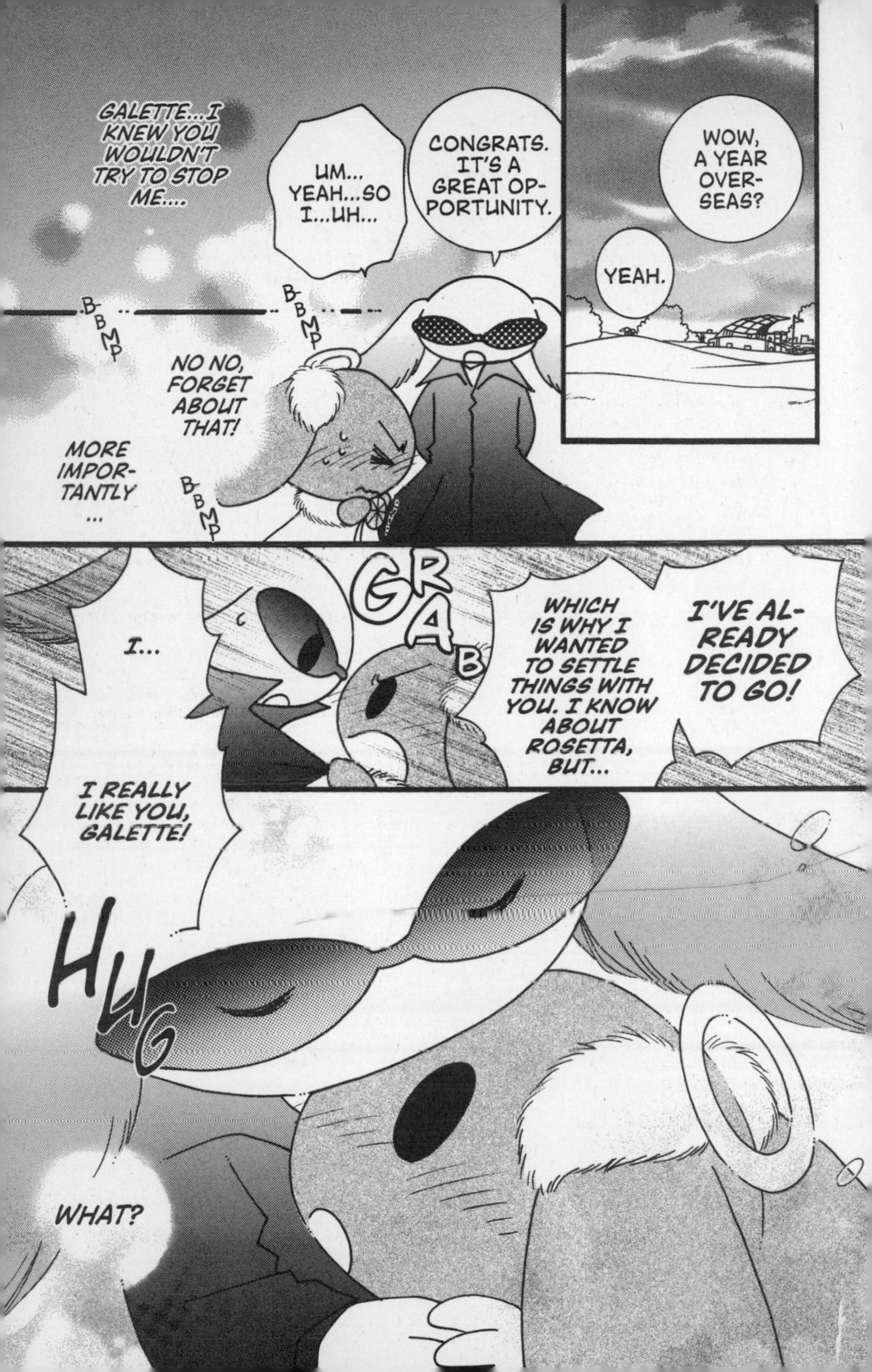
WOW, A YEAR OVER-SEAS?
YEAH.
CONGRATS. IT'S A GREAT OP-PORTUNITY.
UM... YEAH...SO I...UH...
GALETTE...I KNEW YOU WOULDN'T TRY TO STOP ME....
B-BBMP
B-BBMP
NO NO, FORGET ABOUT THAT!
MORE IMPORTANTLY ...
B-BBMP
I'VE AL-READY DECIDED TO GO!
WHICH IS WHY I WANTED TO SETTLE THINGS WITH YOU. I KNOW ABOUT ROSETTA, BUT...
GRAB
I...
I REALLY LIKE YOU, GALETTE!
HUG
WHAT?

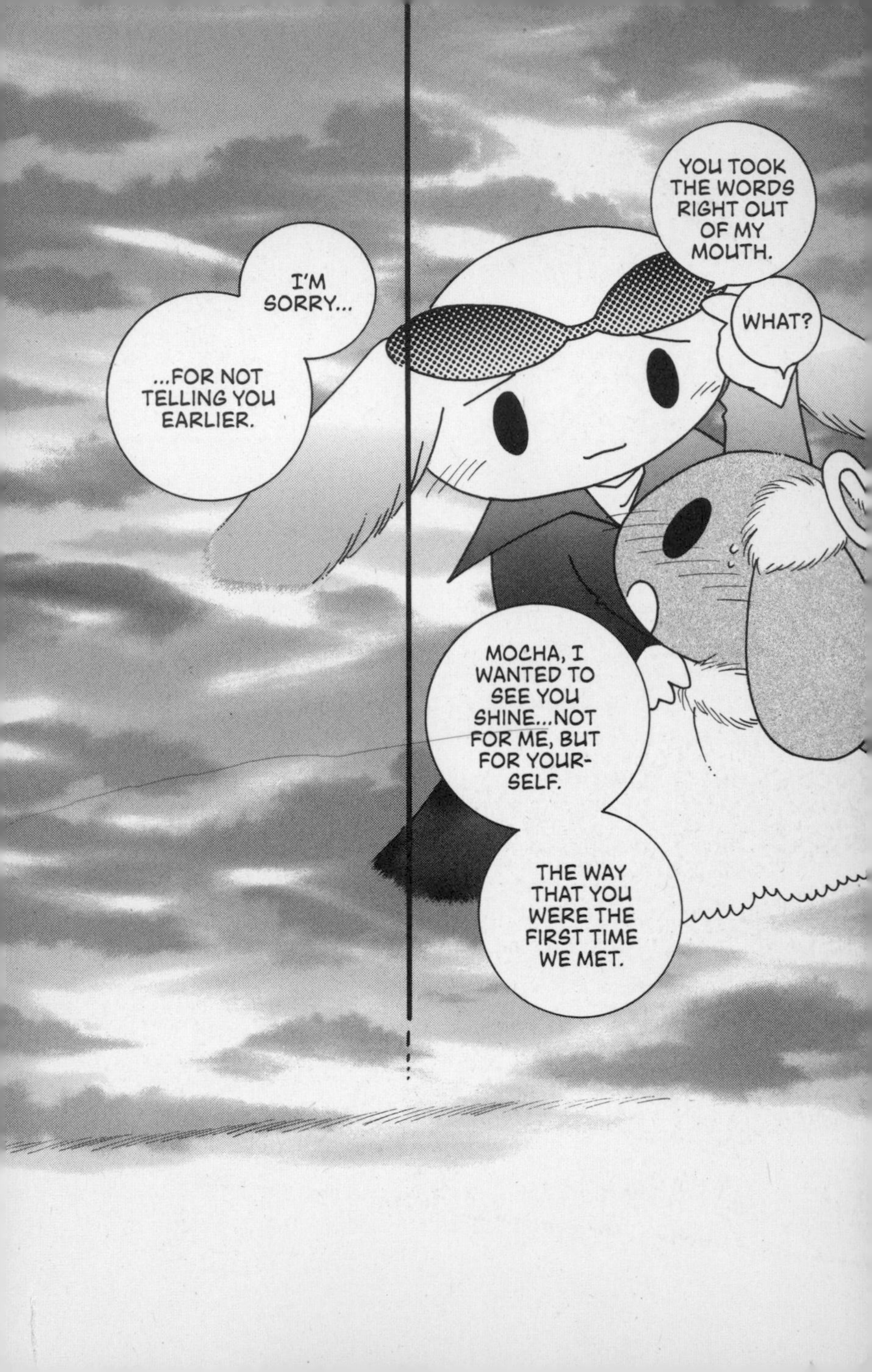
YOU TOOK THE WORDS RIGHT OUT OF MY MOUTH.
WHAT?
I'M SORRY...
...FOR NOT TELLING YOU EARLIER.
MOCHA, I WANTED TO SEE YOU SHINE...NOT FOR ME, BUT FOR YOUR-SELF.
THE WAY THAT YOU WERE THE FIRST TIME WE MET.

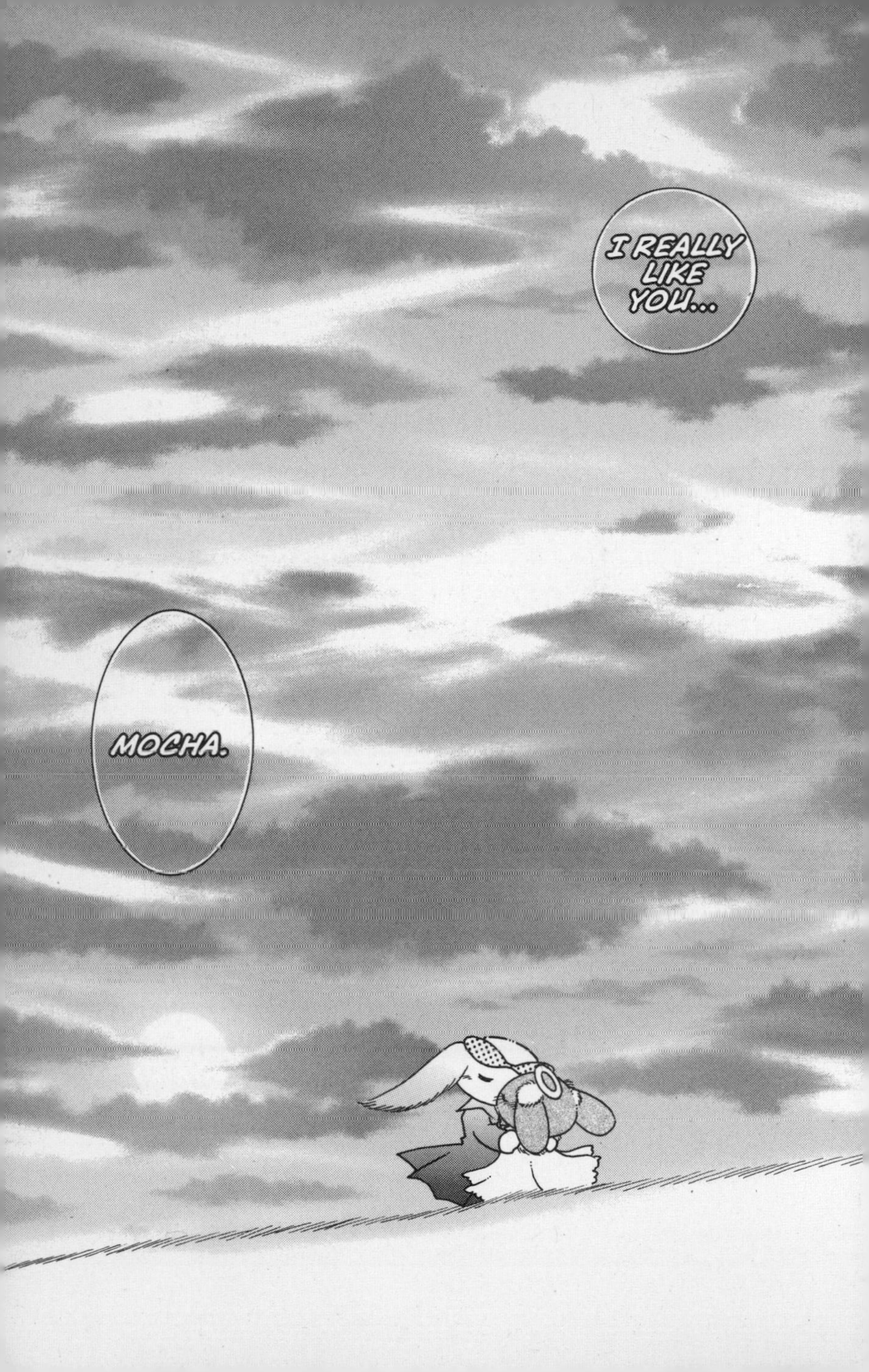
I REALLY LIKE YOU...
MOCHA.

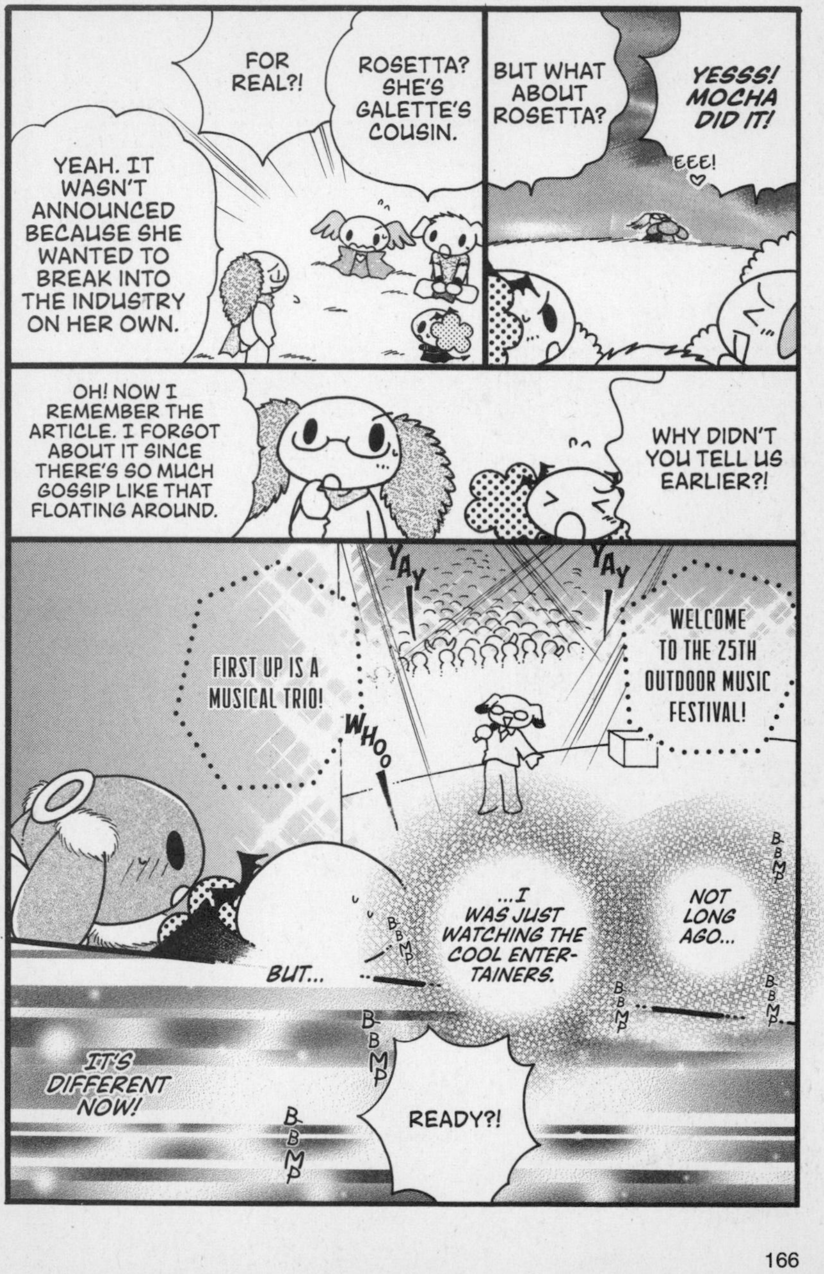
YESSS! MOCHA DID IT!
EEE! ♡
BUT WHAT ABOUT ROSETTA?
ROSETTA? SHE'S GALETTE'S COUSIN.
FOR REAL?!
YEAH. IT WASN'T ANNOUNCED BECAUSE SHE WANTED TO BREAK INTO THE INDUSTRY ON HER OWN.
WHY DIDN'T YOU TELL US EARLIER?!
OH! NOW I REMEMBER THE ARTICLE. I FORGOT ABOUT IT SINCE THERE'S SO MUCH GOSSIP LIKE THAT FLOATING AROUND.
YAY
YAY
WELCOME TO THE 25TH OUTDOOR MUSIC FESTIVAL!
FIRST UP IS A MUSICAL TRIO!
WHOO
BBMP
NOT LONG AGO...
...I WAS JUST WATCHING THE COOL ENTER-TAINERS.
BBMP
BBMP
BUT...
BBMP
BBMP
READY?!
BBMP
IT'S DIFFERENT NOW!

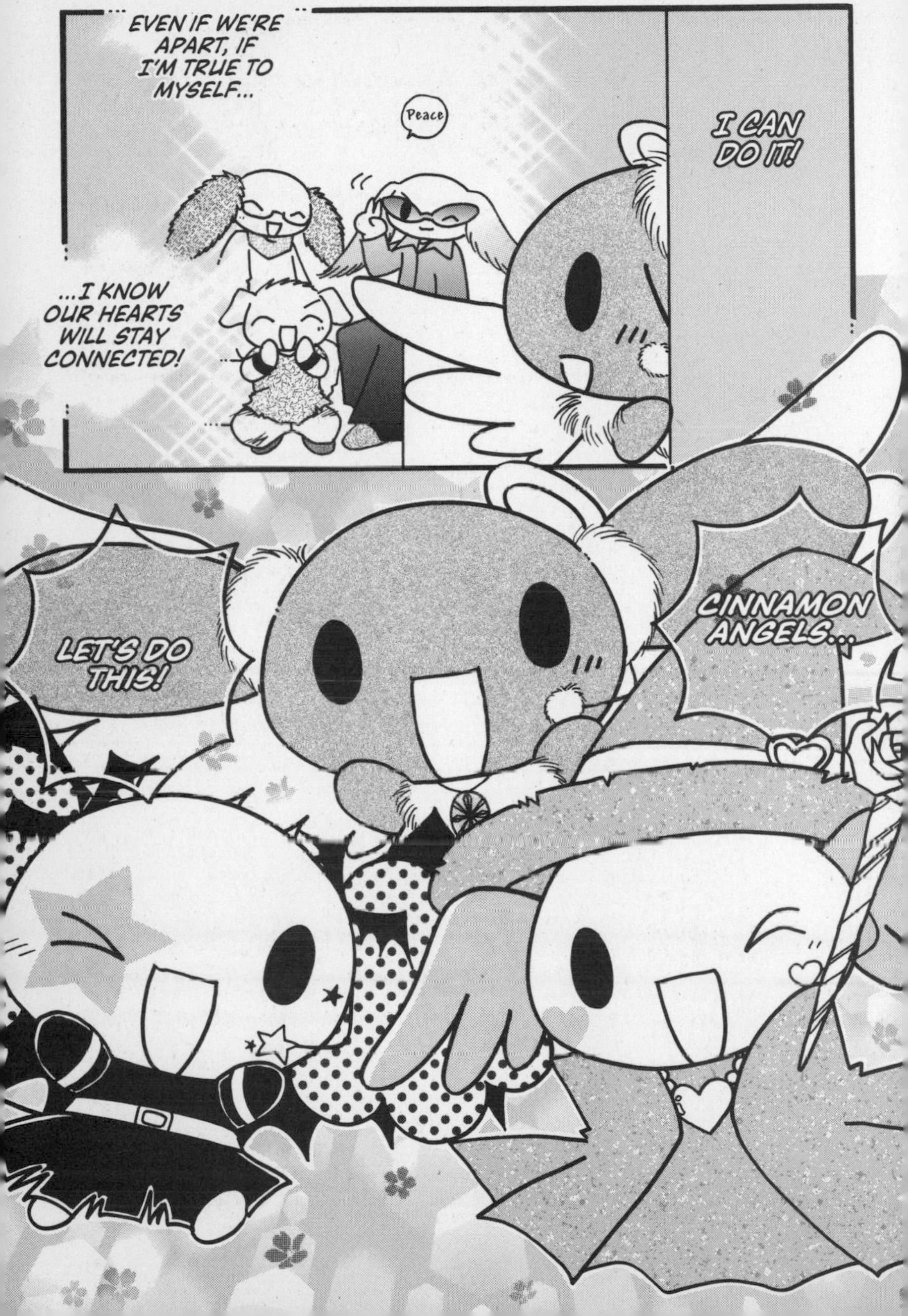
I CAN DO IT!
EVEN IF WE'RE APART, IF I'M TRUE TO MYSELF...
Peace
...I KNOW OUR HEARTS WILL STAY CONNECTED!
CINNAMON ANGELS...
LET'S DO THIS!

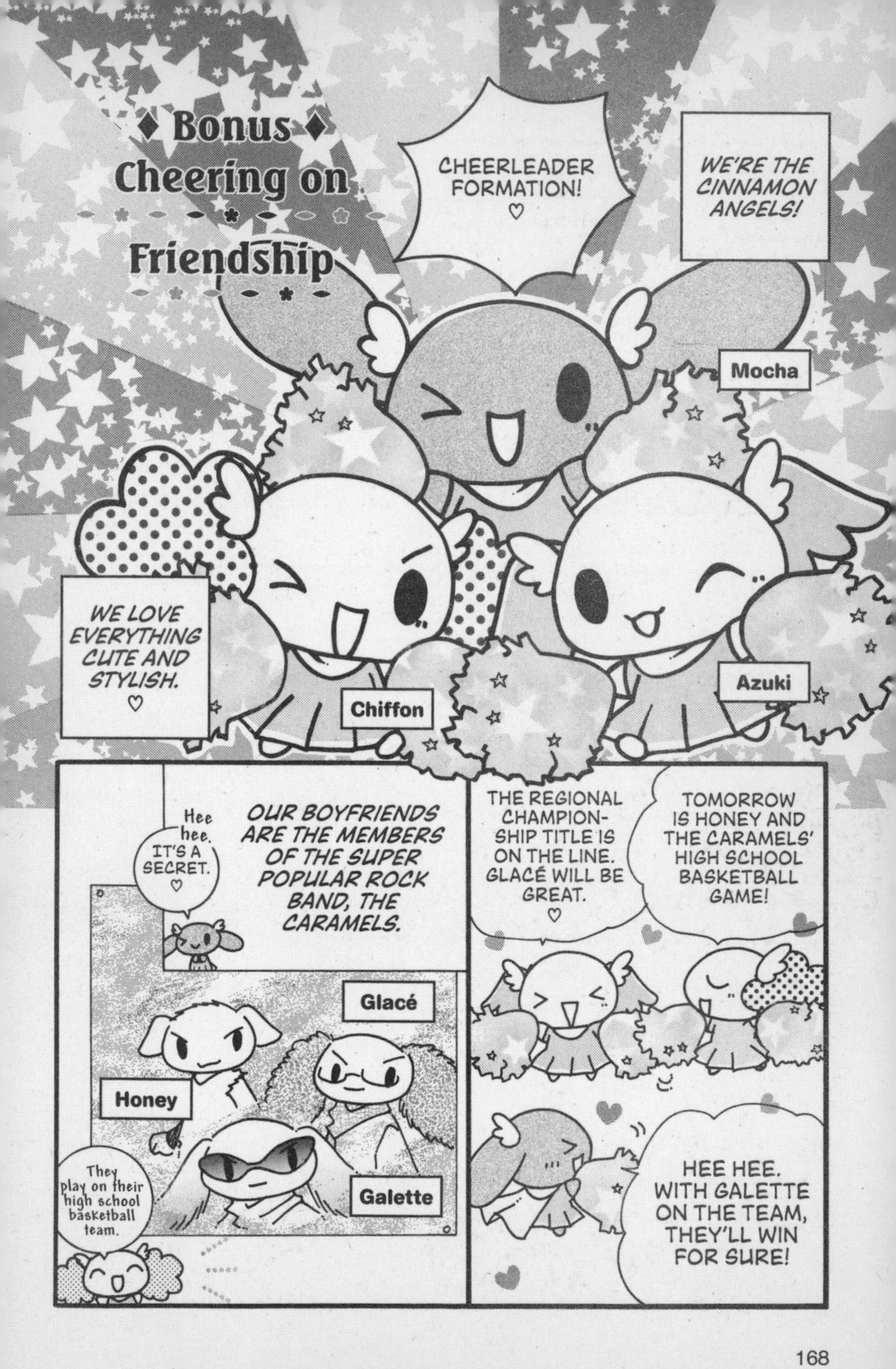
◆ Bonus ◆ Cheering on Friendship
WE'RE THE CINNAMON ANGELS!
CHEERLEADER FORMATION! ♡
Mocha
Azuki
Chiffon
WE LOVE EVERYTHING CUTE AND STYLISH. ♡
TOMORROW IS HONEY AND THE CARAMELS' HIGH SCHOOL BASKETBALL GAME!
THE REGIONAL CHAMPIONSHIP TITLE IS ON THE LINE. GLACÉ WILL BE GREAT. ♡
HEE HEE. WITH GALETTE ON THE TEAM, THEY'LL WIN FOR SURE!
OUR BOYFRIENDS ARE THE MEMBERS OF THE SUPER POPULAR ROCK BAND, THE CARAMELS.
Hee hee. IT'S A SECRET. ♡
Glacé
Honey
Galette
They play on their high school basketball team.

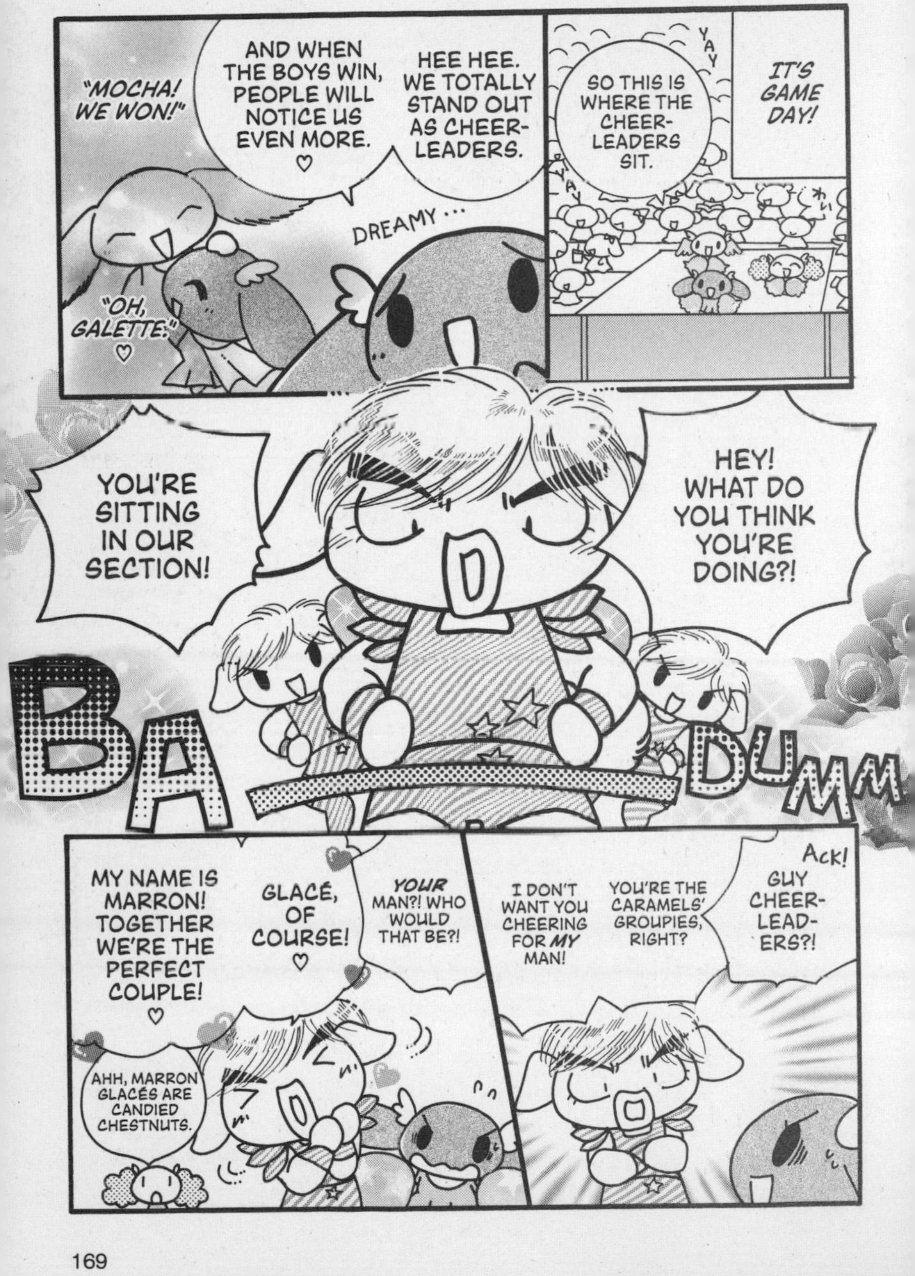
IT'S GAME DAY!
YAY
SO THIS IS WHERE THE CHEER-LEADERS SIT.
YAY
HEE HEE. WE TOTALLY STAND OUT AS CHEER-LEADERS.
AND WHEN THE BOYS WIN, PEOPLE WILL NOTICE US EVEN MORE. ♡
"MOCHA! WE WON!"
"OH, GALETTE." ♡
DREAMY...
HEY! WHAT DO YOU THINK YOU'RE DOING?!
YOU'RE SITTING IN OUR SECTION!
BA DUMM
Ack! GUY CHEER-LEAD-ERS?!
YOU'RE THE CARAMELS' GROUPIES, RIGHT?
I DON'T WANT YOU CHEERING FOR *MY* MAN!
YOUR MAN?! WHO WOULD THAT BE?!
GLACÉ, OF COURSE! ♡
MY NAME IS MARRON! TOGETHER WE'RE THE PERFECT COUPLE! ♡
AHH, MARRON GLACÉS ARE CANDIED CHESTNUTS.

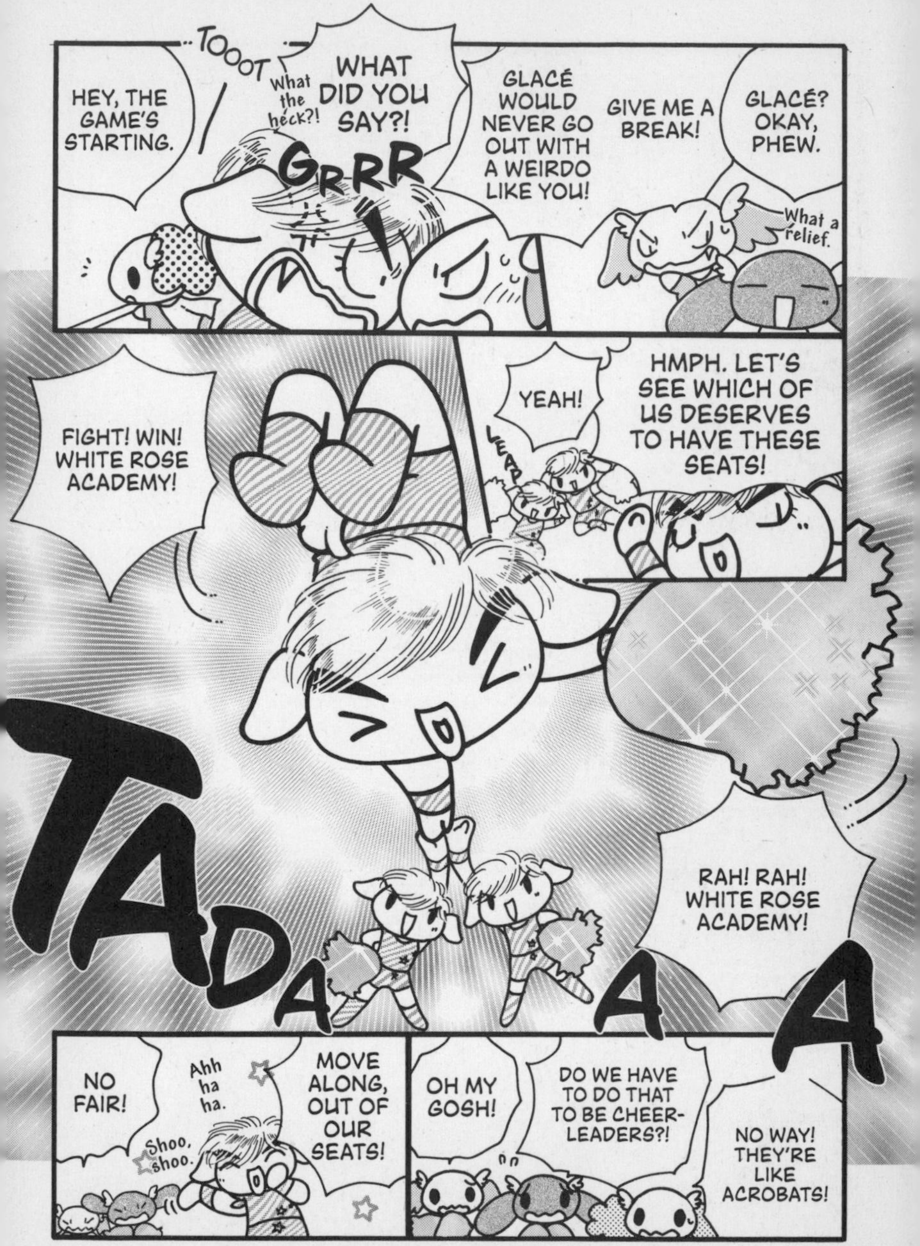
GLACÉ? OKAY, PHEW.
What a relief.
GIVE ME A BREAK!
GLACÉ WOULD NEVER GO OUT WITH A WEIRDO LIKE YOU!
WHAT DID YOU SAY?!
What the heck?!
GRRR
TOOOT
HEY, THE GAME'S STARTING.
HMPH. LET'S SEE WHICH OF US DESERVES TO HAVE THESE SEATS!
YEAH!
LEAP
FIGHT! WIN! WHITE ROSE ACADEMY!
RAH! RAH! WHITE ROSE ACADEMY!
TADAAAA
NO WAY! THEY'RE LIKE ACROBATS!
DO WE HAVE TO DO THAT TO BE CHEER-LEADERS?!
OH MY GOSH!
MOVE ALONG, OUT OF OUR SEATS!
Ahh ha ha.
Shoo, shoo.
NO FAIR!

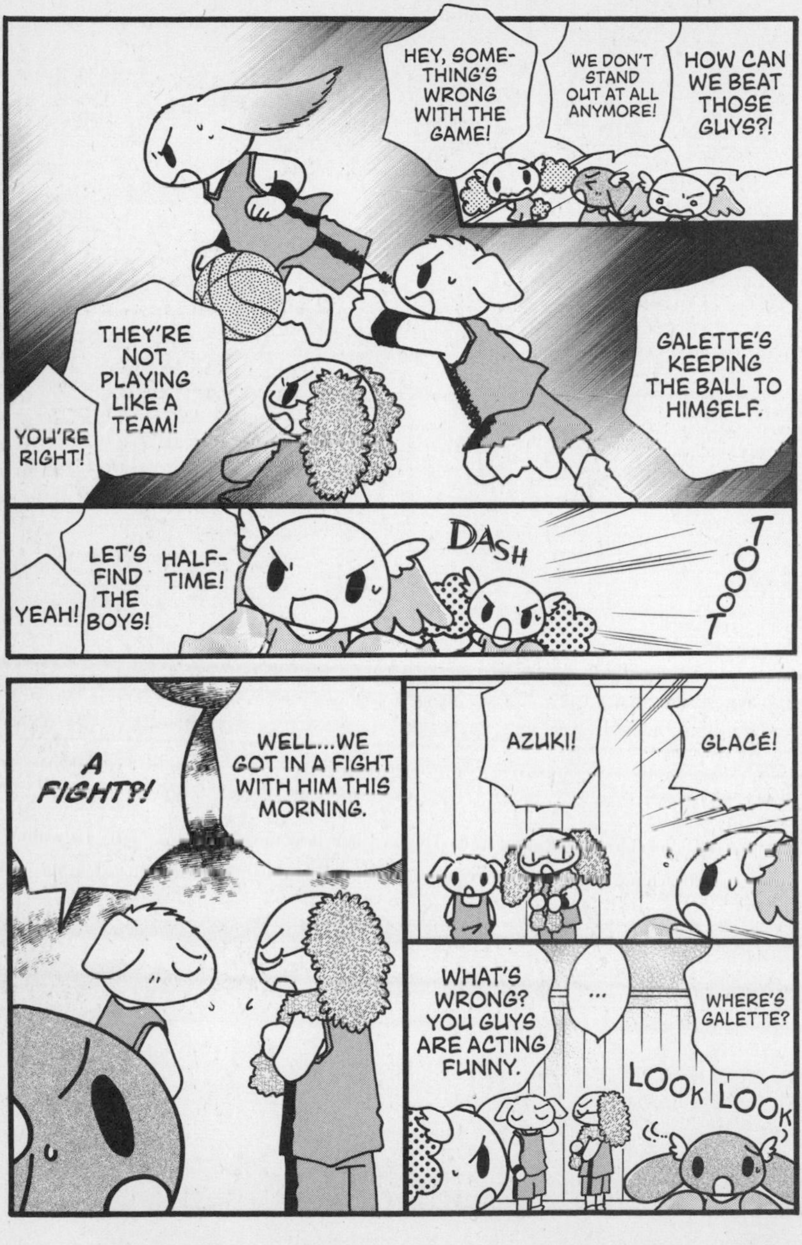
HOW CAN WE BEAT THOSE GUYS?!
WE DON'T STAND OUT AT ALL ANYMORE!
HEY, SOME-THING'S WRONG WITH THE GAME!
GALETTE'S KEEPING THE BALL TO HIMSELF.
THEY'RE NOT PLAYING LIKE A TEAM!
YOU'RE RIGHT!
TOOOT
DASH
HALF-TIME!
LET'S FIND THE BOYS!
YEAH!
GLACÉ!
AZUKI!
WHERE'S GALETTE?
...
WHAT'S WRONG? YOU GUYS ARE ACTING FUNNY.
LOOK LOOK
WELL...WE GOT IN A FIGHT WITH HIM THIS MORNING.
A FIGHT?!

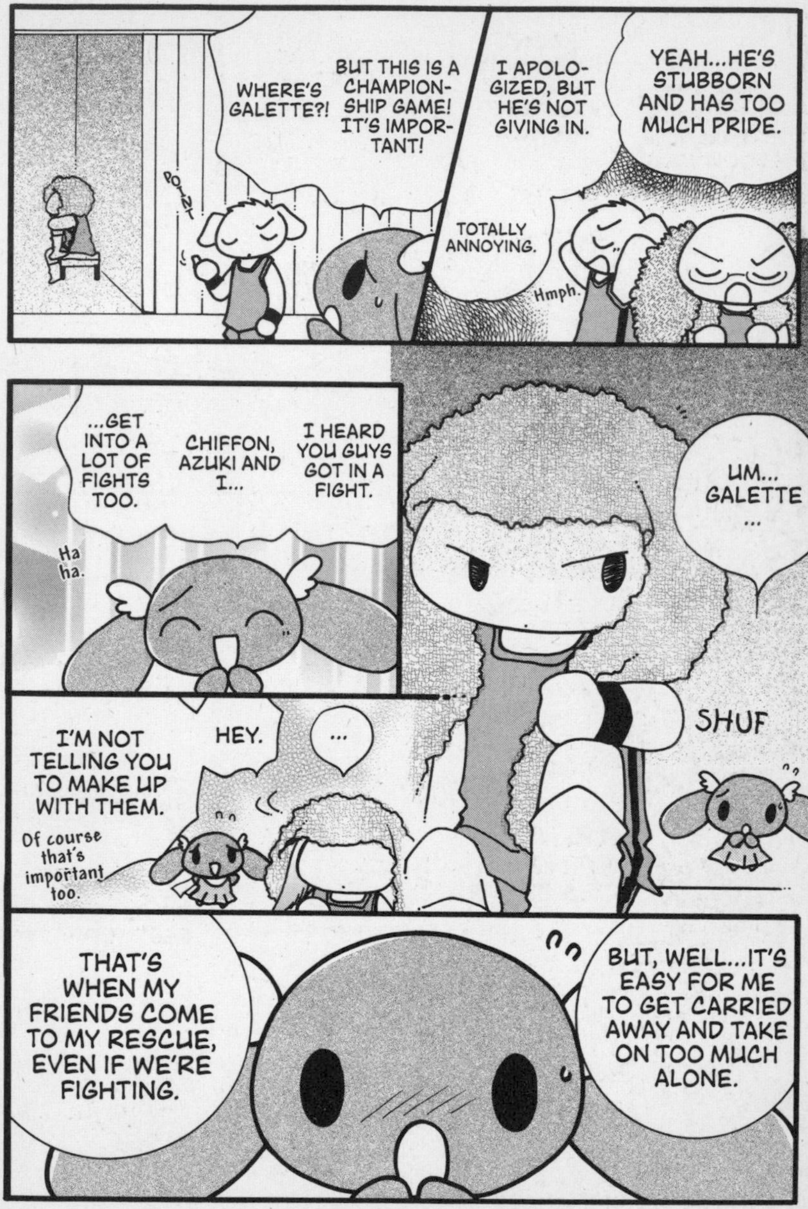
YEAH...HE'S STUBBORN AND HAS TOO MUCH PRIDE.
I APOLOGIZED, BUT HE'S NOT GIVING IN.
TOTALLY ANNOYING.
Hmph.
BUT THIS IS A CHAMPIONSHIP GAME! IT'S IMPORTANT!
WHERE'S GALETTE?!
POINT
UM... GALETTE ...
I HEARD YOU GUYS GOT IN A FIGHT.
CHIFFON, AZUKI AND I...
...GET INTO A LOT OF FIGHTS TOO.
Ha ha.
SHUF
...
HEY.
I'M NOT TELLING YOU TO MAKE UP WITH THEM.
Of course that's important too.
BUT, WELL...IT'S EASY FOR ME TO GET CARRIED AWAY AND TAKE ON TOO MUCH ALONE.
THAT'S WHEN MY FRIENDS COME TO MY RESCUE, EVEN IF WE'RE FIGHTING.

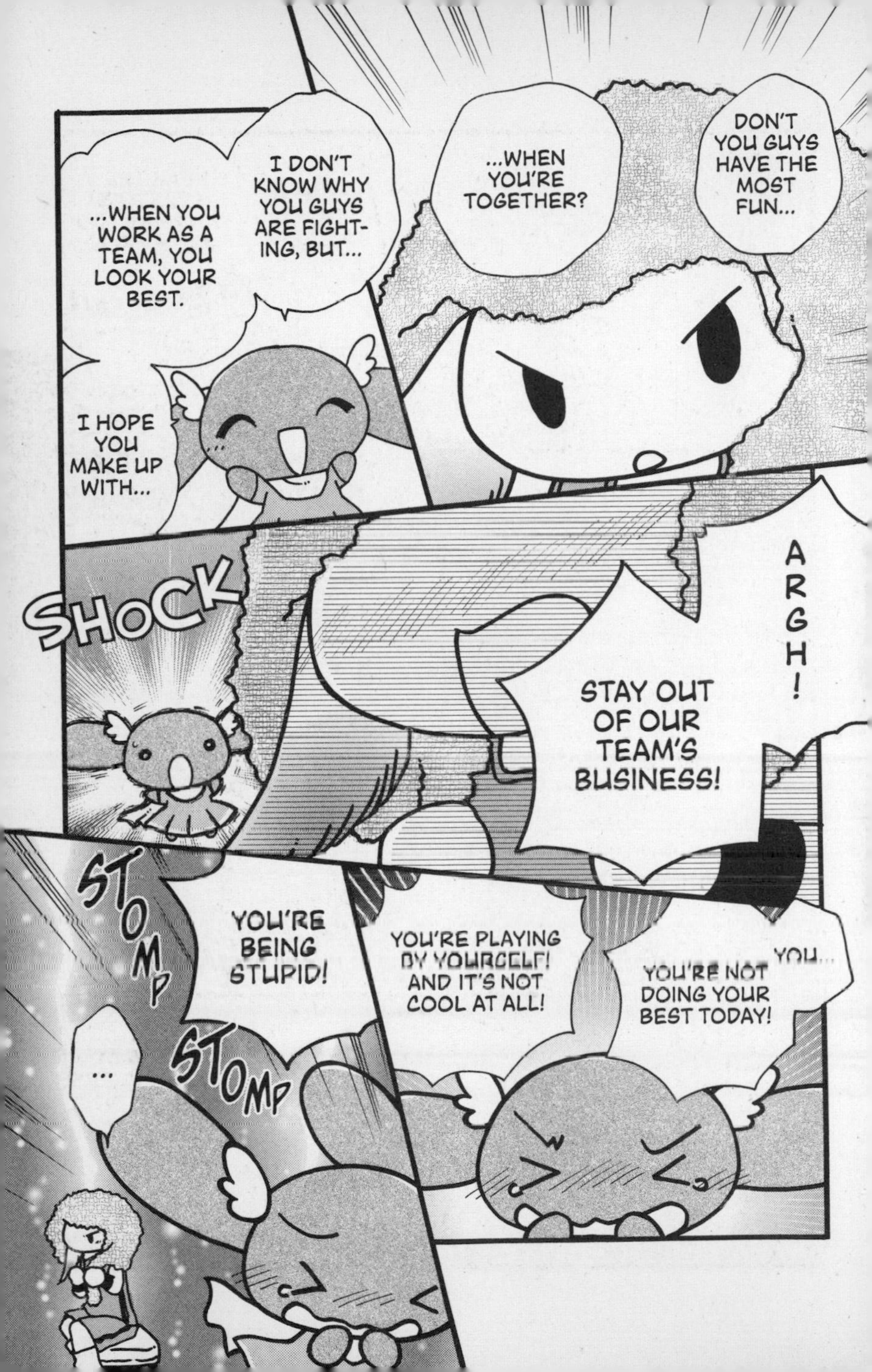
DON'T YOU GUYS HAVE THE MOST FUN...
...WHEN YOU'RE TOGETHER?
I DON'T KNOW WHY YOU GUYS ARE FIGHTING, BUT...
...WHEN YOU WORK AS A TEAM, YOU LOOK YOUR BEST.
I HOPE YOU MAKE UP WITH...
ARGH!
STAY OUT OF OUR TEAM'S BUSINESS!
SHOCK
YOU...
YOU'RE NOT DOING YOUR BEST TODAY!
YOU'RE PLAYING BY YOURSELF! AND IT'S NOT COOL AT ALL!
STOMP
STOMP
YOU'RE BEING STUPID!
...

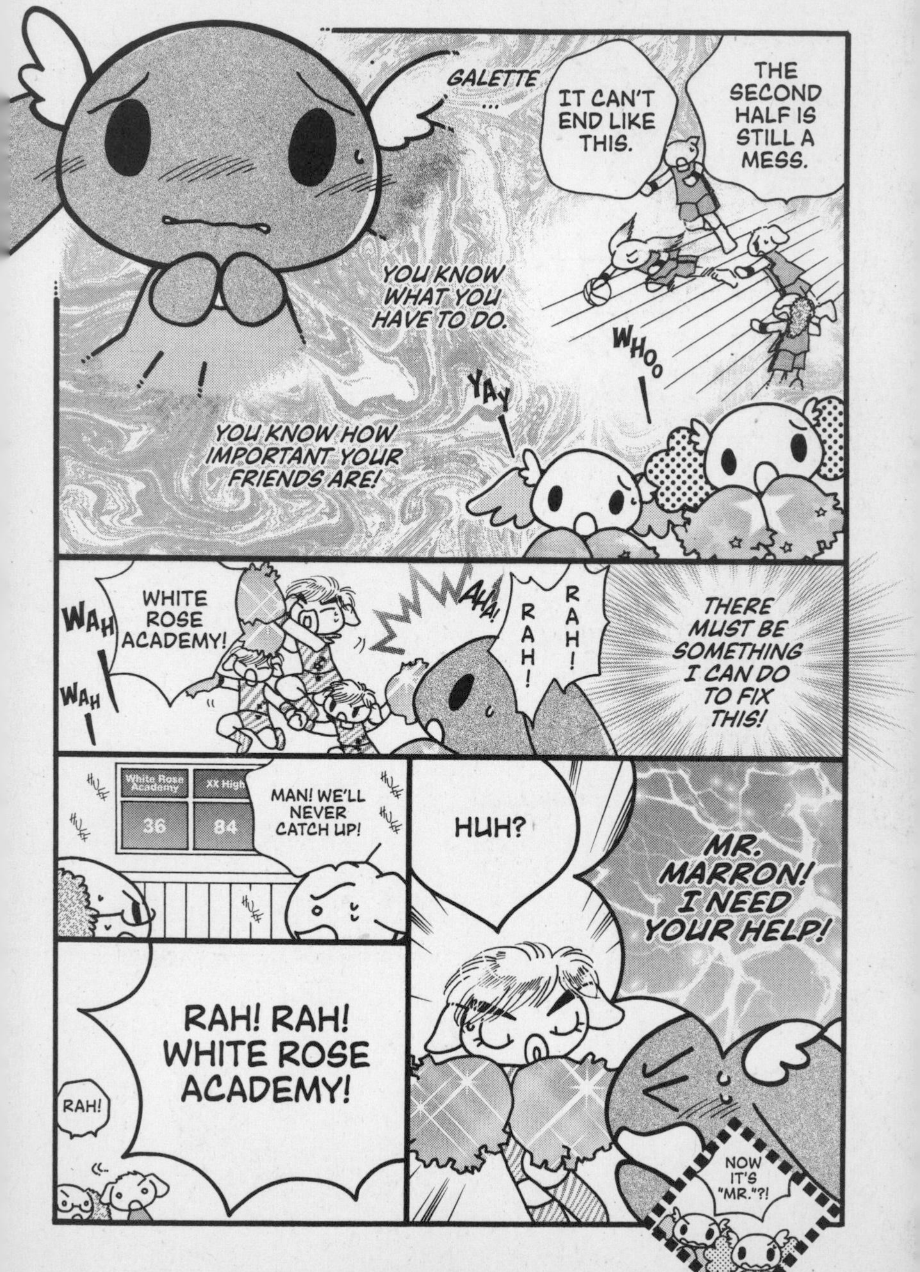
THE SECOND HALF IS STILL A MESS.
IT CAN'T END LIKE THIS.
GALETTE ...
YOU KNOW WHAT YOU HAVE TO DO.
WHOO
YAY
YOU KNOW HOW IMPORTANT YOUR FRIENDS ARE!
THERE MUST BE SOMETHING I CAN DO TO FIX THIS!
RAH! RAH!
WHITE ROSE ACADEMY!
WAH
WAH
MR. MARRON! I NEED YOUR HELP!
HUH?
NOW IT'S "MR."?!
White Rose Academy
XX High
36
84
MAN! WE'LL NEVER CATCH UP!
HUFF
RAH! RAH! WHITE ROSE ACADEMY!
RAH!

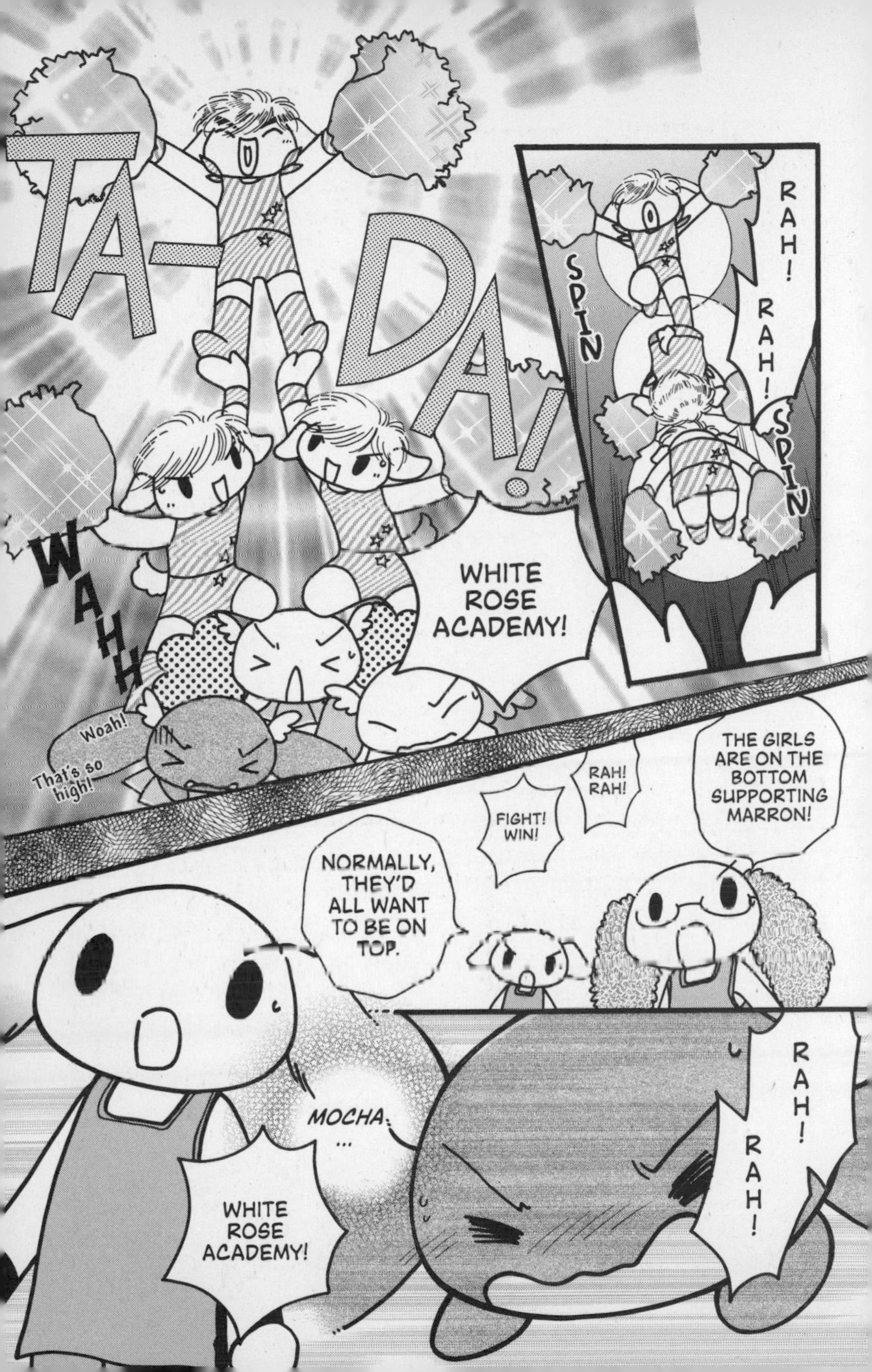
RAH! RAH!
SPIN
SPIN
TA-DA!
WHITE ROSE ACADEMY!
WAHH
Woah!
That's so high!
THE GIRLS ARE ON THE BOTTOM SUPPORTING MARRON!
RAH! RAH!
FIGHT! WIN!
NORMALLY, THEY'D ALL WANT TO BE ON TOP.
RAH! RAH!
MOCHA...
WHITE ROSE ACADEMY!

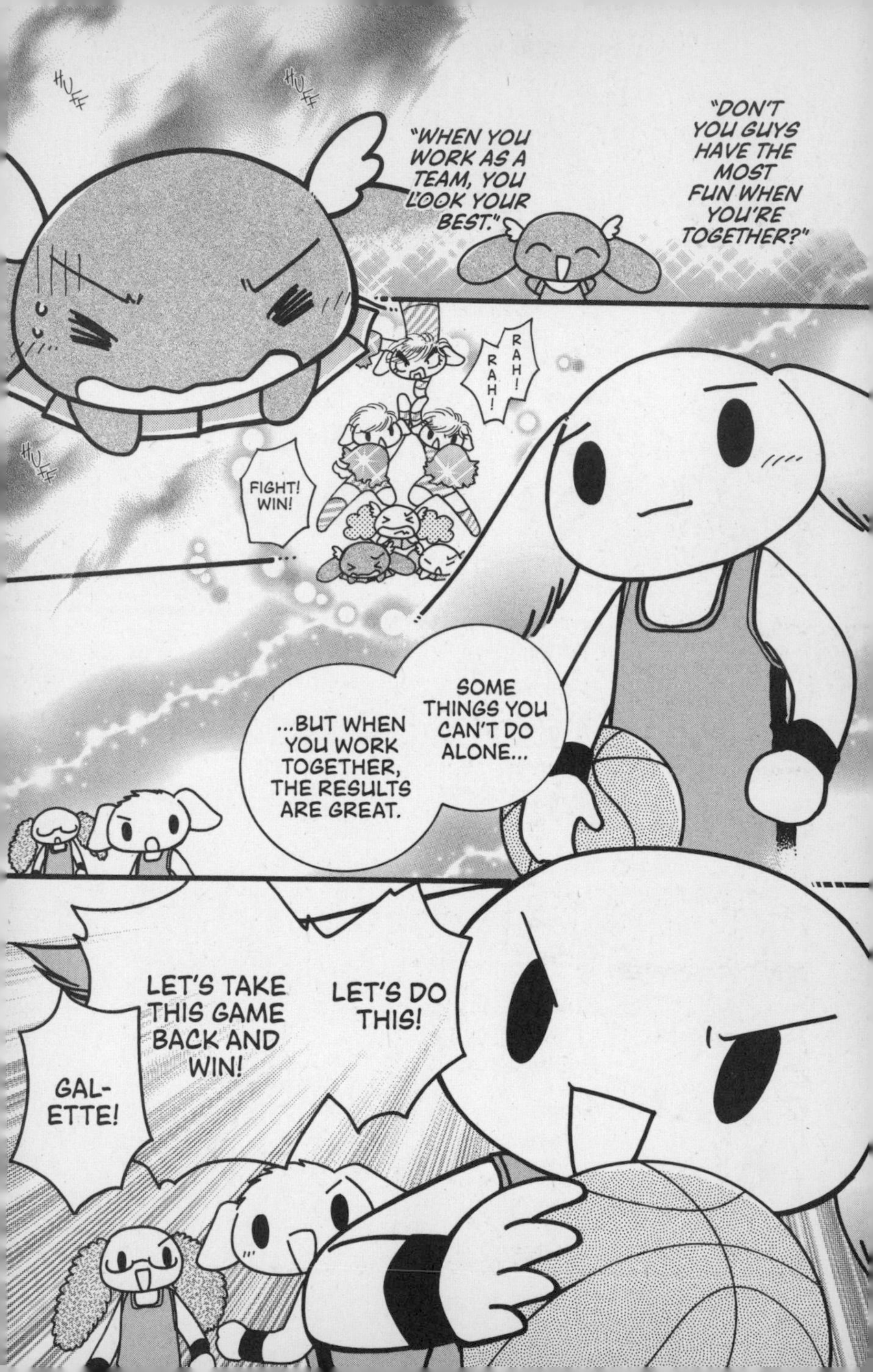
HUFF
HUFF
"DON'T YOU GUYS HAVE THE MOST FUN WHEN YOU'RE TOGETHER?"
"WHEN YOU WORK AS A TEAM, YOU LOOK YOUR BEST."
HUFF
RAH! RAH!
FIGHT! WIN!
SOME THINGS YOU CAN'T DO ALONE...
...BUT WHEN YOU WORK TOGETHER, THE RESULTS ARE GREAT.
LET'S DO THIS!
LET'S TAKE THIS GAME BACK AND WIN!
GAL-ETTE!

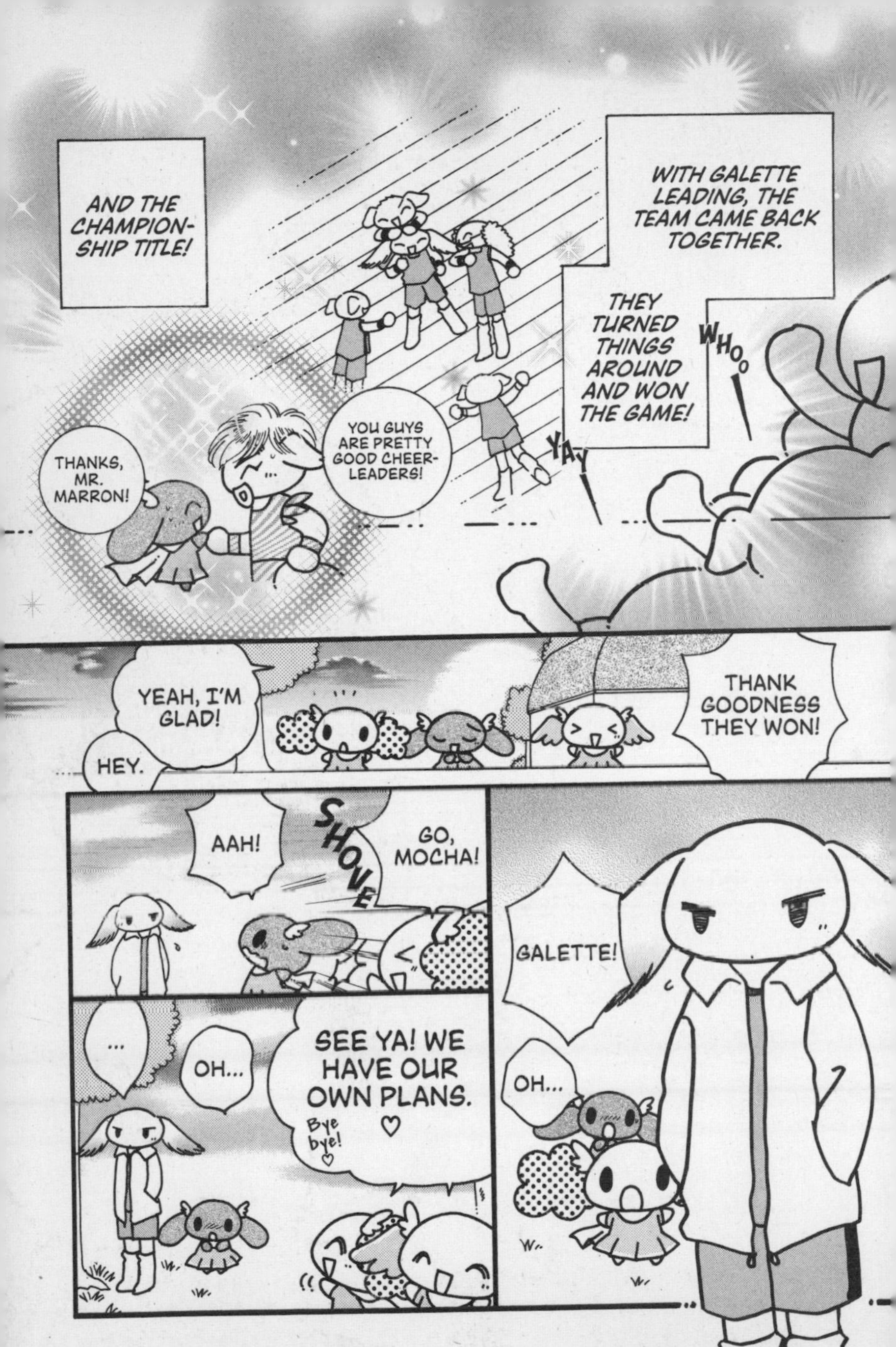
WITH GALETTE LEADING, THE TEAM CAME BACK TOGETHER.
THEY TURNED THINGS AROUND AND WON THE GAME!
WHOOO
YAY
AND THE CHAMPION-SHIP TITLE!
YOU GUYS ARE PRETTY GOOD CHEER-LEADERS!
THANKS, MR. MARRON!
THANK GOODNESS THEY WON!
YEAH, I'M GLAD!
HEY.
GALETTE!
OH...
GO, MOCHA!
SHOVE
AAH!
SEE YA! WE HAVE OUR OWN PLANS.
Bye bye!
OH...
...

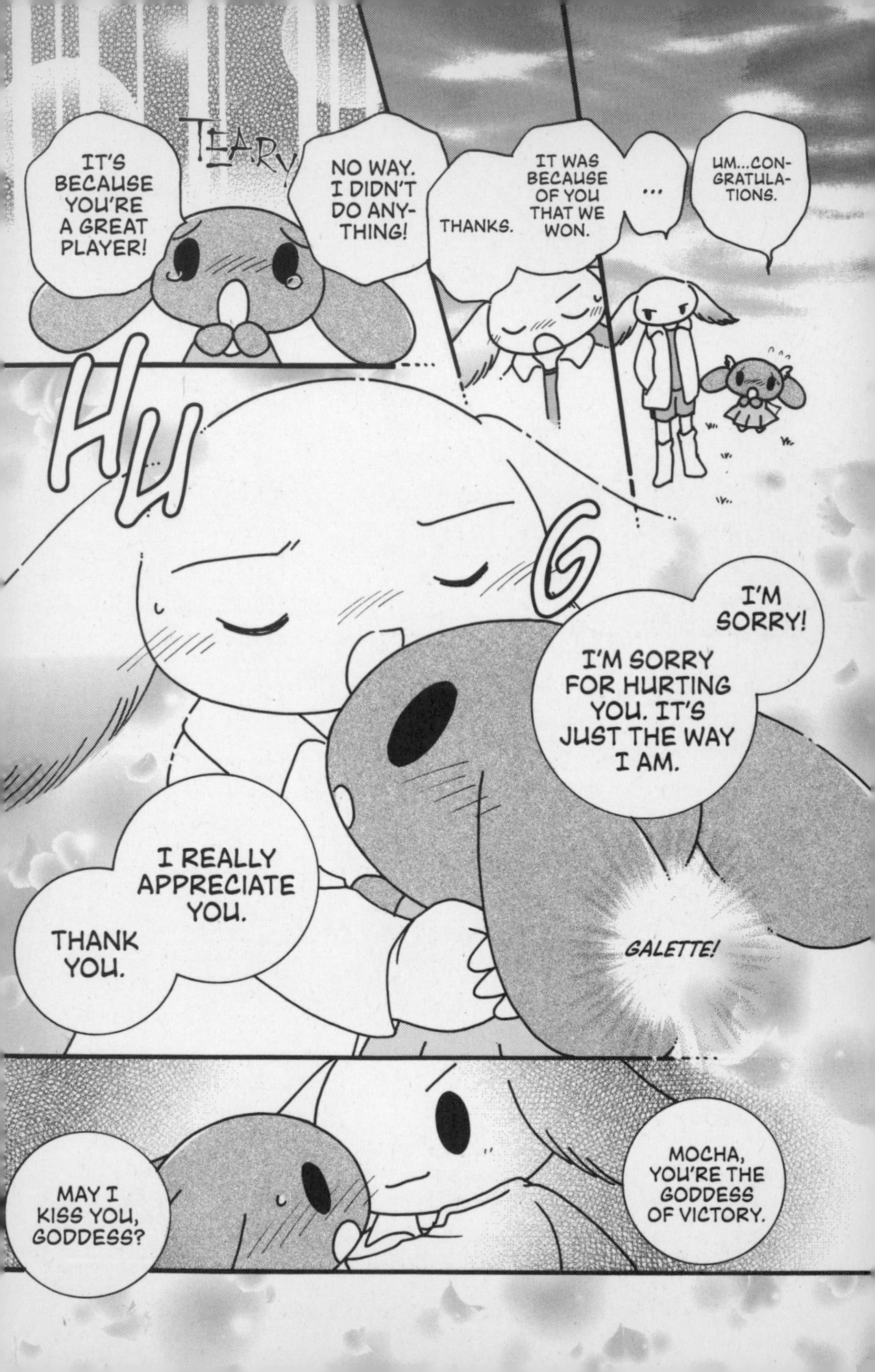
UM...CON-GRATULA-TIONS.
...
IT WAS BECAUSE OF YOU THAT WE WON.
THANKS.
NO WAY. I DIDN'T DO ANY-THING!
TEARY
IT'S BECAUSE YOU'RE A GREAT PLAYER!
HUG
I'M SORRY!
I'M SORRY FOR HURTING YOU. IT'S JUST THE WAY I AM.
GALETTE!
I REALLY APPRECIATE YOU.
THANK YOU.
MOCHA, YOU'RE THE GODDESS OF VICTORY.
MAY I KISS YOU, GODDESS?

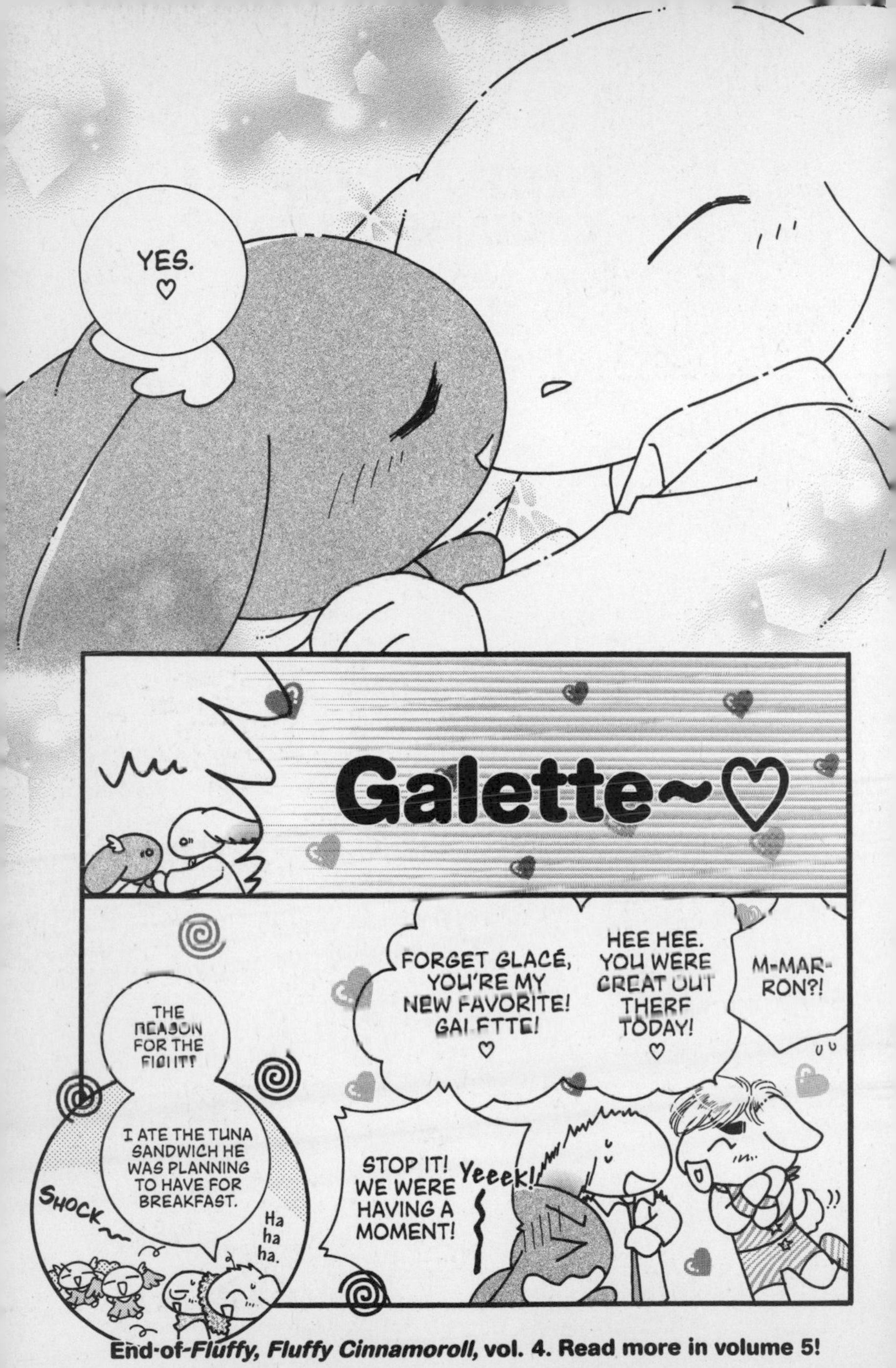
YES. ♡
Galette~♡
M-MAR-RON?!
HEE HEE. YOU WERE GREAT OUT THERE TODAY! ♡
FORGET GLACÉ, YOU'RE MY NEW FAVORITE! GALETTE! ♡
STOP IT! WE WERE HAVING A MOMENT!
Yeeek!
THE REASON FOR THE FIGHT
I ATE THE TUNA SANDWICH HE WAS PLANNING TO HAVE FOR BREAKFAST.
Ha ha ha.
SHOCK

End-of-*Fluffy, Fluffy Cinnamoroll*, vol. 4. Read more in volume 5!

FLUFFY, FLUFFY CINNAMOROLL

Volume 4

VIZ Kids Edition

Story & Art by Yumi Tsukirino
Original Concept by Chisato Seki

© 2005 Yumi TSUKIRINO, Chisato SEKI/Shogakukan
© 2001, 2012 SANRIO CO., LTD.
All rights reserved.
Original Japanese edition "FUWA FUWA CINNAMON"
published by SHOGAKUKAN Inc.

Translation	Emi Louie-Nishikawa
Touch-up & Lettering	Erika Terriquez
Design	Fawn Lau, Chii Maene
Editor	Hope Donovan

Printed in the U.S.A.

Published by VIZ Media, LLC
P.O. Box 77010
San Francisco, CA 94107

10 9 8 7 6 5 4 3 2 1
First printing, June 2012